A
SINGLE
THREAD

ALSO BY TRACY CHEVALIER

The Virgin Blue

Girl with a Pearl Earring

Falling Angels

The Lady and the Unicorn

Burning Bright

Remarkable Creatures

The Last Runaway

At the Edge of the Orchard

New Boy

A
SINGLE
THREAD

Tracy Chevalier

VIKING

VIKING
An imprint of Penguin Random House LLC
penguinrandomhouse.com

"Love Is The Sweetest Thing," written by Ray Noble, published by
Range Road Music and Bienstock Publishing Company o/b/o Redwood Music Ltd.,
rights administered by Round Hill Carlin, LLC

Library of Congress Cataloging-in-Publication Data

Names: Chevalier, Tracy, author.
Title: A single thread / Tracy Chevalier.
Description: First edition. | New York : Viking, [2019] |
Identifiers: LCCN 2019007094 (print) | LCCN 2019009175 (ebook) |
ISBN 9780525558255 (ebook) | ISBN 9780525558248 (hardcover)
Classification: LCC PS3553.H4367 (ebook) | LCC PS3553.H4367 S55 2019 (print) |
DDC 813/.54—dc23
LC record available at https://lccn.loc.gov/2019007094

Printed in the United States of America
1 3 5 7 9 10 8 6 4 2

Designed by Meighan Cavanaugh

For Morag

A

SINGLE

THREAD

S hhh!"

Violet Speedwell frowned. She did not need shushing; she had not said anything.

The shusher, an officious woman sporting a helmet of gray hair, had planted herself squarely in the archway that led into the choir, Violet's favorite part of Winchester Cathedral. The choir was right in the center of the building—the nave extending one way, the presbytery and retrochoir the other, the north and south transepts' short arms fanning out on either side to complete the cross of the whole structure. The other parts of the cathedral had their drawbacks: The nave was enormous, the aisles drafty, the transepts dark, the chapels too reverential, the retrochoir lonely. But the choir had a lower ceiling and carved wood stalls that made the space feel on a more human scale. It was luxurious but not too grand.

Violet peeked over the usher's shoulder. She had only wanted to step in for a moment to look. The choir stalls of seats and benches and the adjacent presbytery seats seemed to be filled mostly with women—far more than she would expect on a Thursday afternoon.

There must be a special service for something. It was the 19th of May 1932; Saint Dunstan's Day, Dunstan being the patron saint of goldsmiths, known for famously fending off the Devil with a pair of tongs. But that was unlikely to draw so many Winchester women.

She studied the congregants she could see. Women always studied other women, and did so far more critically than men ever did. Men didn't notice the run in their stocking, the lipstick on their teeth, the dated, outgrown haircut, the skirt that pulled unflatteringly across the hips, the paste earrings that were a touch too gaudy. Violet registered every flaw, and knew every flaw that was being noted about her. She could provide a list herself: hair too flat and neither one color nor another; sloping shoulders fashionable back in Victorian times; eyes so deep set you could barely see their blue; nose tending to red if she was too hot or had even a sip of sherry. She did not need anyone, male or female, to point out her shortcomings.

Like the usher guarding them, the women in the choir and presbytery were mostly older than Violet. All wore hats, and most had coats draped over their shoulders. Though it was a reasonable day outside, inside the cathedral it was still chilly, as churches and cathedrals always seemed to be, even in high summer. All that stone did not absorb warmth, and kept worshippers alert and a little uncomfortable, as if it did not do to relax too much during the important business of worshipping God. If God were an architect, she wondered, would He be an Old Testament architect of flagstone or a New Testament one of soft furnishings?

They began to sing now—"All Ye Who Seek a Rest Above"— rather like an army, regimental, with a clear sense of the importance of the group. For it *was* a group; Violet could see that. An invisible web ran among the women, binding them fast to their common cause, whatever that might be. There seemed to be a line of command too: Two women sitting in one of the front stall benches in the choir were clearly leaders. One was smiling, one frowning. The frowner was looking around from one line of the hymn to the next, as if ticking off a list in her head of who was there and who was not, who was singing boldly and who faintly, who would need admonishing afterward about wandering attention and who would be praised in some indirect, condescending manner. It felt just like being back at school assembly.

"Who are—"

"Shhh!" The usher's frown deepened. "You will have to *wait*." Her voice was far louder than Violet's mild query had been; a few women in the closest seats turned their heads. This incensed the usher even more. "This is the Presentation of Embroideries," she hissed. "Tourists are *not allowed*."

Violet knew such types, who guarded the gates with a ferocity well beyond what the position required. This woman would simper at deans and bishops and treat everyone else like peasants.

Their standoff was interrupted by an older man approaching along the side aisle from the empty retrochoir at the eastern end of the cathedral. Violet turned to look at him, grateful for the interruption. She noted his white hair and mustache and his stride, which, though purposeful, lacked the vigor of youth, and found herself making the calculation she did with most men. He was in his late fifties or early sixties. Minus the eighteen years since 1914, he would have been in his early forties when the Great War began. Probably he hadn't fought, or at least not till later, when younger recruits were running low. Perhaps he had a son who had fought.

The usher stiffened as he drew near, ready to defend her territory from another invader. But the man passed them with barely a glance, and trotted down the stairs to the south transept. Was he leaving, or would he turn in to the small Fishermen's Chapel, where Izaak Walton was buried? It was where Violet had been heading before her curiosity over the special service waylaid her.

The usher moved away from the archway for a moment to peer down after the man. Violet took the opportunity to slip inside and sit down in the closest empty seat, just as the dean stepped up to the pulpit in the middle of the choir aisle to her left and announced, "The Lord be with you."

"And with Thy spirit," the women around her replied in the measured tempo so familiar from church services.

"Let us pray."

As Violet bowed her head along with the others, she felt a finger poke at her shoulder. She ignored it; surely the usher would not interrupt a prayer.

"Almighty God, who of old didst command that Thy sanctuary be adorned with works of beauty and cunning craftsmanship, for the hallowing of Thy name and the refreshing of men's souls, vouchsafe, we beseech Thee, to accept these offerings at our hands, and grant that we may ever be consecrated to Thy service; for Jesus Christ's sake. Amen."

Violet looked around. Like the choir's, the presbytery chairs were turned inward rather than forward toward the high altar. Across from her were ranks of women in facing seats, and behind them, a stone parclose decorated with tracery in the form of arches and curlicues. On the top of the screen sat stone mortuary chests containing the bones of bishops and kings and queens—unfortunately jumbled together during the Civil War when Cromwell's men apparently opened the chests and threw the bones about. During a tour that

Violet dutifully took after moving to Winchester, the guide had told her the soldiers threw femurs at the Great West Window and destroyed the stained glass. Once Charles II had been restored to the throne in 1660 it too had been restored, using saved shards of glass, but it was remade higgledy-piggledy, with little attempt to re-create the biblical scenes originally depicted. Yet it looked orderly, as did the mortuary chests—so tidy and certain, resting above her head now, as if they had always been and always would be there. This building might look permanent, but parts of it had been taken apart and put back together many times.

It was impossible to imagine that such bad behavior could have taken place in so solid a building, where they were now obediently reciting the Lord's Prayer. But then, it had been impossible to imagine that solid old Britain would go to war with Germany and send so many men off to die. Afterward the country had been put back together like the Great West Window—defiant and superficially repaired, but the damage had been done.

"In the faith of Jesus Christ we dedicate these gifts to the glory of God." As he spoke the dean gestured toward the high altar at the far end of the presbytery. Violet craned her neck to see what gifts he was referring to, then stifled a laugh. Stacked in even, solemn rows on the steps before the altar were dozens of hassocks.

She should not find them funny, she knew. Kneelers were a serious business. Violet had always been grateful for the rectangular leather kneelers the size of picture books at Saint Michael's, the church the Speedwells attended in Southampton. Though worn and compacted into thin hard boards by years of pressing knees, they were at least not as cold as the stone floor. She had never thought they might require a benediction, however. And yet that appeared to be what this special service was for.

She glanced at her watch: She had left the office to buy a typewriter ribbon, with the tacit understanding that she might stop en route for a coffee. Instead of coffee Violet had intended to visit the Fishermen's Chapel in the cathedral. Her late father had been a keen fisherman and kept a copy of Izaak Walton's *The Compleat Angler* on his bedside table—though she had never seen him read it. Now, though, she wondered if kneelers were worth being late for.

The prayer over, she felt another sharp tap on her shoulder. The service might take longer than a coffee or a pilgrimage to Walton, but she could not bear to be bullied by this woman. "I've joined the service," she muttered before the usher could speak.

The woman frowned. "You are a *broderer*? I haven't seen you at the meetings."

Violet had never heard the word and was not entirely sure what it meant. "I'm new," she improvised.

"Well, this is a service for those who have *already* contributed. You will have to wait for the next service in October, once you have actually taken part and put in some *work*."

If the usher hadn't then glanced down at Violet's left hand, she might have accepted that the service was not for her and departed. She should have done anyway—gone for the typewriter ribbon and returned to the office in a timely fashion. Besides, services were often dull, even in a cathedral as magnificent as Winchester's. But she hated the judgment that the usher was forming from her not wearing a wedding ring. She couldn't help it: She glanced in return at the usher's left hand. A ring, of course.

She took a breath to give herself courage. "I was told I could come." Her heart was pounding, as it often did when she rebelled, whether on a large or a small scale. When she'd told her mother six months before that she was moving to Winchester, for instance, her heart had beat so hard and fast that she'd thought it would punch a hole through her chest. Thirty-eight years old and I am still afraid, she thought.

The usher's frown deepened. "*Who* told you that?"

Violet gestured toward one of the fur-wearing women in the front choir stall bench.

"Mrs. Biggins said you could come?" For the first time, the usher's tone faltered.

"Mabel, shhh!" Now others were shushing the usher, who turned scarlet. After one last scowl at Violet, she stepped back to her place guarding the archway.

The dean was midway through his address. "This magnificent cathedral has been blessed with many adornments over the centuries," he was saying, "whether in stone or wood, metal or glass. The effect has been to lift the spirits of those who come to worship, and to remind them of the glory of God here on Earth as in Heaven.

"To this abundance can now be added the kneelers you see before the altar—the start of an ambitious project to bring color and comfort to those who come to services in the choir and presbytery. The Winchester Cathedral Broderers group was formed by Miss Louisa Pesel at my invitation last year. The word *broderer* is taken from the Worshipful Company of Broderers—a guild of embroiderers established in medieval times. This new group of cathedral broderers reflects the noble history of this craft, brought forth by Miss Pesel to unite the past and present. Many of its members are here today. You have clearly been very busy with your needles, embroidering these splendid hassocks for the presbytery, and soon to commence on cushions for the seats and benches in the choir. Not only will we see glorious colors and patterns amongst the more sober wood and stone, but worshippers will find it easier to kneel as they pray." He paused, with a smile that indicated he was about to make a small, deanlike joke. "The cushions may well make it easier for congregants to sit and listen to my sermons."

There was a sedate collective chuckle.

As he went on, Violet glanced at the woman next to her, who had laughed more openly. Her face was thin and angular, like a long isosceles triangle had unfolded between her temples and chin, and her brown hair was shingled into another triangle whose points stuck straight out from her cheeks. She turned to Violet with eager dark eyes, as if the glance were the calling card she had been waiting for. "I haven't seen you before," she whispered. "Are you from the Monday group? Is one of yours up there?"

"Ah—no."

"Not done yet? I managed to finish mine last week—just before the cutoff. Had to run clear across town to get it to them. Miss Pesel and Mrs. Biggins were that strict about it. Handed it straight to Miss Pesel herself."

A woman in the seat in front of them turned her head as if listening, and Violet's neighbor went quiet. A minute later she began again, more softly. "Are you working on a kneeler?"

Violet shook her head.

"What, your stitching wasn't good enough?" The woman made a sympathetic moue. "Mine was returned to me three times before they were satisfied! Have they put you on hanking instead? Or straightening the cupboards? The cupboards always need that, but it's awfully dull. Or maybe you keep records for them. I'll bet that's what you do." She glanced at Violet's hands as if searching for telltale signs of inky fingers. Of course she would also be looking for the ring, just as Violet had already noted that she didn't wear one. "I said no straightaway to record keeping. I do enough of that the rest of the week."

The woman ahead of them turned around. "Shhh!"

Violet and her neighbor smiled at each other. It felt good to have a partner in crime, albeit one who was a little eager.

By the time the service dragged to its conclusion with the end of the dean's address, another hymn ("O Holy Lord, Content to Dwell"), and more blessings, Violet was very late and had to rush away, her thin-faced neighbor calling out her name—"Gilda Hill!"—after her. She ran across the Outer Close, a patch of green surrounding the cathedral, and up the High Street to Warren's stationers, then hurried with the typewriter ribbon back to Southern Counties Insurance, arriving flushed and out of breath.

She needn't have run: The office she shared with two others in the typing pool was empty. When Violet had worked in the larger offices of the same company in Southampton, the manager had been much stricter about the comings and goings of the workers. Here, where the office was so much smaller and more exposed, you might think Violet's absence would be noted. But no. Though she didn't want to be reprimanded, she was mildly disappointed that no one had noticed her empty chair and her black Imperial typewriter with its cream keys so quiet.

She glanced at her office mates' vacant desks. Olive and Maureen— O and Mo, they called themselves, laughing raucously about their nicknames even when no one else did—must be having tea down the hall in the staff kitchen. Violet was desperate for a cup, and a biscuit to plug the hole in her stomach. For lunch she'd had only the

Marmite and margarine sandwiches she'd brought in. They were never enough; she was always hungry again by midafternoon and had to fill up with more cups of tea. Mrs. Speedwell would be appalled that Violet had a hot midday meal only once a week. She could not afford more—though she would never admit that to her mother.

For a moment she considered joining her colleagues in the kitchen. O and Mo were two local girls in their early twenties, and although they were nice enough to Violet, they came from different backgrounds, and treated her like an African violet or an aspidistra, the sort of houseplant a maiden aunt would keep. Both lived at home and so had a more carefree attitude toward money—as Violet herself had once had. One sexy, one plain, they wore new dresses as often as they could afford to, and lived for the dance halls, the cinema dates, the parade of men to choose from. There were plenty of men their age; they didn't walk into a dance hall as Violet had done a few times after the war to find the only dancing partners were old enough to be her grandfather, or far too young, or damaged in a way Violet knew she could never fix. Or just not there, so that women danced with each other to fill the absence. As they typed, O and Mo talked and laughed about the men they met as if it were assumed men should be available. They had each gone through several boyfriends in the six months Violet had worked with them, though recently both had become more serious about their current beaux. Sometimes their high spirits and assumptions made Violet go and boil the kettle in the kitchen even when she didn't want tea, waiting until she had calmed down enough to go back and carry on with her rapid typing. She was a far more efficient typist than the girls—which they seemed to find funny.

Only once had Mo asked her if she'd had a chap, "back then."

"Yes." Violet clipped her reply, refusing to make Laurence into an anecdote.

This week had been worse. Even the prospect of tea and a biscuit did not outweigh the dread Violet felt at having to watch tiny, buxom Olive straighten her fingers in front of her face for the umpteenth time to admire her engagement ring. On the Monday she had come into the office walking differently, pride setting her shoulders back and lifting her tight blond curls. She had exchanged a sly, smug smile with Mo, already installed behind her typewriter, then announced as she shook out her chiffon scarf and hung up her coat, "I'm just off to speak to Mr. Waterman." She pulled off her gloves, and Violet couldn't help it—she searched for the flash of light on O's ring finger. The diamond was minute, but even a tiny sparkle is still a sparkle.

As O clipped down the hall in higher heels than the court shoes Violet wore, Mo—smarter than her friend but less conventionally attractive, with colorless hair, a long face, and a tendency to frown— let her smile fade. If she were feeling kind at that moment, Violet would assure Mo that her current boyfriend—a reticent bank clerk who had stopped by the office once or twice—was sure to propose shortly. But she was not feeling kind, not about this subject; she re- mained silent while Mo stewed in her misery.

Since that day and O's triumphant display of her ring, it was all the girls talked about: how Joe had proposed (at a pub, with the ring at the bottom of her glass of port and lemon), how long they would wait to save up for a proper do (two years), where the party would take place (same pub), what she would wear (white rather than ivory—which Violet knew was a mistake, as white would be too harsh for Olive's complexion), where they would live (with his family until they could afford a place). It was all so banal and repetitive, with no interesting or surprising revelations or dreams or desires, that Violet thought she might go mad if she had to listen to this for two years.

She lit a cigarette to distract herself and suppress her appetite. Then she fed a sheet of paper through the typewriter rollers and began to type, making her way steadily through an application from Mr. Richard Turner of Basingstoke for house insurance, which guaranteed payment if the house and contents were lost to fire or flood or some other act of God. Violet noticed that "war" was not included. She wondered if Mr. Turner understood that not all loss could be replaced.

Mostly, though, she typed without thinking. Violet had typed so many of these applications to insure someone's life, house, automobile, boat, that she rarely considered the meaning of the words. For her, typing was a meaningless, repetitive act that became a soothing meditation, lulling her into a state where she did not think; she simply *was*.

Soon enough O and Mo were back, their chatter preceding them down the hall and interrupting Violet's trancelike peace. "After you, Mrs. Hill." Mo stood aside and gestured Olive through the door. Both wore floral summer dresses, O in peach, Mo in tan, reminding Violet that her plain blue linen dress was three years old, the dropped waist out of date. It was difficult to alter a dropped waist.

"Well, I don't mind if I do, *Miss* Webster—soon to be Mrs. Livingstone, I'm sure."

"Oh, I don't know." Mo looked eager, though.

Olive set down her cup of tea by her typewriter with a clatter, spilling some into the saucer. "Of course you will! You could marry sooner than I do. You may end up my matron of honor rather than my maid!" She held out her hand once more to inspect her ring.

Violet paused in her typing. Mrs. Hill. It was a common enough name. Still . . . "Does your fiancé have a sister?"

"Who, Gilda? What about her? She's just a warped old spins—" Olive seemed to recall whom she was talking to and bit her words back with a laugh, but not before Violet took in her dismissive tone. It made her decide to like Gilda Hill.

2

Violet lived fifteen minutes from the office in an area called the Soke, on the eastern side of Winchester just across the river Itchen. On a single typist's salary, she could not afford the nicer areas in the west with their larger houses and gardens, their swept streets and well-maintained motorcars. The houses in the Soke were smaller yet had more inhabitants. There were fewer motorcars, and the local shops had dustier window displays and sold cheaper goods.

She shared the house with two other women as well as the landlady, who took up the ground floor. There were no men, of course, and even male visitors other than family were discouraged downstairs, and forbidden upstairs. On the rare occasion there were men in the front room, Mrs. Harvey had a tendency to go in and out, looking for the copy of the *Southern Daily Echo* she'd left behind, or her reading glasses, or feeding the budgies she kept in a cage there, or fiddling with the fire when no one had complained of the cold, or reminding them to be in good time for the train. Not that Violet had any male visitors other than her brother Tom, but Mrs. Harvey had given him this treatment until Violet showed her a family photo as evidence. Even then she did not leave them alone for long, but popped her head round the door to remind Tom that petrol stations shut early on Saturdays. Tom took it as a comic turn. "I feel I'm in a play and she'll announce a body's been found coshed over the head in the scullery," he remarked with glee. It was easy for him to enjoy Mrs. Harvey as entertainment since he did not have to live with her. Occasionally Violet wondered if in moving to Winchester she'd simply exchanged her mother for another who was equally tricky. On the other hand, she could go upstairs and shut her door on it all, which was harder to do with her mother. Mrs. Harvey respected a closed door, as long as there was no man behind it; in Southampton her mother had sometimes barged into Violet's bedroom as if the door did not exist.

Back now from work, she declined tea from her landlady but smuggled some milk up and put the kettle on in her own room. This was her seventh cup of the day, even having been out part of the afternoon at the cathedral. Cups of tea punctuated moments, dividing before from after: sleeping from waking, walking to the office from sitting down to work, dinner from typing again, finishing a complicated contract from starting another, ending work from beginning her evening. Sometimes she used cigarettes as punctuation, but they made her giddy rather than settling her as tea did. And they were more expensive.

Sitting with her cup in the one armchair by the unlit fire—it was not cold enough to justify the coal—Violet looked around her cramped room. It was quiet, except for the ticking of a wooden clock she'd picked up at a junk shop a few weeks before. The pale sun sieved through the net curtains and lit up the swirling red and yellow and brown carpet. "Thunder and lightning carpet," her father would have called it. Fawn-colored stockings hung drying on a rack. In the corner an ugly battered wardrobe with a door that wouldn't shut properly revealed the scant selection of dresses and blouses and skirts she had brought with her from Southampton.

Violet sighed. This is not how I was expecting it to be, she thought, this Winchester life.

Her move to Winchester last November had been sudden. After her father's death Violet had limped along for a year and half, living alone with her mother. It was expected of women like her—unwed and unlikely to—to look after their parents. She had done her best, she supposed. But Mrs. Speedwell was impossible; she always had been, even before the loss of her eldest son, George, in the war. She was from an era when daughters were dutiful and deferential to their mothers, at least until they married and deferred to their husbands— not that Mrs. Speedwell had ever deferred much to hers. When they were children, Violet and her brothers had avoided their mother's attention, playing together as a tight gang run with casual authority by George. Violet was often scolded by Mrs. Speedwell for not being feminine enough. "You'll never get a husband with scraped knees and flyaway hair and being mad about books," she declared. Little did she know that when the war came along, there would be worse things than books and scrapes to keep Violet from finding a husband.

As an adult Violet had been able to cope while her father was alive to lighten the atmosphere and absorb her mother's excesses, raising his eyebrows behind her back and smiling at his daughter, making mild jokes when he could. Once he was gone, though, and Mrs.

Speedwell had no target for her scrutiny other than her daughter—her younger son, Tom, having married and escaped years before—Violet had to bear the full weight of her attention.

As they sat by the fire one evening, Violet began to count her mother's complaints. "The light's too dim. The radio isn't loud enough. Why are they laughing when it's not funny? The salad cream at supper was off, I'm sure of it. Your hair looks dreadful—did you try to wave it yourself? Have you gained weight? I am not at all sure Tom and Evelyn should be sending Marjory to that school. What would Geoffrey think? Oh, not more rain! It's bringing out the damp in the hall."

Eight in a row, Violet thought. What depressed her even more than the complaints themselves was that she had counted them. She sighed.

"Sighing makes your face sag, Violet," her mother chided. "It does you no favors."

The next day at work she spied on the notice board a position for a typist in the regional Winchester office, which was doing well despite the depressed economy. Violet clutched her cup of tea and closed her eyes. Don't sigh, she thought. When she opened them she went to see the manager.

Everything about the change was easier than she had expected, at least at first. The manager at Southern Counties Insurance agreed to the move, Tom was supportive ("About bloody time!"), and she found a room to let at Mrs. Harvey's without much fuss. At first her mother took Violet's careful announcement that she was moving to Winchester with a surprising lack of reaction other than to say, "Canada is where you should be going. That is where the husbands are." But on the rainy Saturday in November when Tom drove over with Evelyn and the children and began to load Violet's few possessions into his Austin, Mrs. Speedwell would not get up from her armchair in the sitting room. She sat with a cold, untouched cup of tea beside her and with trembling fingers smoothed the antimacassars covering the arms of the chair. She did not look at Violet as she came in to say good-bye. "When George was taken from us I never thought I would have to go through the ordeal of losing another child," she announced to the room. Marjory and Edward were putting together a jigsaw in front of the coal fire; Violet's solemn niece gazed up at her grandmother, her wide hazel eyes following Mrs. Speedwell's agitated hands as she continued to smooth and resmooth the antimacassars.

"Mother, you're not losing me. I'm moving twelve miles away!" Even as she said it, though, Violet knew that in a way her mother was right.

"And for the child to *choose* for me to lose her," Mrs. Speedwell continued, as if Violet had not spoken and indeed was not even in the room. "Unforgivable. At least poor George had no choice—it was the war; he did it for his country. But this! Treacherous."

"For God's sake, Mum, Violet's not *died*," Tom interjected as he passed by with a box full of plates and cups and cutlery from the kitchen that Violet hoped her mother wouldn't miss.

"Well, it's on her hands. If I don't wake up one morning and no one discovers me dead in my bed for days, she'll be sorry then! Or maybe she won't be. Maybe she'll carry on as usual."

"Mummy, is Granny going to die?" Edward asked, a puzzle piece suspended in the air in the clutch of his hand. He did not appear to be upset by the idea; merely curious.

"That's enough of such talk," Evelyn replied. A brisk brunette, she was used to Mrs. Speedwell, and Violet admired how efficiently she had learned to shut down her mother-in-law. It was always easier when you weren't related. She had sorted out Tom as well, after the war. Violet appreciated her sister-in-law but was a little too intimidated to be true friends with her. "Come, give your Auntie Violet a kiss good-bye. Then we'll go down to the shops while Daddy drives her to Winchester."

Marjory and Edward scrambled to their feet and gave Violet obedient pecks on the cheek that made her smile.

"Why can't we come to Winchester?" Edward asked. "I want to ride in Daddy's car."

"We explained before, Eddie. Auntie Violet has her things to move, so there's no space for us."

Actually, Auntie Violet didn't have so very much to move. She was surprised that her life fitted into so few suitcases and boxes. There was still space on the back seat for another passenger, and she rather wished Edward could come with them. He was a spirited little boy who would keep her cheerful with his non sequiturs and shameless solipsism. If forced to focus on his world, she would not think of her own. But she knew she could not ask for him to come along and not Marjory or Evelyn, and so she said nothing as they began to pull on their shoes and coats for their expedition in the rain.

When it became clear that Mrs. Speedwell was not going to see her off as she normally did, watching from the doorway until visitors were out of sight, Violet went over and kissed her on the forehead. "Good-bye, Mother," she murmured. "I'll see you next Sunday."

Mrs. Speedwell sniffed. "Don't bother. I may be dead by then."

One of Tom's best qualities was that he knew when to keep quiet. On the way to Winchester he let Violet cry without comment. Cocooned by the steamed-up windows and the smell of hot oil and leather, she leaned back in the sprung seat and sobbed. Near Twyford, however, her sobs diminished, then stopped.

She had always loved riding in Tom's handsome brown-and-black car, marveling at how the space held her apart from the world and yet whisked her efficiently from place to place. "Perhaps I'll get a car," she declared, wiping her eyes with a handkerchief embroidered with violets—one of Evelyn's practical Christmas presents to her. Even as she said it she knew she could afford no such luxury: She was going to be dreadfully poor, though as yet that felt like something of a game. "Will you teach me to drive?" she asked, lighting a cigarette and cracking open a window.

"That's the spirit, old girl," Tom replied, changing gears to climb a hill. His affable nature had helped Violet to cope with her mother over the years, as well as with the war and its effects. Tom had turned eighteen shortly after news of his brother's death came through, and joined up without hesitation or fuss. He never talked about his experiences in France; like Violet's loss of her fiancé, they took a back seat to their brother's death. Violet knew she took Tom for granted, as older children always do their younger siblings. They had both looked up to George, following his lead in their play as children. Once he was gone they had found themselves at sea. Was Violet then meant to take on the role of the eldest, to assume command and set the example for Tom to follow? If so, she had made a poor job of it. She was a typist at an insurance company; she had not married and begun a family. Tom had quietly overtaken her—though he never gloated or apologized. He didn't need to: He was a man, and it was expected of him to achieve.

After they had moved her things in under Mrs. Harvey's watchful eye, he took her for fish and chips. "Mum's a tough old boot, you know," he reassured her over their meal. "She got through George, and Dad too. She'll survive this. And so will you. Just don't stay in your room all the time. Don't want to be getting 'one-room-itis'—isn't that what they call it? Get out, meet some people."

Meet some men, he meant. He was more subtle than her mother about the subject, but she knew Tom too wished she would miraculously find a man to marry, even at this late age. A widower, perhaps, with grown children. Or a man who needed help with injuries. The war may have ended thirteen years before, but the injuries lasted a lifetime. Once married, she would be off Tom's hands, a niggling burden he would no longer have to worry about. Otherwise Violet might have to live with her brother one day; it was what spinsters often did.

But it was not easy to meet men, because there were two million fewer of them than women. Violet had read many newspaper articles about these "surplus women," as they were labeled, left single as a result of the war and unlikely to marry—considered a tragedy, and a threat, in a society set up for marriage. Journalists seemed to relish the label, brandishing it like a pin pressed into the skin. Mostly it was an annoyance; occasionally, though, the pin penetrated the protective layers and drew blood. She had assumed it would hurt less as she grew older, and was surprised to find that even at thirty-eight—middle-aged—labels could still wound. But she had been called worse: hoyden, shrew, man hater.

Violet did not hate men, and had not been entirely man-free. Two or three times a year, she had put on her best dress—copper lamé in a scallop pattern—gone alone to a Southampton hotel bar, and sat with a sherry and a cigarette until someone took interest. Her "sherry men," she called them. Sometimes they ended up in an alley or a motorcar or a park; never in his room, certainly not at her parents'. To be desired was welcome, though she did not feel the intense

pleasure from the encounters that she once had with Laurence during the Perseids.

Every August Violet and her father and brothers had watched the
Perseid showers. Violet had never said anything to her father during
those late nights in the garden, watching for streaks in the sky, but
she did not really like stargazing. The cold—even in August—the
dew fall, the crick in the neck: There were never visions spectacular
enough to overcome these discomforts. She would make a terrible
astronomer, for she preferred to be warm.

The Perseid showers she remembered best were in August 1916,
when Laurence had got leave and come to see her. They'd taken a
train out to Romsey, had supper at a pub, then walked out into the
fields and spread out a rug. If anyone happened upon them, they
could be given a mini-lecture by Laurence about the Perseids, how
the earth passed in its orbit through the remnants of a comet every
August and created spectacular meteor showers. They were there in
the field to watch, merely to watch. And they did watch, for a short
while, on their backs holding hands.

After witnessing a few meteors streak across the sky, Violet turned
on her side so that she was facing Laurence, her hip bone digging
into a stone under the blanket, and said to him, "Yes." Though he
had not asked a question aloud, there had been one hanging between
them, ever since they had got engaged the year before.

She could feel him smile, though she couldn't see his face in the
dark. He rolled toward her. After a while Violet was no longer cold,
and no longer cared about the movement of the stars in the sky
above, but only the movement of his body against hers.

They say a woman's first time is painful, bloody, a shock you must
get used to. It was nothing like that for Violet. She exploded, stron-
ger, it seemed, than any Perseids, and Laurence was delighted. They

stayed in the field so long that they missed any possibility of a train back, and had to walk the seven miles, until a veteran of the Boer wars passed them in his motorcar, recognized a soldier's gait, and stopped to give them a lift, smiling at the grass in Violet's hair and her startled happiness.

Only a week later they received the telegram about George's death at Delville Wood. And a year later, Laurence at Passchendaele. He and Violet had not managed to spend more time properly alone together, in a field or a hotel room or even an alley. With each loss she had tumbled into a dark pit, a void opening up inside her that made her feel helpless and hopeless. Her brother was gone, her fiancé was gone, God was gone. It took a long time for the gap to close, if it ever really did.

A few years later when she could face it, she tried to experience again what she'd had with Laurence that night, this time with one of George's old friends, who had come through the war physically unscathed. But there were no Perseids—only a painful awareness of each moment that killed any pleasure and just made her despise his rubbery lips.

She suspected she would never feel pleasure with her sherry men. She had laughed about them with scandalized girlfriends, for a time; but some of her friends managed to marry the few available men, and others withdrew into sexless lives and stopped wanting to hear about her exploits. Marriage in particular brought many changes to her friends, and one was donning a hat of conservatism that made them genuinely and easily shocked and threatened. One of those sherry men could be their husband. And so Violet began to keep quiet about what she got up to those few times a year. Slowly, as husbands and children took over, and the tennis games and cinema trips and dance hall visits dried up, the friendships drifted. When she left Southampton there was really no one left to regret leaving, or give her address to, or invite to tea.

"Violet, where have you gone?" Tom was studying her over the remains of his chips.

Violet shook her head. "Sorry—just, you know."

Her brother reached over and hugged her—a surprise, as they were not the hugging sort of siblings. They walked back to Mrs. Harvey's, where his motorcar was parked. Violet stood in the doorway and watched his Austin hiss away through the wet street, then went upstairs. She had thought she might cry when finally alone in her shabby new room, with a door she could shut against the world. But she had cried her tears out on the trip from Southampton. Instead she looked around at the sparse furnishings, nodded, and put the kettle on.

3

Violet had not really understood how hard it would be to get along on her own on a typist's salary. Or she had, but vowed to manage anyway—the price she paid for her independence from her mother. When she'd lived with her parents, she handed over almost two-thirds of her weekly salary to help with the running of the household, keeping five shillings back for her own expenses— dinner, clothes, cigarettes, sixpenny magazines—and putting another few shillings in the bank. Over the years her savings had gradually built up, but she assumed she would need them for her older years when her parents were gone. She had to eat into them more substantially than she'd expected to pay for the deposit on her lodgings in the Soke, and for some bits and pieces to make the room more comfortable. Her mother had plenty to spare in the Southampton house, but Violet knew better than to ask. Perhaps if she were moving to Canada to find a husband, Mrs. Speedwell would have been willing to ship furniture thousands of miles. But sending anything twelve miles up the road was an affront. Instead Violet had to scour the junk shops of Winchester for a cheap bedside table when there was a pretty rattan one sitting in her old bedroom, or a chunky green ashtray rather than an almost identical one in the Southampton sitting room, or a couple of chipped majolica plates for the mantelpiece when her mother had any number of knickknacks in boxes in the attic. It had not occurred to her to take such extras when she moved out, for she had never had to make a strange room into a home before.

Violet was still earning thirty-five shillings a week at the Winchester office, the same as her Southampton salary. It was considered a good one for a typist—she had been at the company for ten years, and her typing was fast and accurate. It had felt generous when she lived at home; she could have a hot dinner most days and not think too hard before buying cigarettes or a new lipstick. But it was not a salary you could easily live on alone; it was rather like a pair of ill-fitting shoes that could be worn but that pinched and rubbed and left calluses. Now that Violet had to survive on it she understood that, proud as she had been to earn and contribute to the running of the house, her parents must have regarded what she handed over almost as pocket money.

The same amount she'd given to her parents now went to her landlady, and it only covered breakfast; she paid for and cooked her own supper, and she had to pay for laundry and coal—things she'd taken for granted at home. Whenever she left the house she seemed to spend money—just little bits here and there, but it added up. Living was a constant expense. Violet could no longer put aside any money to save. She had to learn to make do, and do without. She began wearing the same clothes over and over, and washing them under the tap to avoid an excessive laundry bill, mending tears and hiding worn patches with brooches or scarves, knowing that whatever she did would never refresh the shabbiness. Only new clothes could do that.

She stopped buying magazines and papers, relying on O and Mo's castoffs, and did not replace her lipsticks. She began to ration her cigarettes to three a day. Many evening meals consisted of sardines on toast or fried sprats rather than a chop, for meat was too dear. Violet was not keen on breakfast—she would have preferred toast and marmalade—but since she was paying for it she forced herself to eat the poached egg Mrs. Harvey served every morning, afterward arriving at work faintly queasy. She took herself to the cinema every week—her one indulgence, which she paid for by going without a meal that day. The first film she saw in Winchester was called *Almost a Honeymoon*, about a man who had to find a woman to marry in twenty-four hours. It was so painful she wanted to leave halfway through, but it was warm in the cinema and she could not justify sacrificing a meal only to walk out early.

Every Sunday she took the train to Southampton to accompany her mother to church, the money for the ticket coming from her slowly diminishing savings. It would never have occurred to Mrs. Speedwell to offer to pay. She never asked Violet about money, nor about her job nor Winchester nor any aspect of her new life, which made a two-way conversation difficult. Indeed, Mrs. Speedwell just spent the afternoons complaining, as if she had been saving up all her grievances for the few hours her daughter was with her. If Tom and Evelyn and the children weren't there, Violet almost always made an excuse and took an earlier train back, defiant and guilty in equal measure. Then she would sit in her room reading a novel (she was making her way through Trollope, her father's favorite), or go for a walk in the water meadows by the river, or catch the end of Evensong at Winchester Cathedral.

Whenever she walked through the front entrance below the Great West Window and into the cathedral, the long nave in front of her and the vast space above bounded by a stunning vaulted ceiling, Violet felt the whole weight of the nine-hundred-year-old building hover over her, and wanted to cry. It was the only place built specifically for spiritual sustenance in which she felt she was indeed being spiritually fed. Not necessarily from the services, which apart from Evensong were formulaic and rigid, though the repetition was comforting. It was more the reverence for the place itself, for the knowledge of the many thousands of people who had come there throughout its history, looking for a place in which to be free to consider the big questions about life and death rather than worrying about paying for the winter's coal or needing a new coat.

She loved it for the more concrete things as well: for its colored windows and elegant arches and carvings, for its old patterned tiles, for the elaborate tombs of bishops and kings and noble families, for the surprising painted bosses that covered the joins between the stone ribs on the distant ceiling, and for all of the energy that had gone into making those things, for the creators throughout history.

Like most smaller services, Evensong was held in the choir. The choirboys with their scrubbed, mischievous faces sat in one set of stall benches, the congregants in the other, with any overflow in the adjacent presbytery seats. Violet suspected Evensong was considered frivolous by regular churchgoers compared to Sunday morning services, but she preferred the lighter touch of music to the booming organ, and the shorter, simpler sermon to the hectoring morning one. She did not pray or listen to the prayers—prayers had died in the war alongside George and Laurence and a nation full of young men. But when she sat in the choir stalls, she liked to study the carved oak arches overhead, decorated with leaves and flowers and animals and even a Green Man whose mustache turned into abundant foliage. Out of the corner of her eye she could see the looming enormity of the nave, but sitting here with the boys' ethereal voices around her, she felt safe from the void that at times threatened to overwhelm her. Sometimes, quietly and unostentatiously, she cried.

One Sunday afternoon a few weeks after the Presentation of Embroideries service, Violet slipped late into the presbytery as a visiting dean was giving the sermon. When she went to sit she moved a kneeler that had been placed on the chair, then held it in her lap and studied it. It was a rectangle about nine by twelve inches with a mustard-colored circle like a medallion in the center surrounded by a mottled field of blue. The medallion design was of a bouquet of branches with checker-capped acorns among blue-green foliage. Checkered acorns had been embroidered in the four corners as well. The colors were surprisingly bright, the pattern cheerful and un-churchlike. It reminded Violet of the background of medieval tapestries, with their intricate millefleur arrangement of leaves and flowers. This design was simpler than that but nonetheless captured an echo from the past.

They all did, she thought, placing the kneeler on the floor and glancing at those around her, each with a central circle of flowers or knots on a blue background. There were not yet enough embroidered kneelers for every chair, and the rest had the usual unmemorable hard lozenges of red-and-black felt. The new embroidered ones lifted the tone of the presbytery, giving it color and a sense of designed purpose.

At the service's end, Violet picked up the kneeler to look at it again, smiling as she traced with her finger the checkered acorns. It always seemed a contradiction to have to be solemn in the cathedral amid the uplifting beauty of the stained glass, the wood carving, the stone sculpture, the glorious architecture, the boys' crystalline tones, and now the kneelers.

A hovering presence made her look up. A woman about her age stood in the aisle next to her, staring at the kneeler Violet held. She was wearing a swagger coat in forest green that swung from her shoulders and had a double row of large black buttons running down the front. Matching it was a dark green felt hat with feathers tucked in the black band. Despite her modish attire, she did not have the appearance of being modern, but looked rather as if she had stepped aside from the flow of the present. Her hair was not waved; her pale gray eyes seemed to float in her face.

"Sorry. Would you mind if I"—she reached out to flip over the kneeler and reveal the dark blue canvas underside—"I just like to look at it when I'm here. It's mine, you see." She tapped on the border. Violet squinted—stitched there were initials and a year: "DJ 1932."

Violet watched her gazing at her handiwork. "How long did it take you to make it?" She asked partly out of politeness, but curiosity too.

"Two months. I had to unpick bits a few times. These kneelers may be used in the cathedral for centuries, and so they must be made correctly from the start." She paused. "Ars longa, vita brevis."

Violet thought back to her Latin at school. "Art is long, life short," she quoted her old Latin teacher.

"Yes."

Violet could not imagine the kneeler being there for hundreds of years. The war had taught her not to assume that anything would last, even something as substantial as a cathedral, much less a mere kneeler. Indeed, just twenty-five years before, a diver, William Walker, had been employed for five years to shore up the foundations of Winchester Cathedral with thousands of sacks of concrete so that the building would not topple in on itself. Nothing could be taken for granted.

She wondered if the builders of the cathedral nine hundred years ago had thought of her, standing under their arches, next to their thick pillars, on top of their medieval tiles, lit by their stained glass— a woman in 1932, living and worshipping so differently from how they did. They would not have conjured up Violet Speedwell; that seemed certain.

She put out a hand as "DJ" set her kneeler on a chair and made to move off. "Are you a member of the Cathedral Broderers?"

DJ paused. "Yes."

"If one wanted to contact them, how . . ."

"There is a sign on the notice board in the porch about the meetings." She looked at Violet directly for a moment, then filed out after the other congregants.

Violet did not intend to look for the notice. She thought she had set aside the kneelers in her mind. But several days later, out for a walk by the cathedral, she found herself drawn to the notice board and the sign about the broderers, written in careful copperplate like her mother's handwriting. Violet copied down a number for Mrs. Humphrey Biggins, and that evening used her landlady's telephone to ring.

"Compton 220." Mrs. Biggins herself answered the telephone. Violet knew immediately it wasn't a daughter, or a housekeeper, or a sister. She sounded so much like Violet's mother in her better days that it silenced her, and Mrs. Biggins had to repeat "Compton 220" with increased irritation until she eventually demanded, "Who is this? I will not tolerate these silences. I shall be phoning the police to report you, you can be sure!"

"I'm sorry," Violet stumbled. "Perhaps I have the wrong number." Though she knew that she did not. "I'm—I'm ringing about the kneelers in the cathedral."

"Young lady, your telephone manner is *dreadful*. You are all of a muddle. You must say your name clearly, and then ask to speak to me, and say what your call concerns. Now try it."

Violet shuddered and almost put down the telephone. When the Speedwells first had a telephone installed, her mother had given her lessons in telephone etiquette, though she had often put off potential callers herself with her impatient manner. But Violet knew she must persist or she would never have her own kneeler in Winchester Cathedral. "My name is Violet Speedwell," she began obediently, feeling like a small child. "I would like to speak to Mrs. Biggins with regard to the embroidery project at the cathedral."

"That's better. But you are ringing very late, and at the wrong time. Our classes finish shortly for the summer and don't resume until the autumn. Miss Pesel and Miss Blunt need time over the summer to work on designs for the next batch."

"All right, I'll ring back then. Sorry to have troubled you."

"Not so hasty, Miss Speedwell. May I assume you are a *Miss* Speedwell?"

Violet gritted her teeth. "Yes."

"Well, you young people are far too quick to give up."

It had been a long time since Violet had been called a young person.

"Now, do you know how to embroider? We do canvas embroidery for the cushions and kneelers. Do you know what that is?"

"No."

"Of course you don't. Why do we attract so many volunteers who have never held a needle? It makes our work so much more time-consuming."

"Perhaps you could think of me as a blank canvas, with no faults to unpick."

Mrs. Biggins's tone softened. "There you may be right, Miss Speedwell. A blank slate can indeed be easier. Now, we hold meetings two days a week, on Mondays and Wednesdays, from half past ten to half past twelve, and then from half past two to four o'clock, both days. Come along to the next and we'll see what we can do. If nothing else we can get you helping out—copying designs, or tidying the cupboards, perhaps."

Violet remembered what Gilda had said about cupboards. "Actually, I'm afraid I am not available then, Mrs. Biggins. I work, you see."

"You *work*? Where?"

"In an office."

"Why, then, have you telephoned me? And so late in the evening, I might add. If your time is taken up elsewhere, then I'm afraid you are of no use to the Cathedral Broderers. We demand total commitment."

"But . . ." Violet hesitated, wondering how to explain to this overbearing woman that she wanted to make a kneeler, one that kept knees from aching during prayers and that she could look out for specially in the cathedral presbytery. One that might last long after she was dead. Over the centuries others had carved heads into the choir stalls, or sculpted elaborate figures of saints from marble, or designed sturdy, memorable columns and arches, or fitted together colored glass for the windows: all glorious additions to a building whose existence was meant to make you raise your eyes to Heaven to thank God. Violet wanted to do what they had done. She was unlikely to have children now, so if she was to make a mark on the world, she would have to do so in another way. A kneeler was a stupid, tiny gesture, but there it was. "I would like to make a kneeler for the cathedral," she finally said in a small voice, then hated herself for it.

Mrs. Biggins sighed. "Everyone would, my dear. But what we really *need*—not what *you* need—are skilled embroiderers to work on the cushions Miss Pesel has planned for the choir seats and benches. Not beginners looking to conquer the cathedral with a simple kneeler."

Violet was silent. From years of experience with her mother, she had learned that silence was often more effective than words.

"What company do you work for?"

"Southern Counties Insurance."

"What, for Mr. Waterman?"

"Yes."

"There shouldn't be a problem, then. He lives in our village. I know him from our local bird-watching society. You tell him Mrs. Humphrey Biggins has asked for you to be allowed to take half a day's leave to attend class."

Violet was not at all sure she wanted to give up her precious annual leave to attend embroidery classes. "Are there no classes outside of work hours—in the evenings, or on a Saturday?"

Mrs. Biggins snorted. "Do you think we're organizing meetings to suit *you*? Some of us have families to look after. Now, you ask Mr. Waterman to let you take time off. I'll expect to see you on Wednesday at half past ten, at Church House in the Inner Close. Good night." She hung up before Violet could reply.

Whose telephone manner needs work? she thought.

It seemed Mrs. Biggins's rules about when to telephone others did not apply to herself. When Violet arrived at the office the next morning, Mr. Waterman had already left a note on her desk giving permission for her to take Wednesday morning off. Despite the hour, Mrs. Biggins must have telephoned him immediately after speaking to Violet, not trusting her to ask her supervisor herself. Later, Violet ran into him in the corridor and thanked him. A nondescript man with brown hair, pasty skin, and a drooping mustache that partially covered his tentative smile, he ducked his head as if Mrs. Biggins were lurking somewhere nearby. "I don't mind how you use your annual leave," he replied, "and for a noble cause, too." He paused, fiddling with his shirt cuffs, which were not as clean as they could be. Mrs. Biggins would bleach them till they gleamed, Violet thought. "Take care, though, Miss Speedwell," he added. "Once Mrs. Biggins gets her claws in you, you'll never be free!" He wheeled around and hurried back the way he had come, as if frightened he'd said too much.

4

Though annoyed by Mrs. Biggins's interference, as well as her mixed messages—Come on Wednesday but you won't be much use to us—Violet found herself looking forward to the broderers' meeting. Her brother had been pestering her ever since she moved to Winchester to join some groups—ramblers, historical societies, benevolent church funds, anything that would bring her into contact with potential friends and suitors. Now she could genuinely answer that she was doing just that—although suitors were rather unlikely at an embroidery group.

On Wednesday morning it felt odd to sleep in on a working day, to dawdle over breakfast and not have to join the queue to wash. Violet sat in her tea-colored dressing gown, lit a cigarette, and listened to the house empty of its inhabitants—the other lodgers to their various employments, her landlady to the shops. Eventually she got dressed, aware that the broderers would note her choice of clothes, her hair, her makeup. After some thought she donned a simple chiffon dress in pale green with yellow flowers, and her beige cardigan in case the embroidery room was chilly.

Church House was one of a row of houses in the Inner Close, to the south of the cathedral. Violet had walked past the buildings before but had never considered what might be going on inside. She felt a little sick as she approached the entrance, a feeling similar to that on her first day of work at the Winchester office—the war in her gut between craving the new and clinging to the comfort of the familiar. The door had a bell to one side with a small handwritten sign that read RING THE BELL. That impertinent sign almost made Violet turn around and hurry away. But hurry away to what—an empty room? Window-shopping with no money in her purse? The office, where they wouldn't even notice she'd not been there?

She rang the bell. After a moment a girl answered, looked her up and down, and before Violet could say a word, commanded, "Up the stairs, right, and all the way down the passage to the last room."

How does she know? Violet thought, and suddenly wished she had worn something different—though what, exactly, she wasn't sure. She found the room and forced herself to enter boldly, like plunging into the cold sea rather than hesitating on the shore. She was not late—as she walked down the corridor Violet had heard the cathedral bells sounding the half hour—but the dozen chairs around the long table were almost full. Some women were already bent over pieces of canvas, glancing at patterns and needling colored wool in and out of the tiny holes. Others were murmuring over embroidered work they held, presumably discussing a technique or comparing results.

No one looked up as she came in. Violet wondered if she had got the time wrong, if they had started at ten or nine thirty. No, she was sure Mrs. Biggins had said ten thirty. These must be the keen ones. The feeling in the room was one of quiet purpose, tinged with a drop of self-satisfaction, which would be denied if anyone accused them of such a thing.

Even if she hadn't recognized her from the broderers' service, Violet immediately guessed who Mrs. Biggins must be from her demeanor, so similar to her telephone manner. She wore a high-necked blouse and hair piled and puffed on top of her head, her style being stranded somewhere around 1910. She was not walking about to peer over each embroiderer's shoulder at her work. Instead she sat at one end of the table, where the chairman of the board would be during meetings, and let workers come to her, placing their bit of stitching before her like an offering. There she scrutinized and pronounced. As Violet watched, she flattened three embroiderers in rapid succession. "No, no, no, you have only used two shades of blue in this corner. You must know Miss Pesel's first principle of background work—three shades must be used throughout, to give texture and shading. You shall have to unpick your work and redo it."

"See now, here you have pulled too hard, so that the stitches are too tight and the tension uneven. That will not do at all—you will have to unpick that section."

"Have you mixed two stitches here? Is that cross-stitch and long-armed cross alternated? Oh my dear, no! Miss Pesel is encouraging us to become more adventurous with the stitches we use, but never on God's green earth should you alternate those two. Start again!"

Each woman nodded and said, "Yes, ma'am, I'll rework it," or some similar response, then scuttled away like dogs scolded for stealing bones from the dinner table. Back at their seats, they frowned and muttered to their neighbors.

"Where is your work?" Mrs. Biggins demanded as Violet approached.

"I've not done any yet. This is my first time. We spoke on the telephone."

"Miss Speedwell, is it? No embroidery experience at all? All right, let's get you started. You can work with Mrs. Way. Mabel!" she called. "Here's Miss Speedwell to help you sort the cupboard."

A thin woman in a gray dress with hair to match stepped back from a large cupboard in the corner. It was the usher who had tried to keep Violet from the broderers' service at the cathedral. She started when she recognized the newcomer. "It's not looking too bad, Mrs. Biggins," she insisted. "I don't really need the help."

"Nonsense. A tidy cupboard sets up the whole endeavor and helps us to work better."

Violet took a deep breath. She had no choice but to stand up for herself, as she had with her mother when she moved to Winchester, and as she had with Mabel Way a few weeks before. Else there was no point being here. "I was hoping to learn embroidery, not tidying." She spoke in a low voice, but it seemed everyone heard, for the room went quiet.

Mrs. Biggins sat up straight, as if to rearrange the rod up her back. "Miss Speedwell, I know you are keen to make your unique contribution to the cathedral with your very own kneeler. But this is a cooperative operation, and in the spirit of cooperation, we all have tasks to perform here, many of which do not involve embroidering but are nonetheless essential to our endeavor. Now, you go over to the cupboard and help Mabel make it the tidiest cupboard in Winchester. Only *then* will we teach you to thread a needle."

Violet turned red during this public dressing-down. If this was to be what embroidering for Winchester Cathedral was like—sorting cupboards and being condescended to—perhaps she should walk out and abandon the idea of a kneeler with her initials on it. She could leave the Cathedral Broderers in their room in Church House and go for a walk instead, along the river through the water meadows, admiring the harebells and poppies and campanula on the verges.

Or watch the Winchester College boys playing cricket on their grounds. Or she could go home and reach for the bottle of cheap sherry she tried not to resort to too often. Or go to the Royal Hotel and have her sherry there, though she could not afford it, waiting for a man to sit down across from her and pay for another.

She did not have to do any of that, for at that moment the smiling woman who had been in the front bench at the Presentation of Embroideries service walked in. Immediately the tension in the room eased. Violet had never known one person to have such a marked effect on an atmosphere. She was a short woman in her early sixties, with spectacles and a soft double chin, her gray hair drawn back in a low, loose bun. Her wide mouth maintained a slight smile that reassured rather than judged. "Ladies, I am delighted to see you here," was all she said, and yet somehow it was enough. As is often the case, a leader comfortable with her authority does not need to be strident, but can afford to be generous. It felt like being visited by the nicest, strictest mother possible. The women who had been scolded went about unpicking their work with renewed energy, and others crowded around, calling, "Miss Pesel, may I have a word? Miss Pesel, I would be grateful if you could check my eyelets—I cannot get them to lie flat. Miss Pesel, have I mixed the yellows as you wanted? Miss Pesel . . ." They were like schoolgirls eager to please a favorite teacher. Even Mrs. Biggins softened.

Eventually, Violet thought, she will get to me. In the meantime, helping Mabel Way with a messy cupboard suddenly did not seem so bad. She did not want Miss Pesel to find her idle. Even as Violet joined her by the enormous wardrobe set against the back wall, Mabel's permanent frown lessened slightly, as if a rubber had been taken to the lines on her brow. "Perhaps it might help me to see what there is in here," Violet suggested, "until I can begin learning to embroider."

Mabel Way nodded, her eyes on Miss Pesel as she made her way around the room, like a bride at a wedding greeting her guests. "I have some work I want to show her. Why don't you continue to separate the hanks of blue wool into piles, making sure they've not got mixed up? Look, I've made a start, light to dark." She gestured at the wool sitting on the wide windowsill next to the wardrobe, then hurried off.

Violet gazed at the hanks. She had not handled wool since she was a girl and went through a phase of learning from her grandmother to knit and crochet. She had made her mother a bed jacket Mrs. Speedwell never even tried on, and her father a muddy yellow-green scarf that he loyally wore to work for two weeks while her mother daily complained that he would be made fun of for humoring his daughter. When the scarf mysteriously disappeared, Mrs. Speedwell denied all knowledge.

Mabel Way had removed the blues from the reds and yellows and oranges and browns, and it seemed to Violet that there were only two shades—light and dark blue—and they were already sorted. She was not sure what more she could do with them, and peered into the cupboard to see if there was anything else she might tidy—though organization was not her forte. Her brothers had always kept their clothes and toys and books in better order than she. George had arranged his books in alphabetical order, Tom by color and size. Violet's ended up jumbled together, books she loved and despised side by side, books she hadn't read next to those she had. Her clothes were similar: She brushed her dresses and skirts and hung them with care, yet somehow they became wrinkled and disordered. Her hair too would not stay in its waves, but went flat too easily. It hadn't mattered so much at home, but now that she was trying to be independent, she noticed these small failures.

The embroiderers' cupboard was a thing of beauty, if you liked your beauty labeled and tidy. It had been fitted out with numerous shelves, each with handwritten labels glued on: "Kneelers"; "Choir Stall Seat Cushions"; "Choir Long Bench Cushions." There were boxes of various sizes, separating the colored wools from one another, and stacks of designs. There were several boxes of models, and rolls of canvas made of hemp (single weave or double weave). If she studied the cupboard for half an hour, Violet would understand how the broderers' project was set up. Perhaps that was why Mrs. Biggins had assigned her to it.

The cupboard reminded her of the lessons on stationery at the secretarial college she had gone to a year or two after the war, when she'd finally accepted marriage was no longer a given and she needed to do something with her time other than be a companion to her mother. Mostly the girls were taught typing and shorthand, but there had also been a few sessions on organizing stationery cupboards, with rules to learn such as always putting the heaviest, bulkiest things on the lower shelves, or using box lids to sort and keep pen nibs and rubber bands and paper clips in. Violet had thought it all beneath her dignity, yet she failed her first exam in stationery organization. She chuckled now, remembering.

"You're here! After the broderers' service I wondered if you might come along to a meeting." Gilda Hill had arrived, and hurried over to her. She wore a floral red-and-white dress with a V-neck that mirrored her triangular face. Her slash of bright red lipstick made Violet aware of her own chewed lips.

"Hello." Violet felt almost shy as she held out her hand. "I'm Violet Speedwell."

Gilda pumped her hand. "Gilda Hill, remember? We'll have such fun together. Now, don't tell me Biggins has put you on cupboard duty! And with Mabel, I expect. Is she having you sort wool? It's best if you hold it in the natural light. That's why Mabel was sorting it on the sill. Didn't she say? Honestly, she's hopeless! And her embroidery! I shouldn't point fingers, as mine's nothing special. Let's just say there's a reason Mabel gets assigned to the cupboard so often. Did she or Mrs. Biggins explain the blues? No? You'd best have a look at what I'm working on; then you'll understand better." From a bag at her feet she pulled out a rectangular frame with canvas stretched across it. "I'm making a kneeler for the presbytery. Nothing fancy—not like the choir cushions."

"What different things are being made?" Violet interjected, already exhausted by her new friend's patter.

"Biggins didn't tell you? Of course not—she'll never tell you anything so practical; she'll just assume you know it. The first thing we began working on was the kneelers for the chairs near the altar in the presbytery, like this." Gilda patted the embroidered rectangle. "There are to be hundreds of them eventually. These are all variations on a theme—a sort of medieval-style knot in the center, circular, with flowers or geometrical shapes in them, set on a background patterned in blue with crosshatching or zigzags. Miss Pesel says we are always to use at least three shades of blue for the background, to give it texture. Those are the blues you're sorting—four there, so when making a kneeler you choose three of the four. Then there are borders, made up of red or brown and cream or yellow squares or rectangles, and the corners have little motifs. They're not too

difficult to make, and there's a surprising amount of variety in stitch
and tone, so that they feel individual but are harmonious when all
together. Miss Pesel is a genius designer."

Violet nodded, wondering if she would get to meet the genius.

"Then there are two types of cushions—stall seat cushions, which
are smaller ones for the seats along the back of the choir; and bench
cushions, which will be much longer. The bench cushions and some
of the seat cushions will have a series of medallions in the centers that
Miss Sybil Blunt is designing. She is a friend of Miss Pesel's—she just
does the designs, so you won't see her much at these meetings. The
medallions are to be scenes from English history, with a Winchester
twist. So there will be kings who have ruled here or are buried here
or have connections here, like Alfred and Canute and Richard the
Lionheart, and one of King Arthur. And there will be famous Winchester bishops like Wykeham and Beaufort and Wodeloke."

"Are there any women?"

"Wives. Emma and Mary Tudor. In terms of embroidery style,
the history medallions will be a mix of large stitches and petit point
using finer wool and silk, and which require more skill. Only the
more experienced broderers will work on them. The rest of us will
fill in the backgrounds and borders. Miss Pesel has done the top of
one of the history cushions to show us what we'll be aiming to make.
Would you like to see it?"

Violet nodded.

"Biggins will have stored it in the cupboard in the hall, I expect.
You go back to your sorting and I'll fetch it." She pulled out two
hanks of blue from the bundle. "Here's your third and fourth blues."

Violet stared. "They look the same to me."

Gilda laughed. "Once you've worked with them for months you
become intimate with each shade." She winked as she hurried away.

Violet studied the wool, straining to distinguish between the different tones of blue. She closed her eyes for a moment, and thought about a drawing class she had taken several years before in Southampton. She had gone with a friend, who married the next year and disappeared into that life, keen not to be reminded by Violet of her previous surplus status. As they scraped their pencils over rough drawing paper, their teacher—a genial man who'd lost an arm in the war ("Not the drawing arm, mind—thank God for His small mercies")—told them to be like soldiers and close the mind while opening the eyes.

It had made Violet wonder if Laurence had done that—followed orders and stopped thinking on the battlefield. There was no information about how he died, no account from his commanding officer or fellow soldiers, no small details ("He made the men smile with his imitations of the Kaiser") or strong adjectives or adverbs ("Lieutenant Furniss fought bravely alongside his comrades and played a major role in defending the territory gained"). Perhaps the officer had written too many of those letters that day and had run dry of uplifting phrases and superlatives. Or maybe no one had seen what happened to Laurence Furniss—he was one of hundreds of British soldiers who died at Passchendaele on the 1st of August 1917. Presumably he had done nothing out of the ordinary; dying that day wasn't special. Although no one said, Violet heard afterward about the terrible mud there, and wondered if he had simply got stuck in it and become an easy target.

One evening at the drawing class the regular teacher was absent and a woman took his place for the evening. Her style was very different: While she set up the usual still lifes of fruit and bottles and glasses, she had them draw quickly, then move around the room to another easel and draw quickly again, and again, then go back to their original easel and spend an hour on the drawing. Violet was not sure what she was meant to learn—that things looked different from different angles, she supposed. It made her want to go outside and smoke.

The new teacher prowled behind them, stopping to peer at their drawings and make comments—few of them complimentary. Violet tried to block the sound of her voice, retreating deep inside her thoughts. She heard her name being called from a distance, but only when a hand was waved in front of her barely begun drawing did she listen.

"Miss Speedwell, what are you thinking of?"

"My brother," she replied, surprised into honesty. George *had* had some words attached: "noble effort," "stalwart in the face of enemy fire," "died bravely defending the most sacred values of this country." She could repeat these phrases because her mother had done so often over the years, sucking every drop of comfort from them until they were dry and meaningless as sticks.

"Stop thinking about him," the teacher commanded. "He is not here." She gestured at the still life. "You should be thinking of nothing more than where the highlight is on the apple, or how to achieve the glassiness of the bottle. Your entire focus should be on what you are looking at—let the rest drain away. It will make for a better drawing—and it will be a relief to you too, to remain in the moment, not to dwell." With these last words she gave Violet permission to set George and Laurence aside for the evening. She made her best drawing that night, and never felt the need to go back again.

Now, with the blue wool to sort, she tried to bring back that feeling of extraneous thoughts draining away to leave her vision clear. It was remarkable how much was knocking about inside her brain: curiosity about what Gilda was going to show her; anxiety that she would not be able to wield a needle well enough to embroider any-thing for the cathedral; rage at Mrs. Biggins for taking such satisfaction in belittling the workers; shyness at trying to find a place among all these women who already knew what they were doing; concern that no one would even notice she was missing from work that morning; calculation about what she could have for supper that didn't involve sardines, beans, or sprats, as she was so sick of them. There were probably more thoughts in there, but Violet cleared out most of her mind, looked at the wool again, and immediately recognized that one of the blues had a tinge of green in it, making it sealike and murky, like her eyes, which she had always wished were a cleaner blue—like the light blue hank she picked out and dropped into its box. Light blue, mid-royal with a hint of gray, green blue, and dark blue. Within a couple of minutes she'd sorted them, so that when Gilda came back, she had finished.

"Here we are," Gilda said, setting down a rectangular piece of canvas embroidery about thirteen by thirty inches. In the central medallion were small, careful petit-point stitches done in subtle shades of brown and cream, depicting a tree, with two blue-and-tan peacocks standing in its branches, pecking at bunches of dangling grapes while a goat and a deer grazed below. The peacock feathers were intricately rendered, and the grapes expertly shaded with just a few dots of color. Surrounding the medallion was bolder, cruder embroidery in a complicated pattern of bold stitches that created blue Celtic knots and red flowers on a background of yellow.

"This is exquisite," Violet declared, tracing the peacock with a finger. "So beautifully done I can't imagine anyone will actually sit on it when it's in use."

There was a laugh—not Gilda's high tinkle, but lower and mellifluous. Violet looked up and found herself staring into two deep brown pools. Louisa Pesel's gaze was direct and focused, despite the clamor in the room and Mrs. Biggins hovering at her elbow. She looked at Violet as if she were the only person here who mattered.

"What part of Winchester history is this?" Violet asked. "I've not lived here long, and this is unfamiliar."

"You must look further afield, to the Bible."

"The Tree of Life?" Violet guessed. Like everyone else here, already she wanted to please Miss Pesel.

The older woman beamed. "Yes. The other historic medallions will be directly connected to Winchester, but I thought the first might be more universal. Luckily Dean Selwyn agreed with me, though I only told him after the medallion was half-done." She chuckled. "This one and another will be for the vergers' seats on either side of the central aisle when you enter the choir. They are just that bit longer than the rest, because the seats are wider. Perhaps vergers are wider than the rest of us!"

"Miss Pesel, this is Miss Speedwell, our newest recruit," Mrs. Biggins interjected. "Though it is rather late in the day for her to start."

"It is never too late," Miss Pesel rejoined. "We have hundreds of cushions and kneelers to make. We shall be stitching for years, and need to put every possible hand to the pump. I see Mrs. Biggins has got you sorting wool. That's all well and good, but if you are to start embroidering over the summer break, you must learn your stitches now. I shall teach you myself. Come and sit." She led the way to two spaces that had miraculously opened up at the table without her having to ask. "Miss Hill, would you kindly fetch a square of canvas and a model for Miss Speedwell? No need for a frame just yet."

Gilda grinned at Violet as she hurried away, her eyes disappearing into slits, her teeth bright and horsey.

"Now, Miss Speedwell, have you ever done any embroidery?" Miss Pesel tilted her head like a bird. "No cross-stitch at school?"

"I don't—" Violet stopped. She could feel a dim memory emerging, of a limp bit of cloth gone gray with handling, scattered with crosses that made up a primitive house, a garland of flowers, the alphabet, and a verse. "'Lord, give me wisdom to direct my ways . . . ,'" she murmured.

"'. . . I beg not riches, nor yet length of days,'" Miss Pesel finished. "Quite an old-fashioned sampler. Very popular. Who taught you?"

"My mother. She still misses Queen Victoria."

Miss Pesel laughed.

"My sampler was not very good," Violet added.

"Well, we shall have to teach you better. We'll start with the main stitches we use for the kneelers and cushions: cross, long-armed cross, tent, rice, upright Gobelin, and eyelets. Though we are adding as we go, for variety. I am determined that we avoid the domestic look of a woodland scene in green and yellow and brown cross-stitch on a chair seat."

Violet smiled: Miss Pesel had accurately described the dining room chairs in use in Mrs. Speedwell's house.

Gilda returned with a square of brown canvas and a similar piece with several different patches of stitching done in blue and yellow. "Italian hemp," Miss Pesel explained as she handed the square to Violet. "And this is a tapestry needle, with a big eye and a blunt end." She held it out, along with a strand of mid-blue wool. "Let's see you thread it. . . . Good, you remember that. This morning I'll teach you tent, Gobelin, cross, and long-armed cross." She tapped at each stitch on the model. "This afternoon, rice and eyelets. If all goes well you may have finished your own model of stitches by the end of the day!"

Violet opened her mouth to protest that she'd only taken the morning off from work, but then thought the better of it. Who would even notice or care that she was gone? O and Mo? Mr. Waterman? She could make up her work easily enough. And if Mr. Waterman complained, she could get Mrs. Biggins to scare him.

"Now, some rules," Miss Pesel continued. "Never use a sharp needle as it will fray the canvas; only a blunt one. Don't leave knots, they will come undone or make a bump; tie one, stitch over it, then cut the knot—I'll show you. Make your stitches close—you are covering every bit of the canvas, so that it is entirely filled in and none of the canvas weave shows. Any gaps between stitches will make the cushion or kneeler weak and it will not last. These cushions and kneelers will be used every day—sometimes two or three times a day—for at least a hundred years, we hope. That is many thousands of times they will be sat on or knelt on. They must be robust to withstand such use for that long.

"Finally, don't forget the back of the canvas. You want the reverse to look almost as neat as the front. You will make mistakes that you can correct back there, and no one will be the wiser. But if it's a dismal tangle at the back, it can affect the front; for instance, you may catch loose threads with your needle and pull them through. A neat back means you've worked a neat front."

Violet recalled the back of her childhood sampler, tangled with wool, the front a field of irregular crosses, her mother's despair.

"Think of your work rather like the services at the cathedral," Louisa Pesel added. "You always see an orderly show of pageantry out in the presbytery or the choir, with the processions and the prayers and hymns and the sermon all beautifully choreographed, mostly thanks to the vergers who run it all, and keep things tidy and organized in the offices away from the public eye as well, so that the public show is smooth and seamless."

Violet nodded.

"All right, let's start with the tent stitch, which you will be using a great deal." Miss Pesel tapped a patch of yellow stitches beading up and down the model. "It is strong, especially done on the diagonal, and fills gaps beautifully."

Violet wrestled with handling the unfamiliar needle and wool and canvas. Miss Pesel was patient, but Violet was clumsy and uncertain, and panicked whenever she got to the end of a row and had to start back up the other way. "One stitch on the diagonal, then two squares down," Miss Pesel repeated several times. "Now going back up the row it's one diagonal and two across. Vertical going down the row, horizontal going up. That's right!" She clapped. "You've got it."

Violet felt stupidly proud.

Miss Pesel left her to practice several rows of tent while she went to help others. The backlog of broderers impatient to see her was a pressure Miss Pesel did not seem to feel, and no one dared to complain to her, but they frowned at Violet over the teacher's shoulder.

She checked back after twenty minutes. "Very good," she said, studying Violet's rows. "You have learned where the needle must go. Now unpick it all and start again."

"What? Why?" Violet bleated. She'd thought she was doing well.

"The tension in each stitch must be the same or it will look uneven and unsightly. Don't despair, Miss Speedwell," she added, taking in Violet's rueful expression. "I can guarantee that every woman in this room has done her share of unpicking. No one manages it straight off. Now, let's sort out what you're doing at the ends of the rows. Then I'll teach you upright Gobelin. That's rather like tent but more straightforward."

It *was* more straightforward and easy to master, so that before lunch Miss Pesel was also able to show her cross-stitch and long-armed cross. "I'm pleased with your progress," she declared as she handed back Violet's canvas. "This afternoon we'll go over rice and eyelets, and then you'll be ready. We start again at half past two."

Violet found herself lapping up the praise like a child.

5

As the broderers gathered together their bits and pieces to go to lunch—some leaving for good, others going out to eat with the intention to return—Violet wondered for a moment what to do. She should go back to the office and ask Mr. Waterman if she could take the afternoon off as well. Then Gilda was at her elbow. "Shall we eat out on the Outer Close?" she suggested, as if they had been friends for years. "There's a yew tree by Thetcher I like to sit under when it's warm. Lets you see the comings and goings of the cathedral, which is no end of entertainment."

"Thetcher?"

"You don't know? You're in for a treat!" Gilda took her arm and began to lead her out. Violet was tempted to pull away: There was something in Gilda's thin face, her prominent teeth, and the fine wrinkles around her eyes that telegraphed . . . not desperation, exactly, but an overpowering insistence.

"I'm meant to be back at work this afternoon," she said as they descended the stairs. "I hadn't realized I would be expected for the whole day. Mrs. Biggins only mentioned the morning."

Gilda grimaced. "Old Biggins probably didn't want you for the day. Honestly, she acts as if a new volunteer is a burden God has placed at her feet, when actually we're desperate for more broderers. Silly woman should be thanking you! Luckily you have Miss Pesel's blessing. Anyway, couldn't you take the afternoon off? Is your supervisor understanding? Where do you work?"

"Southern Counties Insurance."

Gilda stopped in the middle of the Close, the cathedral looming behind her. A group of young scholars from Winchester College in their gowns and straw hats parted in streams around them, clattering across the cobblestones on their way back to classes. "I suppose you know Olive Sanders," she said, looking as if she had bitten into an anticipated apple and found it mushy.

"Yes, we're both typists. We share an office."

"Poor you! Oh, sorry, I shouldn't have said that." Gilda didn't look sorry. "But really," she added as they began walking again, "I can't imagine being in a confined space with her. How do you cope?"

Violet thought of all the silly conversations she'd overheard between O and Mo, the shrieks, the braying laughter over nothing, the casual condescension, the over-sweet perfume, the half-filled teacups with cigarette butts floating in them. "It's not for much longer."

"No, because she's marrying my brother! So the problem of Olive gets transferred to *me*. Do you know she had the gall to suggest she take over my job? I do the books and the appointments for my brother's garage," Gilda explained, guiding them through a passageway of arches made by the cathedral's flying buttresses that led from the Inner to the Outer Close and spat them out in front of the main entrance. "She knows nothing about numbers or motorcars! I put an end to *that* idea." A seam of doubt running through her tone made Violet suspect that this was not the case, and feel for her. A spinster's uncertainty, she thought. It is always there, underlining everything we do.

She glanced up at the cathedral. Its exterior was always a surprise. Violet had visited several times since childhood and knew what to expect, but each time she willed it to be spectacular and was once again disappointed. When she thought of a cathedral in the abstract, it always made a big, bold, dramatic entrance. Everything would be tall: the entrance, the body of the building, and especially the tower or spire. It would shout its presence, and its physical essence would not let anyone forget that it was there for the purpose of worship. Nearby Salisbury Cathedral did so with its impressive spire, the tallest in Britain; so did Chichester, which she had seen when visiting her grandparents. On holiday she had admired the handsome square towers of Canterbury Cathedral, and of Lincoln, which dominated and conquered that city as a cathedral should.

In reality Winchester Cathedral squatted like a gray toad in a forgettable green off the High Street. Given that the town had been the central base of power for many kings, the cathedral was surprisingly easy to miss; Violet often had to direct tourists to it, even when it was just ahead of them. "Oh," they would say. "Oh." Where is the tower? she knew they were thinking. For the cathedral had only a stubby one; it looked like a dog with its tail cut short, or as if the project had run out of funds before they could build higher. It seemed more like an oversize church than a grand cathedral.

"It is better inside," she wanted to say. "It is spectacular inside." But Violet was not in the habit of saying what she thought to strangers. Besides, they would find out soon enough.

The green Outer Close spread out around the cathedral, crisscrossed by two paths lined with lime trees. Everywhere visitors and

workers were taking advantage of the sunshine to sit on handkerchiefs or newspapers on the grass and eat sandwiches. A few old
graves and tombs dotted the Close, and were given a respectful berth
by the picnickers—apart from Gilda, who marched up to one about
fifty yards from the cathedral entrance, under a large yew tree, and
dropped down beside it. "Thetcher," she announced.

Violet studied the waist-high white gravestone. "'Thomas Thetcher,'" she read aloud, "'who died of a violent Fever contracted by
drinking Small Beer when hot the 12th of May 1764.' Gosh."

> *Here sleeps in peace a Hampshire Grenadier,*
> *Who caught his death by drinking cold small Beer.*
> *Soldiers be wise from his untimely fall*
> *And when ye're hot drink Strong or none at all.*

Gilda was able to recite the words from memory rather than looking at the gravestone. "Forget the cathedral," she added. "*This* is the
true Winchester landmark." She patted it fondly, as if it were the
family cat, then opened a wax paper packet and laid it out between
them. "Share?"

"Oh. All right." Violet reluctantly pulled out her offering from her
handbag. Gilda's sandwiches contained thick slices of ham and were
spread generously with butter rather than the slick of cheap margarine and the meager layer of fish paste Violet had used for her own.

But Gilda didn't seem to notice. "I always find sandwiches others
have made much more interesting," she declared, popping a triangle
of fish paste sandwich in her mouth. "Like being made a cup of
coffee—it always tastes better when someone's made it for you, don't
you think?"

"I suppose."

"So, how did you get on with your stitches? Miss Pesel is a brilliant teacher, isn't she? She makes you want to do well."

"She is very good. I'm not sure that I am, though." Violet bit into the ham. It was sweet and delicately smoked, and so delicious she almost cried. The only time she ate well was on the rare occasion she had Sunday lunch at Tom's, when Evelyn cooked a vigorous roast. At home her mother seemed to relish burning the joint, serving too few potatoes, and making watery custard, as a continuing punishment for Violet abandoning her. The succulent, abundant ham made her realize: She was starving.

"Oh, I was terrible at the start!" Gilda interrupted Violet's reverie over the ham. She seemed gleeful about her shortcomings. "I thought I'd be stuck on borders and hanking wool forever. But eventually the stitches become second nature and you can relax as you work. I've noticed that if I'm tense, my embroidery becomes tense too. And we can't have a tense cushion in the cathedral choir, can we? Those choristers need well-made cushions to sit on!"

Violet couldn't help it—she reached for another ham sandwich, though it went against the usual etiquette of sharing where one alternated for an even distribution. Again Gilda did not seem bothered, but proceeded to quiz Violet on her family, her life in Southampton, and what brought her to Winchester.

"My father died two years ago and it became harder to live with my mother," Violet replied to the last.

"Is your mum awful?"

"She is, rather. She never really recovered from my brother's death during the war." There, she had said it.

Gilda nodded. "Joe came through the war all right, but then we lost Mum to the Spanish flu right after he got back. He said he went all the way through the war without crying once, but to get back and lose Mum—that was too much."

"Did you lose . . . anyone else?"

Gilda shook her head, and looked around, as if shrugging off the attention. No fiancé, then, Violet thought.

"Arthur!" Gilda jumped up and waved at two men pushing bicycles along the tree-lined path toward the cathedral entrance. Both had their right trouser legs tucked into their socks to keep them from getting caught in the chains. One was the man with the white hair and mustache Violet had seen at the cathedral during the broderers' service. At the sound of Gilda's voice he stopped, then wheeled his bicycle over to them, followed by a younger, shorter man. Violet scrambled to her feet.

"Hello, Gilda." The man raised his hat at Gilda, then nodded at Violet. His eyes were bright chips of blue, his gaze warm and direct. She felt herself flush red, though she was not sure why: He was much older than she, and—she automatically glanced—he wore a wedding ring.

"Are we going to hear you soon?" Gilda demanded.

"Not this afternoon. We're just meeting with the verger to go over the summer schedule. Beyond the normal, there are a few weddings, and the royal birthdays, of course. This is Keith Bain, often our tenor. I'm not sure you've met—he's lived in Winchester for two years."

The younger man, small and wiry, with ginger hair and a carpet of freckles, nodded at them.

"This is Violet Speedwell. She's just joined the Cathedral Broderers, haven't you, Vi?"

Violet flinched. No one had called her Vi since Laurence died; her family had instinctively understood that his nickname for her was now off-limits. She tried to cover her discomfort by holding out her hand, but as Arthur shook it she suspected he was filing away in his mind: Don't call her Vi.

He smiled at her. "Your name—that was very clever of your parents."

"Clever how?" Gilda wanted to know.

"Speedwell is the common name for veronica, a kind of purple flower. And they named her Violet."

"It was my father's idea," Violet explained. "My brothers have—had—have more traditional names." She did not name them—she did not want to say George's name aloud.

"Good thing they didn't name you Veronica!" Gilda laughed. "Veronica Veronica."

"I see you've chosen Thetcher to sit by." Arthur nodded at the gravestone.

"I'd never seen it before," Violet admitted.

"Ah, then you must not be from Winchester."

"No. Southampton. I moved here seven months ago."

"I thought not. I would have known you otherwise." His tone was neutral but somehow the words were not. Violet's cheeks grew warm again.

"Arthur and I went to the same church for a long time," Gilda explained. "I played with his daughter at Sunday school. She's in Australia now, and Arthur's moved to the country. To Nether Wallop, the most beautiful village in England, and with the funniest name."

Even as Arthur was correcting her—"Technically our cottage is in Middle Wallop"—Violet was remembering a visit to Nether Wallop with her father and brothers when she was a girl. "I have been there," she said. "The Douce pyramid."

Keith Bain and Gilda looked puzzled, but Arthur nodded. "Indeed." He turned to the others. "In the churchyard at Nether Wallop there is a pyramid on the grave of Francis Douce. Apparently the family liked pyramids, as other relatives had them built as well, such as at Farley Mount." He smiled again at Violet, and she silently thanked her father for plotting the route of their short walking holiday so that they passed through Nether Wallop. She would have been eleven, Tom seven, and George thirteen. Mrs. Speedwell had not come with them, which made the holiday more relaxed and put them all in good moods as they'd taken the train to Salisbury and a cart up to Stonehenge, then began walking through woods and skirting newly planted fields of wheat. At Nether Wallop they stayed at the Five Bells, and went to look at the church, where George had got a leg up from their father so he could grab the stone flame that topped the pyramid tombstone, and declared himself the King of Egypt. If any of them had been told that day that eleven years later he and hundreds of thousands of other British men would be dead, they would not have believed it.

To her mortification, sudden tears pricked Violet's eyes, spilling over before she could hide them. She rarely cried over the loss of George and Laurence. Mrs. Speedwell had always been the town crier of the family loss, leaving little room for Violet or Tom or their father to voice their own feelings. When Laurence died a year after George, Mrs. Speedwell not once expressed sorrow or tried to comfort Violet, but managed to make it into a competition, reminding anyone who would listen that a mother's loss of her son was the worst loss there was, the implication being that this trumped a girl losing her fiancé. Violet did not want to play that game, and stifled any tears.

Arthur was holding out a handkerchief with quiet understanding.

Even almost fourteen years after the war's end, no one was surprised by sudden tears.

"Thank you." Violet wiped her eyes. "I'm terribly sorry." Arthur and Keith nodded, and Gilda patted her arm just the right amount. Then they carried on, because that was what you did.

"I haven't been to Farley Mount in years," Gilda remarked. "We used to go all the time on a Sunday afternoon."

"What's Farley Mount, then?" Keith Bain spoke for the first time. To Violet's surprise, he had a Scottish accent.

Gilda and Arthur chuckled. "Beware Chalk Pit!" Gilda cried.

"Unlikely as it sounds, Beware Chalk Pit is a horse's name," Arthur explained. "A relative of the Douces built a pyramid on top of a hill a few miles from Winchester, in honor of his horse who had won a race. Before the race the horse had fallen into a chalk pit, hence the name."

"Maybe I'll walk out to it," Keith Bain said. "I've only been up St. Catherine's Hill. Want to see more of the countryside. Where is it?"

"About five miles west of here. If you fancy a longer walk, you can go straight across the fields to Salisbury. That's twenty-six miles. I call it the cathedral walk. You can stay the night at mine in the Wallops en route if you like."

"I may well do that."

"We'd best get on to see the verger." Arthur turned to Violet. "Very good to meet you, Miss Speedwell."

"And you." Violet watched him wheel his bicycle toward the side of the cathedral. His brief attention had steadied her, like a hand reaching out to still a rocking chair that has been knocked.

Only after he'd gone did she realize she was still clutching his handkerchief. The initials AK had been embroidered in an uneven blue chain stitch in one corner. She could run after him, or give it to

Gilda to give to him. Instead she waited until her new friend wasn't looking, then tucked it in her handbag.

"Are they in a choir of some sort?" she asked when the handkerchief was out of sight.

"Not at all," Gilda replied, folding the waxed paper from the sandwiches. "What made you think that?"

"He mentioned being a tenor."

"No, no, they're bell ringers! For the cathedral. Now, shall we have a coffee? Then I'm going to find a telephone and tell your office you've taken ill—fainted on the Outer Close!"

On their return, Violet found that her privileged position as Miss Pesel's new pupil had been usurped. Several other broderers were crowded around her; indeed, two who saw Violet enter pushed closer, as if to defend their positions and their teacher.

"Which stitches was she going to teach you?" Gilda asked, frowning at the scrum.

Violet picked up the model. "This one. . . . Rice, I think. And eyelets."

"I can teach you those. Miss Pesel always likes us to teach others, says the best way to set in your mind what you've learned is to explain it to someone else."

Both stitches were fiddly but not hard to learn. Then, before she went to consult Miss Pesel about her own work, Gilda suggested Violet make a sampler of the six stitches she had mastered, to show to the teacher at the end of the day.

It was calmer now, more settled. A dozen women—some from the morning, others new—worked around the big table, with Miss

Pesel and Mrs. Biggins fielding questions and making suggestions. Violet focused on her sampler, concentrating on getting each stitch uniform, the tension consistent. After a time she found she could work and also listen to the conversations around her. Mostly the embroiderers talked about their children and grandchildren, their neighbors, their gardens, the meals they made, the holidays they might take. All listened politely; none really cared. They were simply waiting their turn to speak. And, as was usual in these situations, the married women spoke more than the spinsters, assuming a natural authority and higher place in the hierarchy of women that no one questioned. Only Gilda spoke up from time to time, and was tolerated because she was entertaining and knew everyone—though some glanced at each other behind her back. Most were of a certain class, and Violet guessed that they looked down on a family who ran a garage and serviced their motorcars. She herself had become less judgmental, however, for she had discovered that when you were a single woman living on your own on a small salary, background meant little. Gilda might be from a different class, but with her family backing her she could afford to eat much better sandwiches than Violet.

What would happen, she wondered, if I changed the subject and asked the room who they think will form the new German government now that the current Chancellor has resigned? Would anyone here have an opinion? She was not sure she herself had one, but the room was beginning to feel a little airless with its insularity. Perhaps she just needed to get to know the women better.

Mrs. Biggins clapped twice. "All right, ladies, that's enough for today. Leave your place as tidy as it was when you arrived. We don't want bits of wool left behind. Mrs. Way will sign out the materials to you."

The others began lining up by Miss Pesel, who inspected their work before they left. Violet watched, suddenly shy about showing her sampler. She did not want to be told to unpick it again, or to be put on record keeping alongside Mabel Way. Finally, however, she joined the queue behind Gilda and listened as she and Miss Pesel discussed the difference between upright and oblique Gobelin stitches. Then Louisa Pesel held out her hand for Violet's piece. "You have come along nicely," she declared, running a finger over the stitches. "Do be careful on the long-armed cross to pull the long stitch tight; otherwise it puffs out, as it does here. But not too disgraceful—no need to unpick since it's a sampler, and the mistake will serve to remind you." She handed it back. "For next Wednesday, teach someone else the stitches and come back to show me what they've done. You can pick up some canvas and wool and a needle on your way out."

Violet gaped. "Who shall I—" But Miss Pesel had already turned to the next woman.

Gilda was grinning again. "Told you so!"

6

Violet had no idea whom to teach the stitches to. Her mother would never agree, Evelyn had too much to do, and Marjory was probably too young to master anything as complicated as the rice stitch. For a moment she wondered about her landlady, but Mrs. Harvey did not seem the type to sit down with a needle. She might be able to convince one of her fellow lodgers, but wasn't sure she wanted to. Violet had been careful to maintain her distance from Miss Frederick, an English teacher at a local girls' school; and Miss Lancaster, who worked as a clerk at Winchester Crown Court. There was a certain kind of misery that hung about them, a wistfulness she hated to think clung to her as well. To become friends with them would only make that feeling more pronounced. Still, when several days had passed and she had still not found someone to teach, she realized she would have to break her ban and ask Miss Frederick. She pondered this one morning as she sat typing, two days before the next embroidery class. Her office mates had not yet arrived; they were rarely on time.

Mo sloped in as Violet was midway through her second contract, adding fire insurance to an existing policy on a house in Andover. Mo was never as loud and confident when Olive was not with her. Now she seemed even more downcast: Head low, she muttered a hello into her collar and did not look up. Her dress mirrored her mood, puddle brown, with a shapeless skirt and too much fabric hanging at the chest. Violet nodded hello, and after finishing the contract offered to make tea.

"Yes, please," Mo answered in a small voice, and sighed. The sigh was the opening, her way of indicating that she was ready to be quizzed about what was wrong.

First Violet went to the kitchen and made a pot of tea, then brought it back to the office with a plate of Garibaldi biscuits—no one's favorite, but that was all there was. "Right," she said, placing a cup of tea in front of Mo and handing her the sugar bowl. "What is it?" She sat back in her own chair, hands on her cup to warm them, for it was one of those rainy June days that felt like early spring rather than summer. A cardigan day—she alternated between beige and tan. Today she wore tan; though she couldn't afford new, she'd recently refreshed it by changing the buttons to a mother-of-pearl set she'd found in a secondhand shop.

Mo heaped several spoonfuls of sugar into her tea and frowned at the rectangular Garibaldis with their currants that looked like squashed flies. Violet did not press her. They had all day.

"O's handing in her notice," she said at last. "Effective immediately. Her mother is ringing Mr. Waterman this morning." She picked up a biscuit and took a vicious bite.

"I see." This was not what Violet had been expecting. She'd assumed that Mo was moping because of something the bank clerk boyfriend had said or done, and that Olive was out on an errand for the long-off wedding—meeting with a vicar, finding a printer for the invitations, looking at dress fabric—using it as an excuse for a leisurely day out. Violet had expected there to be months, years of this nonsense before the big day itself. Only then would Olive leave; women always left work once they married, but not usually before.

"I may as well tell you—you'll hear soon enough. People are such gossips," Mo added, conveniently ignoring how much she and O discussed and spread rumors. "She's—well, she's getting married soon. Next weekend."

"Ah." Violet pushed at a pen on her desk so that it was square with a stack of paper. There was only one reason why a woman got married so quickly.

"It's not what you think!"

Violet waited a moment, then said quietly, "Of course it is. Poor Olive."

Mo stiffened, as if about to argue, but after a moment she slumped back in her chair and dunked the biscuit in her tea. "It's not as if she didn't want to marry him. Just not so soon, with everyone—talking."

Violet lit a cigarette and felt old. "They'll get over it." And they would. Olive and her man would marry: "We just decided we wanted no fuss, just to be together, because we love each other so," she would say. She would have her baby: "Premature, but look what a big bouncing thing he is anyway; you'd never guess he came two months early!" And people would forget the circumstances, because it happened often enough, and what did it matter anyway? Violet had been careful with her sherry men, using a Dutch cap she'd convinced a married friend to get for her from a doctor. But she'd had a few scares over the years, and knew how easily a girl like Olive could be caught out. At least her fiancé was being honorable. If he was anything like his sister, Gilda, Violet suspected O was very lucky indeed.

At lunch it was raining too hard to go out, and Violet and Mo

remained at their desks with their sandwiches, Mo flicking miserably through a magazine. "I say," Violet finally suggested, "shall I
teach you something that will take your mind off of things?"

It turned out that Mo—or Maureen, for along with Olive's abrupt
departure went the nickname—was better at embroidery than Violet, even though she had never done it before. She had the knack of
remaining focused and somewhat dogged—qualities Violet had
never seen her display while typing. But then, Olive had always been
around to distract her. She was also easily pleased with the results.
"Look at my rows of Gobelin," she announced possessively as they
sat stitching in the office during their break. "Straight as straight!"

Miss Pesel was right: Teaching someone else did help you to learn
the stitches yourself, as your pupil's questions forced you to think
through why you were doing what you were doing, and expose the
things you didn't really understand. "Why does the tension matter so
much?" Maureen demanded as she frowned at her green wool.

"Because, look"—Violet pointed at a rogue stitch—"see how that
sticks out? You haven't pulled it tight enough. It will always be like
that, unless you unpick it."

"Why does it matter if the stitches on the back are straight or
diagonal?"

"Because stitches on the diagonal pull the canvas so it's distorted.
You want the cushions and kneelers to be squared."

"And why must the back be so neat?"

"If there are too many loose threads you may accidentally pull
them through the front with your stitches." Violet could feel herself

parroting Miss Pesel. So far she had managed to answer all of Maureen's questions, but she expected eventually to be caught out.

"Perhaps you should come along to the meeting before the broderers break for the summer," she suggested as they stitched again during their afternoon tea break. It was a remarkably quick transition from being ignored and pitied to becoming Maureen's teacher, and even suggesting an activity together. She could not picture them ever being good friends—Maureen was fifteen years younger—but the atmosphere in their office was already transformed.

"Mr. Waterman won't let us both go," Maureen replied, holding her canvas piece close to her face to peer at her stitches. She was practicing rice, with two different colors of wool. "Oh, blast! I forget which direction to take the overstitches in. Does it matter, clockwise or anticlockwise?"

"No, as long as you stitch each square the same way, so it's consistent." Violet studied her own rice stitches. There seemed to be a lot of canvas showing. "Mr. Waterman might let us go for the morning if we work through lunch and stay late to make up some of the hours."

"With Olive gone, he'll need to hire someone else quickly."

Violet had an idea about that but kept quiet to allow the thought to mature.

Evoking her seemed to conjure up Olive herself, for Violet heard the distinctive click of her heels down the hall. Maureen—or perhaps she was back to Mo—looked up in panic. Throwing down her embroidery, she grabbed a magazine and her cup of tea, and turned her face away. Violet was more amused than hurt.

But Mo was not clever enough to conceal her new hobby. Olive appeared in the doorway, still looking like a sturdy, curvy pony, took in Maureen's awkward pose behind the magazine, glanced at the embroidered sampler on her desk and the one Violet was holding, and snorted. "The second I leave you join the arty-and-crafty lot!" she smirked. "What's this?" Before Mo could stop her, she'd picked up the sampler. The needle slid off the wool and tinkled on the floor.

"Tent, Gobelin, cross, long-armed cross, and rice," Violet replied for Mo. "She'll learn eyelets shortly."

Olive dropped the embroidery as if it were infectious. "Knitting like an old maid!" she cried, gazing down on her erstwhile friend. "What's happened to you?"

Mo lowered her magazine. "You left," she said quietly.

"So? I was always going to leave once I got married. It's just a little sooner, that's all. You'll leave too, one day." Olive looked around and spied her bright chiffon scarf hanging on a hook on the back of the door. "There you are!" she announced in triumph, snatching it up. "Couldn't leave you behind, could I?"

"I'll still be your maid of honor, won't I?" Mo's voice was small and pleading. "Next week?"

"Oh, that. I don't think so." Olive spent a great deal of time tying the scarf around her neck and getting it to hang right. "It's just a small, intimate wedding. Family only."

Mo looked so miserable at this that Violet felt the unusual desire to intervene. "We are not knitting, actually," she said. "We're doing canvas embroidery. The contemporary version of spinning, you might say." At Olive's puzzled frown, she added, "Spinning wool. That's where 'spinster' comes from."

Olive rolled her eyes. "Lord, I'm glad I won't be caught up in any of *that*."

"Well, best of luck," Violet remarked in her briskest voice, "with *that*." She nodded at Olive's still-flat belly.

Olive started, and turned bright red. "I don't know what you mean! Really, that's—" She stopped. Under the flush on her cheeks, she seemed to go green. "Just going up to wash!" She turned and hurried down the hall toward the lavatory.

With another kind of girl, Violet might have made fun of Olive and her abrupt departure. But she knew Mo would not laugh, especially not with the background accompaniment of Olive's distant retching. Instead she said gently, "Shall we move on to eyelets?"

After a moment Maureen leaned down to look for her needle on the floor. "Yes."

Violet fortified herself with a tea biscuit, then went to speak to Mr. Waterman. It was best if she laid out her ideas all in one go—the work and the broderers' classes and Maureen. She was not one to make suggestions at work, but she had not needed to when she lived at home and did not have to pay for her upkeep. If she did not say something now while there was an opportunity, she would slowly starve.

When she knocked on his open door Mr. Waterman was gazing out through the window blinds at the rain. "Hello, Miss Speedwell. I was just admiring the rain. The garden needs it. Now, what can I do for you? Is that a cup of tea you've brought me? Just the ticket, thank you! Take a seat."

Violet knew little about her supervisor's personal life other than that he had a wife and child he never talked about, he liked cricket, and he did not like hot weather. She didn't know what he had done during the war. She could not make small talk with him based on so little. Now as he sat sipping his tea, she chose her words carefully.

"Thank you very much for allowing me to take time off to attend Mrs. Biggins's embroidery meeting last week," she began.

At the mention of Mrs. Biggins, Mr. Waterman sat up straight. "Of course, of course. She was happy, was she? Happy to teach you?"

"Yes, indeed. In fact—"

"But wait: Weren't you ill that afternoon? She didn't make you ill, did she?"

Violet thought quickly. "No, it was the heat. The room was a bit stuffy."

"Ah, the heat, yes. We've been having some scorchers, eh? Not today, though."

"I should have sat by the window. Next time I shall ask to do so."

"Next time? Didn't she teach you what you needed to know?"

"Mrs. Biggins would like me to come once more before they break up for the summer, just to make sure I know what I'm doing. And I'm to bring Maureen as well."

Mr. Waterman's brows shot up. "Miss Webster?"

"Mrs. Biggins is keen to have more broderers for the cathedral work. It seems Miss Webster is quite adept at embroidery."

"I see." Mr. Waterman drummed his fingernails against the teacup in a rapid *tink-tink-tink*. "Mrs. Biggins says that?"

"Mrs. Biggins has not seen her work yet," Violet admitted, for she knew she could only stretch a lie so far. "But she and Miss Pesel—who founded the Winchester Cathedral Broderers—have said more good workers are needed. And Miss Webster's work is exceptional." That was an exaggeration, but Mr. Waterman would not know if he looked at Maureen's sampler; it would seem like hieroglyphs to him, just as embroidery had seemed to her only a week ago.

"Well, far be it from me to stand in the way of good work for the church," Mr. Waterman began. "But there is a problem, what with

Miss Sanders's, er, sudden departure." He gulped down the last of his tea; drops of it hung from his mustache. Olive's mother might have spun a tale of young impetuous love unable to wait to marry, but Mr. Waterman clearly knew what was what.

"I have a suggestion to make about that vacancy," Violet said.

"You do?" Mr. Waterman made no attempt to hide his astonishment—astonishment tinged with disapproval. She would have to hurry to lay out her plan before his annoyance at this female temerity shut down the conversation.

"I was going to suggest that Miss Webster and I handle some of the extra work between ourselves. Miss Sanders was a nice girl, but not the fastest of typists. If I take a shorter lunch break of just half an hour, and work an extra hour on the weekdays, that's seven and a half hours a week more. I can't speak for Miss Webster, of course, but she may want extra hours as well. Then you could hire a part-time typist to make up the difference. And perhaps you'll find you don't even need that." Violet was being polite. Olive was a terrible typist and a lackadaisical employee. Maureen would no longer be distracted by her friend, and together they would more than manage the existing work. But she could not say so.

"You would do that? You would really work more hours for Southern Counties Insurance?" Mr. Waterman's gratitude alarmed her; clearly he had misunderstood a crucial element.

"Of course I would be glad for the rise in pay," she rejoined. "Very glad. It is not easy for a single girl to live on my current salary."

"The rise in pay?" Mr. Waterman's voice rose alongside his thoughts. He wiped his forehead with a handkerchief.

Violet could have said: "Of course, foolish man. Why would I do more work for no pay? Do you know what I eat at lunch? That I never have a hot meal? That my clothes hang off me because I've lost weight and can't afford to buy new? That I either eat or go to the cinema? That I have no pension and no husband to keep me and my savings are being decimated? That I often wonder what will happen when I am too old to work? That I don't dare ask my brother for money because I have good relations with him and want to keep it that way so that I can rely on him and his children to help me when I'm old?"

She said none of those things to Mr. Waterman. "It will save Southern Counties money in the long run," she explained, "not having to pay a third typist's full salary."

"Yes, I suppose that's true," Mr. Waterman conceded after a moment. The tide of his disapproval was slowly diminishing.

It rose again when she suggested her and Maureen's salaries increase by four shillings a week each, and remained high as she patiently took him through the numbers and explained her calculations. "You've clearly given this some thought, Miss Speedwell," he muttered, obviously displeased with this idea.

But when Violet reminded him several times that there would be a saving of Olive's salary minus this increase—provided she and Maureen were more efficient—he reluctantly agreed to set forth this solution to his seniors in Southampton. "But, Miss Speedwell, I shall say this idea came from me, if you don't mind," he added with a frown. "I can't think what management would say about a girl having such a . . . *progressive* idea."

Violet did not expect a response for some time, reasoning that it would take Mr. Waterman a week or two to come round to the idea and in a sense make it his own. She didn't mind if he did so, as long as she got a pay rise. That night as she sat in the front room, listening to Gracie Fields on the wireless, she dreamed of chops.

So she was surprised when two days later he appeared in their office while they were typing—Maureen indeed much faster now that Violet was setting the pace—and announced that Southampton had agreed they would take on Olive's work as a trial run for a month.

"With an additional four shillings a week?" Violet felt she had to ask.

"Yes, yes, Miss Speedwell, with the additional four shillings." Mr. Waterman looked weary, as if imagining he might have to field this sort of demand from his wife or daughter.

After he left they continued to type in silence. But when Violet glanced over, Maureen was smiling.

Violet celebrated by going to Awdry's Tea Rooms on the High Street for lunch, where she had three courses: leek and potato soup, a pork chop with two bread rolls, and spotted dick with extra custard. She scraped every dish clean.

7

At the final embroidery class, Violet was set to work over the summer making borders for cushions: an inch-wide strip of blue, yellow, and red geometric patterns that would create the sides of the cushions being made for the choir seats and benches. "You can't do too much damage there and you won't need a frame," Miss Biggins had declared, still treating Violet as a nuisance rather than a help. It was true, however, that the borders wouldn't be much seen; people would be admiring the history medallions that went on top.

She was given a model of the repeating pattern, canvas, needles, and enough wool to make several yards of border. Gilda nodded at the model, which was beautifully, evenly stitched. "Miss Pesel will have whipped that up in half an hour!"

Violet sighed. Gilda was doubtless right, but it reminded her of how slow her own work was.

She became a little obsessed with embroidery. Stealing an old needle case from her mother, she kept it permanently in her handbag along with a length of border, so that she could work on it whenever she had time. At the office she stitched during tea breaks and after lunch. She stitched on the train to and from Southampton on Sundays. At night after supper she began to spend the evening in the front room with the other residents, listening to the variety shows on the wireless and working on long strips of borders. It was less awkward sitting with others when she had something to do with her hands. Miss Frederick corrected her pupils' essays on Tennyson or *The Canterbury Tales* or made lesson plans for the following term, Miss Lancaster read magazines, and Mrs. Harvey did her usual popping in and out—though she would stop and listen if Al Bowlly was singing. "He's quality," she'd declare, and sing along to her budgies.

Violet found stitching similar to but more satisfying than typing. You had to concentrate, but once you were skilled enough, you could settle into it and empty your mind of all but the work in front of you. Life then boiled down to a row of blue stitches that became a long braid across the canvas, or a sunburst of red that became a flower. Instead of typing in forms about people she would never meet, Violet was making bright patterns grow under her fingers. She began to dream of stitching, of the close square holes of the canvas, of blocks of yellow braid, of red rice stitches and pink Gobelin in even rows.

At work Maureen often stitched alongside her during breaks. She had fitted right in at the Cathedral Broderers' class, proving surprisingly adept at handling Mrs. Biggins by abasing herself before the older woman, agreeing that she was the biggest nuisance for appearing so late in the year and that yes, she would be nothing but trouble, and that no, she didn't know why Mrs. Biggins bothered with her. Then she rolled her eyes behind the teacher's back as if they were all back at school, and made the younger broderers laugh. Even Mabel Way smiled at her exaggerated expressions. By the end of the session she was on her way to replacing Olive with new friends. Violet was astonished at the transformation from plain, downtrodden office worker to confident stitcher larking about with others.

Her coworker had also pulled ahead and was now giving back advice on embroidery. "Blimey, Violet!" she cried one afternoon over cups of tea. "When you're unpicking, don't pull through two holes at once. You'll shred the wool and won't be able to use it again. Pull it out through a hole, then turn the canvas over and pull it out through the next."

Violet frowned. Unpicking was so dispiriting, like having to re-trace your steps after leaving home because you've left behind your purse. But mistakes showed up all too easily, though the gaping hole from a missed stitch was not always noticed until rows later. Violet didn't dare leave the mistakes, knowing they would be noticed by Miss Pesel and have to be fixed.

Without the classes, she turned to Gilda for advice, and they began meeting regularly at Awdry's for coffee at lunch or after work to discuss embroidery, though they strayed into many other topics. Gilda was such a talker that Violet found she rarely had to ask ques-tions. Her new friend was unswerving in her support for Violet's new life in Winchester, and it made her grateful to be encouraged to feel less guilty about leaving her mother. Gilda had her round to the Hills' for tea one night, wrecking the kitchen in her quest to make the perfect shepherd's pie for her guest. It was delicious, but Violet had to eat it under the baleful eye of her old office mate Olive, now installed as the newest Hill, swelling with the next Hill. She pre-ferred to see Gilda elsewhere, at Awdry's or the cinema or on the cathedral green, sunning themselves out on the Outer Close.

During the summer Violet also began to visit the cathedral more often—for practical reasons rather than for spiritual sustenance, to study the kneelers now in use in the choir and presbytery and check her border stitching against them. Gradually she became aware of some of the daily activities taking place there. There was a bustle to the building that had nothing to do with prayer and contemplation. It was more like Plummers, the Southampton department store where she went to buy stockings or gloves or bath salts. Plummers seemed to be filled with shoppers, yet when you looked more closely, there were clerks everywhere, folding clothes, setting out samples, pushing trolleys full of merchandise, sweeping the marble floors. Occasionally when a flu epidemic temporarily reduced staff numbers and dust balls accumulated in the corners and clothes were left in untidy heaps, it became clear how much Plummers relied on its workers to keep it running smoothly.

Violet suspected it was the same with the cathedral workers, who, apart from the vergers, were mostly volunteers. There were the ladies arranging flowers in stands under windows and by pillars. There was the man setting out candles for lighting at shrines and scraping away the old wax from previously lit candles. There was the woman laying out kneelers on the chairs in the presbytery, squaring them so that they sat even. There were two old men gathering up the prayer books and storing them in boxes. There was the man polishing the brass candlesticks on the altars, and another mopping the medieval tiles in the retrochoir. There were the two women who called themselves the Holy Dusters, going around and wiping down every possible surface. There were the vergers, rushing past with a jar of communion wafers, a green robe, a Bible.

One evening after work, Violet sat in the presbytery, inspecting a kneeler to see how the broderer had blended the blues, and considering how to do the same with the yellows in the borders she was working on. As she pulled at the stitches, someone took the seat next to her. She was startled to find it was Louisa Pesel, and let out a little yelp, then apologized.

Miss Pesel smiled. "I like to come here sometimes just to sit and look."

Violet nodded. It felt like having a member of the Royal Family choose to sit by her, though one wearing a brown turban trimmed with a tuft of feathers.

"Sometimes I wonder if we couldn't use even more color here. It's so dark—especially in the choir stalls." Miss Pesel nodded at the wood stalls to their left. "The stone and wood just soak it up; even the mustard yellow some are complaining about."

"People are complaining?"

"Oh, yes." Miss Pesel's laugh was like a low bell ringing through the presbytery. "They say it's vulgar and inappropriate in a religious setting. Not Dean Selwyn, of course. He has always been on our side. Indeed, it was he who asked me to organize making these cushions and kneelers, having seen those I'd made for the chapel at Wolvesey House. I didn't stint on color there. He knew what he would be getting, and he hasn't wavered in his support."

"Have you always embroidered?"

"Since I was a girl, yes. And then I taught it—here and abroad—and that rather set me on the path for life."

"Abroad?"

"I taught embroidery in a girls' school in Greece for several years. I became something of an expert in Greek embroidery."

"Gosh." Miss Pesel seemed so English that it was hard to imagine her in a foreign climate—gently perspiring in blazing sun, teaching a class of Greek girls the rice stitch or long-armed cross in a stark white building against a background of bright blue sea and sky.

Violet wanted to ask about a husband, but didn't, for that was the question she most hated being asked herself.

"I traveled a bit too," Louisa Pesel continued, smiling at the memories. "To Egypt, to India. Glorious. I even rode a camel once! Then during the war I was back in Bradford—"

"Bradford?"

"Indeed. I grew up in Bradford. During the war I taught embroidery there to convalescent soldiers. Do you know, Miss Speedwell, sewing can be so therapeutic when one has had trauma. The bold colors and the repetition of simple stitches had such a soothing effect on the men. There was something about creating a thing of beauty that worked wonders on their nerves. I was very pleased with the results."

Violet had a vision of George and Laurence sitting in a muddy trench, stitching a row of red eyelets, and shuddered.

Louisa Pesel didn't seem to notice, or was too polite to say. "So, is that yours, Miss Speedwell?" she asked, nodding at the kneeler in Violet's lap. "I know the broderers like to come and visit their work in situ, as it were."

"No, I was looking at others' work to see how they handled blending colors." Violet was pleased that Miss Pesel remembered her name.

"Which pattern are you working on over the summer?"

"Oh, I'm not making a kneeler. Mrs. Biggins has assigned me to make borders for the cushions. Lengths and lengths of borders."

"Have you made your sampler?"

Violet nodded.

"And taught the stitches to someone else?"

"Yes. In fact, she has now joined the broderers."

"And would you like to make a kneeler?"

"I would."

"I'm curious, Miss Speedwell. Why? There will be over three hundred kneelers, so yours would get lost in the crowd. Whereas there will be far fewer cushions, and they'll be very striking, and the borders of course will be essential to making them three-dimensional. There is no shame in sewing borders."

"I know. It's just—" Violet stopped.

Miss Pesel said it for her. "You want to make something wholly yours that will be properly seen and used."

"Yes."

Miss Pesel was looking at her expectantly, as if she had handed her a book to read from. Violet realized she was expected to explain herself more fully, though she had not really thought it through. "I grew up in Southampton," she began, "and we attended Saint Michael's. My mother still does."

"I have been. A handsome church."

"Although I have gone all my life—to Sunday school, for Communion classes, to Sunday services—I have never truly been at home there. Especially not after—not after my brother's death during the war. The service for him felt perfunctory. The vicar had performed so many of those services that he could have done it without any notes. He knew George, but he led the service as if it meant nothing."

She stopped.

"That must have been painful," Miss Pesel said.

"It was bewildering. It was not just that it seemed God had abandoned us, but that the Church of England had too. It gave no answers, no comfort. I wanted the vicar to reconcile the loving God he spoke of with the destruction wreaked on a generation of men, and indirectly on us women too, but he did not. After that I got out of attending as often as I could. I managed always to have a headache on Sunday mornings." She shook her head at the thought. "My mother complained, told me I was an insensitive sister and daughter. But my father understood, though he never said anything.

"I suppose I am looking to start again, here." She glanced around at the high stone walls and the vast space above them. "But a cathedral is overwhelming. Spiritually as well as physically. I thought if there was one small part of *me* here, that might help. A contribution that would make me feel connected. And something I could actually use, or that others could use. A border of a cushion is not quite the same as a kneeler."

Miss Pesel nodded. "What you say reminds me of the many people I see who come here and light a candle. That one flame in the great expanse of the cathedral. They look at it, come back to it. It is theirs."

"Yes, but a kneeler lasts longer than a candle."

"Indeed. All right, then." Miss Pesel stood and gestured at the kneelers on the chairs around them. "Choose the design you would like to make."

Although this was the desired outcome, Violet had not expected it to be so quick and definite. But Louisa Pesel was decisive. Now Violet must choose. She already knew, and pointed to the kneeler with the checkered acorn caps—the one made by DJ.

Miss Pesel nodded. "That is a good one. I am pleased with all of the designs, by and large, but like a mother with her children, I secretly have my favorites too. Come, then, let's go to Church House and get your materials. I have a key with me."

"But—Mrs. Biggins . . ."

"I shall handle Mrs. Biggins—though I suggest you stitch the long borders she has assigned you as well, if you have the time. We can't have her master plan go awry, can we?"

8

Mrs. Speedwell's birthday fell on a Saturday in early July, and Tom and Evelyn hosted a celebratory lunch in their garden. It was a hot, bright, glaring day, but Violet's mother insisted on wearing a long-sleeved navy wool dress and thick stockings, as if it were November. "Oh dear, no, I'll be far too hot," she declared as she stepped into the garden and gazed on the table Evelyn had carefully laid with polished silver, ironed linen, and a vase of freshly cut daisies and delphiniums. Marjory was diligently sprinkling plants with a watering can while Edward bashed them with a stick, ignoring her protests. Mrs. Speedwell winced at their shouts.

"We'll seat you in the shade," Evelyn replied, clearly unwilling to reset the table inside. "There's a fan at your place." She was wearing a stylish pink-and-gray floral tea dress that Violet envied, but she looked hot and distracted.

Violet smiled to herself. It was rare for her sister-in-law to make such a blunder. She could have told Evelyn her mother did not like sitting outside when it was hot. Whenever the Speedwells were on holiday on the Isle of Wight, Mrs. Speedwell usually ended up sitting in the window of the guesthouse as the rest took their tea out on the lawn in the sun.

The Speedwells had been going to Ventnor on the Isle of Wight for two weeks in August since Violet was a girl. It was where her father had been happiest, taking them out in hired boats, rambling on Tennyson Down and out to the Needles headland, pottering about among the dinosaur fossils on the beach with his trousers rolled up and a handkerchief tied over his balding head. Because he was happy, Violet was happy. They all were, even her mother, who softened a bit away from the rigidities of home life. Only one year when Violet was twelve did they try a different place—Hastings, with Mrs. Speedwell's sister, Violet's aunt Penelope—and they all missed the Isle of Wight. The tradition was so strong that it survived George's death. Evelyn had to go along with it—which she did with a fixed smile for those two weeks.

"The garden's looking lovely, Evelyn," Violet remarked, acting as mediator for once. "How jolly to be able to eat out in it. Perhaps we could have tea inside afterwards, and Mother could open her presents then."

"Presents now! Presents now!" Edward cried, and Marjory joined him, a notch less exuberantly. "Granny's presents now!"

Granny brightened at the prospect of presents, and sank into her place of honor in the shade.

"Will you take some barley water, Mrs. Speedwell?" Evelyn asked. She had never called her mother-in-law by her first name; nor had she been encouraged to.

"Oh no, dear, only hot tea will do in this heat." Mrs. Speedwell opened the Japanese fan and fluttered it in the direction of her face. "It's the capillary action, you know, that cools one."

Evelyn should know this, Violet thought. Mother lectures about it every summer. It was another slip on her sister-in-law's part.

"All right, now, where's Granny's presents?" Tom cried as he bounded toward them from the French doors, rubbing his hands.

"I'll get them!" Edward ran to a chair, picked up a pile of wrapped shapes, brought them to his grandmother, and dumped them at her feet.

"Careful, Eddie!" Marjory cried, sounding rather like her mother. "You know it's fragile."

"Open this one first!" Edward thrust a large, flat, diamond-shaped package at his grandmother. Violet could guess what it was even before Edward announced, "It's a kite! We made it!"

Mrs. Speedwell gave her grandson a wan smile. "You open it, dear, and show me."

Edward ripped off the gift wrap to reveal a kite made of two sticks and old newspaper they'd painted with splodges of color. The tidiest part of it was the tail: a long piece of string tied with streamers of colored paper. Evelyn's work, no doubt.

"We'll fly it for you, Granny. Watch!" Edward grabbed the end of the string and ran over the lawn, bouncing the kite behind him, Marjory chasing him to try to protect their handiwork. They couldn't get it to fly, though, and came back to the table, disappointed.

"Not enough wind, old man," Tom said. "We'll try later, on the common."

Marjory clapped her hands. "Can we take the kite on holiday to the Isle of Wight? There's always wind there."

"Let's let Granny open the rest of her presents, shall we?" Evelyn interjected, handing her mother-in-law a small flat package neatly wrapped in lilac-colored paper. Inside was a box of three handkerchiefs embroidered at the corners with lilies of the valley, Mrs. Speedwell's favorite flower and scent.

"Oh, you shouldn't have, dear," she said. "I shall have to use one now." She made a show of unfolding one and dabbing her eyes. It was a safe gift: Violet's mother had gone through many handkerchiefs over the years, and her charlady spent a great deal of time ironing them.

Tom gave her a plaid rug to go over her knees when she rode in his car. Summer or winter, Mrs. Speedwell complained of the draft. He patted her knee. "There, now, Mum—no more excuses to coming out for a spin. Maybe later?"

"Oh, it's far too hot to go today," Mrs. Speedwell retorted, fanning herself. "Another time."

She made no move to reach for the last package, wrapped in blue tissue paper, lying on the chair next to her. It was obvious that Violet had yet to give her one, yet her mother sat back and sighed. "I'm very lucky to have people to look after me and give me presents on my birthday. It mitigates the losses I've had."

Violet stared at her forlorn package abandoned on the chair. I am not going to point out the obvious, she thought. I am not going to run after her with my present like a supplicant bearing an offering. I am not.

It felt like a merciful intervention when at last Marjory noticed it. "Look, Granny, you have one more!" She picked up the present and handed it to her grandmother.

It seemed to Violet that her mother opened the package with more reluctance than enthusiasm, letting the embroidered spectacles case drop into her lap without looking at it. "It's for your reading glasses, Mother," she explained. "I made it. It's the canvas embroidery I told you about, same as what I'm doing for the cathedral."

Mrs. Speedwell sighed again. "Just what I need today of all days is another reminder of my failing eyesight." Actually her eyesight was good for a woman of sixty-three; she required only the lowest correction when reading.

Violet had to suppress the urge to reach over and snatch back the case. She had worked hard on it, combining the colors her mother liked—brown, blue, maroon, mauve, pink, and cream—with stitches she had learned from Miss Pesel such as long-armed cross and rice. Gilda had also lent her a book of embroidery stitches, and she'd taught herself some new ones to use. She had been pleased with the result, but her mother's indifference now made her notice the faults— the bits of canvas showing through here and there, the odd stitch sticking up more than it should, the glue that seeped through where she'd adhered felt to the canvas inside the case to make it soft for the spectacles.

"Let's have lunch, shall we?" Evelyn intervened. "Children, wash your hands, please. You stay there in the shade, Mrs. Speedwell. We'll set it out around you. Violet will help me."

Violet was grateful to her sister-in-law for the escape from her mother. Evelyn was too discreet to say anything as they picked up platters of cold sliced tongue, egg salad, dressed lettuce, and a variety of pickles, but even the short break from her mother restored her somewhat. Over the years she had learned that Evelyn's response to her mother-in-law's irritating comments was to change the subject and, if possible, physically move away from the problem.

When Violet took her place back at the table, Marjory had come back from washing her hands, picked up the embroidered case Mrs.

Speedwell had let fall under her chair, and was studying it. She knew her niece well enough to refrain from saying anything lest she scare her away, but when Marjory took great care as she set the case at her grandmother's elbow, Violet wanted to hug her. Throughout the meal Marjory kept glancing at it. Finally, when they'd finished the birth-day cake—Victoria sponge, predictably Mrs. Speedwell's favorite, though with no candles ("far too frivolous; in our day we were grate-ful for even a small slice of cake")—the children were released from the torpid meal. While Edward ran off into the garden to try the kite again with his father, and Evelyn went inside to put things away, Marjory sidled up to her aunt. "Did you make that, Auntie Violet?"

"I did."

Marjory's hazel eyes were fixed on the case. "It's pretty."

"Thank you, darling. Bring it over. We'll look at it together."

Mrs. Speedwell, who had seemed to be asleep in her chair, opened her eyes as Marjory reached for the case. "Don't take other people's things, young lady. Only badly brought-up children do that."

Marjory jerked her hand back as if she'd touched ice. It made Violet's heart contract. "I asked her to, Mother. Surely you don't mind if she looks at it? She's far more interested in it than you."

Her mother sighed. "On one day of the year—just one day—I hope to feel a little special, a little looked after for once, rather than doing the looking after. But it is a mother's lot to be forever hurt by her children." She sighed again. "What would Geoffrey think?"

Violet gritted her teeth, reached over, and picked up the case. Mrs. Speedwell closed her eyes again.

Marjory was now looking at it fearfully, as if it might bite her. No, Violet thought. I will not let Mother ruin embroidery too. "It's all right, dear," she murmured. "Granny's angry at me, not you. Now, which bit do you like best?"

"The zigzag."

"That's called a Florentine stitch. Nice and bold, isn't it? It looks complicated but it's awfully easy to do."

"What's that one called?"

"Hungarian diamonds."

"And that?"

"Rice."

"Rice," Marjory repeated thoughtfully. "Like food?"

"Yes."

"It doesn't look like rice. It looks like exes."

"You're right, it does. Would you like me to teach you to embroider like this?"

She was not at all sure her niece could manage the stitches, but it was worth the suggestion just to see Marjory's face light up in a way Violet wished happened more often. "Oh, yes!"

"No call to teach her old maid's tricks before she needs them," Mrs. Speedwell declared, her eyes still shut.

If Marjory hadn't been gripping her aunt's arm, delighted at the idea of learning to embroider, Violet would have walked out. But she would not let her mother spoil this breakthrough with her earnest niece. "I'll bring the things we need next time I come to visit."

"Promise?"

"Promise, darling. Perhaps we can do it on our summer holiday."

Marjory clapped her hands. "Yes, please!" Her niece was never keen on the long walks along the coastal path that Tom insisted on, much as his father had. Perhaps embroidery could replace them, at least on the rainy days.

"Yes, please, what?" Evelyn set down a tray with a fresh pot of tea and cups.

"Auntie Violet is going to teach me to make this on the Isle of Wight!" Marjory waved the spectacles case at her mother.

Evelyn paused for a moment with her hands on the tray handles—the pause so brief only Violet would have noticed. Her sister-in-law rarely gave away what she was thinking, so Violet had learned to analyze the tiniest gestures. As Evelyn called to Tom to join them and sent Marjory off to play with her brother, Violet guessed what was coming.

Tom sat down. "Yes. So." He gazed helplessly at his wife. They all knew she was better equipped for the hard lifting this conversation required.

"The fact is, we have been invited to accompany my sister and her family to Cornwall for our summer holidays," Evelyn explained. "We won't be going to the Isle of Wight. It will be good for Marjory and Edward to play with their cousins, and go somewhere new. But there is only room for us, I'm afraid. I'm sorry." She had the grace at least to look straight at Violet and appear genuinely sorry. Tom could not meet her eye, but stared miserably into his cup of tea.

Violet had been expecting this announcement for some time. Since Mr. Speedwell's death, the last two holidays to the Isle of Wight hadn't been as successful as in the previous years. Tom had tried and failed to fill his father's role as chief spirit raiser. The children became crabby, Mrs. Speedwell's complaints increased, Evelyn's smile became ever more fixed, and a desultory feeling settled over the holiday like dust. It was only a matter of time before something had to change.

Violet's mother was leaning back in her chair, her eyes closed, not reacting to the news. She already knows, Violet thought, else she would be shrieking and fanning herself and moaning about honoring

Geoffrey's memory. She's probably already done all of that and got it out of her system.

"You might have told me earlier," she muttered. You told Mother, she added silently.

"We only just finalized the plans," Evelyn defended herself, then stopped, perhaps realizing how that sounded. They'd made their plans without consulting Violet.

"You could go to Ventnor anyway!" Tom's tone was too bright. "You and Mum. Stay at the same place, and report back on the comings and goings—who's there this year, what new fossils have been found, which tea shops are doing the best rock cakes." The Speedwells used to argue over the quality of Isle of Wight rock cakes.

"I shall be going with Penelope to Hastings," Mrs. Speedwell announced without opening her eyes.

An unexpected relief washed over Violet. She would not have to go on holiday with her mother alone. She would rather not have a holiday at all than be subjected to that ordeal. Poor Aunt Penelope, she thought. Her aunt, mild mannered and also widowed, was an expert at deferring to her older sister. Violet would be sure to thank her for her sacrifice.

Tom's guilt over the change in holiday plans extended to offering Violet a lift back to Winchester. Evelyn agreed, overly solicitous. "You two go and enjoy the afternoon. I'll look after your mother."

They said nothing until they'd reached the countryside surrounding Southampton, as if needing to put the city between them and the rest of the family, with their announcements and their demands.

Even then Violet was silent. She would let her brother speak first; she wasn't going to help him.

"Look, old girl, I'm sorry about all that!" Tom shouted over the noise of the engine as they turned onto the road to Winchester. "The Isle of Wight and whatnot. Really I am. If it were only up to me I'd be happy to go back there. It's just—well, I'm not meant to tell anyone yet, because it's early days, but Evie's expecting again. Don't say anything!" he added as Violet began to shout her congratulations. "It's better not—oh, blast!" He pulled into a lay-by and switched off the engine. As it grew quiet Violet could hear sheep baa-ing in the field next to the road, hidden by a hedgerow.

"That's better," Tom said. He lit two cigarettes and passed one to her. "Look, I feel awfully bad about not telling you, but we really only just found out yesterday that Cornwall was definitely on. Evelyn— well, you're not to say a word, but we've lost a few since Eddie."

It took a moment for Violet to understand what he meant. "Ah."

"Evie's always wanted three, but that third has been . . . elusive. So we don't say anything now when she—you know. She wants this one to—to take. And she thought it would be better for her to be with her sister, in case there are problems. And it's—well, easier."

"Less stressful for her, you mean," Violet filled in.

"Yes."

"Because of me or because of Mother?" She felt a little childish asking, but wanted reassurance.

Tom was happy to provide it. "Oh, Mum, of course! You're fine! The kiddies love you, and Evie does too."

Violet doubted that but was willing to let it pass. "When did you tell Mother about Cornwall?"

"Yesterday."

"And did she make a fuss?"

"A bit, though less than you might think. Oh, she complained that we were betraying Dad and George's memory, and that the family was falling apart, and all that. But once she got that out of the way, she fixed on the idea of going to Hastings with Aunt Penelope, so much so that she even used our telephone to ring her and begin planning straight off."

They stubbed out their cigarettes. "Do you think you'll go to Ventnor?" Tom asked. "We haven't canceled the rooms yet, so there's still a room for you there if you want. There'll be a surcharge for it being a single, but we'll pay for that, of course," he added as an after-thought.

"I'll think about it."

They were silent for a time. Violet gazed at the puffy clouds on the horizon, trying not to cry. She took a deep breath, breathing in the comforting smell of leather.

"Or perhaps you could go on one of those rambles for single girls, where you all walk and stay at guesthouses along the way," Tom suggested. "They're popular, aren't they?"

"They are—so popular they'll be booked out by now." Violet had seen the posters of smiling red-cheeked women striding along in shorts and berets as they went on their organized rambles. Though she could not bear to wear such a costume, a walk did appeal. And his suggestion gave her an idea. "Do you remember the Wallops? With Father? Over, Middle, and Nether Wallop?"

"Of course. George and I took the word literally, and spent the afternoon walloping each other. And Dad let George have shandy at the pub. I was so jealous."

"You were seven!"

"I know. But we were competitive, even if he was six years older than me. I also remember George and me trying to climb one of the stones at Stonehenge and getting told off by the stewards. That was a good holiday."

"What was the name of the pub at Nether Wallop?"

"The Five Bells. Why?"

"Oh, just a thought." But it cheered her—enough so that back in Winchester she pored over her landlady's local Ordnance Survey maps.

The next day she rang the Christian Alliance of Women and Girls to check if there were any spaces left for their singles holidays to Wales and the Lake District, and was told, as she'd expected, that they were long booked up.

Part of Violet was relieved not to have to go on holiday with strangers, making polite conversation and trying to be jolly together. But now she had two choices if she did not want to end up staying in Winchester, sleeping in and reading and going for desultory walks as she waited for the holiday to end. She could ask to join her mother and aunt in Hastings, where she would be made an object of pity and exasperation by Mrs. Speedwell while Aunt Penelope tried to placate both. Or she could go somewhere on her own. Before she could talk herself out of it, she rang Tom and asked for help to pay for a walking holiday for herself. "Of course, old girl," he replied, chuckling. "Can't have my sister going hungry. What would Dad think?" After a pause he added, "Didn't you get a pay rise recently?"

Violet did not sweeten her reply. "I did. Now I can just about afford to eat a hot dinner most days."

"Yes, I see." Tom hastily changed the subject, perhaps taken aback that his joke about food was taken seriously. "Where will you go, then? Not to Hastings?"

"I am going to walk. First from Winchester to Salisbury, and then down through the New Forest to Lymington. From there I'll take the ferry to the Isle of Wight and stay a few days in Ventnor."

"Gosh, I wish I could go with you!" He lowered his voice. "Cornwall will be fine, of course, but it's different being with Evie's family—and all the kiddies. Going walking would be like old times."

"At least neither of us has to cope with Mother!"

She had a month to prepare: to plot out her route, write to pubs or bed-and-breakfasts to reserve rooms, get her walking boots resoled and buy a new straw hat, borrow a rucksack from the Hills and a compass and penknife from Tom, pack and repack to lighten the load. She had never before had to do the planning—it had always been her father or Tom who sorted out the logistics. But Violet found she rather enjoyed studying Mrs. Harvey's maps, gauging how far she would walk in a day, looking for points of interest to aim for and shortcuts she could take, guessing which villages would have places where she could stay.

She saw her brother and his family only once before the holidays, but she was ready for Marjory, bringing with her canvas, wool in four colors, a needle, and a model she'd made of stitches, much as Miss Pesel made for the Cathedral Broderers. Marjory was thrilled, and was an attentive pupil, sitting close to Violet at the table in the garden and carefully watching her demonstrate how to thread a needle, count squares, make a stitch, tuck an end of the wool behind stitches. When it came time for her to make her own stitches, she took her time, but she got them right, and bit by bit she grew faster and more confident. Violet chided herself for having underestimated Marjory's ability.

As they worked together, focused and absorbed, the rest of the family ranged around them, weeding, drinking tea, reading the paper, tossing a ball in the air. Occasionally one would glance over at aunt and niece. Mrs. Speedwell was also visiting, and took a particular dislike to their industry. "I can't think why you're working with wool in such heat," she declared, even though she was wearing her blue wool dress. "That can't be good for a child. See how flushed she looks."

"Marjory is fine, Mrs. Speedwell," Evelyn said, glancing up from the *Southern Daily Echo*. Since Violet had accepted her exclusion from the Cornwall holiday, Evelyn had gone out of her way to be positive and supportive.

"It's a very peculiar interest, if you ask me. What is the use of such stitching?"

Marjory looked up from her Florentine zigzag with a disarming gaze at her grandmother. "You can make pretty things."

"Tut, child, it's very rude to answer back."

Marjory's eyes widened. "But you asked a question, Granny. And I answered it."

"Now, Marjory," Evelyn interjected. "I'm sure you didn't mean to be rude to Granny. Perhaps you'll make something pretty for her with your stitches."

Marjory looked at Violet. "Of course," Violet agreed. "You could make Granny a little purse for her coins, or a pair of slippers, or a belt. How about that?"

"I can't see that I'd make use of any of those things," Mrs. Speedwell declared.

"Well, then, you can make something for your mother. I'm sure she would love a purse for her pennies. You practice your stitches over the summer, and when you have mastered them I'll help you with a purse." Violet wasn't entirely sure how she would design a purse, but Miss Pesel might be able to help.

Mrs. Speedwell grunted. "Of course, it's much more important to make something for your mother than for your grandmother."

Violet caught Evelyn's eye. Her sister-in-law rolled hers skyward, and Violet started to laugh.

"What are you laughing about?" Mrs. Speedwell demanded, as Evelyn joined her. "There's nothing funny!"

9

It was easy enough to plan a solo trip, but much harder to take that first step out the door. Violet stood in the hall early one August morning, before even her landlady was up, trying to quell her nerves and summon the courage to leave. Ostensibly she was ready: Her rucksack was packed, she was dressed in an old brown linen dress and jacket, and she had laced up her stout boots.

Until a few days before, friends and family had been sanguine about her going walking on her own. As the time drew near, however, her brother rang to ask if she was sure she still wanted to go. "We could probably find you lodgings somewhere near us in Cornwall," Tom suggested in an offhand way, doubtless aware that at this late date everything would be booked, but wanting to make the offer to assuage his guilt.

"Will you be all right out there on your own?" Gilda demanded more directly when they met at Awdry's. "You can always change your plans, you know."

"I'll be fine," Violet replied robustly.

Gilda did not dwell on the point. She was going with her family to Swanage for two weeks, with her new sister-in-law joining them. "Olive will parade her pregnancy as if that was the plan all along," she grumbled, "and will demand as much attention as she can get. If Mum was alive she'd put her in her place. But Dad and Joe are soft on her."

"Then you shall have to be your mother," Violet replied, only later realizing she might have invited Gilda to walk with her.

Mrs. Harvey began fretting the night before. "I don't like to think of one of my girls stranded out there in the fields," she declared, watching as Violet set her rucksack in the hall, ready for the morning. "What if you twist an ankle, or run out of water, or an adder bites you? Then what will you do?" She was voicing concerns Violet had had herself, which made her escape to bed early before her landlady could worry her even more.

Now, Violet was hungry but did not want to linger. If I make some toast, she thought, Mrs. Harvey will get up and start making a fuss again. She swung her rucksack onto her shoulders, tightened the straps, and set off without ceremony or breakfast.

She walked briskly down the hill to the bridge crossing the Itchen. Ahead on a granite plinth was a massive statue of King Alfred, his back to her, facing the High Street and holding his sword blade with its hilt up as if he were blessing the town that lay before him. Violet passed the statue, looked around, then curtseyed to Alfred before she began her walk up through Winchester.

She passed the medieval shop fronts that hung out over the street; passed the butcher and the chemist; passed Awdry's, where for a moment she considered stopping for coffee, but instead pressed on; passed the Buttercross, an octagonal stone structure where women in the Middle Ages used to sell their butter; passed Warren's, where she bought office supplies. The shops were not yet open, so there were few people about: the odd bicyclist, a boy delivering papers, a window washer cleaning a dress shop front. They nodded at her, but no one stopped to chat or ask about her rucksack and where she was going. No one said, "Well done, Violet. That's brave!" or "Are you sure you want to walk on your own?" or "Why don't you come with us to the seaside instead?" She had only lived in Winchester for nine months, so was still a stranger no one was ready yet to invest in. She hadn't thought it mattered, but now she wished there were someone to wave her off on her adventure.

Toward the top of the town she walked through the stone arch of the medieval West Gate that marked her departure from the center, and up to a bridge over the railway line, crossing it just as an early train to London steamed into the station some way to her right. Violet dodged the smuts blown back from the engine, then stood and watched while passengers got on, banging the doors and calling out to one another as they hoisted their suitcases on board. When the train pulled away with a distinctive huff, she wondered if she should have gone to London instead. She could barely afford a night there, though she might have squeezed more funds from her guilty brother so that she could go to a matinee, a concert, a tea dance. She could walk along the Thames and rummage in the bookshops along Charing Cross Road and systematically go through the rooms of the British Museum. She had done all of these things before, but always trailing her parents. Even aged thirty-eight it would be hard— terrifying, if she was honest—to do so alone.

As was this. Violet had gone for walks on her own—on Southampton Common, along the seafront at Portsmouth or on the Isle of Wight, up St. Catherine's Hill outside Winchester—but these were places where there were others about, and people waiting for her to return. She had never walked through fields alone. It had seemed possible when she was simply imagining it, but now that she had to do it, anxiety pushed up from her stomach to the back of her throat.

It was the alternatives—two weeks in Hastings with her mother and aunt, or staying in Winchester, embroidering by the wireless in a stuffy room over pallid cups of tea, accompanied by the budgies' restless chirping—that made Violet set her jaw and walk away from the town.

She headed west up a gradual hill on a road that passed between two substantial Victorian buildings: first the prison with its five arms radiating out like rays of a star from the center, topped by a lantern tower; then the county hospital with its ornate brickwork. Walking past these two institutions felt like saying good-bye to the last outposts of civilization, the places where one might end up if things went wrong. Then the houses fell away and a small road jogged to the right—a Roman road, according to the Ordnance Survey map—and led out into fields. Violet turned in to that road and left behind the last of the houses.

To her left was an orchard, its rows of trees heavy with green apples not yet ripe. There was nothing frightening there. To her right was a large golf course. Though it was hardly eight o'clock, already there were men out knocking balls about in their flat caps, vests, and plus fours, their presence taming the surroundings.

After a gentle curve the Roman road did as the Romans had intended and ran straight, fields rolling out on one side, woods on the other. A motorcar passed her with a friendly toot of its horn, doubtless on its way to Farley Mount, as there was little else out here to drive to. Remaining on the road made Violet feel safer. While she was on a road, in plain sight of people, she could relax and allow herself to enjoy the sun on her arms, a pair of swifts cutting across the sky above her, a tractor puttering in the distance. It was quiet but not silent. She began to hum and think about the breakfast she had missed. She had packed elevenses; she would eat that soon, whatever the time.

After an hour the road kinked left into a small gravel lane toward the monument. Violet followed it to where the motorcar that had passed her was parked. Beyond it a path sloped up to a mound topped with the folly that was Farley Mount. It was a strange thing. Twenty-five feet high, with smooth white walls rising to a point and arched doors emerging from each of the four sides, it looked like a little Wesleyan chapel topped with an Egyptian pyramid.

Violet could see a couple next to the folly at the top of the mound, with two children shouting and laughing as they scrambled up and down the steep slope. For a moment she thought she would bypass the monument, so that the family would not break the spell she was already under out here. But the pyramid seemed to pull like a force that could not be ignored, and Violet found herself striding to it.

A large plaque on the monument reminded her of part of the conversation she'd had with Gilda and Arthur in front of the cathedral: that Farley Mount had been built to commemorate a horse. An eighteenth-century owner out foxhunting had fallen into a chalk pit with his horse. Both survived; the horse, renamed Beware Chalk Pit, won a race the following year, and its proud owner built the pyramid in its honor. Violet smiled. Her father and brothers would have loved such an absurd story. She wondered if they had ever been here.

She climbed the mound and joined the couple. "Glorious day," the man said.

"Yes." Violet gazed out over the rolls of land swelling before her, painted in myriad shades of green and yellow and brown, the sun and sky washing over it all. The English countryside was indeed glorious. But there was also a certain oppressiveness about it in August. The shimmering waves of heat just above the ground, the over-bright sun, the stillness, the yellowed fields of wheat and hay and barley, the clumps of trees where the green had peaked and was now fading: It felt lush yet also on the turn. August was a month off the prime that was July, when the natural world was at its height. It brought with it a melancholy that would deepen in September. Violet preferred October, when the world dropped its leaves and became properly crisp and cold, accepting its fate and no longer trying to hold on to summer.

The woman was giving her a sideways look. "On your own, are you?" She took her husband's arm.

"I am . . . meeting a friend." Violet winced at her inability to say that she was alone. Why was it so shameful?

The man looked around. "What, out here?" His grin was sly; he had decided she was meeting a man.

"At Nether Wallop." Although it was two miles out of the way of the route between Winchester and Salisbury, Violet had written to the Five Bells to book a room.

"And you're walking all the way there? Gosh," the woman remarked, sounding more disapproving than impressed.

Their children were standing in the chamber inside the folly, playing with the echo by shouting. There was an inviting bench nearby that would have been perfect for a breakfast with a view. But Violet wished the husband and wife a pleasant day and left Farley Mount. She would not eat with pity and suspicion accompanying her.

She walked back down to the path, then couldn't help it: She glanced back. The couple was still watching her. Though Violet was now ravenous, she would have to find a place farther away. She followed the footpath down a small hill, and at the bottom rejoined the

Roman road she had left earlier. Now a path bounded by hedgerows, too rough and narrow for motorcars, it led her through a meadow, and there she dropped her rucksack and sat, grateful for a break out of sight of the family. Sheep were grazing in the far corner, but they ignored her.

Before eating, Violet gulped water from a canteen that had been Tom's during the war. It felt odd to use it, but he had offered and she knew she needed one. They had not discussed his experience of the war in any detail. It had been too raw at first, and then too late. Tom just wanted to move on with his life, in a way that Violet found difficult to do: enter a serious career, marry, start a family. Though she couldn't begrudge him these things, she was envious. There was nothing obvious or straightforward in her own life—no clear path to follow.

She got out a luxury she'd allowed herself, though it made the rucksack heavy: a thermos full of coffee. Strong and pungent, it was exactly the jolt she needed after five miles of walking. Even the stale rolls with margarine and jam tasted delicious. Best of all, Violet allowed herself a celebratory square of fudge she'd made for the journey. The Speedwells had always brought fudge with them on their holiday walks, and she felt she'd earned it. It melted on her tongue, leaving a sugary puddle that reminded her of childhood.

After she ate, she packed away the remains of her elevenses, then got out the Ordnance Survey map Mrs. Harvey had lent her. The red-and-brown cover was illustrated with a print of a man in walking clothes, sitting on a hill and consulting his map, an idyllic English landscape spread before him of woods and fields punctuated by an aqueduct in the middle distance and a church spire farther away. Violet studied the route: The way forward was along the course of the Roman road—mostly footpaths now—through fields. From where she sat she could already see the first field—a small one of corn.

Fields made Violet nervous. If you met someone in a field, you wondered what he (for she only imagined a man, never a woman) was doing there alone. Of course he could be on a walking holiday as well, or getting from one place to another—from a farm to a shop, for instance—or walking to see an ailing friend, or looking for a lost cow. There were many reasons a man could be out on his own.

Not so for women. Violet might be unmarried and seem to do things solo, but she was never really alone. There were her landlady and other lodgers in the house; she could sense their presence even behind her closed door. There were colleagues at work. Even when she visited the cathedral on her own, there were always others there, and now she knew a few of the broderers by sight, and even vergers to nod to.

A stile separated her from the field of corn. She stepped up and swung herself over it, then remained seated on the top rung, looking up the path lined on both sides with stalks of corn higher than her head.

Come now, old girl, she thought, pull yourself together. What would Laurence do? She often invoked her late fiancé when she needed a shot of courage that coffee and fudge couldn't supply. Laurence had not been full of obvious bravery, but he had gone to war and never complained about being there or what he witnessed, and that was a kind of English courage.

She jumped off the stile and headed into the corn, stepping carefully along the narrow gap between rows. Cornstalks rustled at her shoulders, their fibrous emerald leaves scratching the sleeves of her jacket and dappling the sunlight. She looked behind her several times to make sure she was alone. The noise and the soft pressure of the leaves and the flickering light and shadows were disorienting. The field seemed endless. Had she been walking across it for minutes or hours?

Then, up ahead, a rabbit appeared from the side and began to run along the row. Violet kept her eyes on its flashing white tail, until it was gone and she was in the sunlight at the edge of the field, hot and out of breath, by a hedgerow covered with brambles offering unripe blackberries. A kissing gate was hemmed in by the bushes, and Violet had to push through, getting scratched through the linen of her sleeves and drawing blood.

The next field was of grass, and the next barley, their heavy beards tipping over, waiting to be cut. Here it was much less oppressive because she could see around her and ahead, where there were farm buildings. She came through the barley to the farm, the path skirting the right edge of the farmyard. No one was visible, but there was laundry hanging out in the sun, and rattling sounds from one of the barns. A horse stood in the field next to the path. He was cropping the grass, but lifted his head to watch her as she passed.

Behind the farm Violet walked through a small scrubby wood, where an old tractor had been left to quietly fall apart and an iron bed frame was rusting, as well as other scraps of metal she could not identify. She didn't like the waste and the untidy maleness of it, and hurried to get back out into the fields—one of cows, one of sheep. She crossed a road, then another field of barley, and then another road, before facing a big field of corn. Violet paused to study it, but only for a moment: With coffee and fudge coursing through her, she felt ready to tackle half a mile of corn. It would only take ten minutes, and then there was a road, and a bridle path through a small field to an inn. She could stop there.

Violet noticed him only when she was well into the field, though it was hard to tell: As with the first field of corn, she was soon disoriented by the noise and dappled light. All she knew was that at some point she looked behind her and a man was there, about forty yards back. She couldn't exactly say that he was following her, because she didn't know if he was just using the same path or if he was there because of her. Where had he come from? The farm with the rusting metal? Had he seen her from one of the barns and come out after her? Or was he looking for a lost cow, or visiting a sick friend, as Violet had suggested to herself that anyone might do? Both possibilities seemed ludicrous now that she was alone with him in an endless field of corn.

She increased her pace while trying not to appear panicked. Stalks of corn edged and crossed the path and blocked a clear view ahead. She considered stopping and waiting for him to catch up with her, which would have the advantage of her being able to see his approach rather than keeping her back to him. Perhaps he would smile and nod and pass her with no incident. But even the brief glance at him told her he was not a smiler. He was not particularly big—just a little taller than Violet—had a sober, focused face, and he walked fast. There was an atmosphere about him of dark corners and rusting metal and an unshaved jaw. She wanted to look back again but didn't dare. She sped up, no longer caring that he would know she was on the verge of flight. She thought she heard the corn rustling nearer. Then she spotted light at the end of the path, and ran.

Bursting out of the corn, Violet scrambled over a stile into a road, then turned and ran along it without looking back. Only after a stitch jabbed in her side did she slow down and look around. He had not followed her out onto the road. She stopped and bent over, hands on her knees, panting, her eyes on the gap where he would appear from the field. When he still did not appear, she felt she had been right to run, for he must be hiding in the corn. Although she hadn't got her breath back, Violet hurried along the road again, hoping a motorcar might come by, or a tractor, or people out walking.

She reached a small road to the right and turned in to it, out of sight of the cornfield, then glanced at her map. This road would take her down to the inn that she'd been aiming for, a quarter of a mile away. She walked quickly along the lane, looking behind her every twenty paces, but the man did not reappear.

She almost cried at the sight of the John O' Gaunt Inn, a simple white building with a slate roof and black-trimmed windows, sited at a crossroads by the river Test. It was only just past eleven, and the pub might not yet have opened. But someone was bound to be about, and might even make her a cup of tea, or a sandwich that she could eat on one of the benches either side of the door. She wanted someone to take pity on her.

Violet pushed at the door and was relieved to find it unlocked. A wave of stale smoke and grease hit her as she entered a room full of empty tables and chairs. To her right was the bar, where the publican was serving someone at the other end but nodded at her in welcome. She was already swinging her rucksack onto the carpeted floor by one of the tables when the customer standing at the bar turned and looked at her. It was the man from the cornfield.

Violet froze and swallowed a gasp. If her rucksack hadn't already touched the ground she might have grabbed it and run back outside. But she felt trapped: by the publican's friendly overture; by her fear of showing her fear; by her concern that she had overreacted in front of an innocent man; by her desire not to be judged a silly girl on her own. So she did not leave, but stood, awkward and turning red, her heart thumping.

The man did not smile or say hello; his silence was much more powerful. He had dark, steady eyes and brown hair longer than was the fashion. His cap was off, sitting next to the pint in front of him. His frame was wiry, his clothes ill-fitting, as if they were second-hand. He had rolled up his sleeves in the heat and Violet could see dense dark hairs on his forearms.

How had he managed to get here before her? And even to have been served a pint? To calm herself, Violet tried to think, retracing her route and recalling the map she'd just looked at. After a moment she was able to work out that the roads she had taken to the inn followed two sides of a triangle. The man had probably cut across a field along the bridle path, taking the third side of the triangle and half the time as she had.

While she'd been thinking this through, the publican had said something, and was looking expectant. "Pardon me, I was . . ." Violet didn't finish; she couldn't say what she was doing.

The publican chuckled. "Just asking what I can get you, love. You must be knackered, carrying that on your own." He nodded at the rucksack.

The man from the cornfield studied his pint.

"I'm fine," Violet muttered. "I'll have a pot of tea, please."

"Have a seat. I'll bring it over."

Violet sat, trapped by her manners. The room felt very small.

"What brings you this way, love?" The publican was busying himself behind the bar with a kettle.

Violet grimaced, though she tried to hide it. Here was the nosy sort of landlord who would cloak his curiosity in overfriendliness. She would now face a barrage of questions she couldn't escape from, and that she didn't want to answer in front of the corn man with his beer.

"I'm . . . walking."

"Where to?"

Violet's mind went blank. She should lie so that the man would not know where she was headed. But she couldn't recall any of the towns north or south of here, and if she said she was going to Winchester, the man would know she was lying since he'd seen her come from that direction. "Salisbury," she found herself saying, to fill the silence that would become suspicious if it went on for too long.

"What, going between the cathedrals, are you?"

Violet nodded, annoyed to hear that her route could be guessed so easily.

"We get a fair number of walkers doing that. The path runs just the other end of the road." The publican nodded in a general direction. "Follows the old Roman road all the way to Old Sarum, just north of Salisbury. But you knew that, of course. Got your map, do you, love?"

Violet waved her Ordnance Survey map.

"And you know how to read it, do you?"

Violet turned bright red. "My father taught me."

"Good on him. Good for a girl to know some skills. Now, you're not walking all the way to Salisbury today, are you? It's much too far to do in a day."

"I'm . . ." Don't say Nether Wallop, Violet warned herself.

"Because there are rooms upstairs if you're looking for a place to stay."

"No, thank you. I'll go on a bit further today before stopping."

The publican brought over a tray with a pot of tea things and a plate of arrowroot biscuits. "There's your tea and that's your hot water."

"Thank you."

"I've got friends do rooms at Broughton. I could ring ahead for you."

"I'm fine, thanks."

"A girl like you, walking alone. You need a place to stay. It's no trouble for me to sort it out for you, love."

"Really, please don't. I have a place to stay."

"Where?" The landlord was standing over her. The man at the bar lifted his pint and took a long drink. Violet couldn't help staring at his profile.

"Nether Wallop." She had always been terrible at lying.

"What, the Five Bells? Tell Bob I said hello, and I'll see him at the cricket Wednesday evening."

Violet nodded.

"Bit out of your way, Nether Wallop, isn't it?"

"I—I have friends there."

"Do you, now? Who, if you don't mind me asking?"

I do mind, Violet thought. I mind very much. He was displaying the kind of friendliness that verged on hostility, as if he thought he could catch her out in a lie. He would have protested that he was just doing his civic duty, keeping an eye on the comings and goings within the community. Violet wished he were actually helpful, that she could say to him, "Who is the man at the bar with the whiff of danger coming off him? I don't trust him. Do you?"

The pause during which she thought all of this was an awkward one, and a frown line appeared between the publican's brows. "Arthur," she said, to fill the gap. Then, realizing she didn't know his surname, she added, "The bell ringer." It was a bit much calling him a friend when she'd only met him once—though she did still carry his handkerchief in her handbag. Somehow she had not managed to get it back to him. She found it comforting to come across it when she was searching for a lipstick or a stray penny. It made her feel looked after.

The publican guffawed. "Arthur the bell ringer," he repeated. "The very one. D'you know, I asked him once to explain it to me, what they do up there with their bells, and didn't understand a word he said. 'Why don't you play us a tune we can sing along to, mate?' I put it to him. I think I offended him." He sounded proud of this.

"Do you know, I might just take my tea outside," Violet declared in as cheerful a tone as she could muster. "It's such glorious weather."

For a moment the publican looked insulted, then hid it behind a professional smile. "Of course, love. I'll carry the tray out for you."

Violet picked up her rucksack, cast a last glance at the man at the bar, then turned her back on him and held the door open for the publican with the tea tray.

Outside she felt both better and worse. Better because the air was fresh and didn't smell of cigarette smoke and fried fish, and she was less trapped. Worse because she no longer knew what the man at the bar was doing, or where he was.

However, at least the publican mercifully left her alone once he'd set the tray down on a bench, going back inside to deal with his other customer. Perhaps they were talking about her. Violet poured her tea, nibbled on an arrowroot biscuit—her least favorite—and looked about. The John O' Gaunt was on the edge of a small village—Horsebridge, she gathered from the map. There were only a handful of houses, but there was a train station. She could probably get a train to Southampton if she wanted, to take her away from the man and the publican and her walking holiday. Her mother was leaving for Hastings this afternoon; she might yet catch her, apologize profusely, and join her. For a moment Violet was tempted.

Just then a young woman came past the pub, pushing a pram. Its hood was covered with white frilly cloth, its occupant asleep. The woman was gazing at the baby with unalloyed adoration. She looked up and took in Violet, her sturdy boots and dress, her map and rucksack, her tea, and smiled. Her face was still full of love for her baby, which overrode any curiosity she might have for this passerby. Violet smiled back.

It was such a normal exchange that it calmed her. This is a place with women and babies, she thought, not just men lifting pints at eleven in the morning. She would drink her tea and head on to Nether Wallop. She studied her map. There were a few ways to walk the five miles to the village along footpaths, but she decided to take roads there. It would not be as immersive, but she did not want a repeat of the cornfield.

She finished her tea and stood, hoisting up her rucksack so that she would be ready to walk away briskly after she paid.

Inside the publican was behind the bar, polishing glasses. The other man was gone. His glass was gone too. Indeed, it was as if he had never been there. Violet tried not to look around or seem bothered, but her stomach knotted. Was he in the gents'? Or gone out a back door to wait and follow her?

Stop it, she scolded herself. There are people about and you're safe. Don't let a man like that intimidate you. Let him go off to find his lost cow. She was able to smile at the idea.

"That's better," the publican declared. "First time you've smiled since you arrived."

Violet stopped smiling.

The publican didn't seem to notice. "A smile makes a girl look years younger," he rattled on. "All those creams and potions and whatnot advertised in the magazines—all nonsense. All you need's a smile. That'll be threepence, love."

Violet set the coin on the bar. "Thank you. Good day."

She turned and walked to the door without engaging in the chitchat expected at the end of an exchange, and heard the barman tut. "Some as don't help themselves, no matter how friendly you are to them," she heard him mutter just as the door swung shut behind her.

The river Test was like a loosened braid of water, and along the road to Broughton Violet crossed strands of it several times. She stopped to gaze down at the bright, clear water running below her. It was prime fly-fishing territory, and men could be seen standing in the river, casting for fish.

There was more traffic now. It was noon, and delivery vans passed, and men in motorcars looking as if they were heading somewhere important, and families out for a drive. An old couple wearing matching straw hats drove past with a honk and a wave. It felt safe, but also as if she were walking to get somewhere rather than out to enjoy being in the countryside. The land too was flatter and less picturesque. And her feet hurt.

At Broughton she stopped alongside a tributary to the Test called Wallop Brook and took off her boots and socks to soak her feet in the icy water. Violet was hot now, and tired. She had walked twelve miles, and had two more to go. She ate the sandwiches she had made for herself and drank the last of the coffee. From now on she would have to buy her meals, and watch her pennies being depleted.

She was still hungry afterward, and gazed longingly at the pub she passed on the High Steet, then at a tea shop where a family was sitting out front in the sunshine, having cream teas and squash, the children flicking crumbs at each other. Violet did not stop at either. She could not afford constant treats.

She didn't recall any of this landscape from when she'd come walking here with her father and brothers. She couldn't remember exactly where they'd gone apart from Nether Wallop. They could have walked down this road. For all she knew they had stopped at the John O' Gaunt, maybe even been served by the same publican, a much younger man then. He would have been deferential to her father, teased her brothers a little, said nothing to her.

Nether Wallop she did remember, and not just for its odd name. She passed a mill along the brook, turned a corner, and there was a vaguely familiar row of thatched cottages, distinctive for the thatch being very thick and hanging over the windows like eyebrows. Some of the houses were of white lime and dark beams, Tudor-like; others were of brick. They made a pretty sight, especially with their small front gardens full of roses and dahlias and daisies.

As she walked down the empty street toward the pub, she felt the strangeness of recognizing a place and yet not knowing it, of it having a similar tone as if nothing had changed, yet everything had changed and aged, including Violet herself. George was dead; Laurence was dead; her father was dead. Violet was thirty-eight years old, not eleven. She was seeing Nether Wallop through eyes that had seen many other things in between. It felt peculiar and sad, and she wondered why she had come.

But she had walked fourteen miles and was tired, and there was the Five Bells, and it too looked both familiar and strange. She went in and met the sort of landlord she preferred—the taciturn type. He handed her a key to her room above the pub and showed no curiosity. Violet went up, dropped her rucksack, kicked off her boots, and was asleep in a minute.

10

When she woke Violet knew the light had broken, that the sun was no longer so insistent overhead, but more subtly aslant. Nearby a bell tolled five times. Her legs were stiff and sore from the long walk. She washed her face in the basin, then changed from her crumpled linen dress into a lighter floral tea dress in cream and green and brown, her beige cardigan, and low pumps that felt cloudlike after the heavy resistance of her boots. It was Violet's plan to change into these clothes after each day of walking. It was like putting on one costume to walk and another to reenter society.

She could not yet face visiting the church, with its memories of George. Instead she turned and wandered up the lane, past the village shop and post office, the butcher, the smith, the village school—all shut—and out past the village green toward what the map had labeled Middle Wallop and Over Wallop. The names were the joyful fodder of comedians, doubtless the butt of many jokes, but Violet loved them.

She reached a clump of houses set back from the road, with substantial front gardens rather than the earlier postage stamps. Peeking over high walls, she spied cottage borders full of hollyhocks and salvia, birches and lime trees and copper beeches. One garden had a large pear tree abundant with fruit. Violet stopped to admire it and saw by the front door of the cottage an older woman sitting on a bench, hatless, her eyes closed, face to the late afternoon sun. She wore a white dress, and her gray hair was longer than most women wore it these days, falling below her shoulders. An unopened magazine lay in her lap. Her whole demeanor reminded Violet of a pilgrim worshipping at a church, except that she appeared to be worshipping the sun.

There was the sound of snipping in the garden, and when Violet looked around she saw Arthur the bell ringer, deadheading roses in one of the borders. Arthur, her friend, she had called him at the John O' Gaunt. This was why she had really come to Nether Wallop, she realized. Of course: She wanted to see him. She opened her mouth to speak, but Arthur must have sensed she was there, for he turned and looked at her. He did not seem surprised to see her, but she was also not sure he knew who she was. Nonetheless, she raised a hand in greeting, and he raised his hand back. The tiny glance he threw toward his wife told Violet a great deal. She was still sitting with her eyes closed, and Violet took a step back so that the pear tree blocked her from view. Arthur set down his secateurs and walked over to the front gate, not hurrying but not bringing attention to himself. He opened the gate and shut it behind him in one fluid movement, careful not to bang it. Then he walked up the road. Violet followed. When they were out of earshot she said, "I was just passing by and admired your pears."

Arthur stopped and looked back at the tree. "It's a Williams. Producing well this year. A crop of 250 pounds, I should think." He had rolled up his sleeves for his gardening; his forearms were covered with white hairs.

"I'm Miss Speedwell. Violet. Gilda introduced us, in front of the cathedral."

"I know who you are, Miss Speedwell."

"I—I'm doing the walk between the cathedrals you mentioned. For my summer holidays."

He was looking at her shoes—pumps that would fall apart at the first sign of rough ground.

"I have boots, back at my room," she added.

"Are you staying at the pub?"

"Yes."

"Good food there. Especially the steak and kidney pie."

"That's good—I'm hungry." Having said it, Violet turned red. It seemed vulgar to acknowledge hunger.

But Arthur just nodded. "Walking will do that. Have you been to the church yet?"

"I'm going now. I was just having a look round the village first."

"Well, then, I'll let you get on with that while I finish the roses."

Violet felt a twinge of disappointment that this was to be the extent of their interaction. But then he added, "I'm likely to be at the pub later. Do you play cribbage?"

Violet nodded. She used to play cribbage with her father, and sometimes still with Tom.

"Good. I'll see you later, then." He turned and went back to his gate, then smiled briefly at her before closing it behind him.

Violet stood still and heard low voices: Arthur's tenor and a light musical alto, the call and answer of a husband reassuring his wife that all was well. She wondered what he was saying but didn't dare go nearer.

As she walked back along the road toward the church, she thought about her instinctive step out of sight of Arthur's wife, understanding that he would not introduce them but would keep them separate. Violet had rarely been in a position of appearing a threat to another woman; the feeling was a novelty that was not entirely pleasant, but there was something thrilling about it too—so thrilling that she stopped at a bench by Wallop Brook to have a cigarette and savor it.

Pubs were generally not places women spent much time in. Never in the public bar side, of course, which was reserved for men and was dingier, darker, and focused on the serious business of drinking. Women could sit in the saloon side, usually with others, but there was always a sense of them being merely tolerated in what was a male preserve. A pub was not a soft place. The wood bar and beams and tables and chairs, the worn carpet, the sharp gleam of the taps and glasses—all gave off an unyielding hardness that was not encouraging to women. That was why Violet went to hotel bars to find her sherry men. In hotels there was a transience that made everyone vulnerable and softer. If hotel bars were like seldom-used but comfortable front parlors, pubs were more like the shed where a man kept his tools. Or so she had always thought when she went to pubs with her family, particularly on walks. Country pubs were easier, with more give to them, but you still saw few women, and none on their own.

The Five Bells was different. Perhaps because she was staying in a room upstairs and so was expected to eat there, Violet felt her purpose in being in the pub was not questioned. When she walked in the publican waved her to a table in the corner and came over to take a drinks order. "A dry sherry and the steak and kidney pie," she said. The barman showed no surprise at this unusual combination, though when he brought her drink she realized it did not go well with the pie, and asked for some water as well.

As she sipped her sherry and waited for her meal, Violet looked around. The Five Bells had not changed much since she'd been there twenty-seven years before. There was a scattering of tables and chairs, horse brasses hanging along the beams, tankards on hooks behind the bar, and a large unlit fireplace with a fat Labrador lying in front of it, probably dreaming of winter blazes. She could remember George and Tom here—George trying bitter for the first time and spitting it out, unaccustomed to the taste, Violet and Tom and her father laughing at him, her father having it sweetened with lemon soda into a shandy.

It was a Saturday night and reasonably busy without being uncomfortably so. Anyone who wanted a seat would be able to find one, and there were a few couples sitting, some eating, some drinking. The women seemed to be drinking either port and lemon or lime and soda. Hers was the only sherry in the room. A scrum of men stood at the bar, and there were sure to be more in the public bar. There were occasional curious glances her way, but not judging or unfriendly. So much of a pub's atmosphere depended on the standard the publican set. If he treated Violet as if she belonged, so would his customers.

She also felt at ease knowing she was meeting someone here. She was expected. And he was a local. Violet did not doubt that when Arthur walked in he would nod to everyone, and have a quiet word with a few. She would be accepted by all because he accepted her. She admitted to herself too that she was looking forward to the jolt of surprise some of those giving her sideways glances now would experience when they saw Arthur join her.

She ate her steak and kidney pie and Arthur was right—it was delicious. The walking and the sunshine, as well as the accumulated months of a rationed diet of sardines and beans on toast, made her appetite enormous. When she finished the pie she hesitated only a moment before ordering jam roly-poly, though she knew it was depleting her budget for the trip. Day one and already she was spending too much. Violet sighed. It ground her down, this constant worry about every transaction and whether she could afford it. It was only a pudding! Why should she have to deny herself a pudding if she wanted one?

When Arthur arrived he found her scraping every bit of roly-poly and custard from her bowl, and smiled. "I like to see a clean plate," he said, taking the seat across from her and setting a cribbage board and a pack of cards between them. "It means you've enjoyed your food. How was the steak and kidney pie?"

Violet sat back. "Excellent. Thank you for suggesting it."

Arthur eyed her sherry glass. "Another of those, or would you like a half of the mild? The local is brewed right down the road. Mr. Trout makes it hoppy but not too bitter."

Violet chose the mild, pleased that he seemed to find nothing odd about her drinking it even when the other women in the Five Bells were not. Up at the bar he indeed knew everyone, and seemed to steer through any awkward comments about Violet's presence with a steady hand.

Soon they were playing crib and drinking and chatting, almost as if they were friends. Violet had noticed that when men met they often did something—played cards or darts or did the crossword together. It made conversation flow more easily because they didn't focus as intently on each other as women sometimes did. It was what had made embroidery sessions for the cathedral pleasurable.

Over the course of the evening, during their games they talked about things they had in common: Gilda ("a grand girl"), the workings of the cathedral, local elections. She was pleased that Arthur assumed she would vote; her mother had never voted since she got the right in 1918, and that made Violet diligent about exercising her own right once she gained it. She told him about transferring to the job in Winchester, and Arthur said she had been lucky, that the town was well-off enough to be less affected by the depressed economy. He talked for a time about unemployment in Britain, on the Continent, in America, and what it would take to shift things. "Germany," he concluded. "That is where the pressure is most concerning, particularly with the rise of the Nazi Party. Winston Churchill has expressed unease, and I rate him."

"He is not in the Cabinet, though, is he?" Violet offered this remark up timidly, for she did not discuss politics with others much, and worried that she was simply repeating what she could recall from the wireless and the occasional newspaper article.

"That does not mean he is not perceptive. Sometimes backbenchers are more sensible, because they don't have to answer to the Cabinet and the Prime Minister. They can say what they really think."

Violet cleared her throat; she was scoring. "Fifteen two, fifteen four, fifteen six, and a pair royale makes twelve." She did not really want to talk about Germany; it was still too painful to think about the country responsible for ruining her past. But she was thrilled that Arthur thought her clever enough to talk to about what was going on in the world. So many men assumed otherwise, even Tom and her father.

Gradually Arthur revealed more personal details: that he had two grandsons he had never met, in Australia. That he was a surveyor but had recently taken early retirement. That he rang bells at the village church as well as at the cathedral, cycling from one to the other on Sundays. "I'll be taking the service ring tomorrow morning," he added. "You may hear them as you walk. Now, whose box is it?"

What she did not find out, because she did not ask and he did not offer, was anything about his wife. It was not that he left her out—he said "we" had lived in Nether Wallop for thirteen years. But he gave no specifics—not her name, nor what she was doing now that meant she did not join them at the pub, nor what she thought of Nether Wallop and whether she missed Winchester. Arthur spoke about concrete things, and did not reveal much about what he felt.

When she'd seen Arthur's wife with her unkempt gray hair and her eyes closed against the sun, Violet had immediately known that something was amiss, though she could not have said what it was, either physical or mental. She had given off the impression of hidden damage, of a pot finely cracked that you could still use but must handle carefully or it might break apart in your hands. Violet suspected Arthur was good at careful handling, the precision required for his job as a surveyor making him an expert at measuring and keeping track of things. But she sensed somewhere a crack in him too, probably from the war; most cracks these days were.

It's over and we don't have to go through such a thing again, Violet reminded herself while Arthur was off at the gents'. She was slightly tipsy from her second half of mild.

She was pleased that he also asked her questions. With her sherry men she had spent many evenings listening to them and realizing at the end that they knew nothing of her apart from a brief physical sensation. But Arthur wanted to know more about what brought her to Winchester and where she worked and how she came to be involved with the broderers. It was hard to avoid the why of her move to Winchester, and she found herself telling him about her father's death, and the difficulty of continuing to live with her mother. That led back to the death of her brother, with a quick skirt over the death of her fiancé. Arthur nodded but did not probe. "Your mother is heartbroken over the loss of her son," he said with such quiet authority that Violet understood he was speaking of his wife too, and of himself, and of the cracks that are never mended.

"Yes," she said. "But she needn't take it out on me and Tom. *We're* still here." She knew she sounded petulant but she couldn't help it. "Tom fought in the war too. She should be glad he survived, and show it."

Arthur was silent for a moment. "It is perhaps difficult to understand if you have not had children yourself. The biological imperative of the parent is to protect the child, and when that is impossible it feels like a failure, whatever the circumstances. It is a complicated feeling to live with for the rest of your life."

"Are you—living with that feeling?"

"Yes. We lost our son."

"I am so very sorry." Her words felt as dry as paper, even though she meant them.

"Yes."

They had been talking earnestly, their game suspended, their heads bent toward each other. As Arthur leaned back, turned over a jack, and declared, "Two for his heels," Violet looked up and caught sight of the man she'd encountered in the corn. He was standing at the edge of the men drinking at the bar, holding a glass that was three-quarters drunk—so he had been there some time—and watching her. Violet started, knocking over her own glass so that the last of her mild spilled over the cribbage cards. "Oh!"

Arthur was the sort of man who had a handkerchief for every spill. He had clearly seen something in her face, though, for even as he pulled one out from his pocket—similar to the handkerchief of his she still had, with his initials embroidered in one corner—he looked around, scanning the crowd at the bar. Then he turned back to the table and began mopping up the beer. Here was the moment when she could give him back his first handkerchief, and apologize for accidentally taking it. But she did not.

"I'm sorry," she said. "Your cards are ruined."

"These cards have had plenty of beer spilled on them over the years. I'm not worried about them. Was it the man with the longish hair who startled you?"

"Yes. Do you know him?"

"Only by sight. He drinks here sometimes. He doesn't live in the village."

"He—I ran into him in a field down near Horsebridge. It was—" Violet was not sure how to describe what had happened.

"He frightened you?"

"Yes."

Arthur looked at her, waiting.

"It's not easy being a woman on your own," Violet explained after a moment. "No one expects it, though there are plenty of us. The 'surplus' women. One would think it would not be such a surprise to see a woman walk through a field, or have a cup of tea at a pub."

Arthur gazed at her, his crystal blue eyes sober. "I'll find out who he is. And if you can wait until after I ring the bells tomorrow morning, I will walk with you some of the way to Salisbury."

"That is kind of you to offer. But aren't you expected elsewhere?"

She was imagining a roast dinner, his wife passing him the gravy boat.

"Nothing I can't change."

Violet glanced over at the corn man, but he was gone, his empty glass still flecked with foam. He had done his disappearing act again.

"Then yes, please," she said. "I would like that very much."

11

Violet hadn't told Arthur, but she had not visited the church during her wander around Nether Wallop. After such an eventful day—the long walk, the man in the cornfield, the surprise of running into Arthur—she had not felt equipped to tackle the memories of a place so connected to her late brother and father. Indeed, she wondered why she'd ever thought it a good idea to re-visit. In the past she had been careful not to go to the dances, the clubs, the fields and villages she'd been to with Laurence.

However, it was easier to go to the church with a purpose: She was meeting Arthur. They had confided in each other in the pub, and she knew him better now. After serving her a substantial break-fast of eggs and beans, sausage, and fried bread, the publican handed her a doorstop of bread, a slice of ham, and a wedge of cheese for lunch, made without her even asking. When she shyly showed him her thermos, he asked, "Coffee or tea?" and filled it for her. Then Violet paid the bill, swung her rucksack onto her back, and waved good-bye to him, grateful for his silent kindnesses.

It was another warm, still day. There were clouds in the distance, but with so little wind they hardly moved. As she walked past the post office, Violet sighed. She had blisters on both little toes, her calves ached, and her walking dress was scratchy with dried sweat. It was sobering to imagine three more mornings where she would have to get up and walk from Salisbury down through the New Forest to the ferry for the Isle of Wight. She had thought of herself as reasonably fit and full of stamina, but walking long distances was a surprisingly tiring business.

Then the bells began to ring the familiar descending scale she had heard from bell towers all her life, and the sound was like a magnet drawing her to the church. It was set on a small slope on the southern edge of the village, and as she approached, Violet's stomach clenched as she remembered George. But seeing it wasn't as bad as she had expected. A compact Anglo-Saxon stone building with a short square tower, it had been altered a bit by the Victorians, added to and taken away from. Though solid and handsome enough, it was not that different from other country churches she'd seen. Its only quirk was the stone pyramid topped with a flame that George had claimed all those years ago. Seeing that did make her pause, but the bells sounding insistently in the tower right next to the pyramid did not allow her to tip into the void of past loss.

She made her way to the church porch, self-conscious with her rucksack. The door was open, and she stepped inside. The church had a nave and two side aisles, and was filled with wooden box pews. Overhead were wide whitewashed Gothic arches and high windows mostly of clear glass so that while it was dark on the ground, sunlight shone overhead. Its size was completely different from Winchester Cathedral's: It was a village rather than a city, with the coziness and claustrophobia that accompanied it.

Two women were setting out hymnals and prayer books, and the vicar was busy shuffling his papers on a wooden pulpit carved in the shape of an eagle. To the right of the entrance, Violet caught a glimpse of movement. She had expected the ringers to be hidden away up in the tower, so was surprised to see Arthur and four other men standing at its base, facing each other in a tight circle and pulling on ropes, each with a long, striped woolen section for them to catch. Each ringer pulled his so that it came down to his waist, then let it snake back up so he was reaching above his head to pull the tail end down again. They stood very still and solid, feet slightly apart, only their arms moving, and watched one another intently. Occasionally one would call out something, though Violet couldn't work out what he said. It was as if the men were privately communicating, yet also taking part in a theatrical public ritual. The vicar and the women setting out the books seemed not to notice, but Violet could not take her eyes off the ringers. She found their movements extraordinary—especially Arthur's, fluid and confident and completely natural. He did not see her, so focused was he on the others.

Suddenly the bells went back to their descending scale. "Stand," someone called, and each bell sounded twice more and went silent. The spell was broken, and the men relaxed, nodding at one another and murmuring. Arthur spotted her then, and moved his head almost imperceptibly. She nodded back, less subtly, for one of the women sorting prayer books stopped and stared at Violet in the way that only happens in a small village.

"Grandsire Doubles," one of the men announced. "David, you take the treble this time. Arthur, take the tenor. All right, lads."

Their focus swung back into their circle. "Look to," David called, pulling on the striped section of his rope. "Treble's going. . . . She's gone." His bell rang and they began ringing down the scale, over and over, until the leader called, "Go Grandsire," and the scale broke down into what sounded to Violet like random sounds. The prayer book woman was still staring, a frown beginning to form, so she withdrew outside to the churchyard. There she found a bench at the top of the graveyard that sloped around on two sides of the church, and sat down.

Though Violet had heard bells ringing many times before, she had never properly listened. She could not make out any pattern in the bells—though each was clearly struck, they seemed to clatter over each other in no particular order. Yet they were deliberate, not chaotic. It was like listening to people speaking German and sensing there was a grammar and structure, a rhythm and logic to it, even if you could not understand the meaning.

People were beginning to come up the path and enter the church. Some studied Violet and her rucksack, possibly struggling between a Christian desire to welcome and a villager's suspicion of a stranger sitting in the churchyard. Finally a tall man in a wool suit detached himself from a group of worshippers and loped up the slope to her. "I say, are you lost? The service will start shortly if you intend to come in." He glanced down at her rucksack.

"Thank you, but I'm waiting for a friend."

"I see." The man gave her a peculiar look. Don't worry, she wanted to say, he is not a sherry man.

At that moment, the bells changed from their unfathomable pattern back into the recognizable descending scale, then rang quicker and quicker until they all stopped, apart from the bell with the lowest tone, which continued to ring insistently. The man hurried away as if it were chivying him along. As he entered the church, a few of the bell ringers were leaving. Arthur was not among them. They headed off into the village, the single bell still sounding urgently. Eventually it too stopped, and the familiar chimes of the hour began on this lowest bell, struck so evenly that Violet suspected a machine had swung into action. The sound was completely different from when the men had been ringing: even and mechanical and soulless, like the difference between homemade biscuits and those from a packet.

After a few minutes she heard the congregation singing the first hymn: "Before the Throne of God Above." As the second verse began, Arthur came out of the church and climbed the slope to her. Violet scrambled to her feet, the rucksack on her back pulling her off-balance.

"Sorry to keep you," he said. "I was stuck on the tenor—that's the lowest bell—and had to get it ready for the clock chime. I call it the Calling All Sinners bell."

Violet smiled. "It had its effect on the stragglers. Are you sure you wouldn't rather stay for the service? I can stay too."

Arthur shook his head. "You have a twelve-mile walk ahead to Salisbury. It's best you don't start too late. Besides, it's a fine tradition for ringers to leave as the service starts. We've done our service to God for the day."

"So I saw. And heard."

"Now, let's have your rucksack." Arthur grasped the shoulder straps and lifted it from her.

"Oh, you don't have to do that."

But he had already swung it onto his back, and was absorbing her sweat and body heat. Violet swallowed at the unexpected intimacy. "You'll be carrying this for much of the walk," he said. "It only makes sense that I should take it some of the way and give you a rest."

She could think of no argument to that, and her sore shoulders silently thanked him. She followed as he led the way up a steep path to a small lane that took them south out of the village. "We'll go on a few small roads and then take a path down to the Roman road," he explained. "Once you're on that you can't go wrong, as it's so straight, and there's an inn for your lunch not too far from where I leave you. Would you like to see on the map?"

"Not yet."

They walked in silence for a time, and she was surprised at how comfortable she was with him, though she hardly knew him. She had not spent so much time alone with a man since Laurence.

"I found out a little about the man at the pub," Arthur said. "His name is Jack Wells. He lives on a farm a few miles south of here. A quiet sort."

Violet bit the inside of her cheek. She did not want the man to have a name—it made him too real. "Thank you," she said, and pointedly changed the subject. "How long have you been ringing bells?"

"Since I was eleven. I grew up at Barton Stacey, about ten miles north of Winchester. My father rang at the church there before me. It was expected."

"So you do it out of duty?"

"Not at all. It's in my blood, is what I meant. It would feel odd not to do it—like not brushing my teeth."

"It must be quite different ringing at a church like this rather than at the cathedral."

"The principle is the same at a church as at a cathedral: You pull a rope, a wheel turns the bell, and the clapper strikes it. But there are twelve bells at the cathedral whereas here there are only five. There's much less you can do with five. Barton Stacey had only five bells as well, and not very good ones at that. Some of the cathedral bells are heavier, so you have to take that into account when you ring. I do like ringing in a village church, though. With fewer people the circle is smaller, so it's easier to see what the others are doing."

"But you are ringing out in the open here."

"It is rather a public display, isn't it? At the cathedral we're tucked away in the tower. It's our own little world up there. I'll show you sometime, if you like. The bells are quite a sight."

"I would like that." She paused. "When I was listening earlier I wasn't sure what it was I was hearing. It wasn't a melody."

"You were hearing patterns. We start by ringing the five bells down the scale, one after the other. These are called rounds. Then we switch the order of two of the bells, so that each sequence of bells is different from the last. We call them changes. One of the rules of change ringing is that no sequence is repeated."

"Why such a rule?"

Arthur shrugged. "It is simply one of the rules of the puzzle. There's a method to it—a mathematical pattern, if you like—that runs us through all the variations. Eventually we get back to the beginning—the descending scale, or rounds."

Violet frowned. Now it was like Arthur was speaking German. "Can you hear the patterns as you ring?"

"I can, because I've been ringing for forty-nine years. Beginners don't, but they learn to discern."

He was sixty. Violet tried not to be surprised, or . . . disappointed. But—sixty. He was twenty-two years older than she. If she was going to be drawn to a man, he should at least be closer to her age, and not have a wife. She shook her head to clear it of these sobering thoughts. They were just friends now, after all. "And the people you are ringing for?"

Arthur looked puzzled.

"Everyone in Nether Wallop or Winchester who can hear the bells," she explained. "They don't know what they're hearing. They don't know what the pattern is."

"No, I suppose they don't."

Violet picked at a bit of goosegrass in the hedgerow. "Isn't it—well, a bit intrusive? For everyone to hear the bells so insistently, but not know what it is about?"

Arthur gave her a sideways glance. "Are you suggesting we are selfishly ringing for ourselves?"

"No, no, I'm not suggesting that." Actually she was.

"Perhaps we are. Would you rather we rang a *tune*?" His mild emphasis made Violet think of the publican at the John O' Gaunt, and she shuddered. She did not want to be placed in the same category.

"Of course not," she hurried to reply. "But there are patterns that are easily recognizable. The descending scale, for instance, is not a tune but it is familiar to most people. And the sound on the quarter hours and before the hour tolls—la-la-la-laaa; la-la-la-laaa," she sang, then stopped, embarrassed to have sung something that a bell ringer of fifty years clearly knew—that indeed, everyone knew. It was like singing "Mary Had a Little Lamb" to an opera singer and asking if they recognized it.

"I know it seems peculiar," Arthur admitted, "but we English *are* peculiar. We like to ring in mathematical sequences rather than melodies. However, if you pay close attention to the bells—which most people don't do—then you may begin to pick out some of the patterns."

"I did, actually. When you first rang this morning I caught snatches of repetitions, but they kept changing and I couldn't keep up."

"There's something quite mysterious about the pattern of bells ringing—more so than if it were a melody, which would be too predictable. A little complexity can be a good thing. I think people sense there is a form holding it all together. Must they know what that form is to enjoy it?"

"Perhaps not."

They had reached a stile along the road, and Arthur climbed over it with ease, Violet following. They had come to the edge of a field full of clover humming with bees in the flowers. "This is awfully pleasant," she remarked as they started along a narrow track, the bees buzzing around them. "I hope the weather is this nice when I go through the New Forest."

Arthur glanced at her. "Have you walked there before?"

"A few times with my family."

"So you know how empty it can be. Even during the summer you can go for hours without seeing anyone."

Violet wiped her brow, for the sun was already making her hot. Arthur had placed his finger right where she was most sensitive. Since the man in the corn, she'd been fretting about that part of her trip. She had never really liked the New Forest. It was some-what misnamed: While there were woods, much of it was actually heathland. Perhaps there had been more trees back when William the Conqueror named it a royal forest. While woods could conceal things, Violet had always found open scrubby pasture unnerved her. It was wilder and more untended, and made her think of unruly hair or a desk with papers scattered everywhere. The disorder threatened to spill into unpredictable behavior. But the New Forest stood be-tween Salisbury and the ferry to the Isle of Wight, and if she was to have a walking holiday, she must go through it.

She wondered if Arthur ever felt uneasy walking on his own. She suspected not. Men walked through the world as if it belonged to them. Though tempted to tell him of her anxiety, instead she said, "I expect there will be holiday makers there. And it's only for two days."

"Have you walked on your own before?"

"Not a long walk, no. Just to St. Catherine's Hill and back—that sort of thing."

"It can be lonely."

Violet shrugged.

Arthur gave her a sad smile, which irritated her. She did not want pity. "I don't mind being alone. I'm used to it." She was sharp—too sharp, for he flinched. "It *is* a little odd walking alone out here," she relented, and waved at the rolling green-and-yellow landscape around them.

"You could always take the train to Lymington. Spend an extra day or two in Salisbury going out on walks."

Violet smiled. "Are you trying to organize me?"

Arthur bowed his head. "My apologies. It's just that I'm not sure the countryside is as open to a woman on her own as you might wish it to be. I would be concerned if my daughter were walking alone."

Violet's smile faded. Bringing up his daughter reminded her that they were probably of a similar age. "I shall manage," she said stiffly, though she wondered if she would.

"I expect you will."

They walked in silence then, and after several stiles and fields they reached the Roman road. While it was not much improved, here a motorcar could more or less drive along it, though there were none; people were likely at church or preparing their Sunday roast.

Arthur gazed along the Roman road where it came from Horsebridge, five miles east. He didn't say, but Violet knew he was looking for the corn man, Jack Wells. She had tried not to think of him as they walked, but now that she was soon to be on her own again, fear flared. To hide it she busied herself with her map, though she fumbled with the folds, taking some time to find the right section and refold it into a reasonably sized rectangle.

"So, we are here." Arthur placed a finger on the map with the decisiveness of a man who understood measurement and the beauty of knowing exactly where he was. He was probably always the navigator when he went walking with others. "It's just a mile and a half straight walk along the road till you reach Winterslow and the Lion's Head. It'll be noon so it will be open for dinner or coffee or whatever you like. I'll walk you along for a mile or so until we reach a path I can take back to Nether Wallop."

Violet nodded. They set off along the Roman road, which had trees on one side and a high hedgerow on the other. They walked quickly now, as if they were hurrying to get away from someone—which she supposed they were. The presence of the man from the cornfield somewhere behind them was strong even when he was not in sight—perhaps *because* he was not in sight.

They passed through a wood, and near its edge a path turned north that would take Arthur home. Ahead in the sunlight she could see the houses of Winterslow, half a mile away. Arthur took off the rucksack and helped her to put it on. It was damp with his sweat.

"Thank you very much for walking me this far," she said.

Arthur nodded. "Of course."

"Do you know, I'm afraid I don't even know your surname."

"Knight. Arthur Knight."

"Well, thank you, Mr. Knight."

"Oh, call me Arthur."

"And me, Violet."

"Violet, then." He gave a little bow. "It was my pleasure, Violet Speedwell." Since mentioning his daughter, they had retreated into formality, even when deciding to use first names. They shook hands, and Arthur held on to hers for a moment. "I should be glad if you could ring tonight to tell me you've got safely to Salisbury. Perhaps it would be best to ring the pub and tell them. I'll be there tonight for darts and they can tell me."

"All right. Thanks again. I'm ever so grateful."

"Have a good rest of your trip. I'll see you in the autumn, at the cathedral."

She nodded, then turned and walked up the road into the sunlight. When she glanced back, Arthur was standing in the road, the gloom of the wood behind him. He raised his hand and she matched it with hers. Ten minutes later when she arrived at the edge of the village, she turned back to look again. The wood was far away now, but she thought she could see a figure still standing guard in the road. Just in case, she waved.

12

Y ou finished this on holiday? Well done!" Gilda and Violet were sitting over rock cakes at Awdry's, and Gilda was examining Violet's kneeler top, the first cathedral broderer to see it. It made Violet nervous, though not as much as the inspection by Mrs. Biggins or Louisa Pesel would later that morning.

The kneeler design was similar to DJ's: a central knot of checkered-cap acorns nestling among stylized oak leaves in different shades of blue, on a background of yellow. Surrounding the knot was a sea of different blue rectangles—the same blues Violet had been assigned to sort the first time she attended a broderers' meeting—crosshatched to look as if the whole thing had been woven. Violet had thought it a handsome design when she had it at home, but now suspected it would sink into anonymity among the other kneelers in the cathedral presbytery. It was not meant to stand out, she reminded herself. The whole idea of the kneelers and the cushions was to provide a consistent sense of color and design and tone. A kneeler that stood out from the others would not be acceptable, just as a stitch that stood out was not. There needed to be overall continuity, though with individual touches. But Violet knew she would be able to find this one in the sea of similar kneelers, like a mother able to spot her own child from a playground full of pupils wearing identical school uniforms, recognizing a certain run or turn of the head or some sticky-out ears as those of her own offspring. Violet knew every stitch of this kneeler. She had worked on it at night in her guesthouse in Salisbury, and in the familiar guesthouse in Ventnor. The weather on the Isle of Wight had been poor, and instead of walking out in the rain as she would have done with Tom or her father, Violet had sat inside in the bay window with a view of the stormy sea and embroidered meticulously, unpicking stitches when she felt they weren't exactly even. Back home she had finished it in her landlady's front room, making the last stitches while listening to Jack Payne and His BBC Dance Orchestra on the wireless.

"Surely you didn't spend all of your time embroidering?" Gilda accused her. "That's not what a holiday is for, is it? It may be what Miss Pesel and old Biggins do on holiday, because they eat and breathe embroidery. But not *us*."

"Oh, I did other things. I went walking, and I stayed in Salisbury for a few days and saw Old Sarum and Stonehenge and the ruins of Clarendon Palace. And the cathedral, of course." She did not mention Arthur and Nether Wallop, though she knew she should, since it was Gilda who had introduced them. It would be suspicious if she did not say she'd seen him. And yet she did not. Such a decision went hand in hand with her stepping back out of sight of Arthur's wife, and phoning the pub rather than his house to tell him she'd arrived safely in Salisbury. When she'd rung the Five Bells and spoken to the publican, he'd said in his gruff way that Arthur was there playing darts and he'd give him the message. Violet could hear in the background the *thup—thup—thup* of the darts hitting the board, and perhaps even Arthur's measured tone, and her heart had contracted. She wanted to ask the publican to put Arthur on, but she couldn't bring herself to because the man hadn't offered to fetch him. Instead she'd been silent, and the publican had waited until at last he'd prompted her—"The message, miss?"—and Violet stammered out that she was well, her walk had been without incident, that she was staying in Salisbury and would take the train to the Isle of Wight. And to thank him.

"Thank him for what?" the publican had asked.

"Thank him for his handkerchief," she'd said, and hung up.

"Don't mention Salisbury Cathedral to any of them in *this* cathedral!" Gilda nodded in the direction of Winchester Cathedral, a few streets away. "They don't like to be compared—because they know they'll come out the worse!"

Violet had been dazzled by Salisbury Cathedral, in particular its ornate spire and its position dominating the skyline from all around the city. It also had a light-filled octagonal chapter house where an original Magna Carta was on display, and a stunning variety of stained glass. "I don't know," she said. "I admired it enormously, but it is a bit—brown inside. There's an awful lot of dark marble. And it doesn't have Jane Austen or Izaak Walton buried there. Or the Great West Window. Or William Walker's diving heroics."

"Or the longest nave in Christendom. Or beautiful kneelers!" Gilda patted Violet's. "What lovely, even stitching. Watch out—Miss Pesel will have you working on the history cushions before long!"

"I doubt that. Only the most experienced broderers work on them, surely?"

"Perhaps. But you could make some of the background of the long bench cushions, at least. Not just the borders." Gilda sat back and sipped her coffee. "I didn't sew half as much as I meant to this summer," she announced. "On holiday I was too busy getting away from awful Olive. You've never known such a tragicomical character!"

You have not met my mother, Violet thought.

"But how was it, being all on your own on holiday?"

"It was—fine." Because it had been, apart from the man in the corn. Violet had seen interesting things and gone interesting places and not felt too lonely. Only at supper was it sometimes hard, when she was surrounded by people eating together and chatting and casting pitying looks at her. She tried bringing a book to the table but it was too clear a signal of attempting not to care and caring dreadfully. A newspaper or magazine was better, as long as she didn't read it in too absorbed a manner, but glanced at it casually. Sometimes curious people at neighboring tables struck up conversations. It was not always pleasant: The women often seemed threatened; the men, amused. "*Where* are you going? All alone? Gosh! Isn't it lonely?"

Violet never admitted that she was lonely, instead brightly claiming she was meeting all sorts of people and having the gayest time. She did not tell them about the nights she sat in her room, smoking and reading Trollope or embroidering or searching her guidebook for one more hillfort she might walk to or church she had not yet visited. Salisbury was new enough to her for there to be plenty to do. But she had been to the Isle of Wight so many times before and could revisit old haunts such as Carisbrooke Castle or the folly at Luccombe Chine only so many times. She began to sleep late and go to bed early, and go to the pictures during the day when it rained. One afternoon she saw *Self Made Lady*, about a fashion designer whose secret admirer was a boxer. It was so silly—so far removed from what it really was like to be self-made—that afterward to cheer herself up Violet went to a hotel and sat with a sherry, waiting. No one came. Perhaps potential men sensed her heart was not in it.

The next day she returned to Winchester a few days early—though she did not tell Gilda this, nor Tom or her mother. Especially not them. Instead she presented her walking holiday as a triumph marred only by blisters that forced her to take the train through the New Forest part of the trip. "Oh, I'm glad, old girl," Tom had said, clearly relieved that abandoning his sister had not damaged her. Violet wondered afterward if perhaps she had overdone her enthusiasm and they might expect her to take her holidays on her own from now on.

Only Marjory seemed to have missed her. When Violet visited them one Sunday in early September, her niece ran to show her the embroidery she'd done while on holiday. It was a tangle of skipped stitches and twisted wool, but she had managed the basics, and the stitches were recognizable. Violet praised it extravagantly and promised to teach Marjory more after tea.

Mrs. Speedwell was more sanguine than Violet had expected about her holiday in Hastings. "Oh, the weather was dismal," she declared when asked, almost gleeful. "But it was good to make a change."

Violet opened her mouth, then stopped. Had her mother not enjoyed the family trips to the Isle of Wight? She had never said. Perhaps they had never asked her. Violet always assumed Mrs. Speedwell would be the first to want to maintain a tradition.

Her mother asked no questions about her daughter's own trip, and though Violet hadn't expected her to, it hurt nonetheless.

Gilda made up for it at Awdry's with lots of questions. Only one unsettled Violet: "So did you meet anyone?" She smiled slyly, tapping her coffee cup.

"I met many people." Violet knew what Gilda was really asking but chose to dodge it.

"You know—someone . . . interesting."

Violet went pink, and for a horrible moment she thought Gilda already knew she'd seen Arthur.

"You did meet someone!" Gilda cried, delighted at Violet's embarrassment.

"No—no, I didn't." She wondered if she should tell her about the sherry men, to distract her.

"You did."

"No—I—" To cover her embarrassment about Arthur, Violet found herself telling Gilda about the man in the cornfield, though she hadn't meant to tell anyone; she was trying to put that episode aside. She left out the part about seeing him again at Nether Wallop, and she did not use his name. He was simply the man in the corn.

"Rotter!" Gilda muttered in sympathy, getting glances from customers at neighboring tables. "Men can be so awful."

"But never mind about that. That's done with." Violet wrenched the conversation onto another track. "What about you? Did you meet someone at Swanage?" It was not the sort of question she would normally ask of a friend Gilda's age, freighted as it was with inappropriate expectations and certain disappointment.

She'd asked it expecting little response, or a brush-off like her own. Instead, Gilda ducked her head. "Not at Swanage." She jumped up. "I've left my embroidery at the garage—I'll just get it and catch up with you!" She ran out before Violet could question her further. For all her chatter, Gilda could be remarkably opaque.

The broderers' room in Church House was standing-room full, the women chattering excitedly and showing off their summer work to each other. With a full three months away, they'd had plenty of time to make more substantial pieces. Violet was dismayed to spy over a dozen completed kneelers around the room, taking the spotlight off her own. Indeed, her office mate Maureen had completed two, one of them using stitches Violet didn't even recognize.

A few others had made history medallions, made up of larger wool stitches and smaller petit point, demonstrating handiwork that made the pictures sing. Violet particularly admired a rectangular cushion top with a central medallion in delicately shaded petit point, depicting a blue shield with three gold crowns on it, and behind it a sword famously stuck in a stone. The words "King Arthur" were picked out in brown cross-stitch. The surrounding design was similar to that of the Tree of Life cushion top: blue Celtic-style knots and clustered red flowers in a grid pattern on the familiar mustard yellow background Louisa Pesel had said there were complaints about. Violet was growing so used to these adventurous colors and patterns that they no longer surprised her; she loved their boldness. I must show Arthur this when it is made into a cushion, she thought.

She was surprised to discover that the maker of the King Arthur medallion was DJ, whom she had not seen since the day she had looked for her kneeler in the presbytery back in the spring. She was wearing her green coat with the big black buttons, and kept her hands in her pockets, modest while other broderers crowded round to study her work. Her hair was rumpled, her cheeks red, and her smile unfocused.

When Gilda appeared—out of breath and shouting hello—DJ started, and suddenly solidified, as if outlined by solid black. She did not stop smiling, but her eyes drifted toward a corner of the room as if to dodge any attention. Gilda too seemed out of sorts, looking everywhere but at DJ, and laughing a little too brightly as she removed her cloche. Violet saw one or two other broderers taking note of both women and their reactions, and revealing their own response—a tiny grimace, the twitch of an eyebrow. Maureen shivered. Mabel Way frowned at her clipboard, where she was writing down who had made what. All of this unrolled in the space of just a few seconds—a moment in which Violet discovered that there was something to discover, though she did not yet understand what it was.

Then the room shook itself and recovered. Gilda walked over to DJ, tapped the King Arthur medallion, and said, "Oh my days, Dorothy, you've smashed it! Once there are borders for it the cushion will be made up in no time."

Dorothy gave a small smile and nod, then busied herself digging about in her bag as if searching for a lost needle or a hank of wool. Gilda turned to Violet. "Budge up, would you," she ordered, indicating Violet's chair. "I don't think I can face standing all the while Biggins lectures us about the glory of doing our duty for the cathedral. And don't worry, there'll soon be more space," she added in a stage whisper, perching on a corner of the chair. "Everyone comes along to the first meeting keen as mustard, but you won't see half of them by Christmas!" She was still a little brittle, and Violet wanted to put a hand on her arm to steady her the way you would a skittish horse.

Mrs. Biggins arrived then, sending a current of anxious expectation through the room that swept aside any other drama. She took her place at the head of the table—the seat left empty for her—and, as Gilda had anticipated, made a short speech about working with diligence and pride for the cathedral. She spent much longer on slackers and time wasters and those who seemed to think embroidering a cushion for the cathedral would give them a special place in the eyes of God or the dean. "If you plan to waste my time, or Miss Pesel's, then I suggest you leave now," she finished. "You will make my life easier if you do." No one left, but Violet wondered if such an off-putting welcome might tempt some to slip away at the break and never return. Mrs. Biggins was the tedious sermon you had to sit through before you could explore a cathedral's beautiful stained glass or wood carvings.

She sat back when Mrs. Biggins announced she would now look over the summer's work; there was no need to rush toward the inevitable scolding she sensed coming her way when it was discovered that she had made a kneeler without permission. Besides, if she waited long enough, Louisa Pesel might arrive and save her from Mrs. Biggins's wrath.

"Where is Miss Pesel?" she asked Gilda, who was unpacking her own summer offering of part of a blue, yellow, green, and red background that a history medallion would be spliced into.

"Still on holiday. Weymouth, I think. Right, here I go. It's like jumping into a cold bath. Wish me luck!" Gilda gathered her embroidery and stepped into the queue waiting for Mrs. Biggins, just behind Dorothy with her King Arthur piece. Dorothy turned slightly so that her side opened to Gilda. There was something around them that made them seem closer than others, though they were not actually standing closer or even looking at each other. It was like an invisible fence, penning them in together.

"That's what can happen when you're a spinster."

It was said quietly, behind Violet, one woman to another. There was sarcasm in the words, and a harshness, and something like fear. Violet didn't turn to see who had spoken, though she recognized Maureen's low chuckle in response. She felt her stomach sour, as if she had drunk milk that was on the turn.

Her confusion was interrupted by Mrs. Biggins, who held the King Arthur embroidery aloft. "*This*, ladies, is what we are striving for," she declared. "This is what can be achieved with a few humble stitches done in the name of our Lord. Well done, Miss—" She frowned at Dorothy, who kept her eyes fixed on the ground.

"Jordan," Gilda supplied. "Miss Dorothy Jordan. Yes, well done, Dorothy. It's a stunner." She beamed at her friend. There was a muffled hiss behind Violet.

Rather than face that snake, Violet gathered her kneeler and borders and joined the queue. To her surprise, Mrs. Biggins did not shout at her for making a kneeler without her permission. She had seen so much work that morning that she seemed to have run out of things to say. "They'll do," she said of the long strips of border, and nodded at the kneeler top. "Now make it into a kneeler proper. The next Presentation of Embroideries service is October twentieth, so it shall have to be ready by then."

"How do I do that?"

"Find someone who has finished theirs to show you—I haven't the time. Move along, now, there are more waiting their turn."

Violet looked around. Everyone seemed busy, sewing or getting new materials. Gilda was searching through a stack of designs. Maureen was helping Mabel Way write down what each broderer had finished and would be starting.

"I'll show you." Dorothy Jordan's soft voice still penetrated the clamor of a roomful of women talking at once. She was standing by the cupboard, an embroidery frame in hand.

"That would be kind of you, thanks." Violet could feel eyes on them from around the room and shuddered involuntarily.

Dorothy ran a hand over her frizzy hair. She seemed unaware of being watched. "There is a kit for finishing kneelers, already made up." She reached into the cupboard and pulled out a rectangular packet. Pulling off the brown paper, she revealed a hard cushion, four strips of heavy blue cloth, and a piece of brown canvas. She took Violet's embroidery—with a brief smile at the familiar acorn pattern—and placed it facedown on the table. "You must first sew a strip along each side. Then take the cushion and place it on the embroidery, like this, with this bit of canvas on top." She showed Violet how to fold over the blue strips and sew them onto the canvas, using strong blue thread to make a tight fit.

"Before you do any of this, though, you must make your mark. Use blue wool to embroider your initials on one of the long strips, and the year on the other, such as you will have seen on the kneelers already in use in the cathedral. Do that before any of the other sewing."

Violet nodded.

"It is important to make one's mark. It may be the only mark we make. Sic parvis magna."

Violet raised her eyebrows. This was not a Latin phrase she had learned.

"From small things, greatness."

Violet nodded. They were silent, gazing at the makings of the kneeler. Violet listened for more hissing, but heard only Gilda saying to someone, "I could murder a cup of tea. Truly I could."

Five minutes later, both women had gone, though they left separately.

That night Violet embroidered "VS" and "1932," and sewed the strips onto her kneeler.

13

It was only when she was not expecting it—one Saturday afternoon in late September, on the High Street to buy marzipan for the Bakewell tart she had promised to bring to her mother's the next day—that Violet walked straight into Arthur Knight as he stepped out of the chemist's.

"Oh!" she cried, stepping back and laughing nervously. She was pleased to see him smile with delight, then cover it up with formality.

"Miss—Violet." He raised his trilby. "What a pleasure to run into you at last."

"Yes." Over the past few weeks Violet had spent more time at the cathedral, ostensibly studying embroidery, but hoping she might see Arthur there. "How have you been?"

"Very well, thanks. I've been wondering how the rest of your holiday was. Do you have time for a cup of tea? I'll just get my bicycle."

They sat in the Old Market Restaurant on the High Street, which Violet had never been to because it was fancier than she could afford, with linen tablecloths and big plate glass windows that made her feel exposed. Arthur seemed to know the middle-aged waitress, who gave her a sideways look as she took their order. "Miss Speedwell has taken an interest in the bells," he explained when she brought their tea and a plate of toasted tea cakes.

"I'm sure she has," the waitress replied, setting out the pitcher of milk and second pot of hot water. "How's your wife, Arthur?"

"She's getting on. We have hopes."

"Give her my regards." The waitress dropped the bill on their table and turned away.

As they ate, Violet told him about her adventures in Salisbury and on the Isle of Wight. She made it sound jollier than it had been, but admitted she'd come back early because of the rain.

"And no trouble along the way? No strange men?"

"No, none of that."

"I was glad to get your message at the pub that night. I was worried."

"No need, but thank you. And thank you for walking with me, and for the crib. I enjoyed that very much." Violet did not add that it had been the highlight of her trip; it would have sounded too pathetic.

They were silent for a moment, Violet relishing the unexpected treat of a generously buttered tea cake. "What brings you to Winchester today? I thought you only came for bell ringing."

"I had to pick up something from the chemist." Arthur patted his jacket pocket.

"Is everything—" Violet stopped. She didn't know him well enough to ask such personal questions.

"It's not for me."

"Oh, of course. I'm sorry." Violet took a breath and forged into difficult territory. "Is your wife poorly?"

Arthur pushed the plate with the last tea cake on it toward her. "Have another." He was acting as if he had not heard her.

"It's yours."

"You have it. You're hungry."

Violet flushed: She had too obviously gobbled hers down. But she took it—as he'd pointed out, she *was* hungry. "Thank you."

She waited to see if he would take up the topic of his wife. He wiped his fingers on his serviette. "Jean is—she suffers with her nerves."

"I'm sorry."

"Yes, well. Everyone has something."

Violet nodded, and wondered if he would say more. But perhaps that was enough.

"Are you cycling all the way here again tomorrow?" she asked. "For the bells?"

"Yes."

"That is a great deal of cycling."

"I had a motorcar until last year when I retired. I'm used to cycling now. It keeps me fit." He paused. "Would you like to come up to the tower to see the bells? I'll be service ringing tomorrow afternoon for Evensong."

"Oh yes, please."

"If we met at a quarter to two, I could show you then."

"I—yes. I'd like that."

"I'll meet you under the Great West Window. There's a door to the left."

"I know it."

"Good. Now, I must be getting back." Arthur patted his pocket again, and picked up the bill.

When she got home, Violet braced herself and borrowed her landlady's telephone.

"Southampton 225." Her mother's imperious tone made it clear that no telephone call was worth disturbing her.

"Hello, Mother, it's me."

"Violet, have you made the Bakewell tart yet? Because the Leightons may come to tea, so be sure to make one big enough to include them. If need be, family holds back. You won't want a slice anyway, will you, not with your figure." Clearly her mother had not noticed Violet's weight loss since she'd moved from Southampton.

"I'm afraid I'm not—"

"Don't tell me you're not making it. Must I do everything myself? And I won't have Evelyn make it—such a disaster in the kitchen, even for something as simple as a Bakewell tart."

"Now that's not fair, Mother. Evelyn is a good, steady cook." Violet could not think of a bad meal Evelyn had ever served—though she did not make memorably delicious meals either. Mrs. Speedwell must still be hurt at being left out of the summer holiday. Given the opportunity, she would bear this grudge for years.

"Anyway," Violet continued, determined not to be deterred from her message, "I'm sorry to say that I'm coming down with a cold, and won't be able to come tomorrow."

"Nonsense, there's nothing wrong with you."

"How do you know what's wrong with me? As it happens, I have a scratchy throat and my nose is running. And I feel a headache coming on. So I'm terribly sorry, Mother, but you'll just have to manage without me tomorrow. Please give my apologies to the Leightons and tell them I'll make a tart for them another time. Now, my landlady needs the line. Bye!" Violet put down the phone before Mrs. Speedwell could reply. She would pay for it next week, but for now she was free.

"Poor you—there's nothing worse than a cold," Mrs. Harvey announced, bustling past her in the hall. "It seems so wrong to be ill when it's still lovely out. Shall I make you a toddy? I won't charge you for it, this time."

"No, thanks, Mrs. Harvey. I expect it's nothing." Violet shrugged off her landlady's interference.

The next day Mrs. Harvey was by turns solicitous and critical, especially when she caught Violet heading out. "You'll come down with pneumonia if you're not careful!" she cried. "A cold is nothing to be sneezed at." When Violet chuckled, Mrs. Harvey frowned, failing to see the joke.

However, she managed to escape, and hurried to the cathedral. The Outer Close was full of families with children and couples out for a hand-in-hand stroll in the early autumn sun. She was a little early, but instead of going to her usual place among the kneelers in the presbytery, Violet wandered up the north aisle to stop at Jane Austen's grave, a simple stone slab in the floor that did not mention her writing. It had been left to others later to put up a memorial brass plaque near the grave, indicating her fame as an author. Austen had not been a Winchester resident, but had been sent there to see doctors when she was ill, and had never gone home again. Her family had paid a little extra for her to be buried inside the cathedral. She died aged forty-one with no husband or children, only a devoted sister. Violet didn't even have that, and she certainly didn't have several novels to her name. She had just three years to catch up with Miss Austen in terms of accomplishments.

Don't wallow, she scolded herself. Jane Austen would never have wallowed. A very kind man is about to show you the bells of this great cathedral, which most people will never see. Jane would have been thrilled to go up to the bell tower.

When Violet got to the small wooden door below the Great West Window, Arthur was waiting for her, holding keys and an electric torch. Accompanying him was the wiry Scotsman she'd seen with Arthur back in the spring. "Hello, Violet. Do you remember Keith Bain? You met once before."

"Of course." Violet and Keith Bain nodded at each other, Violet doing her best to hide her disappointment.

"Keith took my old surveyor's job two years ago," Arthur explained. "We had some overlap and he expressed an interest in bell ringing. They don't do it where he lived in Scotland, and he was curious to try. And he's not half bad for a beginner. He regularly takes the tenor."

"Is it normal to learn to ring on cathedral bells?"

"Ring the best, if you're going to ring at all." Keith Bain spoke with a rougher edge than Arthur.

"Let's head up now. Mind how you go. I'll lead, and Keith will bring up the rear." Arthur unlocked the wooden door, ushered them in, and locked the door behind them. "Remind me not to leave the key upstairs," he said to Keith Bain. "I've done that before and had to go all the way back up."

"We should hide a spare key as we do at the other entrance," Keith Bain remarked.

"The tower captain is concerned a visitor to the cathedral might find it and breach the ramparts." The men chuckled.

They began climbing a spiral stone staircase lit by occasional small lead-paned windows. "You won't have a problem with all the stairs, will you?" Arthur called over his shoulder. "Not after a walking holiday."

"I'll be fine," Violet replied, conscious of Keith Bain behind her. She had imagined being alone with Arthur and the bells for a few minutes before the other ringers arrived. Now she felt awkward, and wondered if Keith Bain had come along as a kind of chaperone or—worse—a potential suitor. She couldn't bear matchmaking. In Southampton friends had tried over the years, and it had never worked. There was normally a reason why the man was still single: overbearing, or humorless, or self-absorbed, or with a disinclination to wash. And she had a perverse reaction to being told she would like someone. When she was a child, if her mother said she would like a particular dress or toy or pudding, Violet almost willed herself to hate it.

They arrived at the top of the spiral stairs, and she was pleased not to be out of breath. Arthur opened a door, and unexpectedly they stepped outside and onto a parapet. To their left was the cathedral roof, with the squat tower beyond. But they turned naturally to the right and the view over the southern part of Winchester. Below them was the Inner Close and Church House, where the broderers met; Violet could see straight into the room at the end where she sometimes worked—empty now on a Sunday. There was the big cupboard she had been told to sort on her first day, and the windowsill where she had laid out the hanks of blue wool. Beyond the Inner Close lay Winchester College, where boys in suits walked between buildings; then houses, the water meadows by the Itchen, and in the distance, St. Catherine's Hill.

"People do like a horizon," Arthur commented. "I could look at this view all day. But we must get on." He opened a door to their left and led them back inside.

Violet held back a gasp. On the left, a bank of clear narrow windows lit the area directly around them, but to the right was a long cavernous space, traversed by a narrow walkway with handrails on each side, extending far ahead into the dark. After a moment, she realized it was the length of the cathedral nave, from the window at her back to the tower over the transepts, where the bells were. All along were huge wooden beams that lined and followed the shape of the cathedral roof. It was like being in the attic of a house, where you could see the wood skeleton holding the whole structure together. But it was the biggest attic imaginable—the size of a football pitch. Violet stood on the edge of it and stared, then sniffed, taking in the smell of many tons of heated wood, for it was warm up here.

"Oak," Arthur said. "Much of it almost a thousand years old, taken from one of William the Conqueror's nearby forests. Apparently the bishop in charge of constructing the cathedral asked the king if they could take wood from his forest. William said they could use three days' worth of cutting. The bishop then gathered as many men as possible, and they cut down the whole forest apart from one oak! The king was not pleased."

"Poor wee William lost his wood," Keith Bain remarked, and Violet snorted. Arthur frowned; he seemed irritated by their frivolity.

"Have a look here." He nodded at one of the windows. "Graffiti." Carved into the stone mullions were names and numbers, a shield, a skull and crossbones. 1871. Barratt. Packer. 1790. Feb 17. All rough yet stylized.

"Gosh, even in a cathedral," she said.

"People like to make their mark. You'll see graffiti everywhere. Down in the presbytery there's even a bell ringer. Next time you're there, look out for 'Harey Coppar.'"

"There's a bit in the ringing chamber as well," Keith Bain added. "I'll show you."

"Old graffiti, of course. William would have our guts for garters if we did such a thing now."

"William?"

"William Carver. Tower captain. He's been ringing here for thirty-nine years—a year longer than me. You'll meet him today."

Arthur has rung here for as long as I have been alive, Violet thought. It was rare that someone made her feel young. Yet Arthur Knight did not seem old to her.

"Best to keep out of Carver's way," Keith Bain said. "He's a stickler, that one. Charges ringers a fine for being late. I wonder what he'll think of a woman in the chamber!"

Arthur grimaced at these words and turned away. Violet wondered if he was regretting Keith Bain's ebullient company. He led them along the wooden walkway, shining his torch at Violet's feet. Below them were huge cement-covered humps that dipped down into valleys, like a giant egg carton, following the vaulted cathedral ceiling they were walking above. As they stepped, the wood creaked under their feet. It was quiet here in the cathedral's attic, without the hubbub of the visitors and worshippers. Violet felt as if she were inside an enormous whale, its ribs the wooden beams.

Eventually they reached another door. Arthur turned and nodded at Violet's camel-colored cloche. "There is an ancient rule in ringing chambers: no hats worn—or spurs!" He removed his trilby, and Violet and Keith Bain followed suit, Violet smoothing down her hair. Then they left the dark cavern behind and stepped into the ringing chamber. It was a large, square room about forty feet across, the stone walls made up of Romanesque arches and columns. Swooping down and up again from a dozen holes in the high ceiling were ropes, the ends looped around two grappling hooks up high, filling the space above their heads like large rope chandeliers decorated with woolly sections striped red, white, and blue, similar to those that Violet had seen at Nether Wallop.

"The striped bit is called the sally," Arthur said as she studied them. "I named my daughter after it."

There was a case full of books and magazines about bell ringing, a notice board, and a line of chairs along one wall. Keith Bain showed her an old carving on one of the walls of a bell ringer wearing a waistcoat. On other walls hung wood plaques painted with gold lettering, mostly listing names of bell ringers and what they rang. Violet studied them: "Ringers at Coronation of King Edward VII, 9th August 1902." "On the Feast of St Stephen, December 26th 1903, Kent Treble Bob Royal, 5,040 changes was rung on these bells in 3 hours & 35 minutes." "On Saturday 8th September 1923, in 3 hours & 55 minutes, was rung upon the bells in this tower, a peal of Stedman Cinques, 5,019 changes." It was like reading medieval English—familiar, yet not.

"Those commemorate peals rung here," Arthur explained.

Violet stared. "A peal takes three hours and fifty-five minutes to ring?"

"Sometimes, depending upon the weight and number of bells. A peal always takes over three hours, and goes through over five thousand changes."

"Without stopping?"

"Without stopping. No time for a break, a cup of tea, any of that."

"My word. Why do you do it?"

"It is my greatest joy. I've rung thirty-seven of them over the years."

"What exactly is a peal?"

Arthur pointed above them. "There are twelve bells up there. Each time they all ring one after the other is a round, or a change.

You remember from Nether Wallop? Now, you know one round that is familiar—the descending scale. Imagine that you are ringing eight bells and you ring that scale. Next you switch the order of two of the bells—say the first and second bells—so that change is slightly different from the last one. Then you switch two more, or two pairs at the same time. Each time it sounds slightly different. Do you know how many variations there are with eight bells?"

Violet shook her head.

"Think back to your maths," Keith Bain put in.

"That was long ago."

The men looked disappointed, so she tried harder.

"Factorials," Keith Bain hinted. "How would you find out how many combinations there are of three numbers?"

A memory floated up to Violet of sitting in a dusty classroom with rows of other girls, scratchy in her school uniform, gazing out the window and not seeming to pay attention to the teacher's explanation that buzzed in the background like a fly. "$3 \times 2 \times 1$. Six combinations."

"That's right. So with eight?"

"$8 \times 7 \times 6 \times 5$, and down to 1."

"What is the answer?"

Violet smiled. "Must I?"

"Good for your brain."

"40,320," Arthur answered.

"I expect you know how many combinations there are with twelve bells?"

"479,001,600," Keith Bain announced, triumphant.

"Which means we shall be here for some time."

Arthur chuckled. "Not this afternoon. We only ring peals on special occasions. Peals are a sequence of changes, each one a different set pattern, depending on the number of bells. Each has a name. Stedman Cinques, for instance, was a pattern created in the seventeenth century by a man called Fabian Stedman; 'Cinques' means it was rung on eleven bells plus the tenor."

Violet was concentrating hard but could follow little of what he said. Arthur smiled at her confusion. "Don't worry—I have a few years' more experience. It takes a long time to understand bell ringing. Now, would you like to see the bells? It's a bit of a climb, mind. Very steep and narrow. Do you think you can manage?"

"Of course."

"Keith, will you bring down the spiders and pull off the chimes?" As Keith Bain began lowering the grappling hooks where the ropes were looped, Arthur showed her to another door across the chamber, where stairs led down. "That's the other entrance, from outside the south transept. The tradesman's entrance, we call it. But we're going up." He led the way up a set of stairs so narrow it was almost like climbing a ladder. Violet was thankful for a rope hanging down the right-hand side, which she clutched on to and used to more or less haul herself up.

The bell chamber had no niceties to make it comfortable—no lighting or chairs or carpet. It was a space for bells, not people, and was lit only by rays of sunlight slicing through the wooden shutters, which had been left slightly open in the Romanesque windows. She could just make out massive wood frames holding bells that stood upside down, their mouths open skyward like those of chicks wanting to be fed. But they were enormous chicks, more like bulls or elephants, made of dusty gray metal, silent and waiting.

"My word," was all she could say. Something about the bells' presence left her speechless.

Arthur seemed to understand. "I have seen these bells for going on forty years, and I never grow tired of the sight of them."

They began walking around the ring of bells. Violet waved at the largest. "This must weigh . . ." She couldn't guess.

"Thirty-five hundredweight. Getting on for two tons. One of the largest tenors in England. Imagine getting it up here. Astonishing to think how they must have lifted heavy bells in medieval times. I saw them bring up two trebles when they augmented the ring back in 1921, but they had machines and chains and the bells were lighter than this. It's a rare sight to see the bells hoisted up through the cathedral. Mind you," he added, "you may do so one of these days. The tower captain wants to convince Dean Selwyn to recast the bells."

"Why?"

"They're out of tune—something of an embarrassment for a cathedral as grand as this. Of course, it's costly and the dean won't be happy about that. He's not fond of bells, says they make a dreadful racket. Makes us keep most of the shutters closed." Arthur pointed to them. "Those control how much sound leaves the tower." He paused, gazing out over the bells. "It's not just the noise, I expect. He's jealous of us."

"Jealous? Why?"

"It's a little world up here—one he doesn't have so much control over as he does below."

Violet thought of the broderers and their cozy relationship with the dean. It was a women's world, softer and more accommodating, looking to create outward beauty and comfort. It was very different from the bells, out of sight in the tower, making a curious sound that vanished as soon as it was created.

They made their way back, Violet shifting sideways down the

steep stairs. Several other men had arrived in the ringing chamber, most a similar age to Arthur. They had removed their jackets and were wearing waistcoats, their sleeves rolled up. They stared openly at Violet. Arthur brought her over to a solid man with intent dark eyes, tidy gray hair, and a beard carefully cut to follow his jaw. "William, this is Miss Speedwell—she's interested in the bells and has come to watch. I telephoned you yesterday about her visiting. Miss Speedwell, this is Mr. Carver, the tower captain."

William Carver gave her a measured nod. "Miss Speedwell, do be sure to sit quietly. We don't encourage talking during the service touch, so if you have any questions, ask them now." He looked at her expectantly. Over his shoulder, Keith Bain was grinning.

"I have no questions. But thank you for allowing me to be here." Violet slunk over to the chairs lining the edge, feeling like a dog that has been scolded for lying on a forbidden bed. She sat and watched as each man went to stand by one of the twelve dangling ropes. William Carver switched a couple of them, and put Keith Bain on a box. One rope remained unmanned. William Carver frowned, switched two more men, then they bowed their heads as he recited: "Almighty God who has called us to fulfill the office of bell ringers of this cathedral, grant us to be united and faithful in Thy service, that our ringing may be dedicated to Thy glory and the benefit of Thy people through Jesus Christ our Lord. Amen."

As he finished, another man slipped in from the walkway. William Carver glanced at his watch. "A shilling in the jar, Gerald, then take the seventh. I don't need to remind you of how important timeliness is for a service touch. We are expected to begin ringing at two thirty—not two thirty and thirty seconds, as it is now. By being tardy you are letting down not only the cathedral, and the city's residents, but us as well."

Though he was well past sixty, the latecomer looked as sheepish as a boy of six. He hurried over to a jar on a filing cabinet in the corner and dropped in a coin, then stepped up to his rope.

William Carver moved to his own rope. "All right, lads, we'll make a start. Rounds and then Grandsire Cinques." He nodded at another man, who called out, "Look to. Treble's going," and as he began to pull, "She's gone." Each bell started to ring in its turn.

There was much more space in this ringing chamber than there had been at Nether Wallop. Here, twelve men were ranged in a wide circle. For a few minutes they rang rounds, with four extra top notes, in the smooth, curious up-and-down movement, all at different times in the circle, following one another. Keith Bain was ringing the lowest, heaviest bell—the tenor, she remembered Arthur calling it. Standing on a box gave him more space and more leverage on his rope for the weight of the bell; he pulled easily, while clearly putting muscle into it. Violet tried to imagine his movement affecting the enormous bell she had just seen up in the belfry. It seemed impossible that pulling on a thin rope down here could make such a beast ring.

Although there was a ceiling between them and the bells, it was still loud, and the tower was shaking slightly. Violet felt as if she were being buffeted about by the wind. She loved it.

"Go Grandsire," William Carver called out, and the order of the bells changed, then changed again, and again, until she was lost in the pattern of bells weaving their way up and down and through one another. All she could make out was that Keith Bain rang the tenor at the end of each change; if she watched him it was like following the beat of a bass drum keeping time.

William Carver shouted something and they changed their way back to the descending scale, then stopped after he called, "Stand." He swapped ringers and had Keith Bain and some others sit out while they rang Stedman Triples. Keith Bain dropped to the chair next to her. He was sweating.

"Does it tire you?" she asked. "Ringing?"

"Och, it's not so bad." He wiped his brow with a handkerchief. "It's just the tenor here gives you a bit of a fight 'cause it's so heavy. It's got a mind of its own, and me with just a rope to control it. Old Carver puts me on it most of the time, or leaves me out, till he can trust me."

"When will that be?"

"When he's in his grave!" Keith Bain answered in a stage whisper, making her laugh. William Carver looked at them, his neutral gaze somehow as powerful as a glare. Violet stopped. Arthur too was watching them, his expression hard to read. Was he pleased she was getting on with Keith Bain, or annoyed that his ringing protégé had managed to catch her attention? She dropped her eyes to her feet, embarrassed, and did not look up again until the ringers were safely away into their changes.

It appeared there was no room to think of anything apart from the ropes—your own and others'—and the rhythm of the pulling. It was mesmerizing, watching the men watch each other. Some looked around quite clearly, turning their heads from one ringer to another. Others did not move at all but stared into the middle distance; yet with their peripheral vision they were aware of their neighbors.

Keith Bain was watching her watch them. "It's called ropesight," he whispered. "Being aware of what the others are doing, who's pulling when and how you fit in."

Violet watched the movement, and listened to the bells, and after a while the two wove together and for a moment it became all one thing, the men pulling and the bells ringing in and out of each other. It was like watching a dance, and listening to it too. Then the bells lost their form back into randomness, which shortly turned into the descending scale. For that brief moment, though, it had made sense to her, and she understood what the draw of bell ringing was. Then William Carver called, "Stand," and they went silent.

I want to do that, she thought.

Keith Bain jumped up and went back to the tenor. This time Arthur had a break and sat down beside her. "Do women ever ring?" she asked.

"A few. The White sisters in Basingstoke rang. Alice White was the first woman to ring a full peal in the country."

"When was there last a woman in this tower?"

There was a pause, then: "That would be my wife, on the twenty-second of January 1919."

The date was so specific that Violet knew there was a tale to go with it. She waited. Arthur would explain in his own time.

The bell ringers started up again, and under the noise he spoke. "There was a memorial service up here for one of the ringers who died in the war. The Russell boy, who contracted pneumonia at Salonika. We tolled the tenor, the thirty-one times, for the age he was when he died. It was mostly ringers who came along, but Jean insisted on coming up too. The next day, we had the letter confirming at last that Jimmy had died. He had been missing for over a year, you see. Jean got it into her head to connect the news in the letter with the cathedral and the bells. She wouldn't go back to the cathedral after that, and asked if we could move. That's why we live in Nether Wallop."

Violet was silent. There were no words that could express how awful she felt for him. She wanted to squeeze his hand, but instead they sat back and listened to the bells, and she looked for a pattern in the chaos.

14

After the bell ringing, Violet visited the cathedral often, but she did not run into Arthur, and so had no way of contacting him, unless she planted herself by the door of the stairs to the ringing chamber when she knew he would be going up for a service ring or to practice. This seemed both desperate and potentially awkward, for the other ringers would wonder. She could picture William Carver's dark stare and frown. But it was hard to imagine the ringers talking about her. Did bell ringers gossip? Did men generally? Her father and Tom never did, though perhaps they were different away from the company of women. When she overheard men at restaurants or hotels or on the train, they were talking about football or cricket, or the economic depression or the political tensions on the Continent—not about each other. The broderers, on the other hand, discussed other broderers—their work, their children, their clothes. Violet did not join in much, but listened, and wondered sometimes what they said about her behind her back. It was easy to talk to others and think you were somehow immune—but the spotlight fell on everyone at some time or another.

One Sunday after attending an early morning service, she was passing down the central aisle of the nave when she saw the group of ringers by the little door below the Great West Window. Her heart pounded. Silly girl, she chided herself.

But Arthur was not among them. She recognized William Carver and a few of the others, and Keith Bain. Before she could duck behind a pillar, he saw her, waved, and strode over.

"You coming to watch another service ring?" he said, smiling.

"No, no, I've just come from the early service. I'm going down to my mother's for lunch."

To her dismay, Keith Bain seemed disappointed. "Och, well, it's not so different from what you saw the other week."

"How is . . . Mr. Knight?"

"Arthur? He's had to take some time off. His wife's not well."

"Oh, I'm sorry. Do you know what's the matter?"

Keith Bain shrugged. "Not sure. She's taken to her bed, is all I've heard." He lowered his voice. "Carver has had to bring in another ringer to take his place. Makes you appreciate a good ringer once you've lost him."

So bell ringers did gossip.

"Erm, you don't fancy a walk sometime, do you?" Keith Bain continued. "To St. Catherine's Hill, or even out to Farley Mount? Before it gets too cold?"

Here it was. Violet had had a few moments with eligible men like this over the years. She had always said yes, even when she didn't want to. There was nothing wrong with Keith Bain. He was a year or two younger than she, he had a Scottish tartness that made her smile, and he was uncomplicated. He was perhaps the most eligible possibility she'd had since Laurence.

And yet, she was feeling something, even if it wasn't the right thing or for the right person. And she did not want to ruin that feeling with an awkward encounter.

"Thank you," she said, "but I think perhaps not."

Keith Bain looked at her, his ginger head cocked to one side.

"I'm sorry, I must run or I'll miss my train." Violet hurried away before he could respond.

The Presentation of Embroideries service took place the following Thursday afternoon, and Violet and Maureen got special permission from Mr. Waterman to leave work and attend. They took seats along the south wall of the presbytery, next to the archway Mabel Way had guarded five months earlier when Violet stumbled across the last special service. Mabel was standing there again—Mabel who had shushed her, keeping out all but the appropriate people, as she was doing now. Violet smiled to herself. Now that she was an appropriate person, this scene did not seem so strange. She could understand why Mabel might bar all but those who had put in hours of stitching and earned their seat at this service. Nor did she find it funny that stacks of kneelers and lengths of cushion borders had been placed before the altar, hers among them. Instead it felt right, and right that she should be here. For Violet was finally part of a group. She was sitting between Maureen and Gilda, she was nodding at others, Mabel no longer hissed at her but had actually greeted her, and she even earned a smile from Louisa Pesel, as well as a frown from Mrs. Biggins. For once she felt she truly had a place in the cathedral.

The organist had been playing introductory music, but changed now to something more processional, and the dean and vergers appeared up the steps from the nave and through the choir. As they passed, Violet saw Dorothy Jordan slip into a seat by the door. She felt Gilda stir. "I convinced Dorothy to come," she whispered, "though she's not normally one for services."

On her other side, Maureen rustled and tutted.

Although Violet was glad to be there, the service itself was not particularly scintillating. Prayers, hymns, a sermon: it followed a familiar pattern. Even the dean's sermon sounded similar to the last time he addressed the special service. Violet found her eyes wandering along with her mind. She gazed at the screen behind the altar, the wood carving in the choir stalls, the mortuary chests on top of the stone parclose around the presbytery. Then she caught sight of crudely carved capital letters on a seemingly bare paneled stone wall across from her:

HAREY · COPPAR · WAS

SUORNE · BELLRYNGAR · IN

THE · YER · OF · OUR · LORD · GOD

1545

It was the bell ringing graffiti Arthur had told her about.

After the service ended and the broderers were standing about and chatting, she went over to study the graffiti more closely, steadying her hand against the wall as she gazed up at it. Harey Coppar was not the best speller but he had managed to make his presence felt at the cathedral. Perhaps he had not wanted his contribution to be so ephemeral as the ringing of bells.

Other men had also carved their names into the wall—John Rowse, William Stempe—though they did not label themselves as bell ringers. Then she froze. Two names had been carved together: George Bathe and Thomas Bathe. Her brothers' Christian names. Had the Bathe brothers both managed to survive to old age, or did something take one or both of them—war, or plague, or starvation? Violet swallowed the lump in her throat.

Miss Pesel clapped her hands. "Ladies, there are so many kneelers to distribute that we could do with your help. Take one or two and place them on the seats, please."

Her suggestion was taken up with gusto. There was a rush to the altar, and as the broderers began looking for their particular kneelers, an unusual party-like atmosphere descended upon the presbytery. Violet joined them, glad to leave behind the Bathe brothers, and was lucky to find her kneeler among the others scattered about. She looked around. Most of the chairs now had new kneelers on them, but a seat under Harey Coppar's graffiti was still empty. She placed her kneeler there, and touched her initials. VS. Her mark.

Gilda appeared at her elbow, Dorothy Jordan with her. Dorothy nodded at Violet's initials. "Dulcius ex asperis," she murmured, nodding at the kneeler. "Sweetness after difficulties."

"Coming to Awdry's with us?" Gilda asked.

"I'm afraid I have to go back to work," Violet explained. "We were lucky to get the time off."

Normally Gilda would have tried to persuade Violet that a cup of tea was essential. Now, however, she just nodded and took Dorothy's arm. "Cheerio, then. Next week!"

Maureen was frowning when Violet found her to walk back to the office together. But it was only when they'd crossed the Outer Close that she spoke. "Watch out for those two," she warned. Gilda and Dorothy were ahead of them in the distance, Gilda's hand still tucked in her friend's elbow. "You don't want to be tarred with the same brush."

Violet winced. Whatever her uncertainty over Gilda and Dorothy's friendship, she was not having a junior tell her what she should and shouldn't do. "You sound like Olive," she remarked. "It doesn't suit you."

They were silent the rest of the way back to the office.

15

Mrs. Harvey's front room had not had such a crowd for months. Gathered round the fire were Marjory and Edward, Tom and Evelyn, drinking eggnog and eating gingerbread Violet had made for the occasion. The children swung between hysterical delight at being allowed to stay up so late and exhaustion. "They'll sleep in tomorrow, thank goodness," Evelyn declared, sitting in a chair farther from the fire and fanning herself with one of Mrs. Harvey's magazines. "No rising early to see what Father Christmas has put in their stockings." Her pregnancy was like having a heater strapped to her, and her widening hips and belly made her fit snug into the chair, like a cork. She stretched out her legs and sighed; her ankles were swollen and she had dark rings under her eyes. Evelyn prided herself on being unflappable, and had managed to keep herself tidy and contained during her first two pregnancies. This one, however, seemed to burgeon beyond her, and Violet caught her looking wild-eyed and bewildered, a queen whose subjects are unruly for no reason. Though she liked her sister-in-law, secretly Violet was amused by this loss of control. The children also sensed their mother's distraction, and took advantage. Edward had become shouty, and Marjory was developing a calculated sideways glance that made Violet want to snort.

"Only four weeks to go, is that right?" she said as she offered more gingerbread. Normally Evelyn would always say no to second helpings, citing her figure. Now, however, she took some gladly. "More eggnog?"

"I'd best not, or I'll fall asleep at the service."

"Mummy snores!" Edward cried.

"She does," Marjory confirmed, fingering the cage where the budgies were flitting back and forth.

"Now, now, let your mother be," Tom intervened, a little wearily.

Violet's landlady popped her head round the door. "Watch your fingers, young lady," she said to Marjory. "Those birds can peck." Marjory snatched her hand back. "Everyone settled?"

"Yes, Mrs. Harvey," Violet replied.

"More coal for the fire?"

"No, thanks, we'll be heading to the cathedral shortly." Violet had already paid extra for coal to make it warmer.

"Best not leave it too late. Midnight Mass is always popular. More so than Christmas morning. People like to get it done with and out of the way."

"Will you be going?"

"Me? No!" Mrs. Harvey looked almost indignant. "I never set foot outside after nine o'clock. It's not decent. Oh, it's all right for you lot—going to church, after all. But a lady out at night on her own—that wouldn't do."

Violet thought back to the times she'd been out after nine that year—to Gilda's for tea, to a concert at the cathedral, to the cinema. She'd refrained from sherry men since moving to Winchester—it was too small a place to be anonymous, and her landlady was doubt-less keeping more of an eye on her movements than even her mother had.

"You're welcome to join us if you like," she offered reluctantly. Tom nodded.

"No, no, you run along. I've got presents to wrap for the little ones." Mrs. Harvey was going to her daughter's for Christmas Day.

It was cold and rainy, and as they hurried down the hill and across the Itchen, Violet was glad that Mrs. Speedwell was not with them to complain about the weather, the walk to the cathedral, the nosi-ness of Mrs. Harvey, the children's behavior, the spiciness of the gingerbread, or the thickness of the eggnog. She would get enough of that the next day, for she was going back to Southampton with her brother and family after Midnight Mass to spend Christmas with them. Mrs. Speedwell had handed Christmas festivities over to Tom and Evelyn, and had not decorated the house—no holly or candles or Christmas tree or baubles. That autumn she had also begun alter-nating Sunday lunch with Evelyn, and more than once canceled at the last minute, blaming colds, headaches, nerves.

"Is Mother all right?" she asked as they walked up the High Street. She had a hand hooked through Tom's elbow; Evelyn held the other. Their shoes clopped on the wet pavement like horse hooves. The children were running along ahead of them, zigzagging from one shop window to another to look at the Christmas decorations.

Tom hesitated. Normally he dismissed concerns about their mother, laughing off her ailments and declaring she was as robust as an ox. "I expect she's a bit low," he replied. "Holidays do that. All alone in that house. It's too big for her, isn't it? I was there the other day and had to get something from George's and my old room. Have you been upstairs recently?" Violet had not. She avoided her old bedroom and its years of accumulated spinsterhood. "It's awfully dusty up there. Grubby, even. I said something to Mum—gently, of course—and she said she'd told the char not to clean up there any longer. And Mum isn't—well, she smells a little musty, shall we say."

"Are you telling me this because you want me to move back?" Violet had to speak carefully so that her voice didn't crack.

"No! No." Tom stopped to emphasize his point. Marjory and Edward kept going, jumping over puddles, and Evelyn pulled his arm so that they would keep up with the children. "I'm only mentioning it because we should keep an eye on her. There may come a time when something needs to be done, that's all. But of course you must stay. Your life is here now. Frankly, old girl, it's been a pleasure watching your transformation. You seem . . . happy. Winchester suits you."

"Well . . ." Violet wasn't sure she would describe herself as happy, exactly. But she did feel more independent, more self-defined. These days she could even feel a little sorry for her mother, especially hearing her called musty. It was an awful word. "But what can be done?"

"I suppose she could sell up and move. . . ."

"Move where?" Violet sensed Evelyn stiffening on Tom's other side, and suddenly understood. Poor Evelyn, she thought. "Perhaps she could move to Aunt Penelope's," she suggested, to assuage them, though she knew it was not really an option. Her aunt was already looking after an ancient mother-in-law, as well as helping with several grandchildren. She was the sort who collected people to rely on her, but there were only so many she could cope with.

"It's not definite, of course."

"Of course," Violet repeated.

"But I wanted to mention it so you can keep it in mind as we go forward, in case it comes up with Mum tomorrow."

"All right." Now it had been laid out before her, without anyone saying it: Mrs. Speedwell would eventually move in with Tom and Evelyn, and they—and possibly the children too—would be made miserable. They would not be if Violet hadn't gone to Winchester; only Violet would be. The price of her happiness—no, not happiness; the price of her freedom—was the misery of at least two people. It was a very high price indeed, and Violet resented having to calculate it in this way. A man never did.

"Hello, Violet!" Mabel Way called from across the street.

Violet waved.

Marjory turned round to stare. "Who's that, Auntie Violet?"

"One of the women I make cushions and kneelers with."

"Oh! Like what you showed me earlier?" Violet had got out the latest border she was working on, and Marjory had sat petting it like a cat until the gingerbread was brought out.

"Yes. You may see some of the kneelers tonight."

As they were crossing the Outer Close they ran into Maureen and her family, and then Gilda, who delighted the children by jumping directly into a puddle and splashing it everywhere. "Are you on your own?" Violet asked. "Would you like to join us?"

"Thanks, but Joe and Dad are inside, saving seats. You can sit with us if you like. It may be a squash but we'll manage."

"Is Olive here? I suppose not, with the new baby."

Gilda made a face. "What a fusser! You'd think awful Olive was the first person ever to have a baby. Still, I do get to be Auntie Gilda now, so that's some consolation. Gilda the giddy aunt. Here we are!" They had reached the cathedral entrance, where a dull roar greeted them. Violet had never before heard so much noise there—a buzzing anticipation, like the sociable sound in a pub, rather than the usual religious hush.

Inside it was warm and bright with people and lights. As they walked up the central aisle of the nave, where the service would take place, it was gratifying to see Tom and Evelyn look up in awe at the vaulted ceiling high above them. "So beautiful," Evelyn breathed. Violet smiled. She had walked above that ceiling. She was at home here now, and seeing others' pleasure in the building felt like being complimented on how you had decorated your front room or planted the borders of your garden. She wished she could show them some of her favorite bits: the bosses on the presbytery ceiling carved with lions and swans and deer, the Green Man with his mustache made of leaves in the choir stalls, the medieval tiles on the retrochoir floor.

The nave was as crowded as Mrs. Harvey had warned it would be, but there was space for them with her family, three-quarters of the way back, if Edward sat on Tom's lap. "Well, now, your auntie has told me she's teaching you to embroider," Gilda said to Marjory as they were removing their wet coats. The fug of damp wool enveloped them.

Marjory nodded.

"Which is your favorite stitch, then?"

Marjory considered the question as if she'd been asked what she thought of the state of German politics. It was a subject to be taken seriously. "Rice," she said at last in her most solemn voice.

"Oh, that's mine too!" Gilda's face lit up with the lie—Violet knew she preferred long-armed cross. "Shall I take you to see some of the kneelers we've made?"

"Yes, please."

"Maybe we'll find your auntie's, too. And if you're a very good girl, you may see more of her work tomorrow morning." Gilda winked

at Violet as she took Marjory's hand. Despite Mrs. Speedwell's luke-
warm response to her birthday gift, Violet had embroidered all of her
Christmas presents to the family: a needle case for Marjory, slippers
for her mother, a coin purse for Evelyn, a belt for Eddie, and a photo
frame for Tom.

"She's sparky," Tom remarked approvingly as he watched Gilda
lead his daughter up the central aisle of the nave. "Not married,
is she?"

"No."

"Shame." With a word he dismissed Gilda, and turned to her father and brother.

Edward was squirming in his father's lap. Violet stood. "Eddie,
shall I take you to explore?" She helped her nephew up, with Evelyn
giving Violet a grateful look. As they walked up the central aisle
toward the altar, Edward took her hand. His was like a small sweaty
animal burrowing into hers to find shelter, and Violet felt a deep
protective thrill. It was pleasing to walk with a child in front of others. There was Miss Pesel smiling at her and Eddie as he jumped on
the gray-and-brown flagstones, trying to avoid the tombstones set
into the floor. There was Mrs. Biggins in a coat with a long fur collar, with her husband, staring at her. This was as close as Violet
would ever get to showing off a son of her own, and it felt good, and
also pathetic.

They turned in to the south aisle. "What's that, Auntie Violet?"
Edward pointed to a stone chapel built between two pillars, with
tall, narrow windows and Gothic arches high above it all.

"That is the Bishop of Wykeham's chantry," she explained. "Long
ago he was a very important man at the cathedral, and they built a
splendid little house for him to be buried in."

"He's in there? Can I see?"

"Not tonight, dear. I'll bring you back another day when it's less crowded. Would you like that?"

Eddie nodded.

Violet led her nephew up the steps to the presbytery's south entrance. Given how full the nave was, the presbytery was surprisingly empty and quiet. Only Marjory was there, crouched on the floor to inspect a row of kneelers; and Gilda, who hovered nearby. She wasn't alone, though; she was with Dorothy Jordan, and she was unwrapping something in tissue paper and smiling at it. They were not talking, but the way they stood together, one angled to the other, was a kind of intimate communication that rattled Violet, as if she were seeing something she shouldn't. When they became aware of an audience, they jumped apart. "Oh!" Gilda crumpled the tissue-wrapped present against her chest. She looked flushed and happy and slightly guilty. "I set out six kneelers and told Marjory to choose which she thought was yours."

Marjory held up Violet's checkered acorns kneeler. "I got it right! Here are your initials: VS. Auntie Violet, I want to make a kneeler and keep it here."

"You'll have to ask Mrs. Biggins, dear. And I'm not sure she'll say yes. First you must practice your stitches and get them perfect."

"Who's Mrs. Biggins?"

Gilda pulled a face. "Old Biggins is a dragon who eats small children!" She jumped out with a roar, claws bared. Marjory and Edward squealed and fled the presbytery, Gilda in pursuit, leaving Violet and Dorothy alone.

Violet turned red, and wished she hadn't. But she had felt awkward around Dorothy ever since seeing her and Gilda together at the broderers' service in October. Dorothy did not come to many embroidery sessions, but she often seemed to cross paths with Violet in town or at the cathedral. They would nod, as they did now, but Violet would hurry on with a mime of being terribly busy or late for something. Now, the service was not due to start for a quarter of an hour, and Gilda was with the children somewhere—back in the retrochoir, Violet guessed from their delighted shrieks—and the two women could do little but stand together and wait.

She peeked out through the choir to the buzzing nave. "I like it when the cathedral is full of people," she commented, to make conversation. "Then it is how I expect the founders imagined it would always be, a place much in use."

Dorothy cocked her head as if listening with great care. Her lips were bitten, and she wore no lipstick to smooth them, or powder to even out her dappled complexion. She was wearing a dark gray winter coat rather like a soldier's overcoat, swamping even her tall frame. The black beret she wore not at an angle over one eye as most did, but pulled straight down over her ears, making it into an ad hoc cloche. She should look frumpy, yet she didn't. It was perhaps being unconscious of how she looked that made her so appealing. Dorothy was the polar opposite of Olive Hill, with her carefully crafted hair and makeup and clothes. Violet could understand Gilda's attraction to her—and felt unnerved by that feeling.

"This was where our ancestors came for their dose of beauty," Dorothy said, "to sustain them."

"Is that why you've come here—for the beauty?"

"For that, and for other things."

They could hear Gilda's approaching laughter on the other side of the parclose. Violet tried to think of something to say about Gilda but every thought seemed an intrusive one. "Will you be at your parents' for Christmas?" she asked, and was immediately ashamed of the bland question and her obvious desperation to steer the conversation to safer shores.

Dorothy ignored her, and gazed at the Great Screen behind the altar. "How did the men who carved that stone feel when it was installed here, do you think? Did they just go to the pub afterwards and say, 'Job well done,' to each other?"

"Perhaps they said, Dulcius ex asperis."

Dorothy clapped her hands. "Bravo! Top of the class."

At that moment, Gilda and the children appeared in the south archway, while at the same time Arthur Knight entered from the north. Violet's heart surged and began to beat so hard her chest hurt.

"Auntie Violet, there are stars and flowers on the floor back there!" Marjory cried.

"Arthur!" Gilda called. "What are you doing here?"

They stepped across and met in the middle next to Violet and Dorothy. "I was coming to have a look round before the service," Arthur replied. "Have you kidnapped some children?"

Gilda squeezed Marjory's and Edward's hands. "I have indeed. I took them to the retrochoir, but now I must deliver them back to their aunt."

Arthur turned to Violet. "Hello again, Miss Speedwell. It's been some time since we last met."

"Yes. Hello, Mr. Knight." Violet shook his proffered hand, embarrassed by the formality of their greeting.

"The medieval tiles you saw back there are rather splendid, aren't they?" Arthur said to Marjory.

She nodded.

"I often go to see them when I visit. Would you like to see something else that is interesting?"

"Yes, please."

He led them over and pointed to "Harey Coppar was suorne bell-ryngar." "Can you read that?"

As Marjory puzzled over the roughly scratched letters, Arthur murmured to Violet, "This is the graffiti I was telling you about."

"Yes, I found it. And I've seen some other graffiti too, back in the retrochoir."

"On Bishop Gardiner's chantry?"

"Yes—even on the statue of him! And elsewhere too. I'm starting to see graffiti everywhere."

Gilda was staring at them, astonished.

"Miss Speedwell has taken an interest in bells," Arthur explained.

"She has?"

"Yes, she came up to the ringing chamber."

"Did she, now?" Gilda's expression was turning shrewd. "She never told me."

"Auntie Violet, can we see the bells too?" Marjory asked.

"When you're a little older, perhaps, dear. There are an awful lot of steps to climb to get to them." Violet's heart was still pounding.

"I have always admired bells," Dorothy said. "They bring a space to life."

Arthur smiled. "Indeed, Miss . . ."

"Jordan," Gilda filled in. "Miss Dorothy Jordan."

"Like the actress."

"Yes! I didn't think you went to the cinema, Arthur."

Arthur looked puzzled. "I was thinking of William IV's mistress. Late eighteenth century."

"Miss Jordan teaches Latin at the Winchester County School for Girls," Gilda explained. "And she makes cushions and kneelers, like Violet and me."

"Ah, the cushions and kneelers. I should like to have a closer look at the cushions. I have seen some of the kneelers."

"It's just kneelers at the moment. Once enough cushions are ready, they'll add them all at once, to make more of an impact. Probably in February. One of them is Dorothy's."

"Have you seen Auntie Violet's kneeler?" Marjory picked it up and held it out to him. Violet could have kissed her.

"I have not." Arthur took the kneeler and studied it, smiling. "I do like the acorns." He tapped a checkered cap.

"Look at the boys!" Edward cried. The choir stall benches were starting to fill with black-robed young choristers from Winchester College. Marjory and Edward stared at them, especially the younger ones, who could not be much older than Violet's niece.

"We'd best get back," she said to the children, and led them down the south steps and back into the nave, the others following. Several rows ahead of their seats she saw William Carver, Keith Bain, and several other bell ringers. Keith Bain nodded at her.

"We rang after the eight o'clock service," Arthur explained. "Most of us thought we would stay on for Midnight Mass. It is a particularly lovely service."

"I'm sorry I didn't hear the bells. We were indoors then."

He nodded. "The rain muffles them as well."

As they spoke Violet's heart began to pound again. She willed it to slow down. "When do you next ring?"

"The band is ringing tomorrow at nine forty-five, but I will be at Nether Wallop then. I'll come up to ring in the New Year."

"You have to cycle all the way back tonight? In the rain?"

"I'm used to it. It clears my head."

Violet didn't dare ask more, as there was a whole nave full of Winchester burghers and bell ringers witnessing their conversation.

"Happy Christmas," he said as he turned to slip into the bell ringers' row.

"And to you."

"Who was that?" Tom asked as she took her place next to him. He sounded suspicious.

"Arthur Knight. He's a bell ringer. I've been up to see the bells here."

"With him?"

"Him and others. The band of ringers." To escape Tom's tone, she turned to Gilda, who had settled in next to her. "Is Dorothy joining us?"

"Dorothy isn't the joining type," Gilda replied. "She only barely comes to the broderers. A big cathedral service is not for her."

"Why did she come, then?"

Gilda laid one bottle-green leather glove on top of the other so that they matched, then stroked them. "To see me."

Those are from Dorothy, Violet thought. A Christmas present. She did not know what to say. To her relief, the congregation began getting to their feet as the dean and vergers processed up the aisle. Violet fumbled with the Order of Service sheet, gazing blankly at the carols they were to sing: "Adeste Fideles," "Hark! The Herald Angels Sing," "O Little Town of Bethlehem."

As they began to sing, "O come all ye faithful, joyful and triumphant," she glanced at her friend. Gilda was holding the gloves tight as she sang loudly and slightly off-key.

16

Violet had not had a memorable New Year's Eve for years. As a girl she had loved staying up and drinking Horlicks by the bonfire her father made in the back garden, even when it was raining or snowing. With Laurence she had gone dancing till her feet hurt. During the war there had been no celebrations, and afterward they had been quieter. She tried going to dance halls with friends but found the high spirits forced, the memories it brought up too painful. She preferred to stay at home, sitting with her father by the bonfire he still made—drinking brandy now. Latterly she had looked after the children for Tom and Evelyn so that they could go out. She had not yet celebrated in Winchester.

When Gilda invited her to join her and some others at a pub for the evening, Violet hesitated at first. "Just before midnight we all go out to the Guildhall," Gilda explained, "and join hands around King Alfred's statue in a long circle up the High Street, and sing 'Auld Lang Syne.' Sometimes there's dancing if a band turns up. It's great fun."

"Will anyone I know be there?"

"My father and brother. And Dorothy."

The thought of spending the evening with Gilda and Dorothy gave Violet pause, Maureen's warning of being associated with them flicking through her mind. But she was not needed for babysitting this year; Evelyn's pregnancy tired her and she wanted to stay in. Violet did not want to sit at home with Mrs. Harvey and the other lodgers, shaking hands formally at midnight and drinking cheap sherry. Or going to bed early with her hot water bottle.

What she really wanted was to have a drink with Arthur and watch him ring the cathedral bells. But she could not do that.

"All right. Yes, I should like that." Violet was not at all sure she would like it, but felt she must make an effort to show she was accepting the state of things between Gilda and Dorothy. She did not know what words to use to describe their relationship other than "the state of things." She couldn't bring herself to think of it as a love affair.

She wore her copper lamé dress and made up her face with care. When she arrived at the Suffolk Arms halfway up the High Street at ten o'clock, the pub was already crowded, with women as well as with men. Someone was playing "High Society Blues" on a piano, and Gilda and Dorothy were sitting with a group in the corner, leaning against each other and singing. When she saw her, Gilda waved and beckoned.

Violet pushed her way through the scrum to them. Gilda had done her hair in a tight wave and was wearing a silver dress with a dropped waist and layers of fringe at the bottom; she looked like a slightly out-of-date flapper. Dorothy wore a plain black dress, with a paste butterfly clasp in her unkempt hair—simple and dowdily elegant, if such a thing were possible.

Gilda's brother, Joe, jumped up, gave Violet his seat next to Gilda, and offered to get her a drink. She looked around: Most women were drinking either sherry or port and lemon. "I'll have half a mild, please."

"What, a shandy?"

"No, just a mild."

Her order of a drink that was not sweetened must have surprised him, but he nodded.

"Have you left Olive at home, then?"

Joe looked sheepish. "Just for an hour or two. The little blighter's been keeping her up. He's a bit of a squaller."

Violet remembered that as a baby Marjory had been too, giving Evelyn a shattered expression that no amount of powder and lipstick could mask. For a moment she felt pity for awful Olive.

Gilda introduced her to a number of people of various ages, most of them neighbors of the Hills. Violet promptly forgot their names, but found it didn't matter. With a drink in front of her and a seat that gave her a view of most of the room, she sat back and watched the goings-on without taking an active part. Gilda and Joe did so for her, joining in with the joking and shouting and singing all around them. The room grew more and more crowded and smoky, packed with people desperate to have a good time. Violet tried not to wince at the shrieks of laughter. She glanced at Dorothy: She had her eyes closed, but she was smiling.

After a second half of mild, bought for her by Gilda's father, Violet began to relax enough that when the pianist—a bald man with a red face and a substantial belly—played "Let's Do It," she joined in with the singing. Gilda and Dorothy were swaying side to side in their seats, and Gilda put her arm around Violet and made her move in time too as they all sang along.

Once the pianist played faster songs, people began to dance. Gilda's father pulled Violet up and danced with her to "If I Had You."

There was little space and they ended up swaying and smiling at each other. Though a little awkward, it made her feel a part of the celebration.

Gilda and Dorothy were dancing too, which was not so unusual. Since the war and the lack of men, women had taken to dancing together without anyone being surprised or upset. Normally they would dance either fast or very formally, with backs straight and hands carefully placed. Gilda and Dorothy did neither. It was impossible to dance vigorously in the crowd, but they did not keep straight and prim. Instead they clasped each other's hands palm to palm, their fingers entwined, and rocked back and forth, the fringe on Gilda's dress shimmering, singing at each other about snow-capped mountains and mighty oceans and burning deserts being no obstacle to true love. Dorothy's butterfly hairpin had come undone and was hanging precariously from the tangle of her hair. Violet was tempted to step over and rescue the butterfly from being crushed underfoot by eager dancers, but it was crowded and she did not want to draw attention to herself, so she stayed in her seat and tried not to stare.

There was something sweet and childlike about the two women. No one but Violet seemed to notice how intimate their dancing was, and at one point Gilda waved a hand at her, as if both acknowledging her and admonishing her for watching.

This is what love looks like, Violet thought, and did not know whether she was appalled or pleased. She knew about women like them. She'd heard comments about unwholesome friendships that were believed to be a result of the lack of men, of grasping at an alternative to spinsterhood. When Gilda and Dorothy were with each other, however, she did not sense any of that. They looked as if they belonged together.

She realized she had stopped dancing and was standing still as Gilda's father moved on his own, embarrassed. Then the pianist segued into a slow song: "Love Is the Sweetest Thing," Al Bowlly's latest hit, which played every night on the wireless. En masse, the crowd began crooning the words:

> *Love is the sweetest thing*
> *What else on earth could ever bring*
> *Such happiness to everything*
> *As love's old story*

Violet thanked Mr. Hill and sat back down, though she continued to hum along as she fanned herself in the heat of so many people crammed together. Gilda and Dorothy were still dancing, but closer now, fluid, with hands on shoulder and waist, almost like a couple. They seemed to have perfected just how close they could get and not cause raised eyebrows, for no one else seemed to be watching them.

After the song ended, another man took over the piano and Gilda and Dorothy came to sit down again. "You all right there?" Gilda murmured to Violet.

"Yes. Yes." She did not want to talk.

The new pianist played older songs, encouraging even more singing. By now most of the men and some of the women had drunk a fair bit, and were becoming rowdier and more sentimental. So it was not really surprising that the man at the piano would eventually play the song Violet least wanted to hear. When he began picking out "It's a Long Way to Tipperary," she gritted her teeth. The song's chipper, nostalgic, insistent cheeriness was jarringly at odds with what the war had actually been for her. It made her stomach clench every time she heard it to think of the soldiers—George and Laurence among them—dutifully singing it when they boarded trains to the Continent or in the trenches.

She seemed to be the only one with this visceral response to the song, however. As the men round the piano began to pound its top with their fists while bellowing, "Good-bye, Piccadilly / Farewell, Leicester Square!" Violet shrugged into her coat. "I'm just going for some air," she said to Gilda, then pushed through the crowd to the door and stumbled outside. As the crisp winter night struck her she took a deep breath and pulled on her hat, then leaned against the wall and lit a cigarette with trembling hands. The smoke reached deep into her lungs and woke her.

She gazed up at the sky, which was dotted with stars but no moon. New Year's Eve revelers passed by on their way down the High Street. Then she heard the bells. They were not the full-throated ringing she'd grown used to. Instead a round sounded normally, and the next was dull, as if heard through an eiderdown. Back and forth, they alternated between loud and soft. They must be half-muffled, Violet thought. She seemed to recall hearing fully muffled bells when she was young and the King had died, and the strangeness of it, like a thud with no tone.

She glanced at her watch in the light from the pub windows. Half past eleven. Would they ring all the way through midnight? Was Arthur one of the ringers? She had a sudden urge to be up in the ringing chamber, high above the city. Perhaps someone at the cathedral would let her in, or the ringers had left a door unlocked. Before she could talk herself out of it, she stubbed out her cigarette and crossed the stream of people to walk in the opposite direction up the High Street, then turned in to Market Street, a narrow passage that led to the Outer Close. It was lined with shops, their windows still decorated with holly and crèches and snowflakes for Christmas. Here there were fewer people, and it was dark. She passed a few laughing couples—why were people always in couples, and always laughing? She hurried along. The Old Market Inn was on the corner, and she could hear people inside singing.

Then she was alone, walking across the Outer Close, the cathedral ahead of her lit by spotlights, though inside it would be dark and deserted, for there was no service tonight. Only there were bells: louder now but still half-muffled, as if a hand were being placed over a mouth but a shout was now and then escaping.

Even as she thought of it, Violet shuddered at the image, and walked faster. Then she heard footsteps, and she instinctively knew it was him.

Jack Wells was whistling "Love Is the Sweetest Thing," and he was doing it so that she would understand he had been in the pub with her, he had probably spent the evening watching her without her knowing, and now he was following her, because he could. It was as if she were back in the cornfield, running through the same thoughts and choices. It was hard not to walk faster, yet she did not want to show him she was afraid. Now he has ruined it, she thought. Ruined a song I love.

There was no one on the Outer Close now, just her and the corn man approaching the cathedral, hunched and dark, with only the muffled bells to comfort and guide her.

Their sequence metamorphosed into the descending scale, repeated a few times, and then they fell silent. The bells' sudden desertion was more than Violet could bear, and she ran.

She was wearing low heels rather than the boots she'd had on in the corn, and they clattered conspicuously. But she also knew where she was going and how far it was. And she surprised him. By the time he recovered and came after her, Violet had rounded the corner of the cathedral and plunged down the narrow passageway that led to the Inner Close. Unfortunately it was also deserted, for it was far from the New Year's celebrations that drew people out. She could have turned right and run across the cobblestones and through the narrow lanes to the Wykeham Arms, but he would catch up with her before she reached the pub. That was not where safety lay.

She kept running parallel to the cathedral, heading for a large archway and a tunnel through the south transept, where there was a door to the tower—the tradesman's entrance, Arthur had called it. She had passed it once or twice on walks. The entrance to the tunnel was a great black mouth, but she could not hesitate. She plunged into it, her footsteps echoing, mingled with his, for he was catching up. Any second she expected to feel his hands grabbing her. She turned to where she thought the door was, and caught her shins on the steep step up to it. "Oh!" she cried, then found a heart-shaped metal handle and pulled at it. The door was locked.

Violet began to whimper as she turned the handle this way and that. It was pitch-black, for they were far from any streetlights. Something was snagging at her memory—something Keith Bain had said about this entrance. There was a spare key hidden, if she could just find it. She ran her hands over the stone wall on each side of the door, feeling for chinks in the mortar.

Jack Wells's footsteps had slowed down. He must have sensed that his quarry was trapped. He began to whistle the song again.

Then, high to her right, her fingers discovered a hole between two stones, and touched cold metal. Violet fished out the key and, hands shaking, quietly inserted it in the lock, trying to focus on what she was doing and not on the man closing in on her. She turned the key and the door gave way. Darting inside, she slammed the door in the face she could not see.

She scrabbled in the dark to find the lock and reinsert the key from the inside. Jack Wells pushed at the door, and Violet threw herself against it, then managed to turn the key. She stood still, leaning against the door, trying to calm her breath so that she could hear him. He rattled the handle and swore. After a moment's silence he sang softly, "This is the tale that never will tire / This is the song without end."

Violet turned and ran blindly up the stairs.

They wound round and round in a tight spiral, the stone walls close around her. She scraped her fingers along the cold stone to maintain a sense of where she was, and tried to listen for what might be behind her, but her pounding heart and wild panting drowned out any sounds of her would-be pursuer.

Long after she thought she should be at the top, she was still climbing, slower now. At last the curved stairs lightened ahead of her and she reached the clerestory, then another flight of steep, narrow steps that led into the ringing chamber. Violet had not really thought further than getting to Arthur, and drew up short, wondering what they would make of her bursting disheveled and terrified into their ordered little world above Winchester.

But she had no choice. She headed up the stairs and paused in the doorway at the top, panting. The band of bell ringers was gathered, all in suits and waistcoats. William Carver glanced over and saw her, and she had to step into the light. The ringers turned en masse and stared. One or two even exclaimed. It was as if a ghost had appeared.

Arthur hurried over. "Violet, what is it?"

She shook her head, unable to speak. Arthur took her arm. "Come and sit down." He led her to the chairs along one wall, where she'd sat before to watch them ring.

"Arthur, this is highly irregular," William Carver announced. "You know any visitors must be agreed upon beforehand with the tower captain."

"I wasn't expecting a visitor," Arthur replied. "Clearly this is an emergency."

There was a clattering of steps, and Violet froze. But it was Keith Bain and a few others, appearing from the stairs above. "Muffles are off!" he announced, then started at the sight of the surprise visitor.

After a minute she began to feel more herself. There was a small electric heater whirring near her feet, and light, and people. Here was safety.

Arthur knelt by her. "Can you tell me what is the matter?"

"Jack Wells was following me," she explained. "Across the Close. He—" She could not explain about whistling Al Bowlly; it sounded too silly. She was beginning to feel sheepish. "Well, I had to get away from him. I ran—and ended up here."

"Did he follow you up?"

"I don't know. I don't think so. I knew about the hidden key, and I locked the door behind me."

"Who told you about the key?" William Carver demanded.

Violet looked down at her feet, for the answer was obvious.

"Where is the key now?"

Violet stared up into William Carver's angry eyes. "I—I left it in the lock, I think."

"I'll nip down and get it," Keith Bain declared, "and make sure he didn't get in. What does he look like?"

"My height," Arthur said. "Dark hair and eyes. Wiry."

"There's no time for that," William Carver interjected. "Gerald's about to ring the hour, and then we're ringing a touch of Stedman Cinques. It's all hands on deck. You're needed."

"Switch to Stedman Caters with nine plus the tenor," Arthur suggested. "Keith and I will sit it out."

"What? You can't do that!"

"Of course we can. Clearly Miss Speedwell needs our help. You wouldn't begrudge her that?"

William Carver looked as if he would indeed begrudge Violet any attention that would take the ringers away from the bells.

Keith Bain looked from one to the other, then hurried out and disappeared down the stairs.

"There's your answer," Arthur said.

"You're both fined," William Carver declared.

"For what?"

"Lateness. You are not ready to ring when it's time, so that's tardiness. A shilling each in the jar. And another shilling each for revealing to an outsider the existence of the hidden key."

"I'll pay," Violet said, though after funding Christmas presents, she didn't have four shillings to spare. "It's my fault."

"You'll do no such thing," Arthur retorted.

"William, it's time," Gerald called.

William Carver strode over to one of the ropes. "Places, gentlemen. After the hour, we will have to ring a touch of Stedman *Caters.*" He glared at Arthur.

Gerald began pulling the rope of the heaviest bell to mark midnight. As the deep, sonorous tone rang out, Violet imagined it being heard across the Outer Close and down the High Street to King Alfred's statue, and the cheering and singing and kissing that would result. She did not wish she were there.

After the twelfth stroke, Gerald stood his bell. Then, after glancing around the circle at the other ringers, William Carver declared, "Treble's going," then began pulling his rope. "She's gone." The descending scale began. After several minutes of rounds he called, "Go Stedman," and the ringers were off. Violet and Arthur sat watching their smooth, coordinated movements. It was soothing to her, and she began to feel more normal.

"Happy New Year," she whispered.

"And you." He was quiet for a moment. "I do like your dress," he murmured. "Very smart. I hope that is not an inappropriate thing to say."

"Thank you." Violet ran her hands over her lap to smooth the scallop-patterned fabric. She didn't know if he was just being kind, but his compliment made her turn red.

A few minutes later Keith Bain returned. "No one about," he announced, taking a seat next to Violet. "If he was there, he's gone now."

If he *was* there . . . Was Keith Bain questioning her account? Violet wondered. And yet, now that she was here in the warmth and light of the ringing chamber, and in the calm and steady vitality of the band of men, she couldn't quite understand how the corn man could have come anywhere near this world. Had she imagined him, walking and whistling and chasing? It did seem a coincidence that he would find her on New Year's Eve, with so many others out, and so many pubs to be in.

On the other hand, Winchester was the nearest large town to where he lived. Perhaps he had simply come to celebrate and seen her walking up the High Street as he was heading for the place everyone went at midnight. And he was whistling Al Bowlly because it was a popular song; everyone was whistling it. Or: Had he come to Winchester deliberately to look for her, because he knew she came from there and there was more of a chance of seeing her out on this night than any other? The thought made her shudder.

"Are you all right, Violet?" Arthur asked. He kept his voice low; William Carver was frowning at them.

"I am now. I was just a bit rattled."

At that moment Arthur and Keith Bain turned their heads in unison toward the ringers. William Carver shouted, "Frank, dodge with the fifth!" Violet could not hear anything different, but from the responses of the men, something had gone wrong. They kept ringing, but there were glances and frowns at poor Frank, who was pulling without the easy confidence of the others. The bells were slightly out of time and, Violet supposed, a sacred sequence had gone wrong.

"Again, Frank!" William Carver shouted. The man in the wrong was sweating now.

Violet opened her mouth, but Arthur held up a hand and shook his head.

Eventually things must have come right, for William Carver nodded and Frank visibly relaxed. Something had been broken, however; the magical method that kept the bells ringing smoothly had failed. The atmosphere had changed: Rather than a careful team satisfied with their work, the ringers were pulling dutifully but no more, and the bells sounded perfunctory, even to Violet's inexperienced ear. William Carver was not looking their way, but he did not have to; Violet knew the fault was theirs—hers, really. If she had not come up to the ringing chamber Arthur and Keith Bain would never have been dragged into her drama. She should have stayed at the pub with Gilda and the others, sat through "Tipperary" and the other war songs they were bound to sing—"Keep the Home Fires Burning," "Take Me Back to Dear Old Blighty"—and the ringers would have rung in the New Year without mishap. She wanted to bolt from the room, but suspected that would only make things worse.

The ringers returned to the descending scale, pulled a few rounds of it, then William Carver called, "Stand," and they halted their bells. There was a short silence. "That was not the performance I would expect of bell ringers on New Year's Eve," he said. "I am disappointed."

"I'm sorry, William," Frank began. "I'm—"

"It's not your fault," William Carver interrupted. "There were unfortunate distractions." He turned to the three sitting along the wall, ignoring Violet as best he could given that she was seated between the two men. "Arthur and Keith, apart from the fines, you will not ring for the next month."

Keith Bain began to protest, but Arthur spoke over him. "I quite understand." He stood and turned to Violet and Keith Bain. "Shall we?"

Violet stood too. "I'm terribly sorry," she said to William Carver and the other ringers.

"Miss Speedwell, I think this incident is proof to you, if you needed it," William Carver replied, "that bell ringing is an activity we do not take lightly. The concentration required to ring successfully is profound and fragile. Any disturbance can mean disaster. For that reason we keep the ringing chamber closed to most. Visitors are the exception, not the rule. I will not expect you to take advantage of us again."

"No, I—I won't." As she said it, Violet held back tears. She was being banned from the place she felt safest.

"We will see you in February, then," Arthur announced. "Happy New Year, gentlemen." He led the way out and switched on a torch as they picked their way down the steep steps to the spiral staircase.

"Fool," Keith Bain muttered as they started down the spiral. "Pompous fool."

Arthur stopped and Violet almost ran into him. "No," he said, making them stand still on the cold, damp stairs. "No, William is many things but he is no fool. He was right. We caused them to be distracted, and we should not have. Our banishment is a perfectly reasonable response."

"I'm sorry," Violet muttered.

"Don't be. You had no choice. What might have happened if you had not come up? I am glad you did. So glad."

His last two words made her heart contract.

At the bottom Arthur held up a hand. "You stay here while Keith and I look around. You'll be quite safe behind the locked door."

"All right." Violet did not feel all right; she felt wobbly. But she did not want to cause yet more problems.

Arthur handed her the torch, then opened the door. Violet shut it firmly behind them. Then she waited in the cold, with the torch's light illuminating little. It seemed a very long time before she heard Arthur's voice again. "It's all right, Violet. We're back."

"We've looked all round and not seen him," Keith Bain said as she stepped out into the tunnel. "I expect he's run off."

"We will walk you home," Arthur added.

"Thank you," Violet answered. "I don't want him to know where I live."

"We've thought of that," Arthur said. "You live in the Soke, is that right?"

"Yes. It's not far."

"We'll walk you via the back route that he is unlikely to know."

Arthur and Keith Bain held out their elbows and she took them. They began to walk, moving past the dark eastern end of the cathedral and through the Close around it. The path narrowed and swerved left, then ended in Colebrook Street, a small lane with a mix of properties along it—a rectory, a school, and rows of two-up two-down houses that opened directly onto the street. Violet rarely used it since she could walk along nearby Broadway, where there were shops and people and she didn't feel she was walking straight through someone's front room. Some of the turnings off it led into slums—surprisingly close to the opulent cathedral. There were few people out now; those who were up would more likely be out on the High Street or in a pub.

The road turned sharply left, and at the end was the familiar bridge over the Itchen, and to the left, King Alfred on his plinth, where she could hear music and singing. Violet slowed down, then stopped, the men forced to stop with her. "If he is anywhere, he'll be there, where everyone else is."

"I'll go and see if I see him." Arthur squeezed her hand with the crook of his elbow, then left them hanging back in the shadows of Colebrook Street.

Violet dropped her hand from Keith Bain's elbow, and they stood awkwardly. *He is probably remembering that I turned down a walk with him,* she thought. To ease the tension, she offered him a cigarette. He took it, got out his lighter, and lit hers, then his.

"I am sorry about all this," she said, waving a hand to encompass everything, and aware that she was apologizing yet again, though she was not exactly sure what was her fault.

"Och, well, it made for a lively New Year's Eve."

"But you won't be able to ring for a month."

"To be honest, you've done me a favor. It's cold up in the chamber in January! This gives me the excuse to put my feet up by the fire rather than get chilblains in the tower."

They were silent again.

"What brought you to Winchester?" Violet asked, for she had wondered what would bring a Scotsman so far south.

Keith Bain exhaled smoke. "My wife died—cancer—and I wanted a change. Put some distance between me and Paisley. I took the job that got me the furthest away."

"I'm so very sorry."

"Well, we've all got our woes, haven't we?"

Violet thought of asking more, but somehow his straightforward answer seemed to ease the awkwardness.

They were stubbing out their cigarettes when Arthur returned. "No sign," he said. "But let's walk quickly. Best if you don't look towards the crowd, Violet."

She nodded, pulled her hat low over her brow, and took their elbows again. As they came out into the open she peeked just briefly. A band had set up by the statue, and people were dancing. Then they were over the bridge, Arthur glancing around to make sure they weren't followed.

A few minutes later they were at Violet's door. "Thank you," she said. "Thank you both for—well, for all of it."

"You've had quite the New Year's Eve," Arthur replied. "Let's hope the next one is calmer. In the meantime, I am going to find out more about Jack Wells. You will tell me if he bothers you again, won't you?"

"Yes." But Violet wondered how she would get in touch with him if he wasn't ringing for a month.

As if reading her thoughts, he added, "You may always telephone the pub, and they will get a message to me."

She nodded.

"Happy New Year, Violet," Keith Bain said.

"And you." Violet held out her hand, and the men shook it in turn.

17

"A visitor for you, Violet!" Mrs. Harvey called as Violet was getting dressed the next morning. The landlady was using her normal voice. If it were a strange man at the door, she would have been more emphatic, her tone tinged with suspicion.

A surprise New Year's visit from Tom? Violet wondered as she smoothed her hair and dress and opened her bedroom door.

Gilda was standing in the hall downstairs, twisting her green gloves and looking anxious, determined, and annoyed all at the same time.

"Gilda!" Violet slowly descended the stairs.

"Happy New Year, Violet. I didn't get the chance to say so last night," her friend added pointedly.

"Does your brother run the garage in the Brooks?" Mrs. Harvey interjected.

"He does."

"Ah well, I knew your mother back when she was alive. Do you know she grew up here in the Soke? Just a few streets away from the

Brooks, but the river in between makes it seem far. Lovely girl, she was." Mrs. Harvey nodded, satisfied with Gilda's Winchester pedigree. "Now, I'm off to my daughter's," she announced, pulling on her coat. "You'll have to make your own tea. Put some more coal on the fire for your friend, Violet. And there are some Garibaldis left. No charge, seeing as it's for Nell Hill's daughter." She stuck a pin through her hat with such force that Violet and Gilda smiled.

"I'll just put the kettle on while you build up the fire," Violet suggested when Mrs. Harvey had gone, then hurried back to the kitchen to make a pot of tea and collect herself. It was clear that Gilda had come to see her for a reason, and not a happy one.

When Violet came through with a pot and a plate of biscuits, Gilda was standing by the birdcage, watching the budgies hop from perch to floor and back to perch again. She was still wearing her coat, though she had laid aside her hat and gloves. Dorothy's gloves. Violet set down the tray and poured the tea, waiting for her friend to start, for Gilda always launched a conversation. This time, however, she did not speak, but moved to a chair and sat hunched by the fire with her coat over her shoulders, hands wrapped around her cup of tea, the saucer abandoned on a side table.

"Thank you for inviting me last night," Violet finally began. "I enjoyed myself very much."

Gilda's thin face was drawn; she looked as if she had not slept. "Tell me, Violet, do you consider yourself a good friend?"

"I—" Violet had been about to say she didn't know what Gilda meant, but stopped herself. This was a serious question that required a proper response rather than one bought off the shelf. "I like you very much, but we don't know each other well," she answered carefully. "It takes time to build up the history that good friends have."

"Well," Gilda replied, "a *friend*—not necessarily even a *good* friend, but a friend—does not leave a party suddenly without explanation."

"I did—I said I was going for some air."

"But you didn't come back!"

"No. There was a—a problem. I'm sorry. I was going to explain when we next met." Violet was surprised that Gilda was so upset— that she cared about what Violet had or hadn't done, when she was so caught up with Dorothy.

Gilda frowned. "There's no need—I *saw* you. With Arthur and that other man—the Scot. By King Alfred. You didn't even stop to say hello or Happy New Year or anything. You just scuttled away. It was like you"—to Violet's astonishment, Gilda choked back a sob—"like you were *ashamed* of me!"

"That is not what it was. Not at all."

"What was it, then? I should like to know." Gilda set down her cup, clasped her hands in her lap, and leaned forward.

"It was 'Tipperary,'" Violet said. Then she explained, first about the effect of the song on her, then about the corn man's reappearance and her escape up the cathedral bell tower, and finally Arthur and Keith Bain walking her back and her care to avoid being seen. "He was whistling 'Love Is the Sweetest Thing,' which made me think he came from the pub," she added. "I worried he might be by King Alfred and follow me home. That's why I didn't come and find you."

Gilda's face softened, then hardened into something different—a fierce protection of her own people. "You mean he was in the pub with us?" she cried. "Well, then, I'll soon find him out! There were plenty of people there—someone will know who he is. Then I'll send Joe and his mates round to sort him out. He'll not be bothering you again."

The thought of Winchester's men swinging into action on her

behalf made Violet feel sick and exposed. "No, please don't do that. I don't want Joe involved. Please."

"Hmph." Gilda shot her a look. "Are you going to explain about Arthur?"

Violet sipped her tea, cold by now. "There is nothing to explain." She set her cup in its saucer, clattering it more than she had intended.

Gilda grimaced. "Arthur is a good man. And he's loyal. And he's married."

"I know that."

"Then you mustn't look at him the way you do. I saw in the cathedral at Midnight Mass."

Violet searched in her cardigan pocket for her cigarettes and offered Gilda one. She needed that small comforting spark of fire in her hands.

"What about the Scot?" Gilda persisted.

Violet exhaled a shaft of smoke. "Keith Bain."

"He seemed nice. Why don't you consider him?"

"Why don't *you*?" She regretted it the moment the words came out.

Gilda contracted her arms and head into her coat like a turtle into its shell.

"Gilda, I'm sorry. I didn't—"

"Please be kind. Please don't judge," Gilda whispered. "That was what I've come to say."

"Then don't judge *me*."

Her friend sat up, indignant. "I'm not!"

"You are. You're making assumptions about Arthur and me."

"But—well, yes, I suppose I am."

"There is nothing between us. We are friends."

"Listen to me." Gilda leaned forward, her eyes overbright. "I know what love looks like. I *know*. And it is there, Violet. I can see it."

Violet thought of what she had seen between Gilda and Dorothy the night before, and at the cathedral—the wordless invisible cord that bound them. Had that grown between her and Arthur too? She should be appalled, but was secretly thrilled.

"Can you tell me something about him?"

"You just want to talk about him, hear his name—the way people do when they're in love."

"I could say the same about you with Dorothy."

Gilda sighed. "What do you want to know?"

"He mentioned to me the memorial service just after the war for the bell ringer and of hearing about their son the next day, and about Mrs. Knight, but he didn't go into detail."

Gilda's face fell. "It was awful for them. Jimmy was declared missing in action for such a long time, which in a way is worse than knowing, because you keep hoping. And Mrs. Knight hoped more than most, even after the war was over. She had this idea that Jimmy was in hospital somewhere with amnesia and no papers, and eventually he would turn up. The mind constructs such elaborate palaces when it wants to, doesn't it? Arthur was more realistic, though of course he wanted to support his wife as well. Then they got a letter saying a tag Jimmy had worn had turned up on the battlefield at Passchendaele, eighteen months after he'd gone missing. It seemed"—Gilda caught her breath—"he'd been hit by mortar fire, and there wasn't anything left. Just the tag."

Violet clutched her glass. Had Jimmy Knight fought alongside Laurence at Passchendaele? Had they patrolled together, lit each other's cigarettes, laughed over a letter from home? She would never know.

"Jimmy was a lovely lad, so funny and kind." Gilda sighed. "Poor Mrs. Knight took it very hard. That's why they moved to Nether

Wallop. She couldn't stand the sight of the cathedral. Arthur wasn't much better. He didn't ring at the cathedral for a few years. Apparently he kept making mistakes and they asked him to take a break. But it was a shame he had to stop, because I think ringing gave him solace, took his mind off things. You know how embroidery can be so absorbing that you put aside your worries? I expect bell ringing is the same."

Violet nodded, taking this in. It was hard to imagine Arthur making a mistake with anything.

"It was quite a sacrifice for him, moving them to Nether Wallop," Gilda added. "Arthur went part-time at his job, and last year took early retirement, so he could look after his wife. That's why he doesn't have a motorcar any longer—no money with just a tiny pension to live on. That's why you'll see him with his bicycle everywhere. Cycling in from Nether Wallop—fourteen miles in rain and snow! And they have no telephone. And they grow most of their fruit and veg—he's forever pickling something."

"Gosh." Violet thought of her jars of fish paste bought on sale and the cheap neck joint she got at the butcher's for broth and the cress sandwiches she ate for lunch. She had never imagined someone like Arthur having to worry about the price of food.

She poured them more tea, and knew it would be unhealthy to talk more about Arthur. "So, do you and Dorothy have a—a plan, for the future?"

"Yes, we want to live together in a little house," Gilda answered promptly. "We've worked it all out. Between us we could just about manage. Dorothy's salary as a teacher isn't half-bad. It's getting so crowded at home now that Olive's had the baby. And there are sure to be more to come. So I have a good excuse to move out. It turns out awful Olive is a blessing in disguise. Who would have thought?" Her eagerness made it plain she wanted to share her plans with someone. It was unlikely she could talk to anyone else.

"Have you told Joe and your father?"

"Not yet. I'm waiting for the right moment—preferably when we're all stacked on top of each other and the baby's crying."

"And Dorothy's family?"

"They both died of the flu in 1918, same as Mum. Dorothy's been living with her sister and her family. They'll be glad of the space and one less mouth to feed. And it's all right, isn't it? Friends do live together sometimes, don't they?" She sounded as if she were trying to convince herself.

"I suppose."

They sat in silence, finishing their cigarettes. Gilda took a bite of a biscuit and laughed. "Why did I do that? I hate Garibaldis!" She was clearly still nervous, and Violet searched for a way to set her at ease. It was difficult, since she was uneasy herself. Somehow during their conversation her relationship with Arthur had got tied to Gilda's with Dorothy. If she expressed shock, dismay, disgust, or anything negative at all, it would be reflected right back at her. How had that happened?

She realized she was frowning, and it was making Gilda frown too. So she asked the first honest question she could think of. "How long have you felt this way?"

"About Dorothy or in general?"

"Both."

"I knew the moment I met Dorothy a year ago at a broderers' session. It's just taken a while to win her round. We met again at Corfe Castle in the summer."

"Near Swanage."

"Yes. And that's where things became clearer, to both of us. She's so different from me! So—well, you know. She doesn't say much, while I talk far too much. She daydreams while I've got my eyes on everything. She's so tall and glamorous in her way, while I'm so—" Gilda waved a hand at herself. "But none of that matters with Dorothy."

"And in general?" Violet pressed, because she was genuinely curious.

Gilda gazed at her. "All my life."

"So—"

"So all of those things you will have heard: that women do this because they can't get a man, that they're desperate and unnatural and unhappy and hysterical because they haven't had—that. The sex act. None of that applies to me. I don't know why, and I don't know if it's unnatural, but it's how I am."

"Does your family know?" Violet was trying to imagine her mother's reaction to such news in the family—or Tom's, or Evelyn's. How would they explain such a relationship to Edward and Marjory? Then she understood: The same applied to any liaison she had with a married man.

"If they do, they've never said anything, bless 'em. I think they don't want to know." Gilda made a face. "Olive's been the problem. She never says it outright, but she insinuates: makes faces behind Dorothy's back, doesn't want me to hold the baby. I think everyone will be relieved when I move, even if they don't quite know why."

Violet thought about how good Gilda had been with her niece and nephew at the cathedral. "What about children?"

Gilda shrugged, though her nonchalance was unconvincing. "I am thirty-five years old. It's too late for me, so it doesn't really matter what I think, does it?"

"Thirty-five is not too late to have a baby."

"It is if you're not going to marry."

They were silent, watching the coal burning bright in the grate.

"So I am asking you what I asked when I arrived," Gilda said at last. "Are you a good friend to me?"

This was the moment when Violet had to decide. She stared at the fiery bricks of coal, crumbling in on themselves.

"Yes," she replied as firmly as she could, if not as she felt. "I am. Yes."

18

January was always a grim month, and January 1933 was particularly so. Deep into winter proper, the trees were stark, the ground either as hard as iron or sodden, and the weather shuffled between cold and wet, but always gray. There were no festivities to look forward to or be distracted by, just the feeling that all energy had been focused on Christmas and now one had to get through the days somehow, depleted. Violet thought about how people used to store up food and sit out the winter, sleeping and eating and waiting. Despite refrigeration and shops where you could buy food year-round, she sometimes felt in January that she was subsisting like her ancestors, waiting for sunlight and its warmth to unclench her and the first shoots of spring to reassure her that life was continuing.

Her room at Mrs. Harvey's was so icy that most evenings when she didn't go to the cinema she sat in the front room with the others. They all paid for coal, but Mrs. Harvey couldn't bear for her budgies to be cold, and added extra so that the room was reasonably warm. Violet read or embroidered with the wireless on, while Miss Frederick marked essays, Miss Lancaster sat with her eyes closed, and Mrs.

Harvey knitted or read the paper and tutted at the wireless. She tutted whether the news was bad or good: deaths in Spain following political protests, Lady Mary Bailey rescued after her plane crashed in the Niger, the Nazi Party doing well in regional elections in Germany. It was all part of the pot to her, like static emerging from the wireless without any hierarchy in terms of importance.

It was pleasant enough, sitting together, the budgies chirping in the background, but sometimes the closeness night after night with people she had little in common with made Violet claustrophobic and irritable. The hesitant scratching of Miss Frederick's pen on her pupils' papers made her want to shout at her to be more definite; Miss Lancaster's occasional snore made her wince. But it was too cold to spend any time in her room other than to sleep, huddled with a hot water bottle. Along with a copy of *Warren's Guide to Winchester*, Tom and Evelyn had given her a bottle of brandy for Christmas. She began having a small glass every other night, but by mid-January and after endless scratching and snores, she was up to two glasses a night and waking with a headache in the morning.

The office was also cold and grim. Violet and Maureen had one small Belling heater between them, and moved their typewriters together so they could share what little warmth emanated from it. Violet typed with her coat on, and there was always a cup of tea at her side. Even so, she developed chilblains on her fingers. They made her think of the ringing chamber and what Keith Bain had said about the cold up there. The men ringing would be getting chilblains on their toes.

Only Church House in the Inner Close seemed to be warm enough. Perhaps Miss Pesel had come to an arrangement with Dean Selwyn, for there was always plenty of coal, and the fire was built some time before the broderers started so that when they arrived it was already warm enough to take their coats off and stitch properly, without the need to stop and warm their hands.

The women were working hard to finish pieces in time for the next Presentation of Embroideries service, in February. Several choir stall seat cushions were almost ready, their history scenes in petit point spliced into a colorful surround. Dozens of kneelers had been completed, and long bench cushions were being made, though they were complicated, and Miss Pesel insisted they be held back and done carefully, even if it meant taking more time. "All eyes will be on those bench cushions," she declared. "If we get them wrong, we fail." To Violet's surprise, Maureen had progressed enough to be working on the long cushions.

She herself was not working on any of those things, however. After a kneeler and many yards of cushion borders, she was pleased to have been chosen by Louisa Pesel to make alms bags—hand-sized pouches sent up and down the rows during services for congregants to put their offerings in. At St. Michael's in Southampton there had been a plate for the purpose, and Violet had always found it mortifying to see and be seen making a donation, and how much. An alms bag made for more discreet giving. Miss Pesel was particularly concerned that they be beautiful and striking. "More than the kneelers, more than the cushions, the alms bags will be noticed," she explained to Violet and the rest of the alms team she had gathered. "They will be passed from hand to hand, and people will stop and look at them closely. They will note the colors and patterns and textures. When those things are successfully married, it brings them pleasure. And pleasure translates into . . ." She rubbed her thumb and two fingers together, and laughed at their surprised expressions. "Now, now, you don't think the cathedral runs on hope and air, do you? It is not just a building—it's an enormous machine, or a small town, with complicated moving parts that need maintenance. The cathedral has many volunteers such as yourselves, but it cannot rely solely on them. The dean must be paid, and the vergers, and chaplains, the cleaners and stonemasons and gardeners. And it costs money to heat the cathedral, and to run the lights, to clean it and maintain it. To buy the prayer books and hymnals and to print service sheets. To buy the polish and the candles and the flowers and to mend the chairs when they break and the roof when it leaks. But the cathedral receives no money from the government. It must ask its people, again and again, at each service. And that is what your alms bags will do—remind them of the beauty of the place, of the love and care that has gone into making every window, every pillar, every chapel and floor tile and, yes, alms bag, so beautiful that the spirit soars and the wallet opens."

There were to be four sets of fourteen bags, in the four colors used in the cathedral vestments throughout the year: green for Ordinary Time, Pentecost, and Trinity; red before Advent; purple for Advent and Lent; and white for Christmas, Epiphany, and Easter. Violet had been assigned purple ("Well, I couldn't have given a Violet any other color, could I?" Miss Pesel said with a smile). The embroidered designs were different from those on the cushions and kneelers, having been modeled on old Elizabethan bags and samplers in the collection at the Victoria and Albert Museum that Louisa Pesel was familiar with, but given a geometric twist. "I am a magpie," she explained to the broderers, "stealing my designs from all sorts of places. I have even been known to take them from soap packets!" They were done mainly in cross-stitch on a diagonal, the pattern mostly of squares and diamonds, with Hungarian diamonds in striking black and white stitches around the edges. Special metal handles in the shape of Celtic knots had been fashioned for the bags, so that when held by the knot, the bag hung down, the mouth open and ready for whatever would be placed in it, the giver's hand caressed by the kidskin lining Miss Pesel insisted upon—another way to make the experience of donating pleasurable.

One evening Violet was working on her alms bag by the fire in the front room with the others, apart from Miss Lancaster, who had been seconded to Portsmouth for a trial. On the wireless the BBC Symphony Orchestra was playing Elgar while the budgies contributed tweets here and there. Cathedral bells rang in the distance, for it was a Wednesday practice night. Miss Frederick was sitting at the table where they ate their poached eggs each morning, working her way through a stack of papers. When she sighed for the third time, Mrs. Harvey cried, "So much sighing! What is it, young lady?"

"I have double the work," Miss Frederick muttered, her hair disheveled and her hands stained with ink. "And half of it in Latin! One of the teachers has left suddenly and I've had to take on some of her classes. My Latin is so rusty, it's hardly better than the pupils'!"

Violet stopped stitching. It felt as if a weight had plummeted through her stomach. She began forming in her mind a benign question, but Mrs. Harvey, who had a keen nose for scandal, beat her to it. "'Left suddenly,' did she?" she tutted, for they all knew what that was code for—like Olive leaving Southern Counties Insurance suddenly.

"Oh no, it wasn't that," Miss Frederick replied. "Far from it. The opposite, if anything!" She went pink and laughed. It was a filthy, disgusted laugh that Violet could never have imagined coming from such a meek character.

Even Mrs. Harvey looked startled. "What do you mean?" she demanded.

"When did she leave?" Violet interjected.

"Today." Miss Frederick answered the easier question. "I was handed these to mark, and I'll be taking half of her classes until the end of term, unless they can find a replacement sooner. And no talk of any extra pay for the extra work! I don't suppose you could teach Latin?" She was casting about wildly.

Violet shook her head, swallowing hard, her supper at the back of her throat. There are a few girls' schools here, she thought, and several Latin teachers. But she knew.

When the knock at the door came, only Violet would have had any reason to connect it to what Miss Frederick had just told them. And yet they all did, staring at each other. Miss Frederick even rose to her feet in a panic and stuffed the papers she was marking on the seat of an adjacent chair, then pushed it in so they were invisible under the table.

"Who on earth can that be?" Mrs. Harvey muttered. "It's almost nine o'clock!"

"I'll get it, Mrs. Harvey," Violet said.

"You will not. I'm the one answers my own door." Mrs. Harvey heaved herself to her feet and disappeared into the hall. Violet sat clutching her embroidery. "It's Nell Hill's daughter for you, Violet," she heard her landlady call after a moment. "Second visit this month!"

Miss Frederick was staring at her. Violet wanted to say something sharp and cruel, but she couldn't think of anything clever enough. Setting her work aside, she left the room, feeling her fellow lodger's gaze drilling into her back.

Gilda was standing in the hall, her eyes red and enormous in her thin face. She was trying to smile and respond cheerfully to Mrs. Harvey's remarks about the coldness of the night. "It is rather late, dear," the landlady said. "Is everything all right?"

"Yes, I'm so sorry to trouble you. I just wanted to have a word with Violet about—about embroidery."

"Come up to my room," Violet suggested.

"Don't do that," Mrs. Harvey said. "Your room will be too cold. Come into the front room."

"We'll manage."

Her landlady was looking from Violet to Gilda and back, her expression shifting gears. "Shall I bring you up some tea?"

"No, thanks, Mrs. Harvey." Violet couldn't bear more scrutiny, and turned and led the way up the stairs. When she glanced back down, Mrs. Harvey was wearing a full frown.

She hurried Gilda into her room and shut the door. "Sit." She gestured to the armchair and went to get the brandy and two glasses from the cupboard. Filling each with a fingerful, she handed a glass to Gilda and perched on the edge of the bed. "Drink," she ordered. "I know what happened to Dorothy," she added as Gilda took a sip.

Her friend winced. "Lord, are people already talking? It's only just happened!" Her voice rose to a wail.

"Shhh. You don't want to give Mrs. Harvey more to talk about," Violet said in a low voice.

Gilda took a shaky breath, trying to compose herself. "How did you know?"

"Miss Frederick, one of the lodgers here, teaches at Dorothy's school. She told us just now. She didn't name names, though, so you're not implicated."

"Oh Violet, it's even worse than Dorothy losing her job. Her family has thrown her out!"

"Thrown her out of where?"

"Out of the house! She has no place to live. I've left her sitting in the Suffolk Arms, where everyone was giving us funny looks. We don't know what to do!" Gilda was crying now.

"Why have you come to me?" Violet wanted to say, but didn't. She got up and found a handkerchief in her chest of drawers. "Could she stay with you for a bit?" she said, handing it to her friend.

Gilda shuddered and pulled her coat close around her. "Dad and Joe said no. They—they know about us now. They're only just letting *me* stay, and only if I agree not to see Dorothy."

"And—did you agree to that?"

"Of course not!" Indignation stopped Gilda's tears. For the first time since she arrived, she looked more like herself. "That is—I didn't agree or disagree. I said we'd discuss it in the morning." She blew her nose.

"So where do they think you are now?"

"I told them there was a broderers' meeting. Violet"—Gilda turned her red eyes on her—"do you think . . . could Dorothy stay here tonight? Just for one night," she added quickly, "until we find a solution."

It was what Violet had been dreading since Gilda arrived, in fact since Miss Frederick had broken the news—that she would get dragged into their mess. "I'm sorry," she replied, "but Mrs. Harvey has a strict policy of no overnight guests." Even as she said it she thought of Miss Lancaster's temporarily empty room.

"We could sneak her in after she's gone to bed."

"It won't work—she's sensitive to noises. And she knows something's amiss, so she'll be extra vigilant. Does Dorothy have other friends she could ask?"

"None that would understand and be kind the way you are."

Violet felt a flush of pride even as she knew she was not as kind and understanding as Gilda assumed.

"Oh, what can we do?" Her friend covered her face with her hands for a moment, though she did not start to cry again.

They were silent for a time, sipping their brandy. Then Violet heard the descending scale of the cathedral bells until they stopped, and the tenor rang nine times.

"I must make a telephone call," Violet announced. "And you must distract Mrs. Harvey."

She stood over the telephone in the hall for some time, hesitating between the call she wanted to make and the call she ought to make. She could hear Gilda in the front room, chatting to Mrs. Harvey and Miss Frederick. Her voice was a tone higher and touched with hysteria. But she was managing to do her part and cover Violet's call, and even to make Mrs. Harvey laugh.

Violet so wanted to hear Arthur's steady voice at the end of the line, pulled from his darts or cribbage and sounding both practical and pleased to hear from her.

But he was fourteen miles away, and a bell ringer, and that was another world. She had to rely on her own world. She picked up the telephone.

"Of course," Louisa Pesel said when Violet explained. "Broderers look after their own." Violet was grateful that she did not ask for details.

"What did you tell her?" Gilda asked as they walked down the hill toward the bridge and the High Street, still stinging from Mrs. Harvey's gimlet eyes and dark remark about the lateness of the hour.

"Only that Dorothy was having family troubles and needed a

room for a night or two. Does she have any money to pay for the room?"

"A bit, in the bank. She was saving for us to go on holiday in the summer. We were going to go to the Lake District."

Violet could imagine them, striding up the fells, visiting Wordsworth's cottage, laughing in tearooms, rowing on one of the lakes. She felt a stab of envy, until she reminded herself of the terrible state they were now in.

It was a quiet night at the Suffolk Arms, very different from New Year's Eve. Everyone looked up as she and Gilda entered. A few men were scattered around the room; Violet couldn't help looking for the corn man, but he was not there. The piano sat silent, its lid closed. Dorothy was sitting in a dim corner, her eyes shut. A glass half-full of sherry and a full glass of water sat on the table in front of her. She looked up as they approached. "Hello, Violet," she said. "Have you come to save me?"

"She has," Gilda butted in. "She's been so clever!"

"I don't know about that. Anyway, I think we'd best go." The eyes on them made Violet uneasy. "We've a bit of a walk, and it's late."

"Let me just finish this." Dorothy picked up the sherry glass, announced, "In vino veritas," and drank. Then she picked up the water glass. "In aqua sanitas," she said and took a sip of water. "All right. I am ready for my next adventure." Grabbing the small bag at her feet, she called, "Via trita, via tuta. The old way is the safe way, and I am not taking the old way."

"She's a bit tipsy," Gilda whispered. "And who can blame her?"

"Dorothy, have you paid for your drink?"

Dorothy shrugged.

Violet sighed. "I'll settle up. You take her outside."

She'd had three sherries, Violet discovered from the barman, the price of her weekly cinema trip if she sat in the nicer seats. He waited until she'd paid, her coins safe in his palm, before he said, "Don't come here again. Any of you."

Violet quickly turned away so that he would not see the shock register on her face. She set her expression to a careful neutral as she joined the other two outside. Dorothy was holding Gilda's face between her hands. "Nil desperandum," she said. "Omnia vincit amor."

"Oh, speak English!" Gilda cried. "You make me feel an idiot."

"Never despair. Love conquers all." Dorothy kissed her on the forehead. "Horace and Virgil."

I am well and truly part of their mess now, Violet thought. She wished she could step back, let Gilda walk Dorothy down to the hotel where Miss Pesel lived while she went home to bed. That is not what Arthur would do, she scolded herself. Or Miss Pesel. Or Gilda.

She pulled her hat tight over her brow. "Come now, let's go. Miss Pesel is expecting us."

Louisa Pesel lived in a hotel in St. Cross, at the southern end of the city. She had moved there the year before, tired of cycling in from Twyford, a village farther south. "I do mean to find somewhere more permanent," she explained as they sat with her in the warm hotel lounge, slowly thawing. She was wearing a thick robe embroidered around the neckline in a geometric pattern; from Greece, Violet suspected. "But the embroidery project has taken up every spare minute. I just haven't had the time to look. I expect eventually I'll move somewhere closer to the cathedral. I want a good-sized garden, for my irises."

"Irises?" Violet repeated politely.

"Yes. I adore them. Always have. I formed an Iris Society in Twyford, and intend to here, once I've got a garden. I've planted a few bulbs for the hotel—some bearded white as well as purple—but I am not entirely sure they will appreciate them next summer."

Gilda and Dorothy were sitting side by side on a sofa, ankles crossed, knees together. Both looked dazed and exhausted, and remained mute. Dorothy had at least sobered up during their cold walk, and was no longer spouting Latin. But it seemed to be left to Violet to make conversation. It was past ten now, and she longed to be in bed, reading Trollope.

"Miss Pesel," she began, then wondered how to go on.

"Of course, dear, I'm sorry. The last thing you need now is a lecture on irises. All right, Dorothy"—she turned to her—"you need a room for a few nights, is that right?"

Dorothy nodded.

"There are quite a number of us living here on a long-term basis, but there are some rooms let by the night. I have asked the manager, and there is a room available. It's very small, but that means it will be less dear. Besides, you don't have much with you, do you?" She glanced at Dorothy's bag. "I trust you packed your embroidery!"

Violet thought she was joking, but when Dorothy nodded, Miss Pesel said, "Good. When there is an upset, there is nothing like needlework to bring calm and focus. Now, I think we should let these two get home to their beds, don't you? I shall take you up and show you the room. I've got the key. Girls, you'll be all right getting back on your own? Or shall I ask the manager to see you home?"

"We'll be fine, thanks," Violet replied.

Louisa Pesel was applying her broderer's briskness to this new situation, and—to Violet's relief—without judgment or, indeed, real curiosity as to why Dorothy needed a room. Perhaps she was just being discreet.

Dorothy got to her feet, looking brighter than she had all evening. She smiled at Gilda. "Dum spiro spero," she murmured.

Louisa Pesel nodded. "Indeed. While I breathe, I hope. Always."

19

Violet did not hurry to Gilda's after work the next day or the day after to see how she and Dorothy were. Doing her shopping on the High Street on Saturday, she did not dawdle or look out for her friends—though she did run into Louisa Pesel at the library, looking over the returned books. She was holding a copy of Gilbert White's *The Natural History of Selborne*. "I reread this so often I should have my own copy," she said. "I was so thrilled to move close to Selborne after knowing it so well in print for so many years. Have you read it?"

"My father did, but I haven't. I should."

Miss Pesel then offered unprompted that Dorothy was still at the hotel. "I've found her a bit of work tutoring friends' daughters in Latin. It will do for now."

Violet wondered what she knew about the circumstances of Dorothy's departure from home and work. Perhaps she did not know and had not asked. Violet was grateful Miss Pesel had taken this problem case so easily in hand; it made her ashamed too at her own lack of generosity.

At Wednesday's broderers' meeting, Gilda appeared, looking thin and wan and tired. Taking the seat beside Violet, she whispered, "It's just me today. Dorothy will come Mondays, when she comes. It's best that we don't appear together for now." Even those brief quiet words seemed to alert the other broderers. The atmosphere in the room shifted: A few women raised eyebrows at each other, and Maureen tittered—though she subsided when Violet frowned and shook her head.

"Shall we have lunch after?" she suggested, thinking it would be easier to talk then.

Gilda nodded, and after that they kept their conversation strictly to embroidery.

"We have to be very careful," Gilda explained as they ate their Welsh rarebit at Awdry's. "We were so carefree before, but now . . . Dorothy can't come anywhere near the house or the garage. It's not Dad and Joe so much as the awful Olive. You'd think the baby would keep her occupied, but I catch her twitching the curtains and looking down the street, no doubt hoping to spy Dorothy lurking outside."

"What will she do?"

"Dorothy? Start looking for a room, but without a job it's difficult to convince a landlady she's reliable. I don't think she will find another teaching post in Winchester. The schools all know one another, and they talk. She may have to go further afield, to Southampton or Portsmouth or Salisbury. No one is hiring in the middle of the year, though. At best she may pick up some supply teaching, and the tutoring. Miss Pesel has been a brick, but even she can't work miracles." Gilda sighed, and Violet felt a pang to see the joie de vivre missing from her friend.

Afterward Gilda went back to the garage and Violet to the office.

Maureen was already there typing, her back rigid with judgment. Violet ignored her and sat down to her pile of applications. The office was cold, the heater weak; she kept her coat on.

"I saw you two in Awdry's," Maureen announced.

Violet continued typing without comment.

"You should be careful, Violet. People talk."

Violet paused. "Are you threatening me?"

"No! It's not me you should be worried about. You want to keep your position here, don't you?"

Fear darted through Violet like an electric current. All of her hard-won independence depended on this ridiculous job typing up documents about other people's desire for security. "Surely Mr. Waterman is only concerned with how fast and accurately I type," she declared, "not who I eat Welsh rarebit with."

Maureen shrugged. "I'm only trying to give you advice, that's all."

"You are talking about a friend of mine, and I would appreciate it if you said nothing more about the matter."

Maureen grunted. "No need to take offense."

They turned back to their typing, frowning and blowing on their hands to warm them.

Both started when Mr. Waterman appeared in the doorway. "Could you step into my office for a moment, Miss Speedwell?"

"Of course." As Violet rose to follow him, she glanced at Maureen, expecting to see triumph that her prediction was coming to pass so soon. But her office mate looked miserable, her eyes on her hands as they rested on her typewriter keys.

"Now, then," Mr. Waterman began after he had shut the door and offered her a seat, "this is rather a delicate matter. Are you all right, Miss Speedwell? You look pale."

"I—I am a little cold."

"Ah! That's soon fixed." He jumped up and turned the floor heater near his desk toward her.

Violet stared. One heater for two typists, she thought. One heater for one supervisor. A sudden fury rose in her and before she could stop herself she said, "It is very cold in our office, Mr. Waterman, and Maureen and I have only one heater. That is why we wear our coats in the office. Might we get another one to keep us warmer?"

"Oh! Goodness, I hadn't realized." Mr. Waterman rustled the papers on his desk and knocked over a cup of pens and pencils.

"Shall I buy one after work at Kingdon's?" she suggested as he hurriedly scooped up the pens and pencils and stuffed them back in the cup. "We have an account there, and I could get us another Belling like this one—for three pounds, I think." Violet had been looking at heaters for her room at Mrs. Harvey's but could not afford one. "Otherwise I'm afraid our productivity will decline for as long as this cold lasts."

"Well, now, I—well."

Violet waited.

"Very well, Miss Speedwell," he said with a sigh. "You know best."

"Thank you." He may be about to let me go, she thought, but at least the typist after me will have a slightly warmer office. A small victory.

They sat in silence for a moment. Mr. Waterman was so flustered by her request that he appeared to have forgotten that he'd called her in. "You wanted to see me?" she prompted.

"Yes. Yes. Well now, it's about the girls you embroider with."

Violet swallowed. Gilda and Dorothy's story had apparently reached even Mr. Waterman's corner of Winchester. "Yes?"

"I—this is very delicate, you see. I don't want to cause alarm, or resentment. I want to do what is right and proper."

Violet waited.

"It seems my wife has taken a shine to the cushions you've been making for the cathedral."

"I'm glad she likes them."

"So much so that she would like some made in that style for our dining room chairs."

"She—she would?"

"Yes, but she doesn't want to ask Mrs. Biggins about it. They had a falling-out, you see, over the church flowers rota. Mrs. Biggins thought my wife was getting all the weeks when her garden flowers were at their best. Anyway, we thought we'd best go down a different route. So I've come to you. We can't ask you or Miss Webster to make them, I'm afraid—as skilled as I'm sure you both are, it wouldn't be appropriate to ask a colleague. But I wondered if you might recommend someone?"

This was so far from what Violet had assumed he would say that her mind froze on the thought of the two women battling over their flower arranging rota.

"Miss Speedwell, are you sure you're all right?"

Violet shook herself. "Sorry. I was just taken by surprise. Let me be sure I understand: You are offering to pay a broderer to make cushions for you?"

"Yes, yes," Mr. Waterman replied with impatience. "It is always about the money with you, isn't it, Miss Speedwell?"

At that Violet almost lost her temper, but did not want to lose this opportunity for a broderer who needed to earn money. And she knew who needed it. "It is not easy living as an independent woman," she answered as mildly as she could manage. "I'm afraid money is often uppermost on one's mind when one has very little of it. At any rate, I know of a skilled broderer who may be able to take it on. And we needn't involve Mrs. Biggins. I can have Miss Louisa Pesel ring you to make the arrangements on the broderer's behalf. She will have a better sense of the value of the labor."

"Excellent," Mr. Waterman said. He seemed embarrassed at his outburst. "All right, then, Miss Speedwell. I shall expect to hear from Miss Pesel. Thank you."

"I'll just go and buy that heater for the office, shall I?" Violet said as she got to her feet. "If I'm quick I can get to Kingdon's and back in the time it takes for a tea break." She hurried away before Mr. Waterman could change his mind, about either the cushions or the heater.

When she popped into the office to fetch her hat and gloves and handbag, Maureen looked up in astonishment. "He hasn't let you go already, has he?" she wailed. "I thought he'd give you a warning, that's all! Violet, I'm awfully sorry. Really I am. I know Gilda and Dorothy can't help themselves. They've no choice, do they, with no men about for them?"

"That is not it at all," Violet replied with vigor. "But never mind all that. We are getting heat!"

20

On the first Wednesday in February, when Arthur would be ringing again, Violet attended an afternoon session with the broderers. When she arrived she was surprised to see that Dorothy was there instead of Gilda, working quietly in the corner. They nodded at each other, but said nothing. Indeed, Dorothy had little interaction with the other stitchers, though there was a less frosty atmosphere around her than there had been with Gilda. Gilda was popular with the other women, so there had been more of a sense of betrayal, that they had invested in someone they could no longer trust; whereas Dorothy had always been a mystery, so was harder to judge.

An hour into the meeting, Louisa Pesel appeared. Clapping her hands to get their attention, she announced, "Fifteen days, ladies. We have fifteen days to complete our work before the Presentation of Embroideries service. We have done well on the kneelers, and the alms bags are almost ready. The embroidery for six stall cushions is ready too, and just needs making up. We have progressed far on several long bench cushions, but they will not be ready for this service. No matter—there are plenty more services to come. Now, if you have work to finish, I ask you to focus on it. If you are free, see me for new assignments. Mrs. Way will note down what you are doing."

Mrs. Biggins had already said much the same thing at the start of the meeting, but the broderers took it much more to heart hearing it from Miss Pesel. A queue quickly formed to see her, with Mabel Way at her side holding a clipboard. Violet had no need—she was still working on the second side of the alms bag, and would need advice only when she was about to sew them together.

When she went to the cupboard for more purple wool, she met Dorothy there, looking at needles. They said hello but their eyes did not meet.

"It seems I have you to thank for work making cushions," Dorothy said as she took two needles from an embroidered case and held them up to compare sizes. "Paid work."

"No need to thank me—I was glad to do it. Did Miss Pesel negotiate for you?"

"Yes. I think the Watermans don't quite understand how much time it takes to make a cushion. But she is going to simplify the designs so the work goes faster. Besides, now I no longer have to mark translations, I have much more time in the evenings."

"Are you all right at the hotel?"

"For the moment." Dorothy put the needle case back on a shelf in the cupboard, gave her a brief smile, and slipped past her to join the queue for Miss Pesel. Although Violet found encounters with Dorothy awkward, she also felt hurt that she had been somewhat dismissed. Gone was the expectation that she would solve Dorothy and Gilda's problems. Real life had intruded.

After the meeting, she slipped into the cathedral to attend the brief weekday Evensong, but hopeful too that she might run into Arthur. She had not seen or heard from him since New Year's Eve, and had spent much of her spare time scolding herself for thinking of him.

Since she was early she stopped in to the Fishermen's Chapel. There was often someone else there, usually an angler paying his respects at Izaak Walton's tomb. This time, to her surprise, it was Arthur, sitting on one of the small benches that faced a stained-glass depiction of Christ on a throne, surrounded by saints. She almost called out his name, but stopped herself, and instead sat down next to him, the bench creaking under her. He turned to look at her, but to her surprise he did not smile. His face was drawn.

"Arthur, whatever is the matter?" Violet whispered.

There was a long pause.

"Hitler," he replied, not bothering to keep his voice low. "Hitler is the bloody matter."

He was not the swearing type. "What do you mean?" she wanted to say. "What does he have to do with anything that is important?" But Violet cared too much about Arthur, and about what he thought of her, to answer so rashly. She gave herself a moment to think. She had heard on the wireless that Hitler had become chancellor of Germany two days before, after weeks of political machinations that she had not followed closely. Someone had been maneuvered out, she recalled.

"Do you think he will last?" she asked, because that much she did know—that people were predicting such a divisive leader of a minority party would not remain in power for long. How could someone with such strong, radical opinions lead a country effectively?

"That he has made it this far attests to his staying power," Arthur answered. "The Germans are looking for an answer to the economic hole they are in—a hole we have helped to dig with our punitive treaties and plans. We have been very stupid, focused on postwar revenge rather than fixing the problem so that the same thing doesn't happen again. Their pride was also wounded by the war, and we have given them no way to regain self-respect. They have been driven to extremism, and we will pay the price."

"Are you suggesting—" Violet stopped, because she did not want to say it. Because when you have been through it once you can never imagine going through it again.

"Hitler's values are not British values, whatever the *Mail* says," Arthur declared. "If the Germans take to him, nothing will depose him but war."

Violet shuddered. She was thinking of Eddie. He was only seven, but wars had a way of eating the young. Thank God they've had another girl, she thought. Tom and Evelyn's new daughter had been born two weeks before. They had given her the middle name Violet, which Violet felt honored by—though it was coupled with the ungainly first name of Gladys.

She wiped away a tear, and then she realized Arthur had placed his hand over hers. A surge of joy swept through her that washed away Gladys and Eddie and Hitler and war. She turned her palm over and laced her fingers through his. Despite the chill of the Fishermen's Chapel, his hand was warm.

It felt so good to have her hand in his that Violet wanted to cry out. She steadied herself by studying the stained glass in front of them. Under Christ and the saints there were various biblical sayings to do with water or fish: "The Lord sitteth above the water flood," "Bring of the fish which ye have now caught," "I will make you fishers of men." The religious sections were handsome enough, but her favorite parts were two portraits in the lower left and right corners of Izaak Walton himself, in puritan black with a white collar and black hat. In both he was sitting by a winding river, with his fishing rod and basket. In one he was with another man and a picnic; under them read "In everything give thanks." In the other he was alone, reading a book, the fishing rod unused; underneath were the words "Study to be quiet."

"I have always loved that Walton is not actually fishing in these windows," she said now, nodding at them. "He would have been very amused by that. The stained glass designer had a sense of humor."

Arthur gave her a sideways look. "Have you read *The Compleat Angler*?"

"Yes, when I was younger."

"I don't think I've ever met a woman who has read it."

"It was more like dipping in and out of it rather than reading it straight through. It was to please my father."

"Did he fish?"

"Yes. And you?"

"Of course. The river Test has the best fly-fishing in the country. One cannot live near it and not partake—though I am not truly a Brother of the Angle. I fish when I want to escape for a few hours and there are no bells to ring."

"Father always said fishing is about *not* fishing as much as fishing."

"Indeed. And about not thinking. We all need to do things that take us out of ourselves."

"Typing is like that for me. And embroidery, which is more satis-fying, of course, because there is something beautiful at the end."

"At the end of fishing there is a fish to eat."

"Yes."

They were silent.

"Arthur, I have your handkerchief from when we first met. I never returned it."

"I know. I like you having it." He paused. "Violet, I had a word with Jack Wells. He came to the Five Bells one evening. I told him to leave you alone or he would be answering to me, and to the police."

Violet tried not to shudder. "How—how did he respond?"

Arthur grimaced. "With threats." At her look of alarm, he added, "Don't worry. Bob—the publican—sent him packing, and has banned him. We won't see him again."

"Thank you." The feeling of knowing that someone was looking out for her and keeping her safe made her want to cry. She was also very aware that they were still firmly clasping hands, and wondered how this would end, and who would end it.

It was the choirboys who did. They began to sing, reminding Violet that she was meant to be at Evensong. Without meaning to, she moved her hand a fraction, and Arthur let go.

They stood, and it could have been awkward, yet it wasn't. The touch of their hands had communicated something concrete that Violet would always feel and treasure, whatever happened. It was like being given a coin that you could hold in your hand and feel its metallic solidity and, spend or not spend, know its value.

"Are you looking forward to ringing here again?" she asked as they left the Fishermen's Chapel.

"I am. I didn't think I would miss it so much since I can still ring at Nether Wallop, but I will be glad to be back with more than five bells."

"Will William Carver still be angry? Will he put you on the worst bell?"

Arthur smiled. "There is no worst bell, though some are more challenging than others. And William will have put it behind him. He will feel he has punished us and that will suffice. Keith is still smarting, though. I shall have to have a word with him beforehand, and keep an eye on him. Perhaps there is something after all in that saying about a redhead's temper."

They reached the south transept aisle, where they could hear the choir just finishing. "Are you coming to Evensong?" Violet whispered.

Arthur shook his head. "I have some ringing business with William to sort out and am meeting him for an early supper."

"Will you come to the Presentation of Embroideries service on the sixteenth?" Violet didn't want to leave without knowing when she would see him again.

Arthur gave her a look. "I don't think that would be wise."

Violet had a vision of the service full of Winchester women, primed to take away the gossip that Arthur Knight had come to the broderers' service. "I expect you're right. But I wanted to show you the work we've done."

A verger standing at the top of the stairs to monitor the service was frowning at them, just as Mabel had at Violet months before.

"And you will," Arthur whispered, taking her elbow and walking her partway along the aisle toward the nave. "Shall we meet in two weeks? You can show me the cushions and we can have supper after, before ringing."

"All right. I would like that." It was not a date; it was something more than that.

They looked at each other. "Thank you," he said.

"There is nothing to thank. It is I who should thank you."

"There is. You listened to me talk about Hitler, and you changed the subject to Izaak Walton. To what really matters. Quite right, too. I am indebted to you, Violet Speedwell."

21

With only a week to go before the broderers' service, one of the stitchers fell ill, and Violet was given her alms bag to finish because it was in the same pattern as the one she'd just made. She began staying up late in the front room after the other lodgers had gone to bed, even outsitting Mrs. Harvey, persuading her that she would remember to bank the fire and switch off the lights. Mrs. Harvey's admiration for the broderers' work for the cathedral outshone her suspicion of Violet and Gilda's doings, though she still muttered about how Nell Hill would be horrified to hear of the rumors spreading about her daughter. Then she looked meaningfully at Violet, as if expecting her to deliver up confirmation or clarification. But Violet simply changed the subject.

She enjoyed sitting by the fire with only the wireless for company, at least until it signed off at midnight with "God Save the King." The silence and her concentration on the stitches cleared her mind of Gilda and Dorothy, and even of Arthur—though she allowed herself a smile at the thought of meeting him for supper soon.

On the Monday night before the Thursday service, Violet had just snipped the last strand of white wool and was admiring her finished side—the next day Miss Pesel would quickly stitch it together with the other side, then line the bag with kidskin—when the telephone rang in the hall. She started and glanced at the clock on the mantelpiece: eleven forty-five. No one rang at that time of night unless there was an emergency. Of course it could be connected with Mrs. Harvey—she had grandchildren who might fall ill, and a son-in-law who apparently drove too fast. But ever since Gilda had appeared at the door, Violet expected whatever emergencies came to the house to be for her.

She did not want her problems to wake everyone, and so after a moment's hesitation she hurried to the telephone, picked it up, and announced, "Winchester 438," trying for the confidence of her landlady.

"Violet." Tom's voice was so clear it was as if he were standing beside her, speaking in her ear. "I'm sorry to ring so late, but it's about Mum."

Violet was so unprepared for this news that she almost laughed, smothering it just in time. "What has happened?"

"She's had a seizure of some sort. Apoplexy, they think. It's not major, but she's had to go to the Borough. That's where I'm ringing from." The Borough Hospital was where Tom had been born, where George had had a broken arm placed in a splint, where Violet's father had died after a heart attack. "It's not major," they'd said then too.

"Oh, dear." She knew she should say more but she felt nothing; she was frozen. "Is Evelyn with you?" It was best to stick with the facts.

"No, she's with the kiddies. It's just me and Mum. The doctors think she's out of danger, but it would still be best if you came down.

I would come and get you if I could, but I can't leave Mum. Do you know of anyone who might run you down? Else you could get the first train in the morning."

Mrs. Harvey had appeared on the stairs in a light blue winceyette dressing gown. She somehow managed to raise her eyebrows and frown at the same time.

"I'll find a way to get to the hospital as soon as I can," Violet declared, emphasising *hospital* for her landlady's benefit. Mrs. Harvey replaced her frown with a sympathetic moue.

"Thanks, old girl. I appreciate it." For all his bluffness, Tom sounded young and scared. Where parents were concerned it was hard to maintain an adult maturity. When Violet's father died, she had cried and fought with her mother and brother as if she were a little girl again.

When she hung up Mrs. Harvey came the rest of the way down the stairs. "What is it, dear?"

"My mother has had an apoplexy." Saying the words aloud, Violet fought off a sob. "I—I need to find a way to get to Southampton."

"I'll just put the kettle on."

As with the crisis concerning Dorothy, what Violet most wanted to do was to pick up the telephone and ring Arthur. It was a completely impractical impulse: He had no telephone, he was fourteen miles away, and he had no car. But she found it hard to think beyond his hand in hers.

It was Mrs. Harvey who came up with a solution over their cups of tea. She had switched into professional landlady mode. "Get Gilda Hill's brother to run you down. He's got motors to spare at his garage, and from what I hear, his sister owes you a favor or two."

Any other time Violet would have worried over what Mrs. Harvey knew and was implying. Now, however, she just nodded and went to pack an overnight bag in case it was needed.

Mrs. Harvey insisted on walking her through the crisp cold night to Gilda's house, breaking her nine o'clock rule. She clearly enjoyed the drama and wanted to play her small part to the full. She even dealt with an astounded Olive, who opened the door, a crying baby draped over her shoulder. "Wake your husband if he's asleep, Olive Hill," she ordered. "And get that baby out of the draft—he'll catch his death." If Violet hadn't been so numbed by her mother's drama, she would have been amused by Olive's stunned face.

Mrs. Speedwell looked both tiny and rotund in the hospital bed, like a little barrel covered with a blanket. Her eyes were closed. Tom was asleep in a chair next to her, and Violet did not wake him, but stood and studied her mother. She seemed to be in a suspended state, neither asleep nor awake nor dead.

Then her eyes opened, and she stared at Violet, her lips moving but making no noise. Well, Mother, Violet thought, you are quiet at last. She felt guilty for thinking it.

She cleared her throat and Tom woke. "Thanks for coming, old girl," he said, jumping up and kissing her cheek. He looked weary. "How did you get here?"

"A friend's brother brought me. Joe Hill—you met him at Midnight Mass." Joe had been surprisingly sanguine about driving Violet to Southampton, having the sense to obey Mrs. Harvey and ignore his wife's scowls. His only dilemma seemed to be which motorcar needed to stretch its legs the most. He didn't say a word as they drove, except to wish her mother better when he dropped her at the hospital.

"Good man," Tom said. "I'll buy him a pint or two when this is all over."

Violet nodded toward the bed. "Mother's awake."

"So she is! Mum," he called loudly, "you've had a bit of a turn, so we've brought you to the Borough. Doctor's not worried, though—says you'll be right as rain soon."

Mrs. Speedwell's pale blue eyes rested on Tom's, expressionless.

"Are you sure she's all right?" Violet whispered. "She isn't . . . showing anything."

"She's disorientated. She'll come around." Tom yawned.

"Why don't you go home and get some sleep?" Violet suggested. "I'll sit with Mother."

Her brother looked relieved. "Thanks, old girl, I will. Just for a few hours."

"Best ring Aunt Penelope in the morning so she knows."

"Of course. And you ring if there's any change."

It became fifteen hours of sitting alone with her mother. Nurses came in and out, to check blood pressure and temperature, to bring a meal left untouched, to empty a bedpan. Violet admired their cheerful efficiency. At one time she had considered a career in nursing, but it required a devotion to others that she did not feel selfless enough to commit to.

Mrs. Speedwell remained silent throughout these ministrations even as the nurses kept up a stream of comments and questions that went unanswered. The patient slept occasionally, during which Violet could slip out and get a bun or a cup of tea. Whenever she returned, however, her mother was again awake, her eyes reproachful.

Violet had not thought to bring any embroidery—though she had none to do for the broderers, since she had left her finished alms bag for Gilda to hand in. Nor had she remembered to pack a book. She managed to scrounge a newspaper from the waiting room, but otherwise simply had to sit. It gave her plenty of time to think about her mother, when she wasn't thinking about Arthur.

It was easier to consider Mrs. Speedwell when she couldn't talk—when there were no "woe is me" comments, or digs at Violet, or complaints about what Evelyn was or wasn't doing with the children, or how Tom wasn't paying her enough attention. The blessed turning off of that running tap of commentary gave Violet the silent space at last to be sympathetic. She found herself remembering what Arthur had said in Nether Wallop: that there was nothing worse for a parent than the loss of a child, and that her mother was having to carry the burden of that grief for the rest of her life.

She can never be really happy again, Violet thought as she watched her sleeping. Most people looked peaceful, with all the daily cares drained from their features. But Mrs. Speedwell wore a frown even in sleep. Violet was tempted to reach over and smooth out her mother's brow.

The doctor arrived midmorning, as old as Mrs. Speedwell and almost as cantankerous. "Where is your brother?" he demanded of Violet, picking up the clipboard that hung at the end of the bed. "I must speak to the head of the house."

"The head is there." Violet nodded at her mother, who had opened her eyes when the doctor spoke.

"Don't be silly," the doctor chided. "I mean the next of kin." He glanced at the clipboard. "Thomas Speedwell. That's who I want."

"My brother is at home, sleeping. I'm his sister. Surely you can speak to me?"

The doctor looked disgusted at the prospect.

"Talk to my daughter."

Violet and the doctor both started. "Mother!" Violet took her hand, unexpectedly moved to hear her voice.

"So, Mrs. Speedwell, you have decided to grace us with your presence," the doctor declared. "How are you feeling?"

"I want to go home. Take me home, Violet. I can't bear another nurse or doctor poking and prodding at me." Her words were a little slurred, but decipherable.

Violet turned to the doctor. "Can she go home?"

"Yes, at the end of the day." He raised his voice and spoke slowly, as if to a child or a foreigner. "There is nothing wrong with you, Mrs. Speedwell. We have checked, and the apoplexy was a minor cerebral insult. With a little rest, you should make a full recovery." He turned to Violet. "Tell your brother that she must have bed rest for at least four weeks, with supervision. A nurse will visit twice a day, but she must be cared for by her family. Will you do that?"

She didn't know if he was asking her to relay the message to Tom or to do the caring, but she nodded, if only to send him away.

When he was gone, Mrs. Speedwell said, "Are you coming home?" Her eyes locked with her daughter's. Violet could not bring herself to answer. She thought of all the pieces of Winchester she had gathered together over the past fifteen months—her room at Mrs. Harvey's, the office with Maureen, the broderers, Louisa Pesel, Gilda, Dorothy, the bell ringers, Keith Bain, and most of all, Arthur. They were small and perhaps insignificant on their own, but placed together they made up a life of sorts. Now with one question they seemed to be dismantled.

When Tom reappeared late that afternoon, rested, shaved, and guilt ridden, Mrs. Speedwell was dressed and sitting on her bed, ready. "Oh! Hello, Mum. Look at you, so much better! Sorry, old girl," he said, turning to Violet. "I had a sleep, then Evie couldn't settle Gladys, and the children needed collecting from school, and time rather got away from me."

"Mother's been discharged and is ready to go," Violet said.

Tom looked a little confused. "Well, now, that's splendid." He lowered his voice. "*Where* is she going to go, though?" Clearly he was reluctant to bring her back to his house already stuffed with dependents.

"Home," Mrs. Speedwell declared. "I'm going home, and Violet is coming with me."

A cup of tea. No, weaker than that. Another pillow for her head. No, a chair by the fire instead. Pish, the doctor doesn't know what he's talking about—bed rest would make her weaker. More coal on the fire. That's too hot; it will scorch her dressing gown! Toast with marmalade. But not Evelyn's marmalade; she never cuts the peel thin enough. Turn on the wireless. Oh no, not more talk about that Hitler, why do they go on about him so? Can't they play music? A book instead, then—read it aloud. No, not Trollope, it puts her to sleep. Ditto Dickens. Wodehouse—too frivolous. Perhaps *The Diary of a Nobody* instead; that is a safe bet.

As Violet read out the daily doings of the hapless Mr. Pooter, his long-suffering wife, and his rebellious son, she marveled that within only an hour Mrs. Speedwell had driven her back to her usual desire to flee home. She tried to recall the feeling she'd had at the hospital for her mother, the pity and the love that Mrs. Speedwell managed to dispense with so effectively as she recovered.

The only change from her old self was that she slept more. During those naps Violet was able to make a few telephone calls. First to Mr. Waterman to explain that she would have to take some time off to care for her mother. "Of course, of course," he said. "It's only proper a daughter should look after her mother. How much unpaid leave will you be taking?"

Who is thinking about money now? Violet wanted to say. "A week," she guessed.

"Not more? In fact, Miss Speedwell, are you sure you are not considering looking after your mother on a permanent basis?"

"I am not."

"This is the problem I have, you see, with lady typists. Always going off to get married or look after their parents. It does make me wonder why girls are so keen to work."

It was only because she did not want to lose her job that she did not retort, "Because I do not want to be a slave."

"It would be a great help if you told me, you see," Mr. Waterman added, "so that I can look for a replacement."

"I am not moving back to my mother's," Violet repeated firmly, though she tried to keep her voice low so Mrs. Speedwell would not hear.

"Well, you must do what you think best." Mr. Waterman's tone implied she did not know what was best and he did.

"I will ring with an update as soon as I can." Violet hung up without saying good-bye. If pressed she could claim to have been upset rather than angry.

Next she rang Mrs. Harvey to inform her, and Gilda to tell her she wouldn't make it to the Presentation of Embroideries service. Gilda was sympathetic and promised to describe it in full when they next met, and to give Violet's apologies to Louisa Pesel and the other broderers. "But mothers come first," she declared, "even over the cathedral. Lucky you have one to look after!"

It was hardest to ring Arthur, the person she most wanted to talk to and the telephone call she least wanted her mother to hear. Mrs. Speedwell did not seem to want to go to bed, insisting on sitting in the front room by the fire when Tom and Evelyn and Gladys visited—the older children deemed too robust a presence and being looked after by a neighbor. It had gone half-nine before they left, and another half hour before Violet could convince Mrs. Speedwell to get into bed. Once there she wanted her daughter to read more from *The Diary of a Nobody*. The book was beginning to feel like a pointed choice, about a parent whose child breaks away from their old-fashioned expectations, at the expense of the parent. But Mrs. Speedwell did not seem to notice. When at last she fell asleep in the middle of the scene in which the son announces his sudden engagement to his surprised parents, it was half-ten.

Violet rang the Five Bells, certain Arthur would have gone home. When the taciturn publican answered, she could barely ask for him, she was so nervous. "I'm terribly sorry to ring so late," she finally managed. "I don't expect Arthur Knight is still there?"

"He's just left. Hang on a minute."

Violet waited, heart pulsing in her throat.

"Violet?" her mother called from upstairs.

Violet swore under her breath. "Just a moment, Mother!" she called, hand over the mouthpiece.

"Violet?"

"Arthur. How did you know it was me?"

"Bob recognized your voice. Are you all right?"

"Yes, yes, I'm fine, thank you. But I'm afraid my mother has taken a bit of a turn. Apoplexy, the doctor thinks. So I am in Southampton, looking after her. It seems I won't be able to see you tomorrow. I'm so sorry." She swallowed a sob.

"Violet!" Mrs. Speedwell was at the top of the stairs.

"Oh. I am sorry too."

His words were a rope she grasped.

"I have to go now. But I'll—I'll—"

"Violet, who are you talking to? Who is Arthur?"

Violet hung up and glowered at her mother, wondering how she would react if she responded, "I'm talking to the only man I've loved since Laurence." Instead she said, "Go back to bed, Mother. You're standing in a draft and it's not good for you."

"It is astonishing that my daughter should be chatting away on the telephone when her mother is so ill."

"It is astonishing that such an ill mother should get up from her sickbed to spy on her daughter's telephone conversations. Perhaps she is not so ill after all."

Mrs. Speedwell clutched at her dressing gown. "How dare you suggest such a thing! How horrid and ungrateful you are!" They glared at each other, brought once more to the familiar battleground of their relationship.

Then her mother's face crumpled. "Oh, how I miss your father," she sighed, her eyes filling with tears.

With that, the floor dropped right out of Violet's anger. She sank onto a step. "I miss him too. And George. And Laurence." She rarely said their names aloud in front of her mother. They gazed at each other, the staircase between them somehow making it easier to be honest. She has lost the love of her life, Violet thought. And the son she was meant to look after. Poor thing. "Get into bed, Mother," she suggested in a gentler tone. "I'll get you some fresh water."

Her mother nodded and shuffled back to her bedroom, missing the sight of Violet wiping away a tear.

Mrs. Speedwell improved rapidly, so that within a few days she was insisting on getting dressed and coming down to sit all day, though she took a short morning nap and a longer one in the afternoon—just like small children, Evelyn remarked when she visited. A nurse came twice a day to take her blood pressure and temperature and to make sure all was progressing as it should. Since their confrontation on the stairs, Violet and her mother were getting along better—or at least had tacitly agreed to a truce. Mrs. Speedwell did not ask about Arthur, and Violet put up with her fussing. She fetched her cups of tea and shawls and spectacles and knitting that her mother held in her lap and never worked on. She sat and read to her—finishing *The Diary of a Nobody* and convincing her mother to try Somerset Maugham. She turned the wireless up or down or off. She tidied the rooms under Mrs. Speedwell's direction, and tried to conquer the musty smell, though it would require a proper airing of the house that she couldn't do in February.

Violet rang neighbors and friends and arranged short visits, putting out biscuits ("Not too many," Mrs. Speedwell insisted, "or they will stay all afternoon eating!") and warming the teapot. She went to the shops and made simple meals from the purchases, of omelets and leek and potato soup and boiled sole, using her mother's money to treat them to tinned peach melba or pineapple chunks with cream.

She became indispensable.

She rang Gilda, who spoke to Miss Pesel and sent her the design and materials for more cushion borders. She rang Mr. Waterman and asked for another week off, and before he could question or chide her, said her mother was calling for her and hung up. She rang Mrs. Harvey, who asked first how her mother was, then if she would still be able to pay her rent. She considered asking her mother for money to pay the rent, but worried it would wreck the fragile equilibrium they had managed to achieve, and that Mrs. Speedwell would simply say, "Move back to Southampton."

She did not ring the Five Bells.

She also looked after Aunt Penelope when she came to visit for a few days—though she did not require much, for she was so used to others making demands on her that her own needs were set aside. Gentle and mild mannered, Penelope chose to respond to her sister's overbearing nature by giggling. It was like watching someone punch a pillow that is so soft their fists make no impact. Violet began to feel she was living in a Jane Austen novel, but at least her aunt's brief presence gave her some respite.

Once Aunt Penelope had gone back to her responsibilities in Horsham, and after a particularly exhausting day of running and fetching and being bossed about, she welcomed a visit one evening from Tom, who had taken to popping in after work before heading home to Evelyn and the children. Mrs. Speedwell was asleep by the fire, having been read Maugham short stories for much of the afternoon. When he called out "Hello!" Violet hurried to shush him at the door. He held up a bottle of brandy. "Thought you might need this, to keep you going," he whispered.

Violet led him back to the kitchen, where the range kept it reasonably warm and they could shut the door and speak without their mother hearing. A mulligatawny soup was bubbling on the hob and giving the room a pleasant meaty fug.

"How's Mum today?" Tom asked as Violet got out two glasses.

"All right. I managed to bore her to sleep with Somerset Maugham, though I rather enjoy him."

"I must say, old girl, you're doing a splendid job looking after her. Much better than I'd expected. Sorry," he added. "That sounded bad. I didn't mean it like that."

"I know what you meant." Violet poured them each a brandy. "I myself didn't think I would possibly manage for this long." She raised her glass to him and they drank.

"And now," she added, "I want to go home."

Tom was silent for a moment. "Isn't this your home? After all, you lived here for thirty-eight years, whereas you've been in Winchester for just over a year."

It was true that Violet knew every sharp corner and squeaky step and faded curtain in this house, to the point where such things were unconsciously imprinted on her brain. But that did not make it home.

"And aren't you of better use looking after Mum than typing forms for people you don't know?" he continued. "What is Southern Counties Insurance to you, or you to it?"

"That is not the only part of my Winchester life," she countered. "There's the broderers too." She couldn't add about the bell ringing or Arthur, or about the sense she had that she was building a life for herself there—building herself there. He wouldn't understand; he was already built.

"Doesn't Mum count for more than embroidery?"

In his way her brother was using similar arguments to those of Mr. Waterman. It pained her. "You said at Christmas that you were glad for me, that I seemed happy in Winchester."

"Yes, but Mum hadn't taken ill then. That rather puts things into perspective, doesn't it?"

They were silent. Violet decided to ignore what Tom had just said. "I must go back to Winchester shortly to resume my life," she declared. "I wanted to speak to you about what to do with Mother. She is much better, and though she may not believe it, I think she can be left alone." Violet was not entirely sure she did think it. Two weeks was certainly not the four weeks' bed rest the doctor had prescribed.

Tom gulped his brandy. "Evie warned me you would say that."

Violet set down her glass. "And you thought I could be bought off with a bottle of brandy? Shame on you, Tom."

"No! No, not at all, old girl. I do understand. But we can't just leave Mum on her own. She's better because you're here. Left alone—even if nurses visit every day and we rehire the char—she would wilt, and have a fall, or stop eating. Evie is worried—we both are—that we'll end up having to take her in. It's hard work with three kiddies. Taking on another person, especially one as difficult as Mum—well, we dread it, to be honest. Surely you can see that."

She could see it. She wondered if they also "dreaded" the possibility of Violet herself coming to live with them one day. They had never discussed it—the few times she'd brought it up, Tom had ducked out of the conversation by saying, "Oh, no need to worry about that just yet. We've a long way to go before we have to think about it."

But now, unless she took a stand—and what others would see as a selfish stand—she would be backed into her old bedroom and a life of looking after her mother. "Tell me," she said, "what if I were married with children? Would we be having this conversation?"

"But you don't have a husband and children," Tom replied. "I'm sorry you don't, but there it is."

"So what would we be saying if I *did* have a family? What would our options be then? Why can't we discuss those options?"

Tom frowned. "Well . . . I suppose we would be considering having someone live in. Not necessarily a nurse, but a companion. Someone who would cook for Mum and sit with her—not all day, but read to her and such. Instead of rent. Someone who would be in situ if there were a problem, and she could call us or the doctor."

"In situ," Violet repeated.

"Yes, in situ. You know what that means, don't you? It's Latin for—"

"I know what it means," Violet interrupted. "Latin."

"What is it?"

"I am thinking of a solution."

22

Violet had never thought she would be so pleased to walk back into the chilly Southern Counties office and see her tan cardigan draped over her chair back; nor to have Maureen stop dead in the doorway, a cup of tea in hand, and her dour face break into a smile.

"Oh my days, I'm glad you're back!" she cried. "I thought I was going to drown in paper." She hurried in, sloshing tea on the floor in her haste, and indicated the massive pile of forms by her typewriter. "Not to mention how terribly boring it's been sitting here alone all day."

Violet smiled—Maureen was making it sound as if they were the closest chums, conveniently forgetting about the frostiness that had recently descended. But Violet was willing to forget that too. "Did Mr. Waterman not tell you I was returning today?"

"Mr. Waterman tells me nothing, only that you were away until further notice and that I must cope as best I could, and only to use one heater for myself." She pointed at the new Belling Violet had managed to purchase. "Now we can have both on again! Here, have this, I'll make another." Maureen thrust her tea at Violet, then knelt to flip on the switch. "I had to find out about your mother from Olive. How is she?"

"Much better, thanks."

"Who is looking after her now?"

"She's got a lodger who cooks for her and keeps her company." Violet did not mention that the lodger was Dorothy Jordan.

She set down the cup and saucer along with her handbag and looked around. She had only been away for two weeks, but the room seemed different: small, drab, uninspiring. Though pleased to be resuming her life after the hiatus in Southampton, Violet realized now that she could not stay here forever. She would need to move on and find some other way to live.

That sudden understanding was why her subsequent meeting with Mr. Waterman did not trouble her as much as it might. He called her to his office to welcome her back, asking after her mother and even commenting on Maureen's efficiency in handling her increased workload. "Of course I am concerned that our typing pool is made up entirely of girls I cannot completely rely upon," he added, turning a glass paperweight on his desk.

Violet felt her spine stiffen. "What do you mean?"

"Well, Maureen is likely to go the way of Olive, isn't she? She'll marry and leave, as will most girls we hire. Spinsters are more reliable"—he did not notice Violet grimace—"but they are likely to be off looking after their Aged Ps, aren't they?"

Violet looked at him. Not even referencing Dickens softened that blow. "What would you have us do, Mr. Waterman? Put our jobs before our families?"

"Of course not, of course not. That indeed is why girls leave when they marry—to focus on family."

"If you didn't have your wife to look after *your* Aged Ps—as I suspect she does"—a glance at Mr. Waterman's surprised face confirmed she had guessed right—"then what would *you* do if they needed you?"

Mr. Waterman sat up. "There, now, Miss Speedwell, there is no need to get personal. No need at all."

"Except that you just have with me."

"Yes, but it is my job as supervisor to look after the best interests of my employees, as well as of Southern Counties Insurance. I am sorry if you do not see it that way."

"Perhaps you would be better off hiring older widows who don't plan to remarry," Violet remarked, only half joking. "Or men."

"Well, now, men are unlikely to want to type all day, are they? It is a—a feminine occupation, I should think, even now when jobs are scarce. But a widow . . ." He gave the paperweight another half-turn, looking thoughtful.

I shall have to give him a headache soon by handing in my notice, Violet thought, aware now that the moment she was back, she was ready to leave again.

Returning to the broderers was more successful. All seemed genuinely pleased to see her—even Mrs. Biggins, who highly approved of Violet working on cushion borders in her spare time at her mother's. "Loyalty and hard work, that is what I like to see in a broderer," she declared. "For cathedral and family."

Mabel Way nodded at her and said, "Come to me for more materials when you are ready."

Gilda hugged her and whispered, "Thanks so much for finding

Dorothy a place to live—you are a true friend!" She then sat with her and as promised described the broderers' service Violet had missed. "You must go and see the cushions in place," she finished. "There are a dozen of them out, and they look splendid, like little bits of stained glass all over the seats. Now you can see what the effect will be when we finish the project and there are many more. And apparently the new alms bags were used on Sunday and they got a third again the usual donations! Of course the vergers complained because the collection took twice as long since everyone wanted to inspect the bags, and that rather threw out the timing of the service. Just think, Violet: your stitches passing hand to hand for years to come!"

They sat together and chatted easily while they worked on their pieces. There was less tension in the room surrounding Gilda now than there had been in January when things had come to a head with Dorothy. The other broderers were no longer throwing her looks or whispering to each other, and had gone back to listening to and laughing at Gilda's stories. Dorothy was not there, and that made it easier to ignore the fact of them as a couple.

"Dorothy told me she has settled in well in Southampton." Gilda spoke in a lower voice.

"Yes, she has." Violet matched her tone. "It took me quite by surprise, as Mother is not the easiest of people to satisfy. I did warn her."

Indeed, from the start Dorothy was unrattled by Mrs. Speedwell. While grateful for a free place to live, she was, in her floating way, clear about maintaining her own time to embroider Mr. and Mrs. Waterman's cushions or to take the train to Winchester to tutor children in Latin. She did not play the victim, and did not allow Mrs. Speedwell to, either. She did not grovel or concede to her barrage of demands and complaints. On her first morning, while Violet was still there to smooth the transition, Dorothy's response to Mrs. Speedwell's order for another cup of tea was: "Later, we'll all have a cup for our elevenses." Violet's mother was so startled that she did not renew her demand. When she complained that her lodger's vegetable soup was not salty enough, Dorothy passed her the saltcellar. "You are very welcome to make the soup if you prefer," she suggested. "That would be fine with me." She refused to read the *Mail* or the *Express* aloud, but handed them back to Mrs. Speedwell, saying, "I do not care for these papers and their opinions, so you will have to read them yourself." She also rejected the books Mrs. Speedwell wanted her to read aloud, instead insisting on Latin classics. As Violet was leaving she was reading from Virgil's *Aeneid*, first a page in Latin, then the English translation. Mrs. Speedwell was fast asleep. She was clearly in the process of being tamed.

"Do you see Dorothy at all?" Violet asked now.

"A little here and there, when she comes to tutor." Gilda frowned. "It's not like before, when we had all the time in the world. But it's better than nothing. We shall have to find a way. Maybe I'll move in with your mother too!"

Violet paused, her needle threaded through two canvas holes. Her mother had once used the word *deviant* to describe two women who lived together in the next street and who Violet now realized must have been a couple. What would Mrs. Speedwell make of such deviance within her own home?

After the broderers' meeting, she went to the cathedral to see the cushions, hurrying up the central aisle and mounting the stairs that led to the choir. She was not entirely surprised to see that Arthur was sitting in one of the choir stalls, an embroidered cushion on his lap. Violet had hoped he might be there waiting for her, yet when she saw him her feelings were mixed. Her heart dropped into her stomach at the sight of him—the sick, joyous feeling she knew was love. There was relief that she could sit with him and tell him of her days with her mother, and of how glad she was to be back where they could meet; and of her tumult at work, of wondering what she could do next. She wanted to lay all of this before him, to talk it over as one does with a husband; as she would have with Laurence if he'd lived. But Arthur was not her husband; he was someone else's husband.

She was also a bit disappointed that he had already seen the cushions. She had wanted to present them to him with a flourish—in particular the one he was holding: the King Arthur cushion Dorothy had made.

Arthur set it to one side and stood up as she approached. "Violet."

"I am so glad you are here," she said. She held out her hand, because she wanted to feel his touch, and he took it and shook it, as if they were being formally introduced. His hand was cold, and Violet noticed now that the cathedral itself was icy, though it was the beginning of March and she'd thought the back of winter was broken. But it always took a huge stone building longer to heat up and to cool down.

A peculiar mix of emotions crossed Arthur's face. He was clearly pleased to see her, and relieved too. She had not been able to speak to him after that one brief and interrupted telephone call. Perhaps he had been waiting here every Wednesday to see if she would appear after embroidery. But there was something else there too: He was upset. Had she done something?

"What is the matter?" she asked.

Arthur waved away whatever was the matter. "How is your mother?" It was the question everyone asked, Violet had noticed. No one asked how she was.

"Mother is recovering. One of the broderers is lodging there now and keeping an eye on her. Dorothy Jordan, whom you met at Midnight Mass."

"Ah, yes, the actress's namesake. Good. Did your mother drive you a little mad?"

"She did. But we—well, we reached a kind of understanding. And it was because of you, really." Arthur raised his eyebrows. "Something you once said," Violet explained, "about losing a child. How it changes a parent. That made it easier for me to see why she is the way she is. Thank you for that."

Arthur bowed. "Glad to be of service."

"So you have seen the cushions, then?"

Arthur nodded. "I have." His jaw tightened. It's the cushions that are the problem, Violet thought, surprised. She couldn't see why: They were very striking, and even though so far there was only a scattering of them in the choir stall seats, they lit up and lifted the dark wood. Beautifully and unusually designed, carefully made, without a stitch out of place—she couldn't guess how they could upset anyone.

Is his wife an embroiderer? she thought. Perhaps he is thinking that she should have been a part of the cathedral cushions project. Violet thought back to the only glimpse she'd had of Jean Knight, sitting with long gray hair and her eyes closed in the garden in Nether Wallop, face gleaming in the sun. Was that the face of a broderer? She had no idea.

She proceeded cautiously, focusing on the subject of the cushion rather than the embroidery. "I thought the King Arthur cushion would please you. But I have wondered how he is connected to Winchester." Violet asked the question deliberately, knowing that, like many men, Arthur enjoyed explaining things to a willing audience.

Indeed, he perked up. "Have you seen the Round Table hanging in the Great Hall—the only remains of Winchester Castle?"

Violet nodded. She had taken Marjory and Edward to see it, with the requisite sword fight afterward using reeds they'd plucked in the water meadows. It was enormous, twenty feet in diameter, and painted in twenty-four green and white segments, with the names of King Arthur's knights labeled in each. A Tudor red-and-white rose was in the center, and a portrait of the king in red, white, and blue robes, holding a sword.

"It is a medieval replica of King Arthur's Round Table, with later decoration by Henry VIII. It has been suggested that Winchester Castle might have been Camelot, although of course there is no historical evidence—indeed, no historical evidence of the existence of King Arthur himself. I expect the cushion is merely playing on those rumors." After this brief flaring of interest, he subsided once more into a sort of gloom, as if talking of the cushion reminded him of something he didn't like.

He didn't ask her any questions, and Violet felt she should fill the awkward silence. She picked up the cushion and ran a hand over it. "The design is very fine, isn't it? Sybil Blunt has designed all of the history medallions. Dorothy Jordan stitched the petit point. The landscape of rocks and trees behind the sword and shield is very skillfully shaded, don't you think? And Miss Pesel designed the surround, which is a combination of larger canvas stitches mixed with petit point, to give it a varied texture. Miss Pesel is clever that way.

Another broderer stitched that. Then the petit-point medallion was spliced in, so carefully you wouldn't know it was made by two different hands." She gazed at the stitching. "See the little dots of yellow within the blue knots? And that little bit of green by the red flowers? And those light blue cross-stitches framing the medallion? All of these choices have been carefully considered by Miss Pesel, and bring the design to life." She was aware that she was lecturing, but Arthur was making her nervous.

"And who designed and stitched the long border?" Arthur turned the cushion so that they were looking at the inch-wide band along the sides that gave the cushion its depth.

Violet smiled. He had picked out the surprise she had been saving. "Miss Pesel designed it, and—well, it was me. I stitched that border." She was thrilled to have made even a small part of the cushion that bore his name.

"You stitched it." Arthur's tight expression made Violet freeze. Something was wrong that she was not taking in. She looked closely at the border for uneven or dropped stitches, for the wrong colors used or an unpleasing aspect of the design. The border was made up of small blue squares outlined in yellow. In alternating squares were four-petal flowers shaded in red and pink with a yellow center. The other squares were of four yellow lines cricked at right angles, looking a bit like spiders.

"I—I suppose I could have made the red and pink stitches in the petals a little cleaner," she confessed. "They are muddled here and there. Miss Pesel didn't seem to mind, and she is quite the perfectionist. We have all had to unpick our work to meet her standards."

"Do you never question her designs?"

"No. She gives us quite a bit of freedom when it comes to choosing colors, but she is very clear on the designs. She knows so much about embroidery, from all over the world, and I do think she knows best what works. I trust her judgment."

"So you did not question her decision to include swastikas in the design?"

Violet stared at him. Arthur's mustache was twitching, a tiny tic of stress. Then she looked at the border and her face grew hot. Of course the yellow lines made up swastikas. She had recognized them as such when she began stitching the border. But it had not occurred to her to define them in terms other than as a design by Louisa Pesel for a cushion border, an assignment Violet accepted without question. The swastikas were not turned on their points and depicted in stark black on a white-and-red background, as the Nazis had designed them. They were in benign, fuzzy yellow wool, stitched in long-armed cross, surrounded by blue, interspersed with flowers. There was nothing threatening or political about them. But, seen through Arthur's eyes, she understood what a jolt they were.

He was watching her; she could sense him registering every expression that crossed her face, looking for the answer that would appease him. Violet did not know what that answer was. "I'm sorry," she said. "I didn't think about them that way when I was making the border. I"—she tried to make light of it—"I thought of them as little yellow running men."

"Little yellow running men," Arthur repeated, and hearing it back, Violet knew it had been the wrong thing to say.

She tried to repair the damage. "They were just part of the pattern. Part of the bigger picture. I didn't associate them with the Nazis."

"No. You didn't." Arthur was silent for a moment, his disappointment in her palpable. Then he set down the King Arthur cushion on the seat next to him, carefully, as if it were porcelain. "I'm afraid I have to go and see one of the vergers now. Will you excuse me?" He nodded at Violet, then turned and left by the north aisle archway, next to Harey Coppar's graffiti.

Violet managed to hold out until he was safely out of earshot before she began to cry.

That was how Louisa Pesel found her, sobbing as she dug in her bag for a handkerchief. "My dear, what is it?" her teacher murmured, dropping into the seat next to her. "What has happened?"

"Oh! Nothing, it's—" Violet pulled out a handkerchief and wiped her eyes. It was Arthur's, the one she had never returned. "I just—oh." She could not speak; it would make her well up again.

Miss Pesel seemed to understand this, and waited.

Violet sighed. "It's the King Arthur cushion."

"Yes?"

"I showed it to someone and he asked me about the—the swastikas, and I didn't know what to say." Her mouth began to wobble.

"Ah." Louisa Pesel looked around. "Is your friend still here?"

"He went to see the vergers about something. That's what he said, at least. Perhaps he's gone."

"And what is his name?"

"Arthur. Arthur Knight."

"All right." Miss Pesel patted her hand. "You wait here. I'll be back directly." She stood and stepped out to the north transept, her court shoes clicking crisply. Violet found the sound comforting. Louisa Pesel was definite, and would have an answer, unlike her own muddled thinking.

Soon she was back, Arthur trailing behind her, a dubious look on his face. Violet stuffed his handkerchief back in her bag before he spotted it.

"It turns out Mr. Knight and I have met before," Miss Pesel announced. "I thought I recognized his name. We were both at the St.

Swithun's service last year, he representing the bell ringers and I the broderers. Now, Miss Speedwell tells me you have a question about the design of the King Arthur cushion, is that right?" Her tone was as firm as a headmistress's, and had the effect of making him stand straighter and Violet want to giggle like a schoolgirl, despite the seriousness of the moment.

"I do. I wonder why you have chosen to include swastikas in the border, given their association with the Nazi Party."

Louisa Pesel nodded. "That is an understandable concern, but it is inaccurate. They are not swastikas. They're fylfots."

"Fylfots," Arthur repeated.

"Yes. An old Anglo-Saxon word. It is an ancient symbol that has been used for thousands of years, in many cultures and religions, from India to Scandinavia, and particularly used in Hinduism and Buddhism. A symbol of light and life and good fortune. I have seen it myself in Greek architecture, on old Greek vases, even in Egypt when I visited. The Coptics used it there."

If Arthur was impressed by her travels, he did not show it.

"Where do you think the Nazi Party took it from?" she added. "They did not make it up themselves."

"The ancient symbol runs anticlockwise, whereas the Nazi emblem has it running clockwise," Arthur retorted. "Like the symbols on this cushion." He picked it up and held it out to her, though Violet could have told him that Louisa Pesel knew every inch of every design, indeed could have described it in details he would not even understand—the stitches used, the wool colors, and, apparently, the background of each symbol. She wanted to wince, for there was something petty about his tone and gesture. But she was in no position to judge: She had not questioned the swastikas when she should have.

Louisa Pesel waved a hand at the cushion, dismissing it. "The direction the symbol runs in is neither here nor there. It has been used both ways for centuries. I will show you." She turned and to Violet's surprise stepped out through the southern archway toward the south transept and the nave. "Bring the cushion!" she called over her shoulder.

Violet and Arthur glanced at each other as they followed Miss Pesel. She led them along the south aisle past the south transept and stopped in front of the chantry of the Bishop of Edington, one of seven chantries built for the cathedral's most powerful and influential bishops. It had been designed in the Gothic style, and had a wood door painted blue that kept out visitors except when prayers were said at the chantry for the bishop. But it was possible to get a good view of his tomb through the rows of narrow windows with scalloped arches that made up the four walls, making the edifice as much air as stone.

"There. Look inside at Edington's tomb," Louisa Pesel commanded. "Apart from it being some of the finest medieval sculpture you'll find anywhere, what do you see?"

Violet and Arthur peeked through adjacent windows. A full-length alabaster statue of the Bishop of Edington lay on the tomb, wearing his vestments and a crown, his head on a stone pillow, hands folded on his chest, hidden by the elaborate draped sleeves of his cassock. The carved alabaster was delicate and shiny and pearly gray. Violet started in astonishment, for she immediately spied what Louisa Pesel had brought them there to see. She had looked at this chantry and statue before, but somehow had not managed to notice the prominent row of swastikas decorating the bishop's stole—the long narrow strip of cloth he wore around his neck that descended over his sleeves. There were also swastikas on his collar, and even on the cloth draped over his feet.

Not only that—what surprised her almost as much was that interspersed between the swastikas were four-petal flowers exactly like those she had embroidered on the cushion border. They were even divided into squares by ridges of alabaster. Miss Pesel had copied exactly that pattern on the border. Violet wanted to laugh aloud, and that was what Arthur did—not a full-bellied laugh, but more than a chuckle. It was a sound of surprise, of bemusement, of concession.

"Those are fylfots," Louisa Pesel declared. "Fourteenth-century swastikas, if you like. And you'll notice they are turning clockwise, long before any Nazi designer chose to make them so."

They studied them in silence. Louisa Pesel must have felt she did not have to say more—the fylfots spoke for themselves.

At last Arthur stepped back from his window. Violet followed suit. "That is truly remarkable," he said. "I have been coming to this cathedral for forty years, and have looked at this tomb dozens of times, and never noticed the swastikas. The fylfots," he corrected himself. "And I thought I was an observant man."

"In my designs for the cathedral cushions and kneelers I have referred to many patterns and symbols," Miss Pesel said. "Some of the central knots in the kneelers come from Elizabethan samplers or a sixteenth-century embroidery pattern book by a printer called Peter Quentel. But I do like to tie in designs to those already existing in the cathedral. So a few came from the medieval tiles in the retrochoir, and also from the wood and stone bosses on the vaulted ceilings of the nave and presbytery. Have you seen them?"

Violet and Arthur nodded. Violet sometimes studied them in the presbytery during Evensong. Though they were high above her and hard to make out, she sensed the bosses depicted patterns and symbols that resonated from the past.

"I believe they are mainly heraldic emblems," Arthur suggested, his tone less certain and more deferential to the more knowledgeable Louisa Pesel.

"Yes, and thirteenth century, but some a little newer. There are several coats of arms of wealthy Winchester families, but also decorative designs of leaves and animals. I believe there is even a lion with a pig in its mouth. I spotted it with binoculars. The craftsmanship is remarkable, especially when you consider the makers knew that once in place no one would ever see the details up close. It was truly a labor of love for the cathedral that the carvers should make something so fine when no one would see it. I expect they didn't ever imagine the invention of binoculars! But you understand that feeling, don't you, Violet? Of wanting to make your stitching the very best it can be, regardless of whether anyone will notice?"

Violet nodded.

"Like bell ringing too," Arthur added. "We ring as best we can, though no one may notice it—the mistakes or the perfect peals. Unlike the carving or the embroidery, though, ringing doesn't last."

"Except in the memory," Louisa Pesel declared. "And that can be very strong indeed."

"Indeed."

"It was clever of you to base the border of the cushion on the design on the bishop's stole," Violet said. "It lends itself to a border."

Arthur held up the cushion so that they could compare the border with the statue.

Louisa Pesel nodded. "It does. Oh, the sculptor was a clever chap. The four petals of the flowers echo the four arms of the fylfot, but provide a still punctuation between the symbol's movement. That is what is very clever about the fylfot—it looks as if it's moving. So the design is not static. I couldn't resist using it."

Arthur lowered the cushion. "I am curious, though. Surely you were aware when you designed them of the growing controversial nature of the swastika as a symbol. One could easily make the mistake of assuming that the designer, or the maker"—he nodded at Violet—"supported the Nazi Party."

Louisa Pesel drew herself up. "That would indeed be an unfortunate supposition. But I am taking the long view—the very long view. Working in a nine-hundred-year-old cathedral does that to you. This symbol"—she gestured at the fylfots on the bishop's statue—"is thousands of years old. It will long outlive a party of fascists. I felt no need to pander to them by not using a good design when I saw it. If I did that, they would have won, wouldn't they? Instead I am reclaiming it for its true meaning. It is not the Nazi Party that gets to decide for me what interpretation to place on the fylfot. I call upon the long history of the symbol; that is what is important to me. I hope that once people see the fylfots, they will think of them every time they sit in the choir stalls, and connect them to the cathedral and to the Bishop of Edington rather than to German fascists. The Edington sculptor used the symbol in all innocence. I have used it as an act of subversion."

Arthur cocked his head to one side. "I don't know if you are brave or foolish, Miss Pesel."

Louisa Pesel laughed. "Possibly a bit of both."

Violet looked at them smiling together, clearly pleased with each other and no longer battling over interpretation. He has met his match, she thought. Miss Pesel was probably in her early sixties, just a year or two older than Arthur, and Violet could imagine them married, sparring over coffee and marmalade toast of a morning, discussing what they had read in the paper or heard on the wireless. Violet herself was superfluous to this moment. These two people were far nobler than she could ever be.

A yawning gap opened up inside—the dark abyss she felt whenever she lost something important—and Violet had to turn away so
that they would not see the tears that pricked at her eyes. "I'm terribly sorry, but I must go. I'm late. . . ." She hurried down the aisle
toward the exit.

"Good-bye, dear, see you next week," Miss Pesel called, oblivious.
Violet did not hear Arthur; she did not want to.

Outside she turned and strode across the Outer Close toward
the High Street. It was just getting dark; people were leaving offices
and shops and heading toward home or trains or buses, raising
umbrellas against the drizzle that had begun while she was in the
cathedral. She had forgotten hers and could feel the damp clinging
to her.

She had just reached the Old Market Inn when Arthur caught up
with her. "Violet."

She kept walking, though she knew it was rude and childish.

Arthur took her arm. "Please."

Violet shook off his hand. "I really am in a hurry." Hurrying to
her drab room and her beans on toast.

Arthur stepped in front of her so that she had to stop, and placed
his hands on her shoulders. "Please, love."

His brief words rooted her, though she could not look at him.
Arthur took her elbow and led them into a quiet passage, so that
they were alone. He had an umbrella, and raised it over their heads,
sheltering them from the rain and creating their own world.

"Why did you leave us?" he said, his face anxious in the dim light
of a distant streetlamp.

Violet sighed, and her breath seemed to forge a path for the words
that followed, emerging slowly and then tumbling out faster and

faster, like a spring that has been unblocked and is finding its way into the river it will become to travel to the sea.

She did not talk about him and Louisa Pesel, because it was too painful. Instead she talked about herself. "I am tired," she said. "I am so very tired. I've been tired since 1916. First George died, and then Laurence. After that I felt as if I were in a deep hole that took me so long to climb out of. It was as if I were sleepwalking, awake but unable to say anything or do anything to make my life—come to life again. Father helped, but Mother made it worse."

Arthur adjusted the umbrella over their heads, but did not speak. "After Father died, it got worse and worse until finally I came here. And then—things improved, bit by bit. The moment it began to feel as if I were no longer being held back was when I was in the ringing chamber with you. Then I felt I was coming back to life at last, like the shift between winter and spring. Or like a day in late spring when you know you can safely leave the house without a coat, when you can stop holding your body tight, clenched against the cold. When you will be warm. That is what I felt with you and the bells."

"Not with the broderers and your kneelers and cushions?"

"They are a help too. I am grateful that they provide a means for me to make some small lasting mark. And they give comfort to people, cushioning them so they can think about things other than aches and pains. I am glad to be able to do that. But that is what we women are trained for—to give to others, to make others comfortable, whatever we feel for ourselves. It can be tiring, thankless, to be so generous all of the time. I would like to be a bell ringer—just to go up in the tower and for an hour concentrate on nothing but the sound of the bells and my place in them. That to me would be heaven."

"Can you ride a bicycle?"

Violet stared at him. Rain was dripping down one of the umbrella spokes and onto his face. Arthur didn't seem to notice. "I don't have one here. Mine is in Southampton."

"Can you get it in the next few weeks?"

"I think so."

"Good. We'll wait a month or two until it's warmer and lighter."

"Wait for what?"

He wouldn't say. Instead he declared, "I know what you need now more than anything."

A kiss, she thought. Your hands on me. The Perseids. She felt her body pulse.

Arthur did not kiss her or touch her. He led the way to the Old Market Restaurant and bought her a three-course meal, with custard on her apple crumble and cream in her coffee. Afterward, she felt almost sated.

23

Violet normally let herself into her mother's house without knocking. However, since Dorothy's arrival she felt more formal and less able to treat the Southampton house so casually. And so on the Sunday closest to her birthday in April, she knocked on her old front door.

Dorothy answered after a moment. "Happy birthday, Violet," she said, standing aside to let her in. She seemed unchanged by her new role as a companion; her hair was still frizzy and ungroomed, her dress hem hung at an angle, and she smiled vaguely, her eyes somewhere over Violet's shoulder. "I have made the cake," she added.

Mrs. Speedwell was sitting by the fire, though it was a warmish spring day. While physically much recovered from her apoplexy two months before, her spirit was rather cowed—by the presence of Dorothy, Violet suspected. "Hello, dear," she said, and held up her cheek to be kissed. "Happy birthday. You know Dorothy made the cake? I told her you liked Victoria sponge, but she would go and make lemon drizzle."

"It is you who likes Victoria sponge," Dorothy countered as she came into the room, "and it is not your birthday. Violet is the sort of person who prefers the sweetness of her cake cut with something tart."

Violet looked at her. Dorothy was gazing into the middle distance. And she was right.

"Sit with me for a moment, Violet," her mother said. "Put the kettle on before you go out, will you, Dorothy?" She sounded tentative rather than bossy.

"I'm not leaving just yet. But I'll put the kettle on."

"I have to be careful what I say around her," Mrs. Speedwell whispered as Dorothy left, "or she can be *difficult.*"

"Why, what does she do?"

"She leaves the room!"

Violet burst out laughing.

"I don't see anything funny about it," Mrs. Speedwell declared, indignant. "There's nothing worse than being ignored."

"I know."

"What do you mean, you know? How can you know what I'm going through?" She was sounding more like her old self.

At that moment Violet heard the front door opening and Tom's familiar "Hello!" She noticed he did not seem to feel the need to knock with Dorothy there. "Happy birthday, old girl!" he cried as he appeared in the doorway, the two older children behind him. He handed her a bouquet of flowers. "Hello, Mum," he added, kissing his mother.

"Happy birthday, Auntie Violet!" Marjory and Edward repeated several times, frisking around her like dogs that need a run. Evelyn came in, solid and steady and exhausted, with Gladys in her arms. The baby was three months old and now able to hold up her head unaided. She was dressed all in white in a variety of knitted items, and looked about her with a thoughtful frown.

"Hello, Gladys," Violet greeted her niece, taking up her little fist and shaking it. Gladys's frown deepened as she stared at her aunt. She had something of her grandmother's indignation about her.

Violet turned and kissed her sister-in-law. "Cup of tea? Dorothy's making it."

Evelyn sighed. "Oh, yes. Thank heavens for Dorothy."

Violet understood her sigh. When a woman wants a cup of tea, usually she has to make it for herself, and for the others around her. There is no better taste than a cup of tea someone else has made for you.

Marjory stood at her elbow and placed a hand on her arm. "Auntie Violet, I want to give you my present now."

"After lunch, Marjory," her mother corrected.

"I want to give it *now*," Marjory repeated. "I know you will love it. I know it!" She had become much more confident in the past year, Violet noticed. The trick was to foster her newfound spirit rather than squash it. She wondered if she could have her to stay in Winchester on her own for a weekend.

"Perhaps I might have one of my presents now, and the rest later?" she suggested. "And if I may, I'd like that present to be Marjory's."

"All right, then," Evelyn agreed. "Marjory, it's in my bag in the hall."

Marjory hurried out. "I'll tell you what your present is from me," Mrs. Speedwell announced, stealing her granddaughter's thunder. "Almond oil for your skin. Dorothy fetched it for me from Plummers. I began using it at your age and that kept it from fading for a few years."

"Thanks awfully, Mother." Violet glanced at Evelyn, and they smirked.

Marjory returned with a package about the size of Violet's hand, crudely wrapped in brown paper. She set it in Violet's lap and hopped from foot to foot, glancing up at Dorothy, who had brought in the tea tray and was leaning in the doorway. Violet felt a twinge of jealousy: She had not expected her niece to have any sort of relationship with Dorothy, but they seemed familiar with each other. If I had stayed to look after Mother, I would have seen more of Marjory, she thought, then stopped herself and focused instead on her present.

She opened the brown paper to reveal a needle case embroidered in purple, pink, and cream, the pattern imitating the alms bag Violet had stitched. It was like a little book, with inside pages of felt for holding needles, similar to the needle case Violet had made for Marjory's Christmas present. "You made this?"

"I did!" Marjory couldn't contain herself and began to jump up and down. "You made one for me and now I've made one for you!"

"Now, Marjory, stop jumping and be honest," Evelyn chided. "Dorothy helped you a great deal, didn't she? Marjory was over here most days, working away on it," she added.

As Violet studied the case more closely, she could see where Dorothy had embroidered and where she had cleverly left dropped stitches and small tangles uncorrected to indicate Marjory's work. She glanced up at Dorothy, who was smiling into the fire, then at her niece, whose face was shining with a pleasure Violet knew well, of having made something useful and beautiful.

"I love it," she said. "Thank you so much, my dear." She gave Marjory a hug. "I am going to put my needles in it straightaway." Knowing children liked instant results, she reached for her handbag and got out the ragged needle case she kept there.

"So that's where my needle case got to!" Mrs. Speedwell glared at her daughter.

"Yes, Mother, it came in very handy to me, thanks." Violet transferred the needles from the old to the new case as Marjory watched, delighted.

"I am going to be a broderer when I grow up," she announced.

"I shall introduce you to Miss Pesel," Violet replied, setting her mother's case aside. "For that is what she does. She even taught embroidery to Greek girls. And she rode a camel once," she added, to make Louisa Pesel's life even more exotic and appealing, however tenuous the connection between stitching and camels.

"That is what I'll do, then," Marjory declared. "It's settled." She glanced sideways at her mother and grandmother, as if expecting to be challenged. But Mrs. Speedwell had not followed the exchange between her daughter and granddaughter, and Evelyn was distracted by Gladys's fussing. Marjory looked at Violet, and they smiled at each other.

There was a knock on the door, and Dorothy disappeared to answer it. She returned as Violet was pouring tea, accompanied by Gilda. To Violet's astonishment, her friend was greeted casually by the rest of the Speedwells, who had clearly met her more than once. "Happy birthday, Violet!" Gilda cried. "I hope you liked Marjory's present. Didn't she do well?"

"She did."

Gilda turned to Violet's brother. "Tom, Joe said he might have something for you. You're to give him a ring and he'll tell you more."

At Violet's questioning look, Tom shrugged. "I'm thinking of getting a bigger car. More room for the kiddies, you know. Gilda's brother is helping me."

"I see." There was a whole layer of family life that Gilda and

Dorothy seemed to be embedded in that Violet was not a part of. The price I pay for remaining in Winchester, she thought, and nodded. She was willing to pay it.

Dorothy had donned her green coat and beret and was waiting by the door. "We'll be off, then," Gilda said.

"What are you seeing?" Evelyn asked.

"*The Indiscretions of Eve.*" Gilda glanced at Dorothy and smiled. "We missed it first time round."

"Lucky. Someday we'll go back to the cinema, won't we, Tom?"

Dorothy nodded at Violet. "Enjoy your lemon drizzle and your afternoon. Panem et circenses."

"Oh, the Latin!" Mrs. Speedwell groaned. "What would Geoffrey think?"

"He would approve," Violet answered.

"Smashing girls," Tom declared after the front door closed.

Violet *did* enjoy her bread and circuses. The mellowing of her mother helped, for she was able to feel less guilty, and could tease and indulge her more. For her part, Mrs. Speedwell told stories about other birthdays, and even managed to mention George. "When your brother first saw you," she said, "he was sorely disappointed that you could not stack building blocks with him. 'Take her away until she can!' he cried. 'Take her away . . . ,'" Mrs. Speedwell repeated, chuckling.

She seemed to be in a good mood, and waited all the way through the lunch, the cake, the tea, and the presents before clearing her throat. "I should like to say something."

Violet was holding Gladys while Marjory leaned against her knee. Aunt and niece were conferring over whether they might remove a layer of knitting from the baby, as it was warm in the room and her face was red. Violet glanced at Gladys's parents: Tom and Edward were playing cards and Evelyn was sitting on the sofa, her eyes closed and her feet up. "I think we might," Violet decided, and began to peel off the white cardigan as Gladys observed her gravely. She did not cry, but reached over and squeezed Violet's nose.

"I have reached a decision," Mrs. Speedwell continued. Tom looked up from his hand, and Evelyn opened her eyes in alarm. "I have decided that it is time for me to leave this house. It is too big for me. I shall be moving to Penelope's in Horsham in the summer. She needs my help. She has far too much to do, looking after her mother-in-law and all of those grandchildren. My presence will be invaluable."

Tom and Evelyn and Violet stared. "Mum! Why didn't you tell us you were considering this?" Tom cried. "You don't have to—" A shake of Evelyn's head stopped him.

You do, Violet thought. You do have to. What a sensible decision. Thank you, Aunt Penelope. She should have felt relieved, but instead she wanted to cry. She buried her face in Gladys's neck, which smelled warm and tangy.

"What about Dorothy?" Marjory asked, a surprisingly adult concern. "Where will she live?"

"Don't you worry about her," Evelyn replied. "I'm sure she'll find somewhere to go."

"Dorothy already knows," Mrs. Speedwell said. "I have discussed it with her. It was she who first suggested the idea to me. Sensible girl. She and Gilda are out now, looking at places before they go to the pictures."

"Do you mean—a place for Dorothy to live—in Southampton?" Violet stammered.

"For them both to live. It's good to have such a good friend, isn't it? Though how Gilda will put up with all of that Latin, I'm sure I don't know!" She did not call them man haters or describe them as deviant. Does Mother know? Violet wondered.

She met Evelyn's steady gaze. *She* knows, Violet thought, though she is sensible enough not to say anything, not even to Tom. "How will they live?" she asked, more to herself than to her mother.

Mrs. Speedwell sat back, smug with knowledge. "They are looking for jobs. Dorothy to teach Latin, and Gilda is answering adverts for bookkeeping. Even in these difficult times, books need to be kept and children taught."

"What about her brother's garage?"

"Her sister-in-law intends to keep the books. 'Awful Olive,' Gilda calls her. She does sound dreadful. Gilda said she wears dresses that are far too tight for a mother." Mrs. Speedwell tutted happily.

This is what Gilda and Dorothy are making, Violet thought, recalling Gilda's bright, happy face as they left. She surprised herself by adding: Good for them. It made her hug Gladys till she cried.

24

Violet had to draw on all of the reserves of her patience while waiting for Arthur. She had brought her bicycle back from Southampton and got Gilda's brother to pump up the tires and oil the chain for her. It now waited for Arthur as well, in Mrs. Harvey's back garden, a tarpaulin covering it from the insistent April rain.

"May," he said when she asked over chops at the Old Market Restaurant, where they had begun meeting every week for supper after her broderers' meetings and before his ringing. He did not take her hand or call her "love," but he did not need to. There was something comforting about sitting formally together in the restaurant, linen napkins in laps, discussing the menu, the services he was to ring for, the embroidery she was working on, her mother's imminent move to Horsham ("A fine set of eight bells at St. Mary's," Arthur commented), the seedlings he was growing in his greenhouse and would soon plant out. We are like an old married couple, she thought, but without the married part. The thought did not bother her.

He was fattening her up with the dinners at the Old Market, he said. A year and a half of living on fish paste and cress sandwiches and Marmite had made her scrawny rather than simply slim. Violet was grateful but worried whether he could afford it on his pension. However, though she felt guilty, she could not limit herself to soup and a main, but always had a pudding as well—stodgy ones such as apple Charlotte or bread and butter pudding, with custard. "Stick to your ribs," Arthur said, nodding in approval. She could feel her hips begin to fill out her skirt, her collarbones soften under a layer of fat, her belly round out.

During the month she waited, she busied herself. She reorganized the typing she and Maureen did so that they played to their strengths—Violet doing reports with long chunks of text, Maureen on fiddly forms that required careful spacing—and made their output efficient enough that Mr. Waterman stopped complaining he might have to hire another typist or move their work to the typing pool in Southampton.

Maureen and her bank clerk had recently broken up, and Violet introduced her to Keith Bain. They went to the pictures one night and never mentioned each other again.

The broderers were working hard on another batch of cushions to be blessed at a Presentation of Embroideries service in May, adding nine to those already there. One Wednesday when Louisa Pesel assigned her more borders, she asked specifically to sew fylfots. Miss Pesel removed her spectacles and regarded Violet as they stood together by the cupboard in the room in Church House, the buzz of broderers working and chatting all around them, Mabel Way hovering nearby, ready to record the work Violet was assigned. "I am content with Edington's fylfots on the Arthur cushion," Miss Pesel began. "However, perhaps we have made our point. There are many other interesting patterns one could use."

"I want to," Violet countered. "This time I will know what I am making—what it means. I want to rebel meaningfully, not unconsciously."

Louisa Pesel smiled. "It is important for you to rebel, is it?"

"Yes." Ever since Arthur spoke of Hitler in the Fishermen's Chapel, Violet had been widening her world by paying closer attention, reading about him and the Nazi Party in the papers, listening to analysis on the wireless, discussing the news with Arthur at the Old Market. She was not sure Hitler would last as a leader of Germany—many thought he was a fanatic who was having his moment and would fade away, to be replaced by a different attempt to solve Germany's economic woes. If that was the case, fylfots on cushions could go back to being the benign ancient symbol they had always been.

"All right," Louisa Pesel conceded. "There is a cushion that still needs a border. I have been holding off on designing one, as it is an important cushion that I expect many will look at. It will sit on the wide chair across from the King Arthur cushion, and the same border on each will link them further."

"The Tree of Life?" Violet guessed—the unfinished cushion Gilda had shown her when she first began with the broderers.

Louisa Pesel nodded. "Indeed. Symbolically the fylfots would work well there. But you'll have to make the borders quickly to be in time for the service." She reached into the cupboard for the box that read "Models" and rummaged about until she found the narrow band of canvas with the fylfots interspersed between the four-petal flowers. Violet had used the model when sewing the King Arthur border. Miss Pesel handed it to her. "Go and rebel, Miss Speedwell."

Afterward Violet sat with Gilda and Dorothy to work. Though they didn't normally appear together at the meetings, Dorothy was up from Southampton to bring one of the finished Waterman cushions for Louisa Pesel to inspect, and stayed to sew. Violet didn't know how much the other broderers knew about their arrangement. Gilda was her usual lively self, telling stories to those nearby while Dorothy sat silent with her half smile. Those around them laughed and made comments and didn't throw odd glances their way. That crisis seemed to have passed, as long as the couple didn't display affection in front of them.

Violet had to wait until after the meeting, when she and Gilda and Dorothy had a cup of tea together at Awdry's, to ask about their plans. "How is Mother?" she inquired first.

"Mrs. Speedwell has gone to Horsham to inspect her living arrangements," Dorothy replied. "I put her on the train, and your aunt is meeting her off it."

"Thank you for suggesting the move to her. I—we are all grateful."

Dorothy shrugged. "It is the logical solution. Mrs. Speedwell just needed to be led to it and make it her own choice."

"While she's away Evelyn and Dorothy and I are going through the house, sorting," Gilda interjected.

"Shouldn't I be helping?"

"It's much easier when you're not emotionally involved. Gosh, Violet—apart from the telephone and the electricity, your mother's house is frozen in about the year 1894!"

"The year I was born."

"It will take some doing to get it unstuck," Dorothy said, "but we'll manage. Aut viam inveniam aut faciam. Hannibal: I will either find a way or make one."

"Does Mother know what you're doing?"

"Yes, and she doesn't seem to mind," Gilda declared. "Oh, she complains, but then doesn't follow through. Dorothy handles her without any trouble. She's had more trouble with pupils than with Mrs. Speedwell." She gazed admiringly at her friend.

"And have you found lodgings yet in Southampton?"

Gilda and Dorothy glanced at each other. "We're going to live in your mother's house, just until it's sold. They think a house sells better when someone's living in it. People have no imagination and find empty rooms off-putting. After that—well, we'll find something. I have a lead on a job, at any rate. I'll be moving soon. Violet, what's wrong?"

For tears were stinging Violet's eyes at the understanding that the one real friend she had made in Winchester was moving away. She cleared her throat and tried to laugh. "It's just that I moved from Southampton and now you're moving there."

Gilda leaned forward over her cup of tea. "Oh, don't you worry, I'll still come back to Winchester. For one thing, I have to keep an eye on awful Olive, don't I, to make sure she's not running the business into the ground! And then there are the broderers, of course. Didn't Miss Pesel say we have another three years' worth of work? I won't be able to come to meetings every week once I get a job, but I'll manage. And you'll come down and see us, won't you?" Though she grabbed Violet's hand, her face was shining at Dorothy.

"Of course I'll come," Violet answered stoutly. "After all, I am a Southampton girl and you need someone to show you round."

At last over supper one Wednesday Arthur asked Violet to meet him at half past seven on Sunday morning by the Thetcher grave, with her bicycle. "I know it's early, but it needs to be," he said apologetically. "At any rate the weather should be fine for cycling."

Violet knew not to ask for more details, contenting herself with the surprise of it. It was only while waiting for him on the soft May morning, the sun lighting up the short cathedral tower but the rest still in shadow, that she realized he was cycling all the way from Nether Wallop so early in the day. When he arrived and they had formally shaken hands, almost like strangers, and she asked, "Where are we going?" and he replied, "Nether Wallop"—then she understood the strength of his character. For he had cycled fourteen miles to fetch her and bring her back to where he had started.

They took the road that led northwest out of Winchester toward Stockbridge. Because it was early there was little traffic, and Violet could get back her bicycle legs after not riding for eighteen months. She wobbled a bit on the hill out of town, but once on the flat road she cycled more confidently, following Arthur's straight back and steady pace. She suspected he was going much more slowly than he usually did. Eventually he moved over and slowed down so that she caught up and they could ride side by side through the gleaming countryside. The sun had been up for a couple of hours and burned the dew away. It would be warm later but for now it was crisp and fresh and the sky blue-white.

The fields rolled alongside and away from them like waves. Some were newly plowed and dark with disturbed soil. In others shoots were turning the land fuzzy. It was much fresher and greener out here than it had been in August when she'd walked to Salisbury. Then the land had been the older woman, wise to the world and a little weary. Now it was the May ingenue, young and new and open to what lay before her. Which month am I? Violet wondered. May no longer, not yet August. I am July, she thought, surprised. I am in my prime, and ready.

"Will we get to Nether Wallop in time for the bells?" she asked Arthur, for she had worked out that much—though not her place in it.

"Should do," he replied, though he sped up slightly. "We'll stop for a breather before Stockbridge. Now, how are the broderers? Did you have anything blessed in the special service last week?"

"Another alms bag, and the border for one of the finished cushions."

"What pattern was it?"

Violet hesitated. "Fylfots."

Arthur's front wheel wobbled.

"It was my knowing act of rebellion," she added, "against the Nazis and all those who support them. As Miss Pesel explained."

"Indeed." After a moment Arthur added, "Are you planning to fill the choir stalls with fylfots, then?"

"No, just this one. The cushion has the Tree of Life on it, and it seemed appropriate. But two such cushions are enough, Miss Pesel and I have decided—though she did say she reserves the right to stitch another border of them herself sometime if she is feeling particularly angry. She rather hopes she won't have to."

They reached Nether Wallop just before nine, Violet slightly out of breath from the exertion, and wondering what the other ringers would make of her presence.

"Now, I must go in to set up," Arthur explained as they stopped up the lane from the church and dismounted from their bicycles. "I suggest you go and listen outside. Then towards the end, at about a quarter to, come into the church and sit on the right towards the back."

Violet nodded, sweating from the ride, confused and disappointed. She'd had a fantasy about ringing the bells, though she knew that was ridiculous. Keith Bain had told her he'd spent a month just learning how to pull the rope: The two-stroke motion was more complicated than it looked. But it seemed Arthur had brought her here just to listen.

He disappeared into the church, and Violet headed for the bench where she had sat nine months before to listen to the bells. Passing the pyramid that dominated the graveyard, she paused and placed a hand on its smooth surface, which had been warmed by the sun. Her brother had tried to climb it almost twenty-eight years ago. He had been dead for seventeen years, and Laurence for sixteen. Perhaps at long last the sting was gone from this knowledge. She was still alive, and glad of it. Her mother too: Mrs. Speedwell had turned a corner as well, though it was not the same corner as Violet's, for a mother's never could be. As she moved on and sat on the bench, the five bells began their short descending scale, and Violet closed her eyes and turned her face to the sun.

At a quarter to ten she got up and walked back through the grave-yard to the church entrance, nervous now, uncertain what was to happen. Was he going to introduce her to his wife? Would they sit like ducks in a row through the service, stared at by the village? Or were they leaving on their bicycles once he had finished ringing? To do what?

The church was cool and dim inside and, apart from the bell ringers, empty. The women had arranged their flowers and dusted the pews and swept the floor and set out the prayer books; the vicar had readied his papers at the pulpit.

The bell ringers were mid-method, pulling smoothly and watching one another with the kind of focused attention Violet had never seen anywhere else. She slipped into a pew out of their sight lines so as not to distract, then sat and listened, picking out the pattern by following the top bell as it moved through the others. It was easier to discern what was happening with fewer bells, and she was able to hear each move into its original place until the last one clicked in and they were playing the descending scale.

"Stand," the caller said, and four bells fell silent, only the tenor continuing, faster now, its urgent call to the village that the service would soon begin. The other ringers filed out, Violet keeping very still so they would not notice her.

When the door shut behind them she heard Arthur say, "Violet, come." She hurried over to the base of the tower, where four ropes dangled and Arthur pulled rhythmically on the tenor bell, down to his waist, then up almost on his tiptoes. "Do you see that curtain?" He nodded to a faded orange velvet curtain that hung in the corner by the entrance to the bells. "Pull it across. Then the congregation won't be distracted by us."

No, Violet thought. Then they won't see me. But she did as he asked, pulling it to shield them from the nave just as the door opened and the tall patrician man in the wool suit who had spoken to her in August entered. She was not sure if he had seen her or not.

She went over to Arthur. "All right," he said. "I am going to teach you how to handle the rope." He pulled his rope and let it go high up between his hands, then stopped it. The silence was startling. Violet could hear people on the other side of the curtain—the church was beginning to fill.

"Stand across from me," Arthur continued in a low voice. They stood facing each other, the rope hanging between them. "I am going to have you pull the sally while I pull the end of the rope. Grasp the sally with both hands at a height above your head—that's it. Then you will pull down until your hands are at your waist, then let go as it comes up. I'll control it with the tail end of the rope, and once the sally comes down again, grab it as it starts to come up, and then pull down once it's above your head. All right?"

"I—"

"We've no time. Just follow me, and trust me. Grab the sally and pull down to your waist." Arthur nodded at the striped part. Violet took a deep breath, took hold of the sally with both hands, and pulled. For a moment nothing happened, though she could feel the weight of the bell through the rope. It was not as heavy as she had expected, and she pulled far too hard.

"Let go!" Arthur hissed. She quickly let go, and as the sally headed toward the ceiling, he added, "Don't watch the rope. Look at me." He pulled the rope's tail so the sally came back down. "Now grab as it comes up and above your head. Now pull again. Keep watching me."

She pulled, and again he had to remind her to let go, and not to watch the rope. It was a curious up-and-down sensation that required complete concentration to get the rhythm right. At first she could not control the rope; it bounced about rather than running smoothly up and down. A few times Arthur had to grab the sally to set it straight. After a couple of minutes she managed to coordinate her movements and get a steady rhythm going, finding it easier if she kept her eyes fixed on Arthur and did not think about anything else. He was standing close to her, pulling and watching her as she was him. It was an intent gaze, focusing on the rope and the bell and each other. It was a little like being on a seesaw with someone, carefully balanced as long as each paid attention to what the other was doing, as well as to the seesaw. For a short while she felt completely in step with Arthur and the rope and the bell.

She was so intent on what was happening with the rope that it took a few minutes for her to become aware of the sound of the bell above them, making its singular music. Only then did she understand in the most visceral way that pulling the rope was creating this sound. "Calling all sinners," she murmured, and smiled at Arthur.

He returned her smile. "Yes, I think we've called them far and wide. You stop pulling, and I'll bring the bell down now."

She did not want to stop. But she could sense the congregation behind the curtain, and knew that this brief and profound connection between her and Arthur and the bell could not be prolonged. She pulled the sally one last time, then let go. Arthur extended his arms as the rope tail climbed to its highest point, pulled down more gently, checking the rope and taking up a coil as he brought the bell in, in ever quicker time, until it went silent. They looked at each other. "Thank you," she said, and he nodded.

He glanced at his watch, and went over to the wall to unhook a long metal cord from a nail. There was a grinding sound, then the bell began to be struck by an automatic mechanism, ten dead chimes. "A little late, but never mind," he said. He unhooked a rope with a grappling hook on the end and lowered it, and Violet helped him loop the ends of the ropes onto it. When all were looped he pulled up the rope to raise the hook, creating a simple version of the rope chandelier she had seen at the cathedral bell tower.

Behind them the congregation began to sing the first hymn. "Best to go out now," Arthur said. "I'll follow in a minute or two and meet you by the bicycles."

Violet nodded, but hesitated. She had a vision of the congregation turned and facing their way, staring at her as she was exposed. We have done nothing wrong, she told herself, though it did not feel as if they had done nothing as they rang, so close and concentrated together on the rope and the bell and each other.

When she slipped behind the curtain back into the nave, the congregation was faced away toward the vicar at the pulpit. Only one person turned as she made her way to the door—the man in the wool suit. He caught her eye before she got there, and his glare felt like a burning cigarette pressed into her skin. The village will know now, she thought. And Arthur's wife.

She considered telling him when he arrived at the bicycles a few minutes later, but he was looking so pleased and exhilarated that she kept quiet.

"What did you think of it?" he asked.

"I loved it. It was like nothing I've done before."

"It is different, isn't it? Everything else falls away."

"That was clever of you to have me ring then, during Calling All Sinners."

"Yes. Normally with beginners we have them along to a practice evening and let them torment the village for a few minutes with their mistakes. But I thought Sunday morning might suit you better. Easier to get here and back during the day."

Yes, and so that you can keep me hidden from the other ringers and the congregation, she thought. But she was not angry. It was a pragmatic solution.

She did not add that she wanted to do it again, for she understood it would be difficult to arrange—perhaps impossible now that the man in the wool suit had seen her. This had been a lone ringing session.

Arthur picked up her bicycle and handed it to her. "We could go back to Winchester along the route we came on, through Stock-bridge," he said. "But there will be Sunday traffic, and it is not so pleasant. There is another route along smaller roads, through Brough-ton and King's Somborne. It's nicer."

"I would like that," she said. "But there's no need for you to ac-company me all the way back. And you would get to Winchester far too early for Evensong ringing. I'm sure I can find the route." She was becoming more formal with him. "I expect you—you have other things you should be spending your Sunday doing." A Sunday roast with your wife, she thought.

"I'm not ringing at Winchester this afternoon. But why don't I cycle with you part of the way? It's a bit tricky getting across the river and to King's Somborne. Once you take the turning there it's more or less straight."

"Would you like me to cycle away first and you follow later?" Like a proper affair? she added to herself.

Arthur smiled. "No need—the village gossips are all inside." He nodded at the church, where the singing had finished.

They rode south, parallel to Wallop Brook, on a road Violet had walked along in the opposite direction the previous summer. Though side by side, they were quiet now. The exuberance she had felt from ringing with him had dissipated, replaced by a growing sadness, like the feeling she got on the last day of a holiday, when she almost wanted it to be over already, to get back to dull, everyday life.

After Broughton they cycled on toward the river Test, which required a few twists and turns to cross. Then they passed over a railway line, and the John O' Gaunt Inn came into sight. The publican was out front, watering tubs of pansies. "Hello, Arthur!" he called, then did a double take when he recognized Violet.

Arthur nodded, but did not stop. When they were out of earshot he swore softly.

"One gossip who is not at church," Violet remarked.

"Indeed."

"Would you rather turn around?"

"No, but I'll take a different route back so I won't have him stop me and ask about you."

They soon reached a bigger road that led them to the village of King's Somborne, a gathering of houses, a pub, and a church. Arthur turned then onto a smaller road, and very quickly the houses disappeared and hedgerows ran alongside the fields beyond. He pulled over and Violet came up beside him and stopped, sliding off the seat and standing with the bicycle still between her legs.

"If you continue along this road for about seven miles, it will lead you to the outskirts of Winchester," Arthur explained. "There will be little traffic, and it's lovely."

"All right." Violet didn't move. "Thank you for this morning. And for all of the meals you've bought me. And for taking me up to see the cathedral bells. For everything." She knew her words were sounding final. Because they were. Something in his demeanor made it clear that this day was unique. It would never happen again. He had brought her to ring, and that was all. He gazed at her a little helplessly now, and that seemed to confirm it. He would say good-bye and cycle back to Nether Wallop.

Violet felt the abyss gaping inside her. She could tumble into it, or she could take charge of the moment. Her act of rebellion.

They were stopped by a metal gate in the hedgerow where a tractor could go through to plow and harvest. The road and the hedgerows and the fields around them were completely silent, waiting. Violet dismounted and rolled her bicycle to lean against the hedge. Then she began to climb the gate.

"Violet."

She got to the top and swung a leg over so that she was sitting astride it, her skirt ballooning out around her. She took a deep breath before she spoke. "Would you come into this field with me? Because I am ready, and we will never have this chance again."

Arthur stared at her.

"You can come or you can ride away." Violet jumped down into the field and moved away from the gate without looking back. She had taken a risk; it was up to him to decide if he would too. She stepped into the field, left fallow with grass and clover, and the perfect height for lying on, as it was neither too high nor too short and prickly. As she waited she thought about all the people who would not understand what she was doing: her mother, Tom and Evelyn, Louisa Pesel, even Gilda and Dorothy. She thought of them, and then set them aside. Only one person was left to reckon with. She closed her eyes and pictured Jean Knight the only time she had seen her, a striking figure with her hair loose and her face drinking in the sun. Forgive me, Violet thought. Forgive me for making my life from the ruins of yours.

After a moment she sensed Arthur standing next to her. She opened her eyes and turned to him so that they were facing each other as they had while ringing. Reaching out, she took his hand, and he took her other. It was like a circuit being completed so that electricity could race through and connect them, sparking strongest at the base of her stomach.

She asked him to leave first. She wanted to be alone in the field, to gather herself together before she carried on with the rest of her life.

"I'm sorry, Violet," Arthur said, scrambling to his feet. "I am no good at this." He waved his hands about, taking in not just them and the field but all of the times they had met and the things they had said and what they had just done. "My wife—"

"I know."

But he insisted on continuing. "Jean has had a time of it. She needs me."

"Of course. But I think it best that we don't meet anymore, or have any contact. It's better that way." Violet's mouth was trembling so much she had to bite her lips to get them under control. "Because it's too hard otherwise, now that we've . . ."

"Yes. That's best." His simple agreement broke her heart, because she wanted him to say otherwise. But he was right, no matter the consequences of this day. They both understood that.

Arthur held her face for a moment, his eyes sad and blue, and smiled. He kissed her, then walked over to the gate and climbed it without looking back. Once he had rattled off on his bicycle, Violet mopped her face with his handkerchief, straightened her clothes, brushed the grass from her hair, calmed her breath. Then she stood, and looked across the field studded with buttercups, the handkerchief crumpled in her hand. Parts of her were still thrumming, alert to the possibility of change and growth.

She was tucking the handkerchief back into her handbag when she heard the gate clank, and wondered why Arthur was returning. She turned around. It was not Arthur. Jack Wells was standing on the bottom rung of the gate. He grasped the top rung, and with a quick hop swung his legs to the side and vaulted it, landing gracefully.

He stood looking at her with his dark staring eyes and his slow smile, and time seemed to freeze. Violet was able to calculate that his farm with its rusting machinery and the cornfield he had followed her through were just a field or two to the south. She had been so full of Arthur and the bells that she had not thought of that summer day, or of New Year's Eve. She had managed to remove him from her thoughts, until now.

No, she thought. You will not take this day away from me. "Go away," she said before he could speak.

His smile grew wider. "Why would I want to do that?"

"Because I have asked you to, and a gentleman does what a lady asks."

"Does he, now? I don't know about that. I think a man can take what he likes."

He stepped toward her. She took a step back. Now was a time to think quickly and clearly. Best not to panic, she heard her father in her ear. Think calmly about all the options and quickly choose which seems best. Don't overanalyze.

She listened. Arthur was gone; there were no houses nearby, and no farmers out working on a Sunday. No one could help her. Could she talk him out of it? Unlikely, judging from her previous encounters with him. Should she let him do what he wanted? That way he might be less violent.

No. She could not countenance it. After what had just happened with Arthur, she could not bear for him to wreck that memory. What had the past eighteen months in Winchester taught her? She would resist.

Violet glanced at the contents of her open handbag: Arthur's handkerchief, her wallet, a lipstick, a compact, some receipts, and a long strip of canvas rolled up that she was embroidering for a cushion border. She had tucked it in so that she had something to do if she had to wait for Arthur. Accompanying it was the needle case Marjory had made for her birthday, with several embroidery needles—short, thick, with rounded ends—stuck through the felt pages. Now she considered the needles.

Jack Wells took another step toward her. "What are you doing here on your own?"

So he had not seen her and Arthur together, she thought with relief.

"I—I am looking at the flowers."

"Why are you on your own so much?"

"That's my business. What's wrong with being alone?"

"A woman shouldn't be. She needs a man to protect her. Otherwise anything can happen."

"Nonsense," Violet retorted, suddenly angry. It seemed to sharpen her. "Anyway, we are not alone. Someone's in the road." She nodded toward the gate. As the man whipped around to look, she reached into her handbag, flipped open the needle case, pulled out the largest needle, and set it along the fold of the case spine so that the tip was poking out. Then she closed the case and held it pinched between her thumb and forefinger, over the part the needle ran along, to keep it in place. The whole maneuver took all of three seconds, but she just barely managed it before he turned his head back, annoyed.

"Think you're clever, do you? Think I'm stupid? Bitch." He strode up so fast Violet had no time to move. When he shoved her she stumbled backward to the ground, banging her elbow and shoulder. Despite that, she managed to hold on to the needle case, though she didn't dare look to see if the needle was still in place.

He stood over her for a moment, blocking the sun so all she could see was his triumphant silhouette. Then he lowered himself onto her, pinning her shoulders with his hands. He was not tall but he was wiry and strong from working outdoors, and he smelled of sweat and cigarettes and the sharp tang of the farmyard. When he pressed his groin against hers, he was hard. Violet lay frozen and terrified.

She was still holding the needle case. Under her fingers was the even pattern of embroidered canvas—the careful, mangled stitches made by her niece who loved her. The feel of those confident stitches snapped Violet back into the moment.

Jack Wells let go of one of her shoulders to reach toward his belt buckle. Now, Violet thought, and pinched the needle case tight and swung her arm up and over as hard as she could, praying as she stabbed into his neck that the needle was still there.

He screamed and rolled off her, clutching his neck. Go! Violet told herself, and jumped up. Ignoring the pain in her elbow, her shoulder, her back, she grabbed her handbag and ran, stumbling at first and then running faster than she ever had, even when her brothers had chased her when she was young. She got to the gate and scrambled over. She did not look back—that would slow her down. Her bicycle was still leaning against the hedge. As she reached it Violet could hear the clang of the gate being vaulted. She did not turn, but jumped on the bicycle and began to pedal hard.

She heard his panting and his swearing and his roaring, closer and closer, then felt a hand on her arm. She resisted wrenching it away, for she might topple from the bicycle. But she dug in hard with her legs, her thighs burning, and as she sped up he lost his grip on her, and Violet burst free.

She rode and rode, her lungs on fire, her mind frozen, not turning to look back, not slowing, pumping up and down on the pedals until she had put a few miles between her and the man. The road was empty, and there were no farms nearby, just fields and woods extending into the distance. The isolation made her thankful for her bicycle, a trusty steed taking her from danger.

Only when she reached a farm that spanned the road, and a turning toward a village, did she slow down. The farm was full of activity—not just the cows cropping grass in the adjacent field and a flurry of chickens pecking in the yard, but also a woman pouring something out into the grass by a side door, a man sitting in a chair in the sun, reading a paper, and three children kicking a ball about. A dog was jumping around the children and barking. The scene before her was so ordinary after what she had just been through that she almost laughed in disbelief.

She had left her hat back in the field, so her hair was everywhere, and the man and woman were staring at her. She cycled on. There was more traffic out now—people coming from church or going to family for Sunday lunch—and Violet tried not to make eye contact with any of the drivers or passengers.

On the outskirts of Winchester she stopped, propped her bicycle against the sign for the town, and scrabbled in her handbag for her compact. Looking at herself in the mirror, she took in her blotchy cheeks and matted hair, bitten lips and the wild look in her eyes, and thought: Powder and lipstick are not going to help. She raked her fingers through her hair to smooth it as best she could. When she put the compact back in her handbag, she realized Marjory's needle case was gone. It would be lying in the field with the hat, and was lost forever, for Violet could not go back there. The thought of the abandoned needle case made her begin to cry, great shuddering gasps that shook her whole body.

But the storm did not last long; it was done.

Violet found Arthur's handkerchief, dried her eyes, and wiped her face. Lighting a cigarette, she breathed in deeply and blew the smoke skyward. For a brief moment she considered going to the police to report Jack Wells. But it would mean explaining to skeptical policemen why she had been alone in a field, and possibly dragging Arthur into the mess. No. She pictured the needle sticking in Jack Wells's neck, and nodded to herself. That was enough. Violet Speedwell, she thought, look what you did.

She got back on her bicycle and coasted down the hill into town—past the railway station, the West Gate, down the High Street, and right at the Buttercross to head across the Outer Close. She hardly had to pedal, but felt pulled along by a magnet to the cathedral.

Leaving her bicycle against a wall, Violet walked into the cool interior and straight up the central aisle of the nave to the steps up to the choir. It was empty, apart from a verger setting out a cloth and candles on the altar at the far end in the presbytery, preparing it for Evensong. Violet looked at the rows of chairs to the left and right of the central entrance. To her left was the Arthur cushion; to her right, the recently finished Tree of Life. On both the rows of fylfots peeked out, though without announcing themselves; you had to look carefully to see them.

Violet considered the two cushions for a moment, then chose. She sat down on the Tree of Life, the seat creaking under her. Closing her eyes, she surveyed herself. Her breathing had slowed down and was almost back to normal. Her elbow still hurt, but the pain in her shoulder had subsided to a dull ache. Her thighs were tight from the long cycling with its sudden frenetic burst. She would have a bath later to relax them.

Down below she was sore, from Arthur and from the cycling. But as she sat and listened to her inner body, she imagined she felt a faint twinge. Violet opened her eyes and rested them on one of the broderers' cushions on a seat in front of her. The mustard yellow and red stood out like jewels from the dark wood.

Now it begins, she thought. Now I begin.

25

"I do like a journey on the train. A train cures everything." Gilda turned from the passing Hampshire countryside and beamed at Violet.

"Yes." Violet smiled back, though she knew it could not hide her exhaustion. For three months she had had so little sleep she wondered how she functioned.

Dorothy was sitting across from them wearing her green coat and faraway eyes. Violet had chosen a Saturday so that they could accompany her; otherwise she was not sure if anyone would come. Tom and Evelyn had said they would, though there was a fuss over getting someone to mind the children—a fuss Violet suspected had been manufactured to give them an excuse not to turn up. She had hoped Marjory and Eddie and Gladys might come, but knew she could not ask her brother to bring them. Of all the changes in the past year, not getting to see them regularly was one of the most painful. She still lived in hopes that Tom and Evelyn's unspoken attitude might shift. With Dorothy's help she had even remade the needle case Marjory had given her, painstakingly re-creating its faults, just in case her niece visited and asked to see it. The month before, Marjory had made her a birthday card, a careful drawing of violets. Violet took heart that Tom and Evelyn were willing to pass it on to her. Indeed, Tom had shaken his head when he described Marjory's ferocious insistence that the card be given to her aunt. "I don't know where she gets it from," he'd said.

"Look, St. Catherine's Hill! We're almost there." Gilda began to gather their things.

For a brief moment Violet wondered what it would be like to stay on the train and go on to London, as she had once considered on a summer day just under two years ago. Would life be easier for her in the big, anonymous city? Perhaps. But in her heart she knew she would never move there, and the feeling passed.

"Thank you for coming with me," she said.

"Of course!" Gilda cried. "We wouldn't miss it, would we, Dorothy?"

"Per angusta, ad augusta. Through difficulties to honors."

Violet and Gilda didn't even exchange a glance. Violet had found that once you lived with someone, you got used to them spouting Latin. Doubtless she had her own quirks that quietly drove Dorothy crazy.

Here was one quirk. She went over to the pram braked by the carriage door and peeked in. Iris was asleep and had been since they'd left the house. While it was a blessing for the other passengers, it meant she was likely to be awake and vocal later. No matter. Violet smiled down at the miracle of her daughter. For her she would put up with a great deal more than crying.

Still, she braced herself for the walk from the station through town to the cathedral. She had not been back to Winchester since her pregnancy had begun to show and she lost her job. The moment Mr. Waterman called her into his office one crisp October day, she knew he had finally noticed that she was not simply gaining weight. She saved them both from an excruciating interview by sitting down and immediately stating, "I shall be having a baby in February. Would you prefer I left now or in January?"

Mr. Waterman's eyes popped. "Miss Speedwell, I—I—"

"Perhaps now is best," she decided. Though saying so robbed her of two months' more pay, she could not bear Mr. Waterman's red-faced sputtering for that long. She had already had to put up with sideways looks from many of the townswomen. Mrs. Harvey, though, had been unexpectedly tolerant. It turned out she had a daughter who'd had a baby without being married, she confided to Violet. "Of course you can't stay on once the baby arrives," she added. "I don't run *that* sort of house."

But the biggest surprise of the day she lost her job was Maureen, who had already guessed that she was pregnant. When Violet came back from her meeting with Mr. Waterman and explained she would be leaving shortly, her office mate grunted and said, "I'm having my own meeting with him soon. I'm getting married."

"Married?" Violet tried not to sound shocked, but there had been no indication over the months that there was a man in Maureen's life. This sudden announcement was far removed from the endless talk of engagements and rings and wedding receptions Mo and O had indulged in just a year and a half before. Maureen has grown up, she thought. "Who are you marrying?"

"Keith, of course." At Violet's astonished expression she snorted. "Why look surprised? You introduced us, after all."

Violet was still getting her head around Keith Bain being referred

to as Keith. He was a man who suited a surname. And he was marrying Maureen. Perhaps he would have a softening effect on her.
"Gosh. Congratulations to you both."

"Thanks. Keith does make me laugh, and think. Oh, I can't wait
to see the look on Mr. Waterman's face when he discovers he's losing
both typists! You'll come to the wedding, won't you? Since you set us
in each other's sights. You ought to be there. If, that is"—she nodded
at Violet's belly—"that doesn't get in the way."

"I hope so."

But she didn't hope so. Arthur would be there, probably as best
man, and she knew she must avoid him, as she had avoided the cathedral and the Old Market Restaurant on Wednesday evenings and
Sunday afternoons.

Only once had she run into Arthur. She had been coming out of
Church House when she saw him through a group of college choristers crossing the Inner Close in a noisy herd. He was leaning against
one of the cathedral's flying buttresses, clearly watching for her. She
stopped, and when the boys moved on, he spotted her, and the bump
emerging from the folds of her coat. They stared at each other across
the Close. More than anything, Violet wanted to step across the
cobblestones separating them and into his arms. But she did not
move, and he did not move, in that way confirming what they had
decided before they even knew the circumstances. After a moment
Violet gave him a little nod, and turned away as Arthur took a handkerchief from his pocket and wiped his eyes.

She did not go to the wedding. By the time Maureen and Keith
Bain married in late December, she had moved back to Southampton and was able to cite weather and puffy ankles as excuses—though
by then they would have guessed the true reason for her absence.
They did not hold it against her. Indeed, the Bains became proper

friends. They were supportive of Violet's pregnancy and of Iris when she arrived—to the extent that Violet asked them to be godparents.

As the train came to a halt, she gazed down at her daughter's face, looking so much like Arthur that Violet was astonished anyone bothered to ask who the father was. Iris opened her eyes: deep-set, like two slivers of sapphire. "Right on time," Violet murmured. She tucked a small white pillow with the initials AK embroidered in the corner under the covers; she had made it from Arthur's handkerchief. "Welcome to Winchester, little one. Sic parvis magna. So great and so small."

Gilda and Dorothy did not appear to be nervous about walking through town. Once they were living in Southampton, settled together and with jobs keeping books and teaching, it seemed Winchester's citizens were relieved not to have to consider the nature of their relationship. Out of sight, out of mind; it suited the town well. Walking down the High Street now, they looked like two friends, strolling and chatting on their way to a christening.

Violet's sin, however, was more obvious. As she pushed the pram toward the Buttercross, she could feel eyes on her, the way she had in Southampton for the last months of her pregnancy and the first months of Iris's life. Her skin was thicker now, but it was still an ordeal she had to brace herself to get through. It helped having Gilda and Dorothy with her, no longer walking together but wordlessly setting her between them. Like guards accompanying me to a prison cell, Violet thought wryly, though she was grateful too.

The best tonic was to keep her eyes on her daughter's face. Iris was watching her equally intently, her blue eyes fierce with the serious business of staying alive; her complete dependence on her mother made Violet walk with a brisk step and a straight back. It was what had made her able to insist to her brother that she and Gilda and Dorothy should live in the Speedwell house in Southampton rather than sell it. Tom had been bewildered by the suggestion, as he had been by the news of her pregnancy. But Violet had cultivated a new firmness that her brother found hard to argue with. "I am going to have a family," she said, "and I need a family house. Mother is not coming back to Southampton. Unless you need the money at the moment, why shouldn't I live there?"

Gilda and Dorothy supported Violet with their salaries. Since they did not have to pay rent, they just about managed, with Violet looking after them, the house, and Iris. It was an eye-opening arrangement, much discussed by the neighbors behind their backs, and more than once Violet had heard them referred to in hissed tones as the "house of sin." While Tom and Evelyn managed to accept Gilda and Dorothy's arrangement by pretending it was just a friendship, they could not ignore the sheer physical fact of Iris, and the absence of a wedding ring or a father. There was no way to hide that from their children. When they visited, they did not bring them, though they always had an excuse ready: illness, or tiredness, or a punishment for being naughty.

Violet coped. From Dorothy she had learned: Suum cuique. To each her own. She fretted, however, for it seemed a temporary arrangement at best. Would she ever be able to work again? Would she have to ask for more from Tom, and pray he would be merciful? It was painful to imagine those conversations, but eventually she would have to talk to him about her and Iris's future so that it did not seem so precarious.

As they crossed the Outer Close, her heart began to pound. Whatever the town thought of her, she cared more about the cathedral's response to her altered life. It had been a source of refuge for so many over the centuries, and had been to Violet while she lived in Winchester. She dreaded any change—the eyes following her, the tuts as she pushed Iris's pram through the nave. Would this be the last time she visited?

But there was Louisa Pesel waiting in the main doorway. It was she who had convinced Dean Selwyn to allow Iris's christening to take place in the cathedral. Violet wondered what she had said, and whether she'd had to bribe him with the promise of a special cushion in his name; but she suspected the dean had simply found it impossible to argue with Miss Pesel.

"Ah, there you are!" she cried, coming forward with a smile. "And where is our little star?" She poked her head into the pram the way people do who never deal with babies, and Iris gazed at her in alarm. Miss Pesel patted her cheek before straightening. "Remarkable blue eyes," she declared. Violet wondered if she was busy making the connection between the baby and the father.

If she did, she did not show it. Indeed, she had never commented at all about the father or Violet's lack of a wedding ring, but had been as innocently welcoming of Iris as her niece Marjory had been to have a new baby cousin to attend to, the one time Tom and Evelyn had allowed them to visit. "You have chosen the most delightful name for her," Miss Pesel continued. "As you know, irises are my second love after embroidery. Later in the year I'm moving to the White House in Colebrook Street—just a stone's throw from here—and I'm already planning the iris garden. You must bring Iris to see her namesakes when they have taken in a year or two. Now, shall we?"

She led them up the side aisle, past the Bishop of Edington's chantry with its alabaster fylfots, and on toward the Fishermen's

Chapel. With Louisa Pesel as their escort, Violet felt more legitimate, and able to push Iris's pram with confidence through the nave.

Waiting for them in the chapel were the Bains, Maureen with a smile on her face rather than a frown. Then there was Mrs. Harvey and, to her astonishment, Mabel Way, from the Cathedral Broderers. Mabel, who had shushed her two years before, just outside the Fishermen's Chapel. She looked uncertain about being there, glancing around in fright; perhaps she had assumed more broderers would be coming besides Gilda and Dorothy and Miss Pesel. Mrs. Biggins was not there, of course; although she could not ban Violet from the broderers' meetings, she had made her feel so uncomfortable that she stopped going once she moved to Southampton—though she continued to work on the choir stall cushions until Iris arrived and her time for such things vanished.

There must be a reason Mabel Way was here. So many people had unknown stories lurking: a husband gone, a surprise baby passed off as a brother or sister, a misplaced passion, a lost wife. Maybe one day Violet would hear Mabel's. How to navigate through life carrying such things without them making you sad and bitter and judgmental— that was the challenge. She nodded now at Mabel to reassure her. Mabel responded with a tentative smile.

Despite the surprise of unexpected guests and the excitement of the occasion, Violet felt a vague disappointment. She had hoped Arthur might be there, though he should not. She had made it clear, and so had he.

She greeted her guests, but then Iris began to cry—a delayed reaction to Louisa Pesel's sudden looming face, she suspected—and Violet had to tend to her daughter and so could not join in the conversations. Luckily it didn't matter, for most knew one another or could be civil—though she did notice that both Mabel and Mrs.

Harvey took care to remain on the other side of the small chapel from Gilda and Dorothy. It couldn't be helped—they might be open-minded enough to come to the christening of the child of an unwed mother, but could not countenance two women together. Violet herself had found it a puzzle at first and could understand their reluctance. But she had lived with Gilda and Dorothy for several months now and no longer questioned the relationship. They were like an old married couple to her. At least Maureen was speaking to them; she had become more generous since marrying Keith Bain.

The vicar from a local village church arrived—a colorless man who was apparently the only vicar nearby willing to perform this baptism, primarily so that he would be able to say he had led a service at Winchester Cathedral. They began to take their places, Gilda and Keith Bain at Violet's side as godparents. Iris was still crying, and Violet looked around, anxious, her teeth on edge from her daughter's wails. Tom and Evelyn were not there; they were not coming.

Then Evelyn bustled in, breathless and apologetic. "You'll understand why we're late in a moment," she explained. When Tom appeared in the doorway with their mother on his arm, Violet almost cried out.

Mrs. Speedwell had refused to see Violet since moving to Horsham. Violet had written a few times and had no reply. Whenever she telephoned, Aunt Penelope was circumspect. "Oh, she's sleeping, dear," she would say. "Best not to disturb her." Even then Violet could hear her mother making comments in the background. During one call, her aunt had whispered, "I'd leave it for now, dear. I'm sure she'll come round, by and by. She always does." How Tom had talked their mother into coming to the christening, Violet had no idea. But it was only when she saw her—Mrs. Speedwell looking older and smaller and slower, her face grim—that Violet understood how much she had wanted her there. Becoming a mother herself had made her truly appreciate the bond between a parent and child. The thought of losing Iris made her shake with a visceral dread. Her mother had lost a son, and had to live beyond that dread. No wonder she had become so bitter.

Violet handed Iris to Gilda, whose variety of pulled faces always quieted her, and walked over to her mother. "Thank you, Tom," she murmured. Her brother nodded. Perhaps this was the start to his bringing the rest of the family back into her life as well.

"Mother," she said, and took Mrs. Speedwell's gloved hands in hers. "I'm so glad you're here."

Her mother's frown deepened and she snatched her hands back. "I am not feeling at all well," she complained. "I should not have come. All of that travel for—this." She looked around the small chapel with distaste. Perhaps Tom and Evelyn had lured her to the christening with the promise of it taking place in a grander part of the cathedral. "What Geoffrey would make of this, I'm sure I don't know."

"This was Father's favorite chapel. That's why I chose it."

"How delightful that you have come, Mrs. Speedwell!" Louisa Pesel stepped up and held out her hand. "We have all been anticipating your arrival. I am Miss Pesel, head of the broderers here at the cathedral. Your daughter has done some splendid work for us, as I'm sure you know."

Violet's mother took in Louisa Pesel's fur collar, her slightly dated hat, and her natural air of authority, and gave her a curt nod. "Pleased to make your acquaintance."

She has found someone to make this gathering legitimate, Violet thought, hiding a smile.

"The relationship a child has with its grandmother is such an important one, don't you think?" Miss Pesel continued. "Mine taught me to embroider my first sampler. I owe her my life's work, truly. Come and say hello to yours."

Mrs. Speedwell allowed herself to be led over to Gilda, whom she regarded with some relief at seeing a familiar face. No one had dared to spell out to her the true nature of Gilda and Dorothy's relationship; it had been tacitly decided that Violet's news was shock enough.

"Here's Iris," Gilda exclaimed, holding out the baby. "She's stopped crying, just for you!"

Mrs. Speedwell regarded her granddaughter with a critical eye. "Is that Violet's christening gown?"

"Yes, Mother." Violet stepped forward.

"It's far too big for her. But then, you were a large child. Fat as a Yorkshire pudding, you were."

Violet caught Keith Bain's eye; he was grinning at this improbable comparison, and winked at her. He had been tickled to be asked to be godfather to Iris.

Iris was staring at her grandmother, her chin jutting. "She has Geoffrey's eyes," Mrs. Speedwell remarked.

Violet's father's eyes had been a faded pale blue, not Iris's crystal glints, but Violet was not about to argue with her. "Do sit, Mother, and we'll begin."

Iris did not appreciate the water on her face—not even holy water—and cried through most of the ceremony, only calming down afterward when Violet took her to an empty chapel next door and fed her. When they were done and her daughter was lolling in her arms, sated, Violet was able to focus on her guests once more. They were mostly gathered round Mrs. Speedwell, indulging her by listening to her tales of her new life in Horsham. Dorothy was on her own, inspecting Izaak Walton's stained glass windows. Maureen was

chatting to Mrs. Harvey. Keith Bain had disappeared, perhaps to
have a cigarette.

"Violet, dear, you must come—we have something to show you."
Louisa Pesel was with Gilda, and beckoned to her. They led her out
of the Fishermen's Chapel, the others following, and up the stairs to
the presbytery. There the chairs were set out with their kneelers,
Violet's checkered acorn caps somewhere among them.

"Look!" Gilda waved a hand at the choir stalls to their left. Violet
caught her breath. The last time she had been there, months before,
there had been twenty cushions on the choir stall seats. Now ten
long cushions had been made for the benches, dazzling in their colors. She went over to look. Each long bench cushion had two history
medallions with elaborate surrounds in blue and yellow and green.
There were depictions of Richard I and Henry VIII, of the Bishops
Edington and Wykeham, of Charles I and the destruction of the
cathedral interior by Civil War soldiers. There was even a medallion
depicting Izaak Walton. There were two dozen more still to make,
but already it looked glorious.

"Did you know, Mrs. Speedwell," Miss Pesel declared, "that
Queen Mary came to visit us last month? She takes a keen interest in
embroidery, and it was a testament to the Cathedral Broderers' skills
that she wanted to see our work for herself. It was truly a highlight
of my career."

Violet's mother nodded. She approved of the King's wife, even if
she wasn't quite Queen Victoria.

Gilda and Dorothy had gone to the Queen's visit, and told Violet
all about it that night: how the dean took over and ushered the
Queen about as if he knew anything about embroidery, how she was
much taller than Louisa Pesel, how she had asked informed questions and singled out Dorothy's work for praise. Violet had been

happy to hear about it, though she knew she could not have gone: Iris was too young to leave with someone, and she expected she would not yet have been welcomed by the Cathedral Broderers. Mrs. Biggins would have glared her out of the presbytery. Someday soon, she hoped Louisa Pesel would be able to muzzle Mrs. Biggins enough that Violet could return to stitching with the others.

When Gilda added, "They rang the bells for the Queen," and gave her a knowing look, Violet felt her chest tighten. They rarely spoke of Arthur, though Gilda of course had guessed immediately that he was Iris's father. Her friend had not chastised her, however.

Violet was gazing at the long cushions when she caught sight of a familiar border—a row of fylfots interspersed with flowers on the cushion dedicated to Bishop Wodeloke.

"I made that one myself." Louisa Pesel was standing beside her. "I haven't had much chance to do any embroidery for this project other than to make models for the other broderers. But when I heard that the German government effectively banned Jews from all sorts of jobs, I thought I'd like to continue our little stand against Mr. Hitler. It was a very satisfying channel for my anger." They gazed at the border, which was more prominent than those of the King Arthur and Tree of Life cushions. "That is enough, however, I think. We have made our point, and there are so many other wonderful designs in the world to use for the rest."

Violet nodded. Unfortunately the chancellor seemed to be consolidating his power rather than disappearing as some had predicted. The strengthening of Germany should worry her, open the abyss inside. But she had Iris, even with all the remarks behind her back and the sideways looks to put up with. Her daughter blotted out that despair and made her stalwart.

High above them a single bell began to ring—tentative at first, like a mistake, then clanging and urgent, like the ringing she and Arthur had done together at Nether Wallop. Calling all sinners.

"That's Arthur," Maureen whispered, sidling up to her. "Keith went up to tell him the christening's finished. It's his gift to Iris."

Violet's eyes widened. Bells were only rung for cathedral services, and for the Royal Family; not for a daughter's christening. "But— what will William Carver make of it? He'll ban him from ringing."

"Arthur will take his chances. If we're lucky, Old Carver may not hear it."

Violet listened, remembering that morning in Nether Wallop and all that went with it. She looked at the consequence of that day, in her arms. Her daughter was alert now, eyes fixed high above her. Was she looking at her mother's face, or listening to her father's bell? When Iris smiled, a wide, toothless grin, Violet thought it might be both.

Acknowledgments

Just to be clear: canvas embroidery as referred to in this book is what we now call needlepoint.

Louisa Pesel did indeed exist, as do the cushions and kneelers (and fylfots) at Winchester Cathedral; they are still in use and can be sat upon or kneeled on most days. I hope I have honored Louisa's work and spirit in a way she and her descendants would approve of.

I used many resources for this book. Here are a few if you want to do a deeper dive.

Louisa Pesel and Winchester Cathedral embroidery: Louisa Pesel Collection at Leeds University: http://library.leeds.ac.uk/special-col lections; *Embroideries of Winchester Cathedral* by Dorothy Carbonell and Hugh Carey (1982); *Crewel Embroidery in England* by Joan Edwards (1975); *Stitched and Woven: The Embroideries of Winchester Cathedral* by Sheila Gray (2006).

Winchester Cathedral: *The Cathedrals of England* by Harry Batsford and Charles Fry, revised by Bryan Little (1960); *The Glories of Winchester Cathedral* by Raymond Birt (1948); *Winchester Cathedral* by John Crook (2001).

Bellringing: "The Ringing Men," in *Akenfield: Portrait of an English Village* by Ronald Blythe (1969); *Discovering Bells and Bellringing* by John Camp (1968); *An Elementary Handbook for Beginners in the Art of Change-Ringing* by the Central Council of Church Bell Ringers (1976); Dove's Guide for Church Bell Ringers: https://dove.cccbr.org.uk/; *Bells and Bellringing* by John Harrison (2016); *The Nine Tailors* by Dorothy L. Sayers (1934).

1930s women: *Diary of a Wartime Affair: The True Story of a Surprisingly Modern Romance* by Doreen Bates (2016); *Testament of Youth* by Vera Brittain (1933); *The English in Love: The Intimate Story of an Emotional Revolution* by Claire Langhamer (2013); *Singled Out* by Virginia Nicholson (2007).

Britain in the 1930s: *The Thirties: An Intimate History* by Juliet Gardiner (2010); *The Long Weekend: A Social History of Great Britain 1918–1939* by Robert Graves and Alan Hodge (1940).

I would like to thank the following:

The Archivists and Librarians. Jo Bartholomew at Winchester Cathedral; Suzanne Foster at Winchester College; David Rymill at the Hampshire Archives and Local Studies, in the Hampshire Record Office; Jill Winder at Leeds University Library's International Textiles Collection, which houses the Louisa Pesel Collection.

The Embroiderers. The current Winchester Broderers, who showed me their work and explained stitches; they are currently cleaning and repairing Louisa Pesel's cushions and kneelers so that they sparkle with their original vitality.

The Bellringers. The Winchester Cathedral bellringers, who allowed me to watch them ring; and in particular, Tower Captain Nick Bucknall and Colin Cook, who both patiently answered my many questions, as well as reading through the bellringing sections and making much needed corrections. (Bellringing is a complicated business.) Also the bellringers at St. Anne's Highgate, for allowing me to attend a practice and try ringing a bell. Finally, my friend Catherine Moore, who knows her bells and gave me a much better understanding of what it feels like to ring; she also read the manuscript and nudged me in the right directions. Any mistakes I have made are all mine.

The Others. Phil Yates, who gave me colorful details about life in 1930s Winchester. Textile restorer Jacqui Hyman, for sharing what she knows about Louisa Pesel. Winchester Cathedral tour guide Jeff Steers and verger Benedict Yeats. Staff of the Documentation Team at the British Film Institute, London.

The Rest. Gemma Elwyn Harris, for winkling out all kinds of information without batting an eye at my odd requests. My husband, Jon Drori, for walking in the rain with me between Winchester and Salisbury cathedrals, all in the name of research.

My editors Andrea Schulz and Suzie Dooré, for wholeheartedly embracing Violet, embroidery, bellringing, and me. My copy editors Kym Surridge and Rhian McKay for quietly fixing the errors large and small. And assistant editor Ore Agbaje-Williams, for calmly finding the right title when the rest of us were despairing.

My agents Jonny Geller and Deborah Schneider, for making the business side of books painless so that the writing side is a lot more fun.

Finally, I would like to thank Keith Bain for the use of his name. Keith bought the privilege of having a character named after him at an auction to raise funds for Freedom from Torture, an admirable UK charity that provides treatment and rehabilitation for survivors of torture. Keith took a generous gamble on me and *A Single Thread*; I hope he feels he won.